WAYS TO
DIE IN
TOKYO

THOMAS RAN GARVER

For my dad.

風が吹けば桶屋が儲かる。

When the wind blows, coffin makers profit.

*Old Japanese proverb meaning any event
can lead to an unpredictable result.*

PART ONE

CHAPTER ONE

Hotel LaSalle
Shibuya Entertainment District, Tokyo

ANDREA NOVAK IS trying to think of the beach and the sun instead of the man lying next to her.

It's not easy, because he's got terrible BO, an awful sour corn smell he's tried to mask with way too much cologne, which just makes it worse. He's short and wiry with buzzed hair and eyes spaced too close together and an intense gaze that creeps Andrea out. She's scooted down a few inches so she doesn't have to look at his face.

His name is Nakano. He's a friend of Shimazu-san, the disgustingly fat owner of Starlight, the club in Kabukicho where she's been working for the past month. Nakano is a regular at Starlight. Kind of a weird guy, he sits by himself most of the time, sipping his drink and staring at the girls with those crazy eyes of his.

Last Friday, Shimazu told Andrea that Nakano wanted to "play" with her. There was fifty thousand yen in it for her if she agreed.

Andrea had laughed off the offer at first, said no thanks. Then she mentioned it to one of the other girls, a chatty Brit named Liz. Liz didn't bat an eye. She said Andrea should do it; it was easy money. All she had to do was meet the guy at a love hotel and give him a hand job. Liz had done it herself. Almost all the girls at Starlight had.

Fifty thousand yen for a hand job? It sounded too good to be true, but Liz said there was nothing to worry about. Check in. Jerk him off. Check out.

Andrea thought about it for maybe a half second, decided hell yes, she'd do it.

"*Motto hayaku*," Nakano says. Faster.

Andrea speeds it up.

Nakano lets out a little moan.

She sees herself lying on a white sand beach, sipping juice from a big green coconut through a red straw. A warm whisper of a breeze in the shade of a palm tree. The turquoise sea and the soft white noise of waves lapping at the shore.

"*Ah! Ah! Ah! Ah! Ah!*" A woman's high-pitched squeal comes through the wall, breaking the spell.

"*Aaaaah!*"

Andrea suppresses the urge to laugh. The girl is really laying it on thick.

Nakano shifts on the bed. He reaches down and grabs her hand, moves it up and down faster. "Like this," he says, sounding irritated.

She rolls her eyes and tugs faster. After this, she's going to go home and crack a beer and watch something on Netflix.

Nakano clucks his tongue.

Andrea thinks, *Shit*, and is about to ask him what's wrong when he grabs her hard by the hair and jerks her head back. She yelps, starts to turn toward him, thinking, *What the fuck?* He jerks her head back again, harder this time, and fear rockets through her veins. She reaches up and grabs his wrist with both hands. Twisting, Andrea tries to pull away, but Nakano tightens his grip. Heart slamming in her chest, she screams and squeezes his wrist as hard as she can, feels her nails go into the flesh, and the fucker gasps in pain. He reaches up and scrabbles at her hand, finds purchase on her little finger, and peels it back, jerks and twists it. There's an audible crack, like a branch snapping, and a blast of pain that feels like a glass bulb shattering in her hand, and the surge of adrenaline that follows gives her a shot of sudden strength. She turns and twists and pulls away in one big motion that catches the man by surprise. He lets go of her hair, and she lunges at him, tearing and clawing at his arms, neck, and face.

"Fucking bitch!" he says, trying to ward off the blows. He tries to punch her in the face. She leans back and the punch goes wide, missing its mark. She falls back onto her hands, barely registering the pain in her broken finger, while he falls forward. Andrea lifts her hips and kicks out at him as hard as she can with her right foot. The kick misses, and he throws himself back against the headboard. In a frenzy, she keeps kicking until one of the kicks catches him square in the side of the face with a loud *chock*. The back of his head thumps against the headboard. He slumps, stunned, his hands palms out in a weird okay-okay gesture. Blood pours onto the white sheets from his nose and mouth. Andrea's heart is slamming her ribs so hard it feels like it's going to leap out of her chest. *Oh fuck.* Her chest is heaving, her whole body shaking. Nakano groans, his eyes rolling around in his head, his mouth open and bloody, a gap where his two front teeth should be. Keeping her eyes on him, Andrea scoots to the edge of the bed.

Through the wall, the sound of muffled voices.

Nakano suddenly sits bolt upright. Andrea lets out a short, sharp scream. With a roar, Nakano lunges for her and grabs hold of one of her legs. Andrea screams again, tries to kick him off, but his grip is too strong. He yanks her leg toward him. Using her free leg she launches herself backward off the edge of the bed and falls headfirst onto the floor, landing upside down between the top of the bed and nightstand.

"I'll kill you!" Nakano says, looming naked and bloody above her on the bed, his fingers digging deep into her calf. She scrabbles at the side of the bed, finds purchase on the bedsheet, and tries to maneuver her free leg around. She reaches her other hand up and grabs the edge of the nightstand as Nakano starts to rise from the bed. The nightstand topples over and crashes to the floor.

Nakano roars again.

He's going to kill her. He's pulling on her leg with both hands, trying to reel her in, making growling noises with every breath. She kicks her leg as hard as she can. He doesn't let go. She kicks again, then once more with a shout of rage and finally jerks her leg free of his grasp. She immediately rolls onto her stomach to crawl away. Nakano slams his fist into her back. Pain shoots up Andrea's spine. *I don't want to die,* she thinks. She searches the floor, desperate for something, *anything*, to use as a weapon. There! The glass beer mug Nakano had emptied and set on the nightstand earlier, is right there, half hidden by the bedspread. She grabs it just as Nakano seizes a fistful of her hair. He gets to his knees and pulls her head back and Andrea whirls, swinging the mug with all her strength. It catches Nakano in the side of the head with a thud. He crumples to the floor.

Andrea drops the mug and leaps to her feet, her breaths coming in ragged gasps.

She has to get out of here.

She rushes to the bathroom. Flips on the light. Her broken little finger is throbbing. Her right foot too. She sees a little cut on her heel, probably from the asshole's teeth. Hot tears spring to her eyes. *Oh God oh God oh God.* He tried to kill her! He fucking tried to kill her! What if he's dead? But it was self-defense! Oh God. Who will believe her? A wave of dizziness hits her, and she feels like she's going to pass out. She leans against the wall, taking deep breaths until the wave passes; then she snatches a washcloth from the rack, dampens it under the faucet, and with a shaking hand wipes the blood away from the cut on her heel. She quickly dresses and grabs her bag.

On her way out of the room, she glances back at Nakano, naked and bloody on the floor. She can still smell him.

CHAPTER TWO

One week later...

❧

THE GYM IS tucked away in a residential neighborhood in Tachikawa, on the outskirts of Tokyo, in a former *kendo* dojo on the basement floor of an apartment complex. There's a tiny sign next to the door that says "Blast Gym," but if it weren't for Google Maps, you might never find it.

Glad to be escaping the early evening heat, Hank Fisher goes down a short flight of stairs to a metal door. He pulls the door open, steps inside, and pulls it closed. He walks to the end of a short hallway and raps twice on the door to the office. "*Hai.*" Yes?

Fisher pops his head in. "Hey." The office is six feet square and contains a desk with a whiteboard behind it, a filing cabinet against one wall, and a metal shelving unit crammed with old cardboard file boxes against the other. Ken Matsumura is hunched over the desk, writing something in a journal. He's a massive man, though not all that tall, born in Oakland and raised in Tokyo. His dad was a Japanese pro wrestler, his mom an African-American army brat. Six feet even with a big brown bald head, everything about him is thick and broad, from his yard-wide shoulders down to his football-sized calves. The overall impression Ken Matsumura conveys is that of a human bulldozer.

Ken looks up from his laptop. "Hey."

"I'll go get changed," Fisher says.

"Hold on." Ken motions for Fisher to enter. "Come on in for a second."

Fisher steps inside, wondering what's up.

Ken clears his throat and looks down at the desk. "I got a call from the promoter."

"Yeah?"

"Inoue popped his ACL in training yesterday. He's gotta have surgery."

Fisher feels something crumble inside him. He's been training for this fight for six weeks, and he feels good. Better, in fact, than he has in a long time. Inoue, a tough young fighter in Fisher's own weight class, had represented a rare opportunity for Fisher to show he still had the goods. Now? *Poof.*

How's that for magic?

Before he can stop himself, he slams the meaty part of his fist into the metal door with a clang that echoes in the hall.

Ken holds his hands out in a placating gesture. "They're looking for someone to step in."

Fisher says, "You think they'll find someone else?" Knowing the answer already.

Ken presses his lips together, opens his mouth to say something, then closes it again.

"What I thought," says Fisher.

"There just aren't that many guys your size over here, dude. You know that."

And just like that, six weeks of hard work go down the drain. "Yeah," Fisher says, looking at the floor. He shakes his head. "*Shou ga nai,* right?" Shit happens. "Is what it is," says Ken. "Go on and get changed."

In the locker room, Fisher slowly changes into spats and a short-sleeved rash guard. Ever since Lisa and the kids left two years ago, his life has been in a kind of slow free-fall. Cancellation of the fight is just more of the same. One more turd on the pile.

There was a time when he thought he could be the next big thing in mixed martial arts. That he was good enough to make the big bucks. But then he had a string of losses, and before he knew it, he was considered a journeyman—good but not great. Now he just gets by, and he's far from alone. The truth is that of the few hundred guys making their living from MMA, only a toddler's fistful pack enough star power to make serious bank. Everybody else is living pretty much fight to fight, paycheck to paycheck. When you consider that the average shelf life of a fighter is four or five years, it doesn't add up to a whole lot of dough, even for the superstars. And that's in the good old U.S. of A, the mecca of mixed martial arts.

In Japan, the pickings are even slimmer.

Journeyman. Yeah, he's on a journey all right. Took a wrong turn somewhere, though, didn't he?

He considers just going home and bingeing on ice cream, but he made the trip out here to Tachikawa, so he might as well do what he came here to do. Plus, training is a welcome distraction from his wreck of a personal life.

He walks down a narrow hall to another sliding door that

opens into the main part of the gym, a long, windowless room twenty feet by thirty feet, green mats covering the entire floor. Three heavy bags are suspended from the ceiling on the left. Inside the big room, the humidity jumps, and the comforting funk of old sweat, feet, leather, and disinfectant hits Fisher's nose and lifts his spirits a little. Twenty people, give or take, are on the mat, mostly working in pairs, boxing, kickboxing, grappling, holding pads, hitting pads. A few work the heavy bags.

Compared to some of the MMA gyms Fisher has seen in the U.S., Australia, and Singapore, the place is a dump. But the work gets done here, and that's all that matters.

Fisher stretches, skips rope, does some shadowboxing until he's got a sweat going. Then Ken grabs a pair of focus mitts from some metal shelving by the door, slips them on. "No power today," he says.

They move around, Fisher throwing combinations of punches and kicks, Ken swatting each blow away. Fisher flicks out a sloppy jab. Ken slaps it down with the padded mitt, stops, and cocks his head, the expression on his face saying *really?*

"I said light and easy, not half-assed."

Fisher throws a one-two-three combination with a little more oomph.

Ken clicks his tongue, annoyed. "Come on." He was one of the first people Fisher had met when he and Lisa moved to Tokyo from San Jose eight years ago and has been Fisher's trainer and friend for most of that time.

Fifteen minutes later, they move to an area reserved for grappling in the far right corner of the room. Three pairs of men are working takedowns, transitions, and submissions.

A big American guy named Dave is stretching in the corner. Ken waves him over. Dave is almost as large as Ken but about

11

ten years younger, which puts him at around thirty. He's blond with a crew cut and a rubbery face Fisher has never seen without a frown. Dave lumbers over and says, "S'up, Coach." He says nothing to Fisher, just chucks his chin at him because Dave is kind of an asshole.

Ken says, "Let's do a couple five-minute rounds of no-*gi*. No leg locks."

Fisher loves training Brazilian jiu-jitsu with the *gi* because of all the nifty ways you can use the uniform to throw, sweep, and strangle your opponent. Dave knows this, because Dave has been on the receiving end of lots of *gi*-based punishment when training with Fisher. He regards Fisher, his face twisting into a pained expression that makes him look like he's trying to take a crap. Dave's version of a smile.

"Smash you without the *gi*, Fish Man."

Fisher is not in the mood. He glares at Dave as they slap hands and bump fists.

Ken says, "Easy this time, Hank."

Dave slaps his chest twice and barks, "*Oss.*" Used in *karate* and other Japanese martial arts as a greeting, the word could also mean "Let's go," or "All right." To Fisher, though, it's just an irritating affectation that has wormed its way into BJJ in recent years.

But everything irritates him these days. At forty, he's been in the fight game for more than ten years now, a damn long run in MMA. He's divorced and living alone and hasn't seen his kids in two years. He's a bitter, banged-up geezer trying to keep the wheels from flying off.

They circle each other, each of them lunging a few times and moving quickly back, gauging the distance and each other's reactions. Fisher lunges again, for real this time, and tries for an ankle pick. Dave steps back to avoid it. Fisher straightens, hops back a step, and waits. When Dave comes forward, Fisher shoots in full speed, no hesitation. He drives his right shoulder into Dave's belly and grips the backs of his knees and continues to drive Dave forward and up, pulling his legs in and using his head to push Dave's torso to the right.

Dave tries to sprawl to defend the double-leg takedown, but he's too late. Fisher dumps him onto the mat and moves immediately to the left and around Dave's legs and drops into the side control position, his body perpendicular to Dave's, chest to chest. Fisher grabs Dave's wrist with his left hand and applies a Kimura lock. Done quickly and with sufficient force, the technique will literally snap an opponent's elbow as well as rip the same-side shoulder from its socket. But this is training, and the goal isn't to hurt each other, so Fisher applies pressure slowly.

Dave taps Fisher's side with his free hand. Fisher immediately lets Dave's arm go and starts to push himself off the man's chest. Apparently it's not fast enough for Dave, though. Dave shoves Fisher back, mutters "Fuck," and pops up to his feet.

Fisher rises and stares at the big man, holds his arms out palms up. *What's your problem?*

Ken says, "Chill, Dave."

Dave wipes the sweat from his face with a hand and then wipes the hand on his shorts. Fisher hold his fist out for Dave to bump. Dave ignores it and sidesteps around him. They crouch, move forward until they bump foreheads and begin fighting for grips, which is mostly Fisher trying to control Dave's wrists and Dave trying to break Fisher's grips. Fisher grabs the back of Dave's neck with his right hand. He seizes Dave's right wrist with his left and drives forward, trying to get Dave to push back. Dave falls for it. He resists, holding his ground, and then steps forward with his right foot. At that moment, Fisher executes a classic arm drag so that he ends up behind Dave with his hands locked around Dave's waist. For a sliver of a moment, Fisher considers tossing Dave with a suplex. When properly executed, the throw will launch an opponent up and backward and land him on his neck and shoulders. It's a high-risk move that could seriously injure Dave, and Fisher really doesn't want to hurt the idiot. So instead he sits on his butt and shoots his right leg out, tripping Dave's right heel. Dave lands on his right side, and Fisher once again achieves side control. Dave squirms under him, making little whistling noises with every breath. He tries to bench press Fisher off, a rookie mistake that even high-level grapplers sometimes make if they're tired enough.

Fisher snatches Dave's near-side arm, throws his right leg over Dave's head and his left leg over Dave's torso. He grips Dave's wrist with the thumb up and stretches his arm between his legs, applying upward pressure with his hips to hyperextend Dave's elbow. *Jujigatame.* A straight armlock.

Fisher slowly applies pressure and waits.

But Dave doesn't tap this time.

Fisher applies more pressure. Dave grunts in pain, but still he doesn't give up. Fisher stops applying pressure and is about to let Dave's arm go when a tightness seizes his right hamstring. Cramp? Dave's head moves under his leg, and the tightness is suddenly a hot, searing pain that takes his breath away, and Fisher realizes the asshole is biting him.

"*AAAH!*"

His reaction is automatic. Fisher reaches up with his right hand and pounds the bridge of Dave's nose with the meaty part of his fist. As soon as Dave's teeth release their hold on his leg, Fisher sits on his chest and hits him in the face with an elbow, and then another, barely registering the chorus of startled shouts issued by the other members, and then half the gym is rushing over and grabbing Fisher's arms and dragging him off Dave.

Dave immediately jumps to his feet, his face bloody and contorted with rage. "Motherfucker!" He charges Fisher and a clamor goes up as three or four guys block his way. Trying to maneuver around them, Dave says, "You're *dead!* You're *fucking dead!*"

Fisher stands there, mouth agape, not quite believing what just happened, until Ken steps in front of him, points a finger in his face, and says, "Office! Now!"

CHAPTER THREE

WAITING IN THE office for Ken, Fisher rubs the back of his thigh where Dave bit him. It smarts a little, but the skin's not broken. The anger Fisher had felt just seconds ago is gone, replaced by a heavy gloom. He thinks of his family. He can't help it. His anger is what had, in the end, dealt the final blow to his and Lisa's marriage. One night she'd told him something devastating and he'd flown into a rage, and it scared her so badly she took the kids and left.

And now he's gone and ruined another good thing. It's not the first time he's lost his shit at the gym, but this time he's really done it. You *never* intentionally hurt a training partner, even if that training partner is a dickhead. Dave *is* a dickhead, and no, you don't bite a training partner. But a little bite that didn't even break the skin? That didn't justify the kind of beatdown Fisher gave him. So who's the bigger dickhead?

Ken walks in a couple of minutes later, shaking his head, and tells Fisher to clean out his locker. Fisher isn't surprised. Silently he nods, then rises from his seat and goes to the door. He loves this gym, it's his sanctuary, and now he's lost it, and he wants to cry, which makes him feel ridiculous and angry and stupid, because he's a grown man, and he's acting like a big ridiculous pussy. This is his own damn fault, just like everything else.

"Hank."

Fisher turns and meets Ken's gaze. There's genuine concern in the man's eyes. He knows Fisher has been in a downward spiral since the divorce. Knows that Fisher has been trying to track down his family's whereabouts for the past year with zero success.

Ken says, "I know you've been through the wringer, but I just can't—"

Fisher holds up a hand. "I get it. I fucked up. Not your problem."

"Look, wait a while for this to blow over. Maybe I can talk Ono-san into letting you back in."

Ono is the owner of the gym. A busy hedge fund manager in his mid-fifties with a passion for MMA, he's famously mercurial, and he's given much bigger-name fighters than Fisher the boot for much smaller offenses than beating a fellow gym member bloody. Fisher reaches for the doorknob. "Thanks."

Ken says, "Hey."

Fisher turns and lifts his eyebrows. "Yeah."

A sheepish expression comes over Ken's face. "You ever think about getting some help?"

"You mean a shrink?"

Ken shrugs. "Yeah. I mean, no. Not a shrink necessarily. Someone to talk to. You know, to get things off your chest."

A weak smile forms on Fisher's lips. "That's what I come here for. *Came* here for."

Ken winces.

Fisher holds up a hand. "That came out wrong. Look, thanks for everything. I appreciate it."

On his way to the locker room, two guys are talking quietly in the hall. One is a good-natured twenty-year-old kickboxer named Toru. The other is an older BJJ enthusiast named Yusuke who's always complimenting people. They stop talking when they see Fisher coming, and as Fisher passes them, they turn their backs on him. Hurrying past the open door to the main training area, he hears Dave say, "I'll see you later, Fish Boy."

Fisher dumps the contents of his locker into his gym bag, leaves without showering, and trudges back to the station in a daze.

Trying not to listen to the little voice in his head saying, *Loser.*

The AC inside the train is blasting, a jolt after the walk in the sweltering heat from the gym to Tachikawa Station. The city scrolls by outside the window, the dark outline of the Okutama Mountains visible in the distance. In the foreground are the Musashi Plains, blanketed with the lights of factories, apartment buildings, and houses.

Fisher rubs the back of his right thigh where Dave bit him, tells himself to forget about getting kicked out of the gym, forget about the fight getting canceled, forget he's over the hill and nearly broke and all alone.

Fuck it.

His shift at Lounge O, the hostess bar where he bounces twice a week, starts at eight. He keeps a change of clothes in the break room, so he'll go there straight. He'll be a couple of hours early, but he has a key and there's a small sofa in the break room, and maybe he can catch a nap if Terry, the owner, isn't there yet. Better than going home to his shitty little apartment.

He checks his phone to see if there's a message from the PI he hired two months ago to find Lisa and the kids. Nothing. No surprise there, but it irritates him nonetheless because every time he looks at his phone, he gets his hopes up just a little, and every time the result is the same: a stab of disappointment followed by a flare of anger. He's paid the fucking PI almost two grand, and he's found exactly nothing so far.

The rustle of a newspaper draws his attention. An old guy, staring at him over his paper.

People stare at him, he gets it. He's a big *gaijin*—a foreigner—physically imposing enough to make people gawk. He meets the old man's gaze and forces himself to smile, his best "friendly foreigner" face. The man is maybe seventy but could pass for sixty. Slender, with a full head of neatly combed gray hair parted down the side, and smooth, pale skin. He's wearing a polo shirt, polyester slacks, and loafers with monogrammed socks.

The smile doesn't work.

The man tongues a molar, keeping his eyes fixed on Fisher's for a second. Then he looks down at his paper again.

Whatever, dude.

Fisher focuses on a banner ad: a splashy headline about a celebrity wedding. A self-taught Japanese speaker, he doesn't speak like a native, but he's fluent for all practical purposes, and he can read and write. He likes to think his *nihongo* ability would have made his mom and dad happy. Mom was *san-sei*, third-generation Japanese-American, and Fisher's paternal grandfather was *ni-sei*, second-generation. Neither of them spoke a lick of Japanese, but Fisher remembers his mom sometimes making *miso* soup and *kappa-maki* sushi rolls with cucumbers from the garden. On New Year's, she would make *ozoni*—soup broth with *mochi*—rice cakes—she had a friend send up from San Francisco.

The conductor announces the next stop. The train slows and comes to a halt. A few people get off, a few get on, and the train pulls out of the station slow, whining its electric whine.

An old lady sits down across from Fisher. She's probably in her eighties, around the same age Fisher's mom would be if she were still alive. Her hair sits atop her head in a tight bun and she has a heavily lined face, but her posture is ramrod straight and she's staring intently at her smartphone as she texts away like a teenager. Fisher's mom would've been a pretty hip old lady too. His dad, on the other hand, would've been one of those stubborn old bastards who constantly rant about how easy the younger generation has it. Fisher smiles at the memory of them, then feels the familiar pit in his stomach. They've been gone thirty years, and he still can't think of them without thinking about how they died: gunned down by the feds on their pot farm in Northern California.

The train stops again.

Fisher checks his phone. Again, nothing.

He breathes in, closing his eyes, pushing the familiar cloud of sadness and guilt and self-loathing away. He opens his eyes, rubs the back of his thigh again. What is he doing? Why is he still fighting? Lisa had asked him to stop so many times over the years. Literally *begged* him after a kick to the left eye left him with a small retinal tear. What if the next time he lost his sight? What if he developed CTE? Why was he doing this to himself? To her, to the kids? To *them*. He was different. He'd become an asshole, she'd said. Sullen, depressed, angry all the time. No longer the cheerful guy she used to know. It wasn't good for the kids, for *any* of them.

Give him a little more time, he would always say. She didn't need to worry, he didn't have CTE. His memory was fine, and he was only moody because he kept losing and he knew he could do better and he was sorry. He'd stop being an asshole. And if he couldn't turn things around, he'd quit fighting. But he had no intention of quitting then. He wasn't young anymore, but he couldn't imagine hanging it up, even as he felt the wheels coming off. He was a good fighter, and in spite of all the losses, he'd never been knocked out. More important, though, win or lose, fighting gave him power, a feeling of control like nothing else he'd ever experienced. It made everything else life had to throw at him easier.

Over the past two years, he's come to understand that it's mostly bullshit, that feeling. Because you can't stop time and you can't control life. You can sure beat yourself up trying, though. And the worst part of it is that the ones you love most end up suffering the most as a result.

Lisa was gearing up to study for the bar exam when he told her he wanted to pursue his dream of going pro. He was closing in on thirty and had worked a succession of boring office jobs, and it was now or never. Lisa thought he was crazy. What if the fight thing didn't work out? she said. Did he have a Plan B to fall back on? Why not go back to school and get a business degree or something?

Fighting was what he loved to do, he told her. And if he was going to make it as a fighter, he didn't have any time to spare. He'd already fought in a few local smokers and done well. His name was getting some play in the MMA scene around the Bay Area, and he was confident that he was good enough to make a living from the sport, but he had a ways to go. Besides, he could always go back to school.

But what about kids? Lisa said. She was five years older than he was, already thirty-three. They'd discussed having kids now and then, but she'd brought the subject up more frequently over the past year or so. Fisher might not have any time to spare to start an MMA career, but, Lisa reminded him, her biological clock was ticking.

The two things weren't mutually exclusive, Fisher argued. He could pursue MMA and they could still have kids. They'd lived on the cheap and scratched and saved and as a result had fifty grand in the bank. That was a lot of money. Fisher would work part time and train part time, he assured her, and Lisa could keep working her job at a tech start-up, and if she got pregnant, they'd make it work. It would take a bit of time, but eventually he was going to be making a lot of money, enough for her to stop working if she wanted to. Just watch him, he told her.

He kept hammering away like that, all upbeat, and finally got her to say okay.

"If that's what you really want to do," she said. "Of course I'll support you."

At Shinjuku Station he transfers to the Oedo Line and rides to Roppongi. He climbs the stairs and exits the subway station.

Famous for its nightlife, Roppongi is crowded with revelers even this early on a Wednesday evening.

Lisa kept her promise to support him. She became a working mom, paid most of the bills, and he took her for granted, took the kids for granted so he could chase *his* dream, and look where that's gotten him.

At a crosswalk, Fisher waits in a throng of people for the light to change. On the side of a building across the street, a family of four smiles down from a billboard advertisement for a dental office. Big, toothy smiles.

It's not too late, he tells himself. He can get a full-time job, teaching English maybe, or translating. His resume is pretty thin, but he's bound to land something eventually. He'll save up his money, maybe go back to school. Then he can be the husband and father Lisa and the boys need him to be.

The light turns to green.

He moves with the crowd into the street. He's got to get out of this rut, though. It's the only way he's going to be able to get his family back.

CHAPTER FOUR

LOUNGE O IS filled with the sounds of conversation and laughter and the clink of ice cubes in glasses. Bouncy J-Pop emanates from speakers suspended from the ceiling and reverberates off the mirrored walls.

It's just after 9 p.m., and Fisher and the owner, Terry, pour mixed nuts from plastic bags into little glass bowls. The cook is out sick tonight, so Terry and Hank are having to fill in for the guy, and it's not pretty. Unable to find anything, Terry has been walking around in more than his usual state of irritation. He fumbles his bag and sends a shower of salted peanuts, almonds, walnuts, and macadamias skittering over the counter and onto the tile floor.

Fisher grins. "Damn."

Terry narrows his eyes at him. Light glints a soft white off his polished dome. "Don't say it."

Fisher's grin widens. He can't help himself. "That was nuts."

Terry closes his eyes and winces. He wipes his hands, which are the size of mallets, with a towel and signals to Yuki, the floor manager, to come get the bowls.

Fisher grabs a broom and dustpan from the storage closet next to the kitchen and goes to clean up the spilled nuts.

Lounge O is on the fifth floor of a skinny building a stone's throw from the ritzy Tokyo Midtown shopping complex. A long, narrow room of less than a thousand square feet, it's got a row of four plush, red velvet booths on one side and a long, dark wood bar on the other. Behind the bar is a narrow doorway that opens into a closet-sized kitchen. A slim corridor at the far end of the room leads to a pair of tiny restrooms and a break room.

Eight girls are working tonight: Mari, Erika, Ayako, and Kiyomi, who are all Japanese, and Sarah, Liz, Rosalind, and Maria, who hail from Detroit, San Jose, Manila, and Brazil, respectively. Each of the booths is occupied by two or three salarymen and two of the girls. At three of the tables sit bottles of Chivas Regal, necklaced with little name tags on which Yuki has printed in neat uppercase letters the names of the regulars who paid for them in advance. Called *botoru keepu*—literally "bottle keep"—the system enables regulars to come in anytime and party with their favorite hostesses and not have to worry about paying for their booze.

Occasionally a group of foreigners will come in, shit-faced and loud, looking for sex. Fisher tells them, always nicely at first, to kindly leave because Lounge O is not that kind of place. Which they usually do without much fuss. When they don't, Fisher switches to scary mode and informs them that if they don't get out *right now,* he'll make sure they spend the rest of the evening in the ER. Luckily he's never had to make good on the threat, because if he ever did, the cops would come and he'd probably be in trouble, but more important, so would Terry.

Sex is not on the menu at a normal hostess bar. Sex *appeal,* for sure, but as a rule the women working at places like Lounge

O don't sleep with customers. Fisher has come to think of them more as amateur psychologists. Their job is to talk with the men, drink with them, laugh at their jokes. Listen to their complaints about their bosses, their wives, their kids.

Yuki approaches the bar, a harried expression on his face. He's heavyset with slicked-back hair and a unibrow shaped like an arc that the girls are constantly imploring him to do something about. "So busy," he says to Fisher and Terry, waggling his head like he's trying to follow something spinning around it and can't keep up.

Terry sets several bowls of nuts on a tray, and Yuki picks the tray up and hurries off to set them out on some recently vacated tables. Terry bought Lounge O six years ago from a friend who owed a bunch of money to the wrong people.

Fisher empties the dustpan into the trash bin under the bar, then puts it back in the storage closet along with the broom and returns to the counter.

Terry chucks his chin at Fisher. "How you feeling?"

Fisher grabs a towel, shrugs, and starts wiping the marble countertop. "All right."

"Sorry to hear about the fight. Would have been a good one."

Terry should know. A hulking six feet even, with a shaved head and a perpetual scowl that belies a fundamentally friendly nature, he's a former light-heavyweight U.S. Muay Thai champion and BJJ black belt who at fifty-something still looks every bit the part. Fisher met him at the Brazilian jiu-jitsu school where they both used to train, and Terry offered Fisher the bouncing job shortly after he and Lisa split.

"Yeah," says Fisher. "Next time." He thinks of the three grand he'd stood to earn, win or lose, from the fight. Roughly half of it would have gone to the gym and various expenses, and Fisher had earmarked most of the rest of it to pay Terry back for the grand he'd borrowed from him two months ago, the same grand he'd used to hire the PI to search for his family. Fisher's face flushes with embarrassment. He'd told Terry he'd pay him back after the fight, and now he can't. He clears his throat. "Listen, Terry, about the money—"

Terry gives a dismissive wave. "Pay me back when you can."

A mix of gratitude and shame fills Fisher's chest. "Thanks. I just need a couple more weeks."

Terry places his palms on the counter and gives Fisher a serious look. "You know what BL would say at a time like this?"

Fisher fixes him with a skeptical look. Terry is fond of tossing out Bruce Lee quotes, no matter the occasion.

"I'm dying to know."

Terry slowly traces a large circle in the air and then holds his hands out palms up, as if offering Fisher something small but extremely precious. "Take things as they come."

"That's deep. The Little Dragon actually came up with that?"

"No, that's me, channeling him."

"Ah. Good he has you as a go-between. Makes the message much…simpler."

"There is no fixed teaching, my friend," says Terry, making air quotes. "All I can provide is an appropriate medicine for a particular ailment."

"You channel that too?"

"No, *that's* BL."

Fisher chuckles. This is why Monday and Wednesday nights have become his favorite nights of the week. Nominally, he is "security" for Lounge O, but in the year and a half he's been working here, he's only had to actually put his hands on someone a handful of times, either because a customer was belligerently drunk or hassling one of the girls. Most of the time he ends up just hanging out like he's doing right now, shooting the bull with Terry, chatting with the girls when they have a free moment.

Yuki runs up, his unibrow a straight line of consternation. "Table four," he says, motioning with his head. "Guy is getting grabby with Mari."

Fisher exchanges a quick glance with Terry, then turns and immediately sees what's happening. The grabby guy is seated at the end of the booth. He's short and stout, with the kind of ruddy complexion you don't often see on a Japanese person. He's in an expensive-looking, charcoal gray suit with sparkly cuff links and has slicked-back hair so shiny it looks as though it's been lacquered. He's wearing glasses and has a booming voice. One of his arms is draped heavily over Mari's shoulder.

Among the eight hostesses working at Lounge O, Mari has been there the longest. She's in her early thirties and is quick-witted and funny, which has made her popular with the salarymen. It's mainly Mari Fisher chats up when things are slow because she's cute as hell and he digs her sense of humor, a combination of warmth and sarcasm, nuttiness and insight. And he seems to be able to make her laugh too.

Seated with Mari and Cuff Links are another salaryman, thirtyish with thinning hair, and Erika, who has a beautiful singing voice and always gets a big applause during karaoke. "No way!" Mari says to Cuff Links. She's still smiling but Fisher can see she's trying to gently remove his arm from her shoulder.

They went out for a drink a few months back, after which Fisher walked her home and she invited him up to her apartment. He almost took her up on the invitation. He really dug her, and that was exactly the problem. He felt—*feels*—guilty about how much he's attracted to her, because he still considers himself married despite the divorce, and getting his family back is his number one priority. So he made up some lame excuse about having to be in Yokohama early the next morning to train. Now it feels like she's pulled back from him a bit. She's still friendly, but the flirty banter has all but stopped, and he misses it.

Cuff Links guffaws and says, "I'm serious!" Then he reaches up and squeezes one of Mari's tits. Anger flashes across her face as she pushes the hand away.

"Did you see that?" Fisher says to Terry.

"Yeah, I saw it," Terry says. "Shit."

Fisher launches himself off his stool. Non-sexual, flirtatious touching between the girls and the customers is permitted and expected at legit hostess bars like Lounge O. A sympathetic pat on the arm of a businessman who's had a rough day at work. A head on the shoulder of a shy young guy who can't muster the courage to ask a girl out. What is neither permitted nor expected, however, is sexual contact of any kind.

Cuff Links either doesn't know this or doesn't care, though, because before Fisher can get to Table 4, he tries to run his hand up under Mari's skirt.

Fisher says, "Hey!" He's never been able to stand idly by while a person is attacked by someone stronger. The fact that it's Mari who's being assaulted trips a circuit in his head.

A flurry of movement. Mari pushes Cuff Links away. Undeterred, he jams his hand up her skirt again, hard this time. Mari says, "Ow!" then in a flash seizes the guy's arm with one hand and punches him in the nose with the other.

Crack!

Erika lets out a startled yelp.

The force of the blow knocks Cuff Links's glasses off. "Ah!" he says, his hand flying up to his cheek.

For a brief moment it's as if time has stopped. Everyone in the place freezes, focusing on Table 4, the only sound the fast thump of the J-Pop pumping from the speakers.

Blood is already pouring from Cuff Links's nose and through his hands by the time Fisher gets to the table. The man's eyes are wide with shock and anger. "Bitch! What the fuck?!" he shouts into his cupped hands.

His pulse thumping, Fisher grabs Cuff Links by the scruff of the collar.

"Asshole!" Mari says, and then Cuff Links lunges toward her, the top button of his shirt popping as his collar jerks against Fisher's grip. A collective scream echoes off the mirrored walls.

Suddenly filled with rage, Fisher grabs Cuff Links and launches him out of the booth. The man lands hard on the tiled floor.

More screams, barely audible to Fisher as he approaches Cuff Links. He leans over, seizes a fistful of the man's hair. *How does it feel, motherfucker?* He raises his other fist.

Terry's voice, as if through a paper tube: "Hank!"

Fisher stops. Looks down. Cuff Links is covered in blood. Terry moving between him and Cuff Links now.

"Jesus Christ," says Terry. He turns to Yuki. "Go get some towels."

Yuki runs off and comes back a moment later with several rolled-up cold towels, unrolls and hands them to Cuff Links, who takes them without a word and presses them to his nose.

Cuff Links's friend scrambles out of the booth. "Kobayashi-san! Are you okay?"

Terry gives Fisher a withering look and shakes his head.

"I'm sorry," the friend says to Terry as he helps Kobayashi to his feet. "He's very drunk."

"Don't apologize for me, dumbass," says Kobayashi as his friend escorts him to the elevator, and before the doors slide shut, the asshole shouts, "I'm going to run you out of fucking business!"

Terry looks over at Mari, who's being comforted by Erika and the other girls. "You okay?"

"I'm okay," she says and then hurries out of the booth and walks with Erika back to the break room.

Terry sighs long and deep, then stares at Fisher, an *I-don't-even-know-what-to-say* expression on his face.

Fisher holds his hands out, palms up, feeling guilty and stupid and pissed at himself for almost losing his temper again. "Terry, I—"

Terry cuts him off. "I can't have you losing it like that, Hank. Take the rest of the night off."

CHAPTER FIVE

"YOU LITTLE PIECE of shit," says the old man, sitting there behind his desk in that stupid green leather suit of his.

Aoyama Shota fixes his gaze on an obsidian paperweight on the desk, chewing the inside of his cheek. When he was a kid, Uncle Jun's words would leave him on the verge of tears every time. Now he's thirty-five and they just piss him off. And he's angry at the old man, yeah, but he's also angry at himself, because while the words don't hurt like they used to, they still have the ability to make a part of him feel like a tiny, helpless child.

The office reeks of cologne—Axe or some other scent way too young for a sixty-eight-year-old man—and tobacco. Uncle Jun's desk is in front of the only window, a scuffed-up mahogany thing too large for the room. There's an antique grandfather clock in one corner that Shota doesn't remember ever working, a framed picture of Half Dome on the wall facing the desk, and underneath the photo, an incongruous-looking metal filing cabinet. Uncle Jun thinks he's cool, but he has no fucking style.

"Sorry, Uncle," Shota forces himself to say.

"Sorry's what you always say. It's what you said the last time. Remember? Sorry from you means nothing." Uncle Jun says something about Shota's lack of common sense and sophistication and uses a bunch of hard words he knows damn well are beyond Shota's elementary Japanese ability.

When Shota was in fourth grade, he got suspended for smashing a kid over the head with a chair. He bit a teacher in fifth grade, because this fucking guy hit him across the face, and Shota ran at him like a Tasmanian devil, jumped on him, and sank his teeth into the fucker's forearm, bit a nice chunk out. They kicked him out after that. Uncle Jun pulls an e-cigarette from his inside jacket pocket, jabs it between his lips and takes a drag and lets the vapor drift out of his mouth in a flattened waterfall. He strokes his chin for a moment, staring at Shota, then stabs the air with the vape pen. "I should've cut you loose when you killed that stripper. I should've let you face the consequences."

Here we go again, Shota thinks. What was he, twenty back then? Twenty-one? And it wasn't even his fault. He and this chick were at his apartment and it got a little rough, and Shota bit her tit, just enough to draw a little blood, no big deal, and she screamed like he'd stabbed her and the bitch wouldn't shut up, just wouldn't stop screaming, so Shota had to strangle her. Then of course he had to call Uncle Jun, because what else was he supposed to do, and Uncle Jun sent some guys to come and clean things up. And ever since that fucking day, the old man has never let Shota live it down. Like it was such a big deal, which it definitely wasn't, because the organization disappeared people all the time.

He's been working for his uncle for fifteen years now, doing the same kinds of bullshit, and he's not much higher on the totem pole than he was when he started out. Which is why he started his own gang. Spiral isn't well-known yet, but that's going to change.

"It's always something. I used to think you'd snap out of it when you got older, that you'd grow up. But no." Uncle Jun emits a long sigh, and the mix of weariness, disappointment, and derision contained in the sound of it puts Shota on the defensive.

After he got kicked out of school, his mom called Uncle Jun, her older brother. Uncle Jun pulled some strings, got Shota into one of the international schools in Tokyo where they only spoke English. But he kept getting into fights, and the teachers were always sending him to the office, giving him detention. In high school he got caught selling crank to an American kid who happened to be the son of somebody important at the U.S. Embassy. The school called the cops, and if it weren't for Uncle Jun's connections, Shota would've gone to jail. He was expelled five months short of graduation.

"It's not my fault," he says.

"It's never your fault!" Uncle Jun slaps the desk with the palm of his hand, then reaches for his phone. He swipes his thumb a few times across the screen and then holds it up for Shota to see.

On the screen is a photo of an ear, covered in blood. Or most of an ear, anyway. The lobe is missing, clearly and cleanly severed from the rest of the ear.

"You're going to tell me *this* isn't your fault?"

Two nights ago, Shota had been coming out of a bar when a guy bumped into him and didn't say sorry. Shota might have just punched the guy in the face and left it at that, but he'd been in a bad mood. He had Matchan hold the guy down on the ground while Shota cut off his earlobe. He'd used his stiletto, so it was a clean cut and just the lobe, not the whole ear for fuck's sake. Not a big deal. But the asshole had to be threatened, and Uncle Jun had to pay him a ridiculous amount of money not to go to the cops and instead go straight to the ER and tell the doctor that he got plastered and accidentally cut his own earlobe off while trying to trim his hair.

Uncle Jun shakes his head. "You're a disgrace. A blemish on my sister's memory. If you weren't her son, I would have nothing to do with you."

Shota bows his head in a half-assed effort to look contrite. What he really feels like doing is grabbing the letter opener sitting there on the desk next to Uncle Jun's phone, leaping over the desk, and stabbing the old fucker in the heart. Over and over and over, sewing machine style. He doesn't, of course. Instead, Shota apologizes again, in response to which the old man makes a spitting sound.

But it's okay.

The old man can say whatever he wants, because soon, very soon, he's going to be dead, and the Tanabe-*kai* will crumble like the brittle relic it is. And when that happens, everyone on the street will know who Spiral is.

"Get out of my sight," Uncle Jun says.

Shota rises to leave, thinking, *Sure thing, you fucking dinosaur.*

"What did he say?" Tsukahara says from the front passenger seat as Matchan pulls away from the curb.

Shota makes a dismissive motion with his hand. "Fuck it." He looks out the window. It's almost midnight, and there are only a few late-night stragglers walking about. Salarymen trying to catch cabs. Young couples looking for love hotels. Shota homes in on one such couple, a tall, delicate-looking pretty boy in his twenties with carefully mussed hair, arm in arm with a long-haired girl who looks to be about the same age.

She's cute, but what catches Shota's eye is the backpack the boy is carrying. In the light of the streetlamp, he can see it's a vintage indigo Michael Kors flap pack. He tells Matchan to pull over.

Tsukahara says, "What is it?"

Once the car stops, Shota gets out without a word and walks quickly toward the young couple, scanning the street for cops as he goes. Seeing none, he reaches into his pants pocket and pulls out his knife. He flicks the blade out with an audible *snick* just as the boy and girl see him coming. They both freeze, their eyes huge and innocent as anime characters. The girl makes a little squeaking sound and buries the side of her face into the boy's chest.

Pulling the girl tightly into him, the boy says, "W-What do you want?" His face is pale under the streetlight. Poor fucker looks like he might pass out.

"Give me your backpack."

"What?"

Shota takes a step forward, menacing. "Your backpack, fucker."

The boy quickly shrugs the backpack off and hands it to Shota. Shota undoes the flap, turns the pack upside down, dumps the contents onto the sidewalk at the couple's feet, and walks back to the car.

As Matchan pulls away from the curb, Shota inspects his new backpack. He notices Tsukahara giving him his usual exasperated what-the-fuck expression. Normally Shota ignores it, but after getting the third degree from Uncle Jun tonight, he's not in the mood.

"Fuck off," Shota says without looking up at Tsukahara. He goes back to admiring the backpack and decides it will be a good present for Ryo.

CHAPTER SIX

It's a short train ride to Shinjuku Station, followed by a short walk home from the south exit, Fisher cursing himself the whole way.

First he beats Dave up and then...what just happened? What is wrong with him? He'd come close to giving that guy Kobayashi a real beating. If he'd actually done it, Terry could have lost his business license. Fisher is lucky Terry didn't fire him on the spot. He's relieved, though, that Mari seemed to be okay. She really nailed that idiot with that punch. Might have broken his nose.

Pedestrians fan themselves and mop their brows as they move up and down the sidewalk. Ten at night and the sticky heat hasn't let up a bit.

Should he call Mari to see if she's okay? He pictures her again, popping that guy. She takes no shit from anyone, and he finds it attractive as hell. If he'd accepted her invitation that night a few months ago, would something have developed between them? Regret claws at him for a moment, and then Lisa's face floats up and he shakes his head free of the thought.

Home is a redbrick-colored fifteen-story apartment building

whose best days were probably already well behind it by the early 70s. Sunshine Mansion is flanked by two shabby office buildings, one of which houses a cheap ramen place on the ground floor. The apartment complex and its neighbors face the Koshu Kaido, one of the roads built during the Edo Period to connect Tokyo (then Edo) to what is now Yamanashi Prefecture, and above it, the ugly hulk of the Chuo Expressway.

Each floor of the complex is a row of ten units. Fisher's room is the fifth one down from the elevator on his floor, sandwiched between Kawano-san, a guy in his thirties Fisher has only actually seen twice since he moved in, and Wakabayashi-san, an older woman who lives with her seven-year-old grandson, Atsushi.

As he's opening his door, the next-door neighbor's dog starts barking. Then Wakabayashi-san's lock rattles and a second later, her grandson Atsushi—"Akkun" for short—pokes his head out and flashes Fisher a big grin.

"*Konbanwa!*" he says. Hi! He's missing his two front teeth, and it somehow makes his face light up even more than before he lost them.

Cute kid. Of course, seeing that smile of his always makes Fisher wistful for Justin and James. The way they would beam when he came home from the gym. How they'd jump on him, Lisa laughing as she watched them try to wrestle him to the ground.

Wakabayashi-san inside, shushing the dog, an excitable gray toy poodle that reminds Fisher of Brownie, the too-friendly-for-his-own-good dog he and Lisa adopted as a puppy when the twins were a year old. Brownie grew up thinking he was one of the kids, and until a certain age Justin and James seemed to think of him the same way.

Fisher releases an internal sigh. He smiles back at Akkun. "Konbanwa." He squints at the boy, a mock-skeptical look. "Shouldn't you be in bed?"

Akkun shakes his head, his smile widening.

"*Akkun!*" says his grandmother from inside their apartment. "Don't bother him!" Wakabayashi-san's face appears above Akkun's, wearing an embarrassed smile-frown. "*Sumimasen nee,*" she says. I'm sorry.

She's in her early sixties. She's got long hair streaked with gray and is painfully thin. Sugimoto told Fisher shortly after he'd moved in that her daughter was really young and rarely came around. Fisher smiles and shakes his head, says like he always does, "No, no, it's okay."

He looks down at Akkun, who's waggling his tongue around the gap in his teeth. "Have they started to come in?"

"Yeah!" Akkun says. "Look!" He tilts his head back and points so Fisher can see the little sliver of tooth peeping from his gums.

"Oh yeah! Wow, look at that!"

Wakabayashi-san says, "It's time for bed. Say bye-bye."

Fisher winks at him and waves. "See you later."

Akkun flashes that brilliant smile again and winks back. "Bye-bye!"

Inside, Fisher turns on the lights, drops his bag on the floor, kicks off his shoes, and sighs. He steps up into the room from the stamp-sized foyer. He empties his pockets and tosses his wallet, his keys, his phone onto the narrow counter. As he turns to strip off his sweat-soaked clothes, his elbow knocks his only coffee cup off the tiny dish rack. He spins, tries to catch it, misses, and the cup shatters on the floor.

The image kicks up a memory: a glass exploding against

the wall, Lisa screaming. Brownie yelping, startled at the noise, the kids waking up, James immediately starting to cry. It was the only time he'd ever been violent around her. But what she'd told him that night…

His throat clutches. He grabs the broom and dust pan and sweeps up the pieces of the cup and dumps them in a plastic bag. Then he strips off his clothes and tosses them onto the pile in the corner and turns on the AC before stepping into the shower.

He towels off in front of the AC and then stretches out on the *tatami* and stares up at the ceiling. He replays the scene at Lounge O in his mind, then hears Ken's voice suggesting he talk to someone to get things off his chest. The childish way he'd brushed it off—turned it around, laying a guilt trip on Ken for kicking him out of the gym—makes him cringe. The truth was that about a year ago he did make an appointment with a shrink. But he canceled at the last minute, having convinced himself that discussing his problems with a stranger wasn't going to fix things. Instead he joined a yoga class, which helped him relax but didn't really take his mind off the things that had been eating at him.

Yeah, maybe he should see someone.

His gaze gravitates, like it always does, to the picture he keeps on top of the bookshelf in the corner. It's a photo from a family trip to Hawaii three years ago. In it are the four of them, Fisher and Lisa and the twins, all of them tan and smiling, except for James, who's on the verge of tears for some reason Fisher can no longer remember. Things were rocky at the time but not beyond repair, and it had been an amazing trip. Fisher and Lisa lay on the beach during the day, taking turns playing in the surf with the twins, cracking up at how they frolicked like puppy dogs in the water. In the evening, they strolled, ate ice cream after dinner, made love in their hotel room after the boys fell asleep, trying not to wake them with their giggles. Lisa remarking that this was how he used to be. Happy, relaxed, fun. She wanted the old Hank back. Fisher promising he'd change. This is always the part of the day that sucks the worst. Whenever he's here in his shitty little rabbit hutch, it doesn't matter what he starts out thinking about; inevitably his thoughts turn to his family. To what he had and lost and more than anything wants back.

After months of searching, it's starting to seem like he's never going to find his family. Even if he does, how can he make good on his promise to himself to change when he's driven his life into a ditch?

He gets up and goes to the fridge. Inside is a dish of lasagna that Terry's wife, Laura, made for him because she's a sweetheart, a half-dozen eggs, and a little container of vanilla custard from FamilyMart. There's also a bag of plain scones and two overripe bananas on the counter, but that's it, because Fisher hasn't been shopping in days.

He closes the fridge. He's not hungry after all.

He grabs the remote and turns on the TV. He notices the little red light blinking on the phone on his desk. The PI is the only one who calls him on his landline, even though Fisher told him to call him on his mobile instead. He holds his breath in anticipation and hits play. "*Mr. Fisher, this is private investigator Watanabe,*" the message says. "*I have some good news for you.*"

Fisher's heart leaps. He'd tried at first to track his family down himself, but everywhere he turned was a dead end. Lisa was an only child and both of her parents were long dead. Fisher went to every friend and coworker of hers he could think of, but if any of them knew where she'd gone, none were willing to tell him. It was the same story at the boys' school, where the principal informed Fisher that even if she did know where his wife and kids were, she wouldn't be able to tell him because that was "personal information." He'd lived in Japan long enough to know that the rules were the rules. When people divorced in Japan, more often than not Mom took the kids and Dad was cut out of the picture. And not just figuratively. He literally became *tanin*—an outsider. It wasn't uncommon for a divorced father to never see his children again, or at least not while they were still children. "*En wo kiru*" was the Japanese expression for it. To cut ties. It was an accepted reality in Japan, because that's just the way things were.

And if Dad was a foreigner who wanted to remain part of his kids' lives? Well, good luck with that.

That was what Fisher's lawyer had told him, anyway, although not exactly in those words.

Watanabe's message continues: *I went to the address in Nakameguro and talked with the landlord. She told me your ex-wife and sons moved out a month ago. However, I am happy to say that I managed to get a forwarding address from her.*

He's found them!

It was a very difficult case. Very time-consuming. I'm sorry but before I can give you the address I will need another two hundred thousand yen. Please understand. I know you are very anxious to see your family, so please deposit the money into my account as soon as possible and I will send you the address.

Fisher has already paid Watanabe almost two grand U.S., half of which he'd had to borrow from Terry. The deal was that the guy would find Lisa and the boys or Fisher would get his money back. Now the fucker has located them and is holding their whereabouts for ransom. Is that even legal? He should've known. He'd sensed something oily about the man from the start. The bad comb-over, the shifty eyes. The shabby hole-in-the-wall office in Ikebukuro that Fisher would've walked right by if it hadn't been for the handwritten sign outside saying "Private Investigator. English spoken!"

He chews the inside of his cheek as he dials Watanabe's number. No way he can afford another two grand. The phone rings and rings.

Fisher hangs up. How the fuck is he going to come up with another two thousand bucks? His bank account balance is close to zero, and he's got fifty thousand yen—about five hundred bucks—in his wallet to carry him through his next payday, which is three weeks away. Three weeks. He can't wait that long. He's also maxed out his two credit cards.

He looks at the family photo again. It's been two years since he last saw them. He wants to know that they're okay, to wrap the three of them in a huge hug.

There's one guy Fisher can call.

Akio Igawa is the cousin of a former training partner from Fisher's days at the Ralph Gracie Jiu-Jitsu Academy in California. Akio is in the "entertainment business," although he's never been clear about what exactly this means. He used to toss Fisher the occasional odd job—a bouncing gig here, a modeling job there. They always paid well, but the more of them Fisher did, the sketchier they seemed to get. The last one was about six months ago. Fisher had spent five straight hours on the basement floor of a Ginza department store, posing on some chintzy exercise equipment with a bikini-clad young blonde from Ukraine. The photographer asked him afterward if he wanted to do some nude shots at his studio.

Uh, thanks, but no thanks.

After that, he swore he wouldn't do any more of Akio's jobs. Yeah, he could've used the money, but debasing himself wasn't going to get him closer to his goal of being the man his family needed him to be.

Fisher grabs his cell. Extraordinary circumstances. He pulls up the number and hits dial.

CHAPTER SEVEN

"Yo, Killer!" Akio says, amped even at 11 p.m. Dub music plays loud in the background.

Fisher puts the phone on speaker and holds it away from his ear. "Dude, you ever heard of a quiet evening at home?"

Akio laughs. "A *what*?"

Same old Akio.

"One of these days," he says, "you gotta come out with me. Dude, I *guarantee* you'll get laid."

Fisher chuckles. "Sure." Akio has thrown him the same offer more times than Fisher can count. Fisher hasn't been with a woman since Lisa left, and that's the way it's going to be.

Akio makes a dismissive sound, like air rushing out of a punctured tire. "That's what you always say. So, what's up?"

"Well, I'm a little light on cash this month and, uh, I was thinking I could use one of those gigs of yours to help make ends meet." There's a queasy feeling in the pit of his stomach as soon as the words are out of his mouth.

Akio laughs. "My memory serves, 'Never again' is what you said the last time. What's up? Everything okay?"

"Yeah. No, everything's fine. Just got hit with some expenses I didn't plan for."

"Shit, wish you'd called me last week. Had a sweet one lined up. English voice-coaching gig on the set of this TV show. Ended up giving it to this Brit girl I know who does an amazing American accent. I don't know, man. Let me think." There's a long pause. Then: "You know, there is something, but I don't think you'd want to do it."

"Why's that?"

Akio makes a high-pitched skeptical noise. "It's kind of an acting-slash-bodyguard gig. Sort of up your alley I guess, the bodyguard part anyway, but...I don't know, dude."

Acting-slash-bodyguard gig. The description pricks up Fisher's antennae. It already sounds shady. Which is probably why Akio is hesitant. But this is about Fisher being able to see his family again. And it's not like any of Akio's jobs ever required him to do anything illegal. "How much does it pay?"

Akio laughs. "Wow. You *are* desperate. Tell you what, what're you doing right now?"

"Now? Nothing."

"There's a ramen joint in Roppongi called Afuri. Meet me there in an hour and I'll fill you in on the details."

The ramen joint is a sleek, modern-looking place on the basement floor of Hollywood Plaza: black stools around a wooden counter facing an open kitchen that's all gleaming steel.

Fisher gets there fifteen minutes early, anxious to meet Akio and learn about this job.

He takes a seat at the counter. There are eight or nine people in the place. Two young chefs dressed in black T-shirts move around each other with choreographed precision as they prepare bowls of ramen noodles.

Fisher absently looks out the window on his left while he waits for Akio. A muscular kid with a gym bag slung over his shoulder passes by. Looks like a fighter, maybe on his way home from a late-night training session.

Three years ago, Fisher was always grinding at the gym, but especially during the eight weeks leading up to a fight. Up and out the door for a run at 5 a.m. Back at six for a quick bowl of oatmeal, a piece of fruit, a bunch of eggs, and black coffee. Kiss Lisa and the kids and out the door again at ten after six and on the mat an hour later to stretch, work the kinks out, then one or more of the following for the next two hours: wrestling, jiu-jitsu, Muay Thai, boxing, weight training, wind sprints, gymnastics. Shower and leave the gym by ten. Home by ten thirty, watch TV for a half hour or so. Eat. Nap. Out the door again at two thirty and back on the mat by 3:30 for the same basic routine as the morning plus maybe a jog. Off the mat by 5 p.m. and home for dinner by six.

Eight weeks of *that* shit and you're in fighting shape.

Your marriage? Not so much.

By that point he'd lost his last eight fights and was feeling useless and ashamed, his promise to Lisa to make enough as a pro to provide for her and the kids broken. But the more he lost, the more his desperation to turn things around grew, and the less time he spent at home being a husband and a father.

A little cloud of steam rolls up in the kitchen as one of the chefs plucks a helping of noodles from a big pot of boiling water, sets it in a flat strainer, and gives the strainer three brisk shakes.

"Yo!" a familiar voice says and in walks Akio. The offspring of an Irish expat mother and a Japanese father, Akio is forty-five with perfect hair, slightly graying at the temples, and the knock-out looks of a movie star. Resplendent in an expensive-looking gray suit and loafers, he saunters over and pulls out the chair next to Fisher. He holds his fist out for Fisher to bump.

"What's up, Killer?!" He turns to one of the chefs behind the counter, flashes his million-dollar smile, and dips his head. "*Domo*." Hi there.

The chef beams back and bows. A couple of the other patrons stare.

Fisher can't help but chuckle. Akio is so full of charisma, the stuff is probably in his shit.

The chef takes their order: a bowl of spicy *yuzu-ra tanmen* noodles for Fisher, salty *yuzu*-flavored ramen for Akio.

Fisher gives Akio's suit the once-over, as if he'd know whatever brand it is, and says, "Looking good as always."

There's that smile again. "Give me fashion or give me death, baby."

Fisher shakes his head and chuckles. Part of him thinks Akio really means it. The most casual thing he's ever seen the man wear is an expensive-looking sports jacket and slacks. His feet would probably shrivel up if he wore sneakers.

Akio asks him how he's feeling about the upcoming fight.

"It's off."

"Oh no!"

Fisher winces internally. He gives a dismissive wave and asks what Akio has been up to. Akio launches into a story about a girl he met at a club the other night who turned out to be into S&M, emphasis on the "S." Their food comes, and they dig in, Fisher listening with amusement as Akio describes how he and the girl tongue-wrestled, pawing at each other like animals, and his shock when she pushed him hard onto the sofa and pulled a bullwhip out of her bag. By the time Akio has finished relating the story, Fisher is literally choking on his noodles he's laughing so hard.

"So," Fisher says once his mirth has subsided, "this 'acting-slash-bodyguard gig'…" Using air quotes around the words. Akio says, "All you really gotta do is sit there at a meeting and act like the scary foreigner." He nudges Fisher with his elbow. "Not a stretch for you." With a delicate motion of his fingers, he picks up a tangle of noodles with his chopsticks. Fisher wants to know more, especially why Akio was hesitant on the phone, but he pops the most important question first. Everything else is just details. "How much?"

Akio's eyebrows go up. He slurps the last of his noodles and sets his chopsticks down and clears his throat. He dabs the corners of his mouth with a napkin and gives Fisher a conspiratorial grin. "Spill it," Fisher says. He takes a sip of tea.

"A million yen, dude."

Fisher coughs, choking on his tea. A million yen. Ten thousand U.S. "Come on, Akio."

"I kid you not."

"A million yen for one night's work?" Fisher smirks. "What's the catch?"

Akio finishes his noodles and says, "Come on." He stands up to pay the bill. "Let's take a ride."

⁓

They're cruising around Shin-Okubo, Tokyo's Korea Town, in Akio's immaculate black BMW 3-series. The inside of the car smells like leather and cologne. Some too-cool-for-school jazz is playing on the stereo. Whatever Akio is into, he's either making a killing at it or is doing a really good job of faking it.

Even on a Wednesday night, Shin-Okubo is hopping. The

sidewalks and narrow backstreets branching off Okubo Boulevard are crowded with bright-eyed locals and tourists on the
prowl for good eats and cheap prices. Fisher spots a queue of
teenage fashionistas in front of a little shop serving up *hotteok*—
brown sugar syrup-filled crispy pancakes—fresh off the griddle.

Fisher listens to Akio give him the rundown: Two groups
of club owners are in the middle of a dispute over a wayward
stripper. They're going to have a sit-down to resolve the matter.
The two groups are on relatively good terms, so the meeting will
be friendly and shouldn't last more than an hour or two, tops.

In and out. Easy money.

A feeling of unease settles in Fisher's gut. He's been in Tokyo
long enough to know that "club owner" potentially means
"gangster." The job doesn't sound easy. It sounds dangerous.
This, he realizes, is why Akio thought Fisher wouldn't want to
do the job. He fixes Akio with a look.

"What's your connection to these guys?"

Akio laughs. "It's not what you're thinking."

"What am I thinking, Akio?"

"Dude, I'm not a gangster, okay?"

"I didn't say you were."

"You don't have to say it. That look you're giving me says
it all. Listen, this is why I said you probably wouldn't want the
job, and, dude, if you don't, that's fine."

Fisher holds a hand up. "No, no. I'm not saying I don't
want to do it. I just want to know what I'm getting myself
into." Knowing as he says this that it doesn't matter because he's
already made up his mind. He's doing this job.

Akio says, "I have a friend who works for one of the organizations, okay? I've known him since middle school."

"What does your friend *do* for the *organization?*"

Akio's expression turns deadly serious. "He's a hit man."

Fisher's mouth drops open, and Akio bursts out laughing.

"I'm *kidding*. He's an accountant."

"Asshole."

Akio laughs again and slaps his knee. "Dude, the look on your face..." He explains that the Tanabe Group is involved mostly in the consumer finance and real estate businesses. They also own and manage restaurants, bars, and clubs in the entertainment districts of Roppongi, Shinjuku, and Shibuya. He doesn't mention drugs or prostitution, guns or murder, which are the kinds of things Fisher associates with the word *yakuza*. Fisher wonders what "mostly" means but decides it's probably better not to ask. A million yen is a million yen. He could use some of it to pay the PI, some to pay Terry back. Maybe he could use the rest as a partial tuition payment for business school. He could apply for student loans to cover the rest. Besides, the way Akio describes it, this yakuza group doesn't sound like a gang anyway. It sounds like a big company.

They turn right onto Koshu Kaido. Office buildings line both sides of the boulevard, keeping watch like giant robot sentries. "Dude, I'm telling you," says Akio. "Easy-peasy. These guys will make a big show of parading you around. It'll be fun."

Finally starting to relax a little, Fisher asks why they need a foreigner for this. Akio explains that the rival gang has recently been seen around town with a big *gaijin*. Word on the street is that he's from Serbia and affiliated with a Serbian organization the Tanabe Group is trying to establish ties with.

"A 'Serbian organization'? You gotta be kidding me."

"Hank, it's not even work. You go and hang out with these guys, play the part and act tough for a couple hours." He claps his hands once and smiles. "A million yen, baby!"

They stop at a light, and Fisher looks out the window at a homeless guy shuffling along the sidewalk amid throngs of men and women who give him a wide berth, like he's a rock or a bush in their path. His hair is long and matted, his clothes in tatters. It's a rare and disconcerting image, the jarring contrast between this bum and the well-dressed people all around him, the ultra-clean office buildings and hotels and stores lining the orderly street.

A million yen.

"Okay," he says.

Akio holds his fist out. "My man!"

As Fisher touches his knuckles to his friend's, the reality of what he's just agreed to hits him. He's just hopped into bed with gangsters. A ripple of unease runs up his spine. He fights the feeling down.

He's got to do this.

CHAPTER EIGHT

UNCOMFORTABLE IN THE only suit he owns, Fisher sits in the smoky VIP room of Club Deluxe and regards the tableau before him in the gaudy Akasaka nightclub: two groups of Japanese men growling at each other over a shiny black table covered with empty sake and beer bottles.

What did Akio get him into here? Muffled house music from the front of the club thumps softly in the room.

There are four men from Kabukicho plus the Serbian dude on one side of the table. Fisher and five guys from the Tanabe-*kai* on the other.

The Serbian is tall and lean with dark, short-cropped hair, scarred-up eyebrows, and a crooked nose. His ears aren't cauliflowered, which could mean the guy's not a grappler. Could be a boxer. Or maybe a kickboxer. Definitely a fighter, though.

With the exception of Fisher and the Serbian, every face at the table is beet red—*makka*, as the Japanese say—from the alcohol being put away like it's the end of the world.

"That bitch was hazardous material and you assholes knew it," says one of the Kabukicho guys. He's got short, spiky hair, manicured eyebrows, and what looks like a spray-on tan.

"We told you we didn't know," says the man sitting two seats to the left of Fisher.

"Fucking liar!"

Akio's words echo in Fisher's head: *They're mostly into consumer finance and real estate*. Though they're all dressed in suits, these guys don't look or sound like finance or real estate types to Fisher.

He'd met Akio's accountant friend and another man in front of the building thirty minutes earlier as he'd been instructed via text message. The neighboring buildings were all crammed with hostess bars, swanky strip clubs, pubs, and restaurants. In his forties with graying hair parted to one side and wearing a tan suit, the accountant introduced himself as Takahashi. The other man, a tall guy in his thirties with a man bun and diamond earrings, stood off to the side, regarding Fisher with an expression of barely concealed hostility. Takahashi shook Fisher's hand, took a step back, and looked him up and down. He smiled, nodded once, and said, "Good," then, in a dismissive tone, told the guy with the man bun to wait outside.

On the way up in the elevator, Takahashi said to Fisher, "You don't have to do anything. Just sit with them and look tough. And don't speak unless you're spoken to."

Takahashi led Fisher through the club to the VIP room in back, where a man he introduced as Sato-san, "the Boss," was waiting with three other men. A short, pudgy man with dark sunglasses and a thick pink scar on the left side of his nose, Sato nodded at Fisher and said in heavily accented English, "Do you understand my English?"

"Yes."

Sato said, "Okay," and pointed to an empty chair on his left, indicating Fisher should sit there. Fisher took his seat. The three men accompanying him briefly introduced themselves, and he immediately forgot their names.

When the Kabukicho group arrived, the two groups went through the ritual of elaborately polite greetings Fisher has grown accustomed to seeing in Japan. A cordial affair, if a bit stiff. No tension between the men that Fisher could detect. Business cards were exchanged, and both sides got a laugh when the Serbian dude started passing out his own cards. He even gave Fisher one, and for a moment Fisher thought Oh shit, because Akio hadn't said anything about having to bring business cards, which Fisher didn't even have anyway, and his embarrassment must have been apparent, because someone from his side of the table slapped him on the shoulder and said, "It's okay, you don't need one." Which prompted everyone to laugh even louder.

The last of the ice having been broken at Fisher's expense, everyone took their seats. Food and drink and small talk followed, and Fisher relaxed, thinking, *Cool.* Every once in a while he glanced at the Serbian guy, and judging from the impassive look on his face, he wasn't stressing either.

Now, twenty minutes later, the men around the table are mad-dogging each other, shifting in their seats like fidgety schoolboys.

Not good. Part of Fisher wants to get the hell out of there.

But a bigger part of him wants that ten grand.

So he stays put and listens. From what he's heard so far, the Tanabe group has been shelling out a lot of money to bring girls over from Eastern Europe to work in its strip clubs in Roppongi, Shibuya, and Shinjuku. A month ago, one of those girls, a twenty-year-old Czech named Andrea, had quit her job at a club in Shibuya and applied for a gig at a club in Kabukicho owned by the rival gang. Not wanting to make waves, the rival gang reached out to the Tanabe group to discuss the issue before hiring the Czech girl. Reps from the two organizations met and talked and agreed on a "transfer fee." The Kabukicho gang paid the fee, hired the girl, and that was that. Until three days ago, when the girl attacked a customer and left him bloody and unconscious in a room in a love hotel and then skipped town.

Fingers point and accusations fly until the spokesman for the Kabukicho group, a tall guy with a horsey face and long, slicked-back hair, slams his palm down on the table.

Fisher's heart tics in his chest. This is not going down the way it was supposed to.

"Let me say this," he says. His voice is deep like a radio DJ's.

The room goes quiet, and Horseface explains that his people have talked with some of the girls who'd worked with the Czech girl at the Shibuya club, and they said she'd been a constant source of drama there, stealing from the other girls, talking trash, spreading rumors—always stirring up shit. To top it off, she'd started turning tricks on the side. The Tanabe gang had to have known all this since they owned the club. As a matter of common courtesy, they should have informed the Kabukicho group about the girl's history. Horseface says his people are entitled to a refund of the transfer fee, as well as damages to cover the customer's medical and dental expenses and the resulting downturn in business at their own club.

Everyone on Fisher's side of the table turns to Sato, who sits there with the same blank expression he's worn for the past half hour. The only difference Fisher can see is that the scar on the side of his nose has gone from pink to a deep red.

Sato stares at Horseface for a moment, then draws in a long breath, shifts his gaze upward, and lets out a little sigh.

The air in the room changes, a sudden static charge. Then

a clamor goes up, the men on either side of Sato-san screaming at the Kabukicho gang.

"Motherfucker!"

"Fuck you!"

Dread floods Fisher's veins. He can feel his heart beating in his throat.

The man on his right pops up out of his seat, his face twisted into a grimace, his right hand inside his suit jacket. Two guys on the other side of the table jump up in response, reaching inside their own jackets. Then everyone's standing, each side glaring at the other. Except for Fisher and the Serbian, neither of whom moves a muscle.

Things have gone very bad, very fast. Too fast for Fisher to believe what's happening. *Come on! It'll be fun!* He should have known. Everything he touches turns to shit. He searches the Serbian's face, thinking they're both outsiders here, he's probably feeling as alarmed as Fisher is, but if the Serbian shares Fisher's sentiments, he isn't showing it. He sits there with his hands flat on the shiny table, wearing a look of supreme indifference as the shouting ratchets up and up, like he's seen all this before.

Fisher glances down at the guy's hands. They are comically big, like mallets, the fingers adorned with chunky gold rings. If he ends up having to fight this guy, it's going to hurt.

A tense silence descends on the room, and then one of the gangsters breaks it by kicking the underside of the table.

Fisher jumps as if hit by a jolt of electricity. He rises reflexively, his eyes flicking around the room.

The Serbian gets up too. He has at least three inches and twenty pounds on Fisher.

A diamond flash streaks through the air.

Fisher realizes too late that it's a glass ashtray, and it's coming right at him. He averts his face to avoid it, but the ashtray glances off the top of his forehead, arcs up, and smacks the mirrored wall behind him with a crack.

His hand shoots up to feel the spot the ashtray struck, finds no blood.

The room has erupted into a free-for-all.

The guys on Fisher's side of the table quickly stand in front of Sato, shielding him from the melee. Two of the Kabukicho guys cover the horse-faced man in the same way.

A thick guy in dark sunglasses on Fisher's side of the table grabs a beer bottle by the neck and smashes a guy with a perm in the side of the head with it.

Two more guys in a corner have each other by the lapels, beating each other in the face like hockey players.

Over on the right, two men are kicking another man on the floor.

A woman's muffled scream from another part of the club, and then a noisy stampede outside the door as the patrons bolt, apparently aware that something bad is happening, their running footfalls mixed with the sound of slamming doors and shouting.

The noise distracts Fisher, and from out of nowhere, a fist connects with his left cheekbone. It jars him, makes him see double for a fraction of a second.

And then something clicks in his head and he goes into overdrive, punching and kicking people with abandon.

He senses someone behind him, spins, and grabs hold of the guy's left wrist with his right hand. He steps in with his left foot, shoots the crook of his elbow under the guy's left armpit. He snaps his hips around so his back is flush with the guy's chest, simultaneously dropping his hips, fast and low, and then popping up and sending the man sailing over him in a modified judo throw known as *ippon-seioi*. The man lands on top of the table headfirst with a loud *crack*, followed by the rest of him, sending bottles and glasses and plates of finger food scattering and crashing to the floor.

A punch comes out of nowhere, and Fisher sees it just in time and ducks out of the way. He drops into a crouch and glances down at the man he just tossed. The man is sprawled facedown on the table, his sunglasses lying broken next to his head. Fisher can see enough of the left side of his face to make out the puffy pink scar on the side of his nose.

Oh shit.

It's Sato, and Fisher just threw him on his head.

And Sato is not moving.

No no no.

Two of Sato's crew rush to him, pull him off the table. "Sato-*san*! Are you okay?!"

Fisher stands frozen while the two men try to revive their boss. His heart thuds in his chest, his mind seesawing between anguish at having screwed up yet again and fear as he waits for the inevitable moment when, any second now, the gangsters he's supposed to be helping will realize he's the one who hurt their boss.

But neither of the two men so much as glances at him.

From the corner of his eye, movement by the door. He turns his head just in time to see the Serbian guy slip out. Homie has the right idea. Fisher moves quickly to the door and ducks out into the hallway as another beer bottle sails through the air, crashes into a wall, and shatters.

At the end of the hallway is a fire exit. Fisher goes to it, bumps the horizontal silver bar with his hip, and pushes open the door, which triggers the fire alarm. Once in the stairwell, he remembers he's on the fifth floor and takes the stairs two at a time until he reaches the ground floor and bursts out the door and onto a narrow side street.

The nearest station is Akasaka Mitsuke Station. He checks over his shoulder every minute or two until he's halfway there and then pulls out his phone and dials Akio.

No answer.

He leaves Akio a voicemail: *Dude, your acting gig didn't go so well. Call me.*

CHAPTER NINE

SHOTA LEANS AGAINST the car, gazing up at the pink and purple Club Deluxe sign as he smokes, half listening to Tsukahara go on and on about his mother-in-law, who's been living with him and his wife and their eight-year-old daughter for the past six months. For most of the day he's managed not to think about the way Uncle Jun berated him yesterday, but it's starting to eat at him again.

"Every night, I come home and she and Atsuko are screaming at each other," Tsukahara says. "My daughter's like, can you guys please shut the fuck up so I can do my homework, and they just keep going at it, so she goes and hides in her room and listens to her music."

Parked next to Shota's car is another black Mercedes, in front of which stand two more low-level Tanabe-*kai* guys: a beefy prick nicknamed Ogui—"Big Eater"—because he once won a ramen-eating contest, and a suck-up named Momotani, whom everyone calls Mimi—"Ear"—because he was born with one ear. Both of them are looking down at their phones.

They've all been standing outside in the sticky heat with their thumbs up their asses for almost an hour, waiting for their bosses to finish talking with Aikawa, a.k.a. Horseface, about who's going to eat the cost of cleaning up the mess left behind by that Czech stripper. Shota is bored out of his mind and sweating his balls off. Who the fuck knows how much longer this meeting is going to last.

Across the street are four of Aikawa's bodyguards, almost a mirror image of Shota and the three other Tanabe-*kai* men, leaning against their own cars, looking as bored as the rest of them.

Tsukahara shakes his head. "That is not what I signed up for, boss. Know what I'm saying? It's like, damn, either kill each other and get it over with or shut the fuck up." He stabs his cigarette into his mouth, reaches up with both hands, and removes the scrunchy from his ponytail. He shakes his hair out like a girl, then re-scrunchies it into a new ponytail. "Pain in my fucking ass. But man, I tell you. My MIL? That bitch can really fucking cook."

Shota takes a drag off his smoke. He's that close to telling Tsukahara to shut the fuck up, because he's heard all this before, and Tsukahara should stop being a pussy and just kick both those bitches out. More than that, though, Shota's pissed that he has to wait out here like a fucking lap dog while Uncle Jun's ass-lickers sit in that air-conditioned room up there and pretend to be working.

The building's fire alarm goes off.

Clang-clang-clang-clang-clang! Shota pushes himself off the car and looks up at the fifth floor. What the fuck?

Tsukahara looks up too.

Clang-clang-clang-clang-clang!

The sound is deafening. Shota flicks the remains of his cigarette away. Is it a fire? He doesn't smell smoke. He glances back at Aikawa's guys. They're all looking up at the building too, wondering what the hell is going on. Pedestrians stop and look up, open-mouthed.

Tsukahara says, "Should we go up, boss?"

Clang-clang-clang-clang-clang!

What a pain in the ass, thinks Shota. He's about to tell Tsukahara to wait a minute because he wants to see how this plays out. Maybe it *is* a fire. He's imagining how satisfying and funny it would be if Uncle Jun's guys got burned to a crisp when suddenly the *gaijin* dude the accountant led into the building earlier comes barreling around the side of the building. He runs past the mouth of the street like he's being chased by a pit bull and disappears around the corner. "What the fuck?"

Tsukahara's eyes go wide. He drops his cigarette and crushes it with his shoe. "Should I go after him?"

"Nah. Fuck it."

Above the noise of the alarm comes the sound of shouting, talking, laughing as people pour out of the bars and pubs from the emergency exits on each floor, the clatter of their footsteps echoing as they descend the building's external staircase.

Clang-clang-clang-clang-clang!

Shota's phone buzzes. It's Masa. He hits Accept and puts the phone to his ear, cupping his other ear against the noise. "Not a good time," he says, loud, into the receiver.

Masa says, "We got the little fucker, boss."

Shota feels a buzz of excitement. Two of his guys, twins named Masa and Yuki, have been scouring the city for the operator of one of the Tanabe-*kai*'s stash houses. Three days ago it was discovered that the operator, a mousy guy named Gen, might be skimming the cash he was charged with keeping safe. Shota had been ordered by Uncle Jun to track the guy down and take appropriate measures if it turned out to be true—in other words, get rid of him. But Shota has other plans for him.

Clang-clang-clang-clang-clang!

"Where are you?" he shouts into the phone.

"We're at the A-frame."

The A-frame is an abandoned café in a grove near Lake Sagami, an eighties-era resort community that's now a virtual ghost town. Shota bought the place for next to nothing three years ago, and Spiral, his gang, uses it occasionally as its own little interrogation center.

A small crowd has spilled out onto the sidewalk. Aikawa's bodyguards jog past Shota and Tsukahara and push their way through to the elevator. Shota still doesn't smell any smoke. He scans the crowd for Uncle Jun's guys and sees none of them. He doesn't see any of Aikawa's people either. He glances at Ogui and Mimi. Both of them are standing there with confused looks on their faces. Ogui meets his gaze, looks at him like he wants Shota to tell him what to do. Shota shrugs. He can do whatever the fuck he wants. Ogui opens his mouth, closes it, then opens it again and motions for Mimi to follow him, and the two of them start for the elevator.

Tsukahara says, "Boss? What are we doing?"

Shota gestures for Tsukahara to wait a second, then says into the phone to Masa, "We'll be there in an hour," and hangs up.

The crowd on the sidewalk is bigger now. Mostly young couples, they chatter and laugh as they wait for someone to give the coast-is-clear sign so they can go back inside the building and resume drinking.

Somebody probably accidentally tripped the fire alarm, thinks Shota. Whatever. Let Ogui and Mimi handle it. Uncle Jun said he wanted Shota to handle the stash house operator, so that's what he's going to do.

He motions for Tsukahara to get in the car. "Let's go."

Tsukahara shrugs. He goes around to the driver's side and opens the door. "Where we going, boss?"

"Going to get rich," says Shota.

An hour later, Shota stands before Gen, who's duct-taped naked to a chair in the middle of what used to be the café's dining area.

"Please," the little man says in a quavering, high-pitched voice.

Matchan shifts from foot to foot behind him, looking like a bear looming over a child. Tsukahara is waiting in the car. Masa and Yuki are standing guard outside.

It's hot and the place smells like piss and mildew and wet dirt. Ragged holes riddle the mold-splotched plywood walls. The floorboards are rotting and littered with cigarette butts, used tissues, crumpled beer cans.

Sweat rolls down Gen's face and chest, glistening in the light of an LED lantern atop a small table a few feet away. "I took the money," he says. "I'm so sorry."

Shota unscrews the cap on a bottle of water and takes a long swallow. Screws the cap back on, sets the bottle down on the table next to the lantern, and studies the little man. He's about Shota's age, with delicate features under a stupid-looking bowl haircut. He looks like a hunger case. He's got bony knees and a chest so sunken, Shota can almost see his heart beat. Little fucker can't weigh more than a hundred pounds.

Two weeks ago, Shota had heard from a connection of his on one of the U.S. military bases—a guy named Bobby—about hundreds of old handguns—Beretta M-9s—that were being phased out by the U.S. Army and destined for scrap. The guy said he could get his hands on them for the right price and wanted to know if Shota was interested. Maybe, he told the guy. They haggled, settled on a million even. Bobby wanted a hundred grand down, nonrefundable, the balance on delivery in two weeks' time. Shota emptied his savings to pony up the down payment and until three days ago had been trying to figure out how he was going to come up with the rest of the money.

Then, what do you know, the stars lined up, and Gen landed in his lap like a skinny little luck charm. Shota's plan is to jack the stash house with Gen's help; use the cash to buy the guns; kill the old man and watch the Tanabe-*kai* implode.

Shota takes his knife from his waistband—a mean-looking Zero Tolerance titanium folding knife Bobby gave him—and clicks the blade open.

Gen starts to bawl. "Please! My daughter needs surgery! I was going to pay it back!"

Shota is disgusted. This is the kind of people Uncle Jun hires to watch over his money? He gestures to Matchan.

Matchan wraps a massive arm around Gen's neck.

"Please!" The operator looks at Shota, eyes filled with terror.

Shota steps forward. He quickly hooks the point of the knife in the curl of cartilage at the top of Gen's right ear and flicks it up hard.

"AAAAH!"

Matchan releases Gen's neck and steps back.

It's only a nick, but ears bleed a lot, and in a matter of seconds, the whole side of Gen's head is covered in blood.

"When's the next cash delivery?" says Shota.

"I don't know!" says Gen, panic in his voice. His expression is that of a terrified five-year-old. "The couriers come several times a week. I never know when. They bring the money in gym bags and they always come with bodyguards."

Smart, thinks Shota. The couriers come unannounced and with muscle to avoid getting jacked en route. It's going to make things more difficult for him, but that's okay, because a plan is already taking shape in his head. He tells Gen that he's got a choice: he can either die right here, or he can go back to the stash house and Shota will tell the boss that Gen wasn't skimming after all. But Gen will have to do something for Shota.

Snot runs from Gen's nose. He sniffles and swallows. "Anything." His voice is a squeak.

Shota pats Gen on the shoulder. "Good boy."

CHAPTER TEN

WALKING THROUGH THE lobby of Sunshine Mansion, Fisher tells himself to chill. In all the confusion during the brawl at the club, no one had seen him throw Sato, and he's pretty sure none of the gangsters standing around out in front of the building had gotten a good look at him when he ran past them after coming down the stairs. Nor had anyone followed him to the station. And once on the train, he'd faced the wall to hide the lumps forming on his cheek and forehead, his heart jumping around in his chest, but no one seemed to pay him any attention.

He rides the ancient elevator up to the seventh floor, his pulse still thumping, and lets himself into his room and closes the door.

It's going to be okay.

He flips on the light, takes off his shoes, and sets his phone on the counter. He turns on the AC, peels off his sweat-soaked suit and tie, and leaves them in a pile on the floor. Grabs a two-liter bottle of water from the fridge and downs half of it in one go. He gets into the shower, and after a couple of minutes, the adrenaline flooding his veins finally recedes, and that's when he realizes he's not getting the million yen he was supposed to make tonight. The dominoes fall in his head: he won't be able to pay the PI, which means the PI won't give him Lisa's contact info, which means he's not going to be able to see her and the kids, which means he can't show her that he can be the man she wants him to be. He hears himself scoff. He was just involved in a brawl between a bunch of gangsters over a runaway prostitute. He threw one of them on his head and ran away like a criminal himself, all for the sake of making a quick buck. Who's he trying to fool? He's not a changed man. He doesn't deserve to get his family back.

As he's drying himself off, cursing himself, cursing the world, his phone buzzes on the counter. It's Akio. He drops the towel, grabs the phone, and thumbs the button. "That was no goddamn acting—"

Akio cuts him off. "Hank, what the fuck?" His voice has an edge to it that Fisher has never heard before. "What happened?"

"What happened? A fucking brawl is what happened. You said it would be—"

"Where are you?"

"Home. Why?"

"Get out of there."

"What?"

"I said get the fuck out of there!"

"Why?!"

"Because they're coming for you! Hank, you threw Sato-san on his head! He's in the hospital!"

Panic floods Fisher's veins. "Oh Jesus. It was an accident, Akio! He came at me. I didn't even get a look at his face, I just reacted. I didn't think anyone saw me do it. It was total chaos."

"And then you bolted?"

"I panicked." The image of Sato pops into his brain, unconscious in a hospital bed, tubes going in and out of him. It gives Fisher a sick feeling in the pit of his stomach. "I should just go to the police."

"No."

"It was an accident. I didn't mean to hurt anyone. I'll just tell them what happened." Take responsibility for his actions. That's what a good husband, a good father, a good man does.

"Hank, *no*. You can't do that."

"Why the fuck not?"

"Think about it. You tell the police you hurt a guy in a brawl, and they're going to start asking you for details. Where did it happen? Who was involved? Why were you there? What was the fight about? Trust me, you don't want to go there. You'll only end up making things worse for yourself."

"You mean worse for the gangsters."

"Yeah, which means worse for you!"

Suddenly it's as though the walls of the room have started to close in on him. "Wait," he says to Akio. "How did they know it was me who hurt Sato?"

"Somebody recorded it with their phone."

For a moment it's as though Fisher has lost the ability to form words.

Akio says, "Listen, just get out of there, okay?! They're probably already there!"

Fisher moves to the sliding glass door. Hooks a finger on the edge of the curtain and pulls it aside an inch and looks down at the street.

"These guys don't screw around, Hank."

Parked at the curb is a big black Mercedes-Benz. A stocky guy with a shaved head stands on the sidewalk next to the car, talking on the phone. Another black sedan pulls up behind the

Mercedes and stops and puts its hazards on. Three more guys get out and huddle with the shaven-headed guy.

Fisher's scalp tightens. "Yeah, they're here," he says in a low tone as he releases the curtain. "*Don't worry, Hank, it'll be fun.* Jesus fucking Christ."

"I know," says Akio, his tone full of remorse. "I'm sorry, Hank. I'm really sorry."

Sunshine Mansion has a back entrance that leads through a bicycle parking area to a narrow street lined with shops. Fisher will try to slip out that way. But then what? Things are happening too fast, damn it.

"Where am I supposed to go?" he says.

Akio sighs. "You should get out of the country."

"Are you serious?"

"Yes I'm serious! Take the first flight you can get. Go somewhere you won't stand out and lie low for a while. Anywhere. Hell, I don't know. Thailand? Australia?"

Yeah, on whose dime? But more important, as long as Lisa, Justin, and James are here in Japan, he's not going anywhere. "What do you think they'll do if they find me?" he says, thinking maybe it's better if he faces the consequences. How bad could they be? Christ, it was an accident, wasn't it? He didn't mean to hurt anyone.

"I don't know, but these people don't play games. And it's not *if*, it's *when*."

It occurs to Fisher that since Akio is the one who'd introduced him to the gangsters, he's in trouble too. "How about you? What're they going to do to you?"

"You mean after they beat the fuck out of me?" Akio draws a shaky breath, blows it out. "My business...I know how they work. They'll leach me dry. Once these guys sink their fangs into you, they don't let go. I'm basically screwed."

Fisher doesn't know what to say to this. He feels terrible for Akio. On the other hand, he wouldn't be in this mess in the first place if it weren't for the rosy picture Akio had painted for him. *An acting job!*

A moment passes, then Akio says, "I'm sorry, man."

"Yeah. Me too."

Fisher rushes around inside the room, telling himself to think think think, randomly stuffing things into an old backpack: from his dresser, a pair of shorts, a pair of jeans, three T-shirts, socks, and underwear. Then he moves to the desk in the corner and pulls the top drawer out, scoops up a few bucks' worth of loose change from the tray inside, and pockets it. He checks his wallet. He's still got the fifty thousand yen that was supposed to tide him over till the end of the month.

The distant slam of a car door outside.

They're coming.

He shrugs the backpack over his shoulders, grabs a black Nike baseball cap from a hook next to the door and pulls it down low on his head, then slips on his shoes and lets himself out. He jogs to the end of the hall, opens the door to the stairwell, and takes the stairs two at a time to the ground floor. There are two doors here, one leading into the lobby, the other providing access to a covered bicycle parking area in the back of the building.

Fisher takes a step toward the metal door to the lobby, pauses, and listens. A muffled clatter of footsteps and gruff voices in the lobby. At least three men out there, maybe more.

One of the men stabs the elevator button. Then the hum-rattle of the elevator car making its descent.

They think he's still in his room. Good.

Fisher opens the door to the bicycle parking lot a smidge, peeks out, and confirms the coast is clear. Then he slips out and starts to run.

CHAPTER ELEVEN

FISHER RUNS A hundred yards before he notices people stopping to gawk at him, alarmed expressions on their faces.

Why is that big foreigner running? he imagines them thinking. *Suspicious!*

He abruptly stops running.

Tokyo is home to some 550,000 foreigners. It's not an insignificant number in and of itself, but it's a drop in the bucket compared with the city's population of thirteen million. So it's pretty hard for a *gaijin* to blend in.

Especially when he's a big, scary-looking one running down the street.

Fisher ducks around a corner and wends his way through a warren of side streets until one dumps him out onto Yamate Dori, just south of the big thoroughfare of Koshu Kaido. Sweat is already running down his face, his T-shirt soaked and clinging to his back.

A black BMW sedan zooms past and stops at a light a hundred yards ahead.

Fisher keeps walking, his gaze fixed on the car, alert to any sign his pursuers are inside.

The light turns green but the car doesn't move. A cold finger of fear runs up his neck. He slows his pace, watching the car, ready to bolt in the other direction if any of the doors open. The car zooms off.

He lets out a long breath of relief and continues south. Traffic whizzes past, taxis appearing in two- to three-vehicle intervals.

He passes a *koban*, one of Japan's small neighborhood police stations. A single cop sits behind a desk inside the tiny office. The cop looks up at Fisher, locks eyes with him for a moment. Fisher averts his gaze, his heart kicking in his chest. *Keep walking*, he tells himself, fighting the urge to look back over his shoulder to see if the cop is still watching him. He needs to get somewhere safe for the night, somewhere he can figure out his next move.

Damn it, he needs to get off the street. He turns and hails the first cab he sees. Fisher climbs in and tells the driver to just drive. He's drenched in sweat. The driver gives him a suspicious glance in the rearview mirror and says, "*Hai.*" Fisher unzips his backpack, pulls out one of the clean socks he'd stuffed inside, and wipes his face dry with it, little jabs of pain in his forehead and left cheek making him wince. Using the browser on his phone, he finds a cheap hotel in Roppongi, then tells the driver, who is still eyeing him suspiciously, to take him there.

Fifteen minutes later, they pull up in front of the hotel. Fisher pays the cab fare and then jogs up the steps and into the lobby.

Behind the reception desk is a short, stocky woman who eyes him warily as she checks him in.

"Did you fall down?" she says. Fisher's hand moves unconsciously up to the bump on his cheekbone. "Yeah, um, a little accident."

The woman nods.

Fisher pays her in cash.

She hands him his key. "Room 514. A complimentary continental breakfast is served in the café from six to nine a.m."

"Thank you."

"Take care, sir."

⤐

The room is basic and small but clean. Fisher tosses his backpack on top of the bed, cranks the AC to max. He's wrung out from all the adrenaline, and the lumps on his forehead and cheek hurt.

After a quick shower, he stretches out on the bed. He sees Sato lying on the floor, his sunglasses in pieces next to his face. Akio had said the guy was in the hospital. A suffocating dread fills his chest. He pushes himself up off the bed. He paces back and forth between the door and the window. Again wonders what he's supposed to do. Where he's supposed to go.

He grabs his phone and scrolls through his contacts, most of whom he's been out of touch with since the divorce. The rest are people he knows more or less casually, hey-how-you-doing-pretty-good-how-about-this-weather types, certainly not people he can reach out to for help. There's really only Ken and Terry, and he doesn't want to call Ken because his wife just had a kid. As for Terry, he's probably still pissed at Fisher for almost losing his shit with that customer last night. Plus, Terry has warned him more times than he can count about Akio.

He dials Terry anyway, because what choice does he have? Terry picks up on the first ring, and instead of his usual boisterous bellow of *Hank the Tank!* or *What's up, mi amigo?!* he says, "Yeah."

The uncharacteristically curt greeting doesn't come as a total surprise. Yeah, he's still pissed. Fisher hesitates a moment, then says, stupidly, "Hey. Terry. It's me, Hank."

"Yeah, I can see your name on the screen."

Shit. He sounds really pissed. "Um, I'm in a bit of a jam, Terry."

Terry says, "Hold on a sec."

The background noise fades, and Fisher guesses that Terry has gone into the break room to talk. When he comes back on the line, his tone is sharp. "This wouldn't have anything to do with the guys who were just here asking about you, would it?"

Oh no. They've already managed to find out where he works? How? It dawns on him, his pulse thudding in his ears: Akio. Akio must have told them. "They were there?"

"They haven't left. They're waiting outside in their car. They don't look like nice guys, Hank."

"They're not."

"Shit. What happened?"

"Akio set me up with this job and—"

Terry cuts Fisher off. "Wait. Akio? Aw, for Christ's sake, Hank."

"He said it'd be easy," Fisher protests. "A couple hours, just sit there at this meeting with these gangster guys and look tough."

"Yeah, the word 'gangster' would've given me pause. But I don't know, maybe that's just me."

"I needed the money, Terry." The words tumbling out of Fisher now. "That PI I hired located Lisa and the kids, said he wouldn't give me their address unless I paid him another two hundred thousand yen." Fisher groans. "Look, I know I'm an idiot."

Terry says, "Not going to argue with you there." He blows out a long, exasperated breath. "So let me guess: the job didn't go quite like Akio said it would."

"Yeah, you could say that. A fight broke out. I ended up throwing a guy. Turned out he was some kind of bigwig."

Terry says, "Shit."

"That's not the worst of it. Akio says the guy's in the hospital."

"What?! What the fuck, Hank?!"

Fisher closes his eyes. "I know, Terry. Goddamn it, I know."

Terry says, "You gotta go to the cops."

"Akio said that'd make things worse."

"Worse for who? That's nonsense. The guy is in the hospital, for God's sake. Go to the police and tell them what happened."

Fisher draws in a long breath. Terry's right. After he'd left the club, Fisher should have gone straight to the cops. "Yeah. You're right."

"Where are you?"

"Roppongi Hills. The APA Hotel."

Terry says, "Okay. Tell you what. I'll meet you at Azabu Police Station."

Azabu Police Station is about a ten-minute walk from the hotel.

"Those guys know me over there," says Terry. "Might help if I vouched for you."

Terry maintains good relations with the local cops. It's a necessity in *mizu-shobai*, or the "water trade"—the colloquial term for the night-time entertainment business. Still, the gangsters have already paid Terry an unwelcome visit. They're still there, for Christ's sake. Fisher doesn't want to drag him into

this any further and he says so. "Don't worry about me," Terry
says. "I can handle myself. Let's worry about getting you out
of this jam."

"I appreciate this, Terry."

"Don't thank me. Like I said, the cops over there know me,
but you hurt this gangster guy bad. I'm pretty sure they're going
to hold you until they can confirm your story. After that I don't
know what'll happen."

"Not a very positive picture you're painting for me."

"You think Akio's is better? I'm just trying to be realistic
here. What's your room number?"

"Five fourteen."

"Give me an hour. I'll come get you."

Fisher sits on the bed, a gray cloud of fatigue settling over him.
He thinks of Justin and James.

He pictures the two of them fast asleep under their Thomas
the Tank Engine and Spiderman blankets, Justin sawing logs
like an old man, James purring softly like a little cat. Identical
twins, yet so different in almost every way. Justin was the bold
one, open and friendly and at times too generous for his own
good. When he was with other kids, he would share whatever
toy he was playing with and sometimes never get it back. James,
on the other hand, was much more guarded. He was naturally
wary of people and not afraid to defend himself, and while he
wasn't mean to other kids, he would never let another kid take
a toy away from him.

A happy, funny memory: When the boys were three or four,
Fisher and Lisa took them trick-or-treating to Azabu, a wealthy
enclave in central Tokyo with enough foreign expats for Hal-
loween to have become a tradition of sorts, even among some

of the Japanese residents. Justin was dressed as a pirate, James as Thomas the Tank Engine. They were so excited. Each time they stopped at a house, Fisher and Lisa would hang back and watch them run up and knock on the door. He remembers one house where a lady in her sixties came out onto the porch with a big bowl of individually wrapped *ramune* candies. "Dozo!" she said with a big smile. Help yourself! Justin stepped forward, a big smile on his face. He reached into the bowl, carefully picked out a single candy, said thank you, and put it in his bag. Then James approached the lady, cautious. He reached into the bowl, his eyes locked on the lady's face the whole time, and pulled out a huge handful of the sweets. Lisa said, "That's too many, James!" and the lady laughed and said it was fine and asked Justin if he wanted some more, in response to which Justin took two more candies. For the rest of the night, Fisher and Lisa laughed about it, marveling at how two kids with the exact same DNA could be such polar opposites.

They'd begun arguing a lot by that point. Lisa always upset that Fisher was never around, that she had to do everything—work a full-time job *and* take care of the kids *and* do all the housework. Fisher always bent out of shape that she didn't seem to understand that the only way he could provide for them like he'd promised her was to start winning again, and that meant he needed to train more, not less. Not only had trick-or-treating with the kids provided him with an opportunity to be a real dad and a real husband, but it had given the two of them a rare interlude of mutual joy, and they'd both seized on it like a piece of shared treasure.

If only Fisher hadn't let it go.

Eventually, he drifts into an uneasy slumber, zombie-like hordes of *yakuza* armed with thousands of shiny silver blades, chasing him through a warren of dead, dark streets.

CHAPTER TWELVE

A BAR OF early morning sunlight shines through the gap at the bottom of the blinds and creeps up the side of the bed until it hits Fisher's sleeping face like a slap.

He's sore. Jesus, everything hurts. He pushes himself onto an elbow and looks around the room, winces as he runs his fingers over the lumps on his head. His thoughts are disordered, he's unsure where he is. Then with a blast of clarity like the sunlight that just woke him, he remembers: *Terry*.

He grabs his phone. It's 5:30 a.m. He has no calls, no texts, no emails. Nothing. He reaches for the phone on the nightstand and calls the front desk.

"No, sir, no messages" is the response. He feels a flutter of dread. He dials Terry's number and gets his voicemail. "Terry, I dozed off last night and just woke up. Did you come by? I don't see any messages from you. Everything okay? Give me a call." Next, he pulls up the number of Terry's girlfriend, Laura, and, forgetting how early it is, dials it. The phone rings six times and goes to her voicemail. He clicks off and dials again. This time, Laura answers on the fourth ring.

"Hello?" she says, her voice a groggy rasp.

"Laura, it's Hank Fisher."

"Hank?"

"I'm sorry I woke you, but is Terry there?"

Laura groans. "Terry?" she says, irritation in her voice. "Hold on." A moment later, Laura comes back on the line. "Huh. No, he's not here. He called last night, said he had to do something before he came home. What's going on? Is something wrong?"

You could say that. "No, probably not. It's just that he was supposed to meet me last night, and I dozed off. I just woke up a few minutes ago myself. Probably just missed him."

Laura chuckles. "Well, I'm sure he's okay. Maybe something came up with one of the girls or something."

The calm in Laura's tone contrasts sharply with the panic rising in Fisher's chest. Last night on the phone, Terry had said the gangsters were parked right outside the bar. What if he had a run-in with them on his way out? What if they beat him up and now he's lying unconscious in an alley somewhere?

Fisher has a sudden urge to tell Laura everything. He tamps it down, thinking, hoping, maybe she's right. Maybe something did come up with one of the girls.

"Yeah," he says. "You're probably right." But no, he doesn't really believe it. "Listen, if Terry calls could you please tell him to give me a call right away?"

"Okay. I'm sure he's fine, Hank. You know how he is. Always 'Daddy to the rescue' whenever one of the girls is having a crisis."

"Yeah, I know," he says, forcing a laugh, then thanks her and clicks off.

His heart thumping in his chest, Fisher steps to the window, opens the blinds, and looks down the side of the building at the empty alley below, half expecting to see Terry on the ground, the Tanabe-*kai* goons standing around his crumpled body.

An inebriated young couple staggers arm in arm down the alley past the closed bars and restaurants, then disappears around a corner. Fisher locates the number of Yuki, the uni-browed waiter at Lounge O, in his contacts and dials it. He apologizes for waking Yuki up and asks if he knows where Terry is. Yuki says sorry, no, he doesn't. Is there something wrong? Fisher thanks him, tells him no, no, everything is fine, and hangs up.

He moves away from the window, unable to fully shake the feeling that something horrible has happened to Terry. He forces himself to push it down for the moment and decides to walk to Azabu Police Station by himself. He'll try calling Terry again later. He puts on a fresh pair of boxers, shorts, and one of the clean T-shirts from his backpack, and slings the backpack over his shoulder. As he approaches the door, a wave of trepidation rolls over him. What if the goons are out there waiting for him? He puts his eye to the peephole. There's no one in the hallway.

Get a grip.

The Tanabe-*kai* goons have no idea where he is, and there's no way they would know to look for him here in the APA Hotel. He can't imagine them out at the crack of dawn, canvassing neighborhoods for him. He's always thought of the *yakuza* as creatures of the night. Allergic to sunlight, like vampires. Still, he can't shake the feeling he's in a scary new world without a map.

He hurries out and takes the elevator down to the lobby.

At the reception counter is a thirtyish man with graying temples. The man gestures toward the café adjoining the lobby and tells Fisher to please help himself to breakfast. The mention of food makes his stomach growl, and he realizes he hasn't eaten anything since early yesterday evening. He approaches the entrance to the café, cautious, and peeks his head inside.

It's empty. A long, rectangular room with clean white walls and a black and white checked floor, it has a separate entrance fronted by French windows in the rear leading to a narrow street behind the hotel. A flat-screen TV hangs from the ceiling in back. Fronting an empty open kitchen is a counter set with a modest breakfast buffet.

Fisher goes to the coffee machine, pours himself a cup to go, then grabs two hard-boiled eggs, half an orange, and a banana, which he eats on the spot. The shot of calories lifts his mood almost instantly. Laura is probably right about Terry, he thinks, quickly wrapping the eggs and the orange half in a couple of napkins before sticking them in the front pouch of his backpack. One of the Lounge O girls probably got fall-down drunk and called Terry to come and get her. It's happened before. In fact, that was exactly what had happened a week ago with the new girl from Detroit, Sarah. Sarah had called Terry at 2:00 a.m., drunk and crying, saying she was at a bar with a friend and her friend had left and now she didn't know how to get home or what to do and would Terry please come get her. So that's what he did.

Fisher turns to leave and his blood freezes.

There's a man sitting at a table behind a tall partition just to the left of the café entrance. The table is positioned in such a way that the man had been hidden from Fisher's view when he came in. Dressed in a beige summer suit, he's on the thick side with long, slicked-back hair. He's holding a cup of coffee in one hand, pinky up, intently reading a sports newspaper in the other. Fisher can't put his finger on it, but there's something off about him.

A news flash on the TV draws Fisher's eye. The tagline at the bottom of the screen says in Japanese, "*Stabbing in Roppongi.*" A video runs, showing several uniformed police officers in a narrow alley, going to and fro behind yellow crime scene tape. Parked at the mouth of the alley is an ambulance, red light strobing.

A picture of Terry appears on the screen and next to it the following caption:

Roppongi hostess bar owner Terry Nishikawa (age 51) in critical condition after being stabbed by unknown assailants. Police are investigating the matter.

Fisher jumps like he's been injected with ice water. Coffee sloshes out of his cup and burns his hand. He reads the caption again. Terry's name is spelled out in *katakana*, as all foreign names are. There's no mistaking it. Terry was stabbed.

Shit oh shit oh shit.

He sets the coffee down and wipes his hand off with a napkin, and that's when he notices the guy in the beige suit is staring at him.

Fisher looks down, pretending not to notice. The guy sets his coffee cup down, and as he does this, Fisher catches sight of the ponytail trailing down his back.

Ponytail sees Fisher looking at him, and his lips curl into a smile.

CHAPTER THIRTEEN

COLD PANIC WASHES over Fisher. Could they have found him already? He averts his gaze and starts to lift his own coffee cup, trying to look casual, but his hand is shaking so badly he has to set it back down. Visible through the French doors is a shiny black Mercedes-Benz with tinted rear windows parked outside at the curb.

The only thing he can think to do is leave the café through the lobby and continue out the hotel entrance to Roppongi Dori, but in order to do that, he'll have to walk right past Ponytail.

Fisher shoulders his backpack. As he approaches the doorway to the lobby, Ponytail says in English, "Bad accident."

The words stop Fisher like a wall. He looks at Ponytail. "What did you say?"

Ponytail gestures toward the TV. "Your friend," he says, like he's gloating. "Bad accident."

Fury roars through Fisher like a flash flood. He walks briskly toward the entrance, the coffee in his left hand. When he's almost to the doorway, he takes a big step to his left and with a quick motion throws the steaming coffee into Ponytail's face.

Ponytail lets out a piercing shriek. His hands fly up to his face, and his coffee cup bounces off the table and shatters on the floor.

Fisher runs into the lobby and almost collides with the hotel clerk, who is running in the opposite direction toward the café to see what's happened. The clerk looks wide-eyed at him. Fisher mirrors his expression, gestures toward the café.

The clerk hurries on into the café as Ponytail's screaming ratchets up, more from rage now than pain from the sound of it, the echoes punctuated by the startled cries of the clerk. "Sir, what happened?! Are you okay?!"

A few feet from the hotel entrance, Fisher halts and peers out the glass doors. The driver of the Mercedes is engrossed in something on his phone, frantically swiping away at the screen.

Fisher scans the street, heart jackhammering in his chest. Where should he go? They stabbed Terry. Jesus, they fucking stabbed him! Roppongi Dori Avenue is empty this early in the morning, its east-bound and west-bound lanes cloaked in the shadow of the elevated hulk of the Shuto Expressway. The sedan is parked on this side of the street, facing west, and because the boulevard, like most Tokyo streets, offers few opportunities to hook a U-turn, there's no way for the goon to conveniently turn the car around if Fisher heads east, toward Akasaka.

No sooner is Fisher out the door than Ponytail comes barreling out the entrance after him, shouting to the driver of the Mercedes, who looks at him and then at Fisher and scrambles out of the car.

Nerves pulsing, Fisher leaps from the top of the steps and cuts right when he lands and breaks into a sprint, his backpack flopping and thumping his back as he goes. The gangsters are shouting behind him. The car's engine roars.

He turns right into a side street that leads up a gentle slope. A taxi up ahead is letting a young woman out in front of an apartment building. Fisher glances back over his shoulder in time to see the gangsters round the corner. One of them points at him.

"There he is!"

The discharged passenger disappears into the lobby of the apartment building, and the cab begins to pull away. It's at least fifty yards ahead. Fisher breaks into a sprint, waves his right arm, hoping the driver will see him in his rearview.

The cab's brake lights come on and the rear door opens, but Fisher's still forty yards away, the gangsters' shouts echoing behind him.

"Stop, motherfucker!"

Thirty yards. Twenty.

The cab driver's face is visible in the vehicle's side mirror, alarm in his eyes.

Fisher says, "Wait!" But the driver wants no part of this. He closes the door and speeds off.

Fisher keeps running. A woman pushing a chihuahua in a stroller looks up, startled, as he passes, tells the dog in a little voice not to worry, everything's okay. At the top of the hill, he goes left. Azabu Dori is up ahead, an Eneos gas station on the corner. He tries to pick up the speed, his lungs starting to burn. He turns the corner at the gas station, continues running toward the big intersection at Iigura Katamachi, scans the street. Not a single cab in sight. Then he spots one coming toward him and starts waving his arm. The cab's hazard lights come on. Fisher slows to a jog as the cab pulls to the curb. The rear door opens for him.

Fisher jumps into the back seat. The door closes. He's about to tell the driver where to take him when there's a squeal of tires and the roar of revved engines and two big black sedans with smoked windows race up from behind.

The driver says, "What's going on?"

"Go!"

But it's too late. One of the black cars skids to a stop in front of the cab, cutting it off. The other stops behind it. Fisher looks back and forth between the two cars, his chest tight with panic. He feels like a rabbit dropped into a den of rattlesnakes. The doors fly open; two men in suits pile out of each of them. One of them is Ponytail, who's holding a white towel to one side of his face.

Fisher gropes for the door latch. He finds it, yanks it hard, but it's locked. "Let me out!" he says to the driver.

The driver doesn't seem to hear him, turning this way and that in his seat, his eyes wide with fear, too, as he watches the four men surround the car. The two on the driver's side have shaved heads. One is tall with a doughy face, and the other is short and missing his two front teeth. On the passenger side are Ponytail and a guy with short, slicked-back hair and a diamond stud in his left ear.

Panic cyclones in Fisher's chest. They've boxed him in and are pounding on the windows now, all four of them shouting at the driver. "Open the door, asshole!"

Animal fear swamps his brain as he realizes he's going to have to fight his way past them. And then he thinks of Terry in the ICU somewhere, remembers these fuckers are the ones who stabbed him, and in an instant his fear changes to anger, like water flash-freezing into ice.

"Okay, okay!" says the driver.

Fisher readies himself. Whoever opens one of the back doors first is going to get mule-kicked in the face.

The driver unlocks his door and starts to open it slowly, holding up a hand in a gesture of surrender. The tall skinhead jerks the door the rest of the way open. The driver yelps. The gangster grabs him by the wrist and the back of the collar and yanks him out of his seat onto the ground.

The driver says, "Ow! Stop! Please!"

Fisher says, "Hey! Leave him alone!"

The skinhead leans in and smirks at Fisher. He presses a button on the dash, and the back door on the side where the guy with the earring stands waiting opens slightly.

Heart thumping, Fisher turns slightly in his seat, getting ready to lift his legs up and ring Earring's bell. But Earring takes a step back as he yanks the door the rest of the way open, then reaches inside his suit jacket and produces a sword with a foot-long blade.

An electric charge runs through Fisher. He's no authority on traditional Japanese weaponry, but he knows a *tanto* when he sees one. Carried by the samurai during Japan's feudal era, the short swords were used for close combat. Not, however, the kind of close combat Fisher is used to. He puts his hands up, the rage he felt just a moment ago morphing back into raw fear.

Earring glares at Fisher. "Out," he says in perfect American English. Ponytail is shifting from foot to foot in anticipation behind him.

Fisher glances over the seat and through the open driver's side door sees the tan man standing over the cab driver, who's sitting on the ground, his eyes wide with terror.

"Now," Earring says. "Nice and slow."

Fisher swings his legs off the seat. He scoots forward, slow, considers running for it as he places his feet on the ground, but the thought of getting slashed with the sword, of Terry, of the helpless driver and what these men are capable of, crumbles his resolve and suddenly he's trembling. His mind throws up the image of Justin and James watching TV, a news flash cutting in to report on the stabbing death of their father. It would leave them scarred, just like Fisher himself was scarred by his own parents' deaths.

Earring moves back a step to give him room, and as Fisher slowly pushes himself out of the cab, Ponytail jumps between him and Earring and takes a wild swing at Fisher's head. Fisher ducks. Still holding the towel to his face, Ponytail loses his balance and tumbles to the ground.

"Motherfucker!" he says.

Earring says, "Tsukahara! Stop!"

Tsukahara makes an anguished noise and picks himself up off the ground. He removes the towel from his face and glares at Fisher. The whole right side of his face is deep red, and he's squeezing his right eye shut. "I'm going to kill you," he says to Fisher.

Earring says, "Tsukahara, give him room." Slowly Tsukahara sidesteps out of Fisher's way.

Earring motions for Fisher to turn around with a twirl of his finger. "Hands behind your back."

"That's not necessary."

"Turn around. Now."

Fisher turns around and puts his hands behind his back and feels Earring cinch a zip tie over his wrists so tight, it cuts into his skin. His heart is slamming so hard in his chest, it feels like it might burst out of his mouth.

Earring leads him by the elbow to the black Mercedes parked behind the taxi. He opens the rear passenger door and motions for Fisher to get in.

Fisher does as instructed. This is it. They're going to take him somewhere and kill him. His sons will never know him. He'll die having failed them as a father.

Earring closes the door. Behind the wheel is a big round dude, fat but solid-looking, like a sumo wrestler. Earring gets in the front passenger seat, while Tsukahara slides in next to Fisher. The inside of the car smells like clove cigarettes.

As they pull away from the curb and around the cab, the cab driver stands there next to the open door of his vehicle, frowning as he brushes his pants off with slaps of his palms.

Earring opens the glove box and takes out a black cloth bag, which he hands over the seat to Tsukahara. Gripping the cloth bag, Tsukahara slams his fist into Fisher's chest. It doesn't hurt, but it jars him. Tsukahara jerks the bag down over Fisher's head and says, through clenched teeth, "Motherfucker."

Lisa, Justin, James, I love you. I'm sorry. I'm so sorry. Fisher hears himself say, "Where are—"

Crack.

The blow lands on his left ear, a burst of pain rocketing through his head. Stars whirl against the black backdrop of the cloth bag as Fisher realizes Tsukahara has just elbowed him in the head.

"Shut up," says Tsukahara.

He shuts up.

CHAPTER FOURTEEN

THE DRIVE TAKES about twenty minutes. The driver makes so many turns that it's impossible for Fisher to work out where they're headed. The left side of his head throbs from the blow to the ear Tsukahara gave him. Sweat rolls down his sides despite the coolness inside the car. He's been thinking of Terry, waves of guilt and fear and panic crashing over him. Different scenarios play out in his head, all of them ending the same: with Fisher shot or stabbed or strangled to death, the pieces of his chopped-up corpse scattered around the countryside. His fate never to be known to his family. Justin and James growing up thinking he abandoned them.

Fisher closes his eyes and sways with the motion of the car, his own breath spreading hot against his face inside the bag. It suddenly occurs to him that if they wanted to kill him, why would they bother with the hood?

Eventually the car slows, turns left, and descends a short slope and stops. The front passenger door opens.

Fisher feels a small jolt of fight-or-flight, and then it's gone, replaced by the heavy weight of helplessness and resignation. Who knows where they've taken him, and even if he knew, what could he possibly do blindfolded with his hands bound behind his back? And it doesn't really even matter, does it? Because Lisa was right about him all along, wasn't she? He deserves to be sitting here in this car, with these people.

Loser.

Earring says in Japanese, "Tsukahara, go put something on your face."

Tsukahara leans into Fisher and says, "I'll see you later," then climbs out of the car.

Fisher's door opens, and a big hand grabs him by the left elbow and the back of the neck and yanks him out of the back seat. Fisher goes airborne for a moment and lands hard on the concrete, barely avoiding hitting his head.

"Oops," Earring says.

A moment later, the same big hand picks Fisher up like he's nothing and sets him on his feet. His shoulders are stiff from the stress imposed by the cuffs on his bound wrists. He tries to rotate them to loosen them up but achieves only a shrug. His hands are numb, the sting and stickiness of the blood from where the cuffs have dug into his wrists the only sensation he has in them.

He feels the big hand pull him forward.

Earring says, "Walk."

They lead him to an elevator. The doors clatter closed and the car rises for a moment. Where are they taking him? Why?

Ding.

The doors open, and he's led by the elbow for a few seconds and then is told to stop. A door closes behind him, and the hood is yanked off his head.

Squinting, Fisher scans the room. It's a rectangular meeting room with dirty gray carpeting, tacky wood paneling on the walls, and two worn black leather sofas sandwiching a heavy-looking coffee table. Two-thirds of the wall on the left is taken up by an amateurish-looking painting of some European coastal city. Monaco, maybe, or the French Riviera.

The room smells of stale cigarette smoke, cold air blasting from a dirty old AC unit on one wall.

Fisher suddenly gets it: They've brought him here to meet their boss. But what for? To make him apologize before they kill him?

Earring instructs Fisher to sit on the couch facing the door. Fisher does as he's told as Earring and Sumo take up position behind him, and a thickly muscled man in a gray pinstriped suit walks in through the open door carrying a white paper Isetan department store bag. He's a little shorter than Fisher, in his thirties with a crew cut and yard-wide shoulders. With slits for eyes, both of his ears are cauliflowered to the point of being unrecognizable as auditory organs, his left eyebrow is missing, and his jaw is comic book large.

Bodyguard. And from the look of his ears, probably a *judo* guy.

Judo steps aside to make way for a short, stout man in his seventies. Resplendent in an expensive-looking charcoal gray suit and purple tie, he's got short, perfectly combed silver hair and is thick around the shoulders and neck.

So Fisher guessed right. This guy is obviously the boss.

The old man takes a seat in one of the chairs across from Fisher, crosses his legs, and looks back over his shoulder at the empty doorway and says, in a smoky baritone, "*Ocha.*" Green tea.

Judo, Earring, and Sumo remain standing. The old man stares at Fisher.

Jumpy and confused, Fisher swallows hard and shifts in his seat. Wonders what they're waiting for and then realizes they're drawing this out on purpose, making *him* wait.

A pretty young woman with hair down to the middle of her back hurries in with a tray on which are a pot of green tea and three cups. She sets the cups on the coffee table, fills them, and hurries out.

"My name is Suzuki," the older man finally says in heavily accented English. He gestures toward the cup in front of Fisher, a gold Rolex peeping out from his cuff. "Please."

Fisher gives the man a questioning look, unclear whether the offer is intended as a joke or the old man really hasn't noticed that Fisher's hands are still bound behind his back. Apparently it's the latter, because the old man's gaze flicks down Fisher's torso and then he frowns.

"Kei," he says, addressing the bodyguard. "Take those things off him."

Kei walks over, reaches into his pocket, and produces a stubby knife. He leans over Fisher and cuts him free with a *snick*. Fisher winces as the blood returns to his hands, feeling a measure of calm as he realizes, okay, maybe they're not going to kill him. But then what the hell is this?

Suzuki leans back and crosses his legs. Takes an e-cigarette from his inside coat pocket, uncaps it, and sticks it in his mouth. He returns his gaze to Fisher and inhales, causing the little orange light at the tip of the device to glow. A wisp of vapor leaves his mouth as he exhales, and a charged silence falls over the room.

A car horn honks outside.

Suzuki stares at Fisher as he inhales the vapor from the e-cigarette and blows it out in streams that dissolve into nothing as soon as they leave his mouth. His gaze takes Fisher in head to toe and back again. He studies Fisher's cauliflower ears, then gestures at Earring. "My nephew tells me you are a fighter."

Fisher says nothing, his mind juggling anxiety and confusion.

"Is that true?"

Fisher gives a little nod.

Shota says, "A shitty one."

Suzuki frowns. "Shut up," he says to his nephew, then returns his attention to Fisher. "I watch all the fights. Boxing. Kickboxing. MMA. I don't recognize you." What is this? "I'm not a household name."

Earring chuckles.

Suzuki nods. He seems to study Fisher for a moment; then he motions at the cup of tea on the table in front of him. "Please."

"No, thank you." Fisher's paranoia sharpens to a point. Suzuki is playing with him. What does he want? Does he want him to fight someone? If that's what this is, Fisher will fight anyone they want him to.

Suzuki's eyes flick over to Earring and back to Fisher. Suzuki examines his e-cigarette, sighs deep, and says, "The man you hurt is in very bad condition."

Fisher shifts in his seat. There it is. Suddenly the air in the room is freezing. The thudding in his ears so loud, a part of him worries the old man can hear it too. He swallows and his throat clicks. "I'm sorry I hurt him," he says, "It was an accident."

One leg jackknifed over the other, Suzuki draws another lungful of vapor, lets it drift out his nose. With his free hand, he strokes his chin. His fingers are short and thick, but the nails, Fisher notices, are polished.

Suzuki motions with the vape pen and furrows his brow as though he's decided to get to the heart of the matter. "What do you think of Japan?"

The disconnect between Fisher's interpretation of the gesture and Suzuki's question throws Fisher. "Excuse me?"

Suzuki recaps the vape, puts it back in his pocket. He tilts his head as he regards Fisher. "Do you think Japan is safe?"

Fisher is silent for a moment, then says, "I'm not so sure anymore."

Suzuki nods and a smile spreads across his lips, like he's a teacher and Fisher a bright student who's just given a very insightful answer to a difficult question. "There are actually two Japans." He makes a sweeping gesture at the wall with his arm. "One is out there. That Japan has a rule book, and everyone watches each other to make sure everyone is following the rules. That Japan is very safe." Then the smile disappears and Suzuki's gaze goes dead and he holds up a forefinger. "But the other Japan is different. It has a different rule book. If you don't ever enter this Japan, fine." He holds out his palms. "No problem. You don't have to follow our rules. You are safe." Suzuki holds his forefinger out again for emphasis. "*But.* If you enter this Japan and break the rules, you are not safe. You cannot say, 'I'm sorry, I didn't know the rules.' You cannot say, 'But I'm a foreigner.'"

A sick feeling spreads from the pit of Fisher's stomach into his chest and throat. Suddenly he pictures Terry in the ICU, tubes going in and out of him. It's one thing for Fisher to have gotten himself into such a mess. It's another to have gotten Terry mixed up in it. "What do you want from me?"

Suzuki leans forward so suddenly, it makes Fisher flinch. Palms on his knees, he looks Fisher dead in the eye and says, low and slow, "You are mine now." Rising, he tells Shota to take Fisher home, and on his way to the door, Suzuki pats Fisher once on the shoulder.

"Welcome to the other Japan."

CHAPTER FIFTEEN

FROM THE FRONT passenger seat, Shota commandeers the rearview to get a look at Fisher in back. From the look on the guy's face—skin taut and pale and beaded with sweat—he's shitting bricks.

Shota chuckles to himself as he replays the scene in Uncle Jun's office. He had to hand it to the old fuck. He could still put on a good show. Acting all smooth and nice and reasonable, explaining the two Japans and all that shit, and then BAM!

You are mine.

But no, you old cocksucker, thinks Shota. Hank Fisher isn't yours, he's *mine*.

The countdown has begun. Uncle Jun's days are numbered, and when he's gone the Tanabe-*kai* will crumble, because with Sato out of the immediate picture—thank you, Hank Fisher— and no designated number three, there's going to be a power vacuum. The organization will implode like so many other *yakuza* groups have in the past decade. It's inevitable. Splinter groups will form, and turf wars will break out. Chaos will reign, and Spiral will be there in the eye of the storm, armed and ready to make their mark.

Last night, on the way back to Tokyo from the A-frame, he'd gotten a call from Uncle Jun. The old man was pissed. Said there'd been a fight during the meeting at Club Deluxe and Sato had been seriously injured. Where the fuck had Shota gone? Who told him he could just abandon his post like that? Shota responded that he'd found the stash house operator and had gone to interrogate him. Would Uncle Jun have preferred for Shota let the operator go? Uncle Jun made a dissatisfied noise, then asked Shota what he'd found out about the missing money. Shota told him he thought Gen was innocent. It looked like the problem was with one of the couriers. Uncle Jun harrumphed. Then he ordered Shota to find the courier and fix the goddamn problem.

Shota glances at Fisher again in the rearview and smiles to himself. Oh, he's fixed the goddamn problem all right. Gen is going to call him immediately after the next cash delivery. He will then leave the stash house with the door unlocked. Shota will send someone into the stash house to get the money. The only issue is that Uncle Jun has eyes everywhere, so Shota can't use any of his guys to make the grab. He needs a fall guy.

Enter Hank Fisher.

It's so perfect, just thinking about it gives Shota a hard-on.

Fisher's voice from the back seat: "Turn right at the light here."

The light turns red, Matchan slows the car to a stop, and Shota watches the hundred or so people on either side of the street pour into the crosswalk, stupid people with stupid faces.

A moment later, the light changes to green, Matchan turns right.

Fisher pipes up again, pointing to an ancient shit-brown apartment building: "This is it up here."

Matchan stops at the curb, Shota thinking, Jesus. What a dump. He looks at Fisher in the rearview. "You live *here?*" Fisher ignores the question and reaches for the door latch. Tsukahara grabs him by the ear and gives it a hard twist. "The fuck you think you're going?" Fisher takes his hand away from the latch. "Stay a minute," says Shota. "We need to chat." Fisher's pretending to look at something outside his window. Shota snaps his fingers. "Hey." The fighter's gaze travels slowly until it meets Shota's in the mirror.

"You're gonna do a job for me," Shota says.

Fisher's Adam's apple bobs once. "What kind of job?"

Shota smiles. "Simple. Something even you can do."

Fisher's face goes slack for a split second, then tightens again. "If it's so simple, what do you need me for?"

Shota chucks his chin at Matchan, who's staring straight ahead out the windshield. "You think I need him to drive me around?" He makes a scoffing noise. "You're gonna do it because I say so. And when that's done, you'll do something else for me."

Fisher works his jaw. "What if I say no?"

The guy has balls, Shota will give him that.

Tsukahara says, "What did you say, motherfucker?" He reaches for Fisher's ear again. Fisher knocks his hand away, and Tsukahara pulls out his Glock and sticks it in Fisher's face. Fisher freezes. Tsukahara jams the barrel of the pistol under Fisher's ear. "Okay," Fisher says, in a strangled voice, slowly lowering his hands into his lap. "Okay, okay."

Shota smiles. "Do you believe in heaven, Hank?" He lifts his eyebrows. "You believe in an afterlife?"

"No."

Shota purses his lips and nods. "Yeah, me neither. You live, you die. That's it, there's nothing else." His eyes wander off for a second, then flick back to the mirror. "I'll just kill you if you say no." He lifts his chin at Tsukahara.

Tsukahara takes the gun away from Fisher's neck.

Fisher glares at Tsukahara, then at Shota in the mirror. "When am I supposed to do this?"

"A day or two. Maybe three. Give me your cell number."

Fisher recites the number, his voice hardly more than a whisper.

"Be ready to go when I call. Now go on, go home. You look like you're going to barf, and I don't want you fouling up my ride."

CHAPTER SIXTEEN

FISHER CLOSES THE door and stands there trembling in the dark. He turns, places his palms on the door's cool metal surface, and hangs his head and thinks of his family. He feels like he's been strapped to a rocket, and he can see Lisa, Justin, and James getting smaller and smaller below as he hurtles toward space. His kids are going to grow up without a dad, just like he did, and they're going to feel abandoned, just like he did.

Crack-crack-crack.

The memory of the gunshots is as fresh in his mind as it was that day more than thirty years ago. He sees his mom running, rifle in her arms, screaming:

Run, Henry!

Her last words to him.

His dad kneeling beside her, shouting *Jean!* His dad returning fire at the men in camouflage. His dad crumpling, then lying still in the mud beside his mom.

Suddenly Fisher is gasping for breath, guilt and fear and anger churning inside him, and then it all ignites and he explodes in a flash of rage. He kicks the door.

Boom!

A muted yelp from next door startles him, brings him back. He just frightened poor Akkun and Wakabayashi-san. He feels a rush of guilt and shame. He knows what it's like to be a kid and scared witless.

He takes his shoes off and steps up into the room, the image of his parents lying dead in the mud stuck in his mind like a splinter that can't be removed. He goes to the window and looks down at the street. He rubs the spot on his neck, still sore, where Tsukahara jammed the barrel of the gun.

A gun. Here in Japan.

It's insane. Firearms are no more a part of the average person's life in this country than tea ceremony is a part of the average American's. Seeing Tsukahara's pistol was surreal. Like seeing a dog with wings. But there was nothing imaginary about it. Fisher can still feel the cold, hard steel under his ear.

His heart pounds again.

Two Japans.

One night when he was six or seven, he was up in the loft over the living room of their converted barn, unable to sleep because the neighbors' dog, a big black lab named Pete, started barking at something and wouldn't shut up. Fisher overheard his parents talking quietly on the sofa below about his brother, Danny. Twelve years older, Danny was seldom around when Fisher was growing up. Always in and out of trouble, he'd been arrested the day before for what Fisher later found out was a burglary. Fisher's mom said to his dad that she'd always thought Danny would straighten out someday, and now it looked like he was turning into a criminal, and it was their fault, wasn't it? After all, they were criminals themselves, weren't they? Fisher's dad made a soft scoffing noise and told her not to say that. Growing pot was different. If they were criminals, they were "criminals light."

Fisher knew the word "criminal," and *criminals light* sounded cool to his six-year-old ears. He fell asleep imagining a special type of flashlight used by bank robbers. He asked his mom the next morning what she and his dad had been talking about. Nothing, she said, her back to him as she washed dishes at the sink. Daddy was just being silly. Fisher dipped his spoon into his granola and said, Am I a criminal light? Her back stiffened, and she stopped wiping the plate in her hands. She set it down, turned, and stepped over to Fisher and grabbed his chin hard.

You are no kind of criminal, she said, staring into his eyes. *You never will be. Understand?*

Yes, Mom.

He thinks of his brother, stabbed to death in a bar shortly after Fisher and Lisa got married. Danny became his legal guardian after their parents died, and if the new responsibility mitigated his criminal tendencies, Fisher never noticed. If anything it had made them worse. By the time Fisher was in high school and the two of them were living in a shitty one-bedroom in Sacramento—Fisher sleeping on a hide-a-bed in the living room, eating Cap'n Crunch and baloney sandwiches—Danny was doing a bit of unlicensed construction work, but mostly he dealt drugs, stole cars, robbed houses. Fisher knew this because Danny came home every once in a while, usually with his knucklehead friends in tow, and they liked to talk, and Fisher had ears attached to his head.

Fisher loved his parents and he loved his brother. But he never wanted to be like them. He'd ended up relocating to the country with the lowest crime rate in the world, and now he's mixed up with a bunch of gangsters, and whatever it is they want him to do, it's going to make him a criminal. Hell, he's already a criminal. He threw Sato on his head and ran away.

A Japanese saying comes to him: *Kaeru no ko wa kaeru.* The child of a frog is a frog. In other words, the apple doesn't fall far from the tree.

His stomach churns. Will Shota really kill him if he refuses to do what he wants?

You are mine now.

His heart pumping madly, he steps away from the window. He pulls off his clothes and lets them fall to the floor. He takes a long, hot shower, his ear throbbing from the blow Tsukahara dealt him and his shoulders and wrists still aching from the cuffs. He dries off, puts a pair of boxers on, and dials Laura again, desperate to hear that Terry is going to be okay, but she doesn't pick up. He leaves her a message, asking her to call him as soon as possible. Then he pops three ibuprofen and lies down on the *tatami* and closes his eyes. With his thumbs he rubs his eyes, the tide of adrenaline finally receding from his veins, bone-deep exhaustion taking its place.

Akio's words on the phone last night float into his head: *Once these guys sink their fangs into you, they don't let go.*

Fisher feels a twinge of anger toward his friend. None of this would be happening if it weren't for his so-called "acting-slash-bodyguard gig." Fisher sits up and slowly pulls air into his lungs and lets it out. Deep, slow breaths.

Inhale. Pause. Exhale.

No, it's not Akio's fault. Neither is it his mom and dad's fault, or Danny's.

This is no one's fault but his own.

He looks over at the Hawaii picture. He and Lisa and Justin and James, happy. He wants another chance at that life.

He'll do this job Shota wants him to do, whatever it is. But after that, he's done. He's going to get Lisa's address from the PI.

He's going to prove to Lisa he's the man she wants him to be. He's going to show Justin and James that he hasn't abandoned them. He's here, and he's not going anywhere.

PART TWO

CHAPTER SEVENTEEN

Two days later
8:00 p.m.
In a Doutor Coffee shop in Yotsuya, Tokyo

෨

FROM HIS SEAT by the window, Fisher stares at a skinny apartment tower across the street, hunched in his seat, trying to look inconspicuous as he waits for Shota to call with the all-clear.

There are five other people in the café, and they all seem to be looking at him. Are they looking at him? His nerves are crackling and popping like the snapped wires of a downed telephone pole.

Outside, pedestrians trudge up and down the sidewalk in the stubborn evening heat, mopping their brows with handkerchiefs.

On the table in front of Fisher is a plastic cup of iced coffee that he hasn't touched since he sat down twenty minutes ago. Condensation runs down the sides of the cup, soaking the little doily it sits on. Fisher doesn't know why he bought the coffee.

Caffeine is the last thing he needs right now. Next to the coffee is a slip of paper with a room number scribbled on it and the phone Shota gave him.

When the gangsters arrived at six, Matchan was driving with Shota in the passenger seat again, Tsukahara in back. The right side of Tsukahara's face was looking even worse, burgundy red and glistening under some kind of ointment, a gauze patch over his right eye. "One Love" by Bob Marley and the Wailers thumped softly on the stereo. No sooner did Matchan speed off than Shota started to go over the details of the burglary Fisher was going to commit.

Fisher listened, unable to believe this was actually happening. It was crazy. He was to wait for Shota to call and then leave the coffee shop, walk across the street, and enter the lobby of Excel Mansion. It was an older building, Shota had explained, so it had no security other than a single surveillance camera facing the entrance. When Fisher entered the lobby, he was to keep his hoodie pulled low and his head down and go directly to the elevators and up to the twelfth floor. The bag he was supposed to steal was in No. 1205. Shota said the door would be unlocked.

"Go inside, find the bag, and get out of there," he said. "Talk to no one. Understand?"

"What if I can't find the bag?"

"It'll be in there. It's a one-room apartment, shouldn't take you long to find it. Once you're out and clear of the building, call me. I'll tell you where to go from there."

"What if something—"

"*It won't.* Just do what I tell you."

Matchan handed Fisher a pair of work gloves. Shota took his wallet and phone and said he'd get them back after the job was done. Then he gave Fisher a nicked-up smartphone and told him to call him with it when he had the bag.

Before getting out of the car, Fisher turned to Shota. "After I do this, I'm done."

Shota just smiled.

The smartphone vibrates on the table. Fisher grabs it.

"Go now," Shota says and hangs up.

An old lady with a bad dye job gets up from her seat and takes her tray to a cubby above the trash receptacle.

Fisher feels like he might pop out of his skin, but he can't seem to move. Here he is, a big, conspicuous foreigner, and he's about to break into someone's apartment. What if something goes wrong and he gets caught? He's going to jail, that's what.

Goddamn it.

It's all way too simple. A million things could go wrong. And if something does, he'll be fucked. If he's caught there won't be anything except his word to tie him to Suzuki. And who are the cops going to believe: a down-on-his-luck foreign MMA fighter known for his hot temper and frequent run-ins? Or the head of one of the biggest organized crime groups in the city with connections at the highest levels of the department?

The phone buzzes again, startling him. He looks around to see if anyone noticed him jump, but every pair of eyes in the place is glued to a screen. He picks up the phone.

"What the fuck are you waiting for?" Shota says. "*Go.*"

Fisher stuffs the phone in his pocket, tosses the untouched coffee in the trash, and leaves.

Outside, it's a steam-bath, Fisher's hoodie nearly soaked through with sweat before he even crosses the street. It's full dark now, but there are people everywhere.

Panic twists in his chest. He keeps his head down as he hurries into the lobby. On the way in through the glass doors, he catches a glimpse of his reflection. Quasimodo in a sweat-stained hoodie.

He almost runs into a young woman holding a phone up in front of her face. The woman shoots a quick, uninterested glance at him as he steps around her, then returns her attention to her phone and continues on out the doors.

Did she see his face?

He moves past more people, his paranoia ratcheting higher and higher. A shuffling man in his sixties. A college-age kid with bedhead.

Witnesses, all of them.

He walks into the lobby of the building. The elevator is on his right. Nerves throbbing with fear, he pushes the up button and waits for the car to descend from the seventh floor, the only sounds in his ears the gusts of his breathing over the heavy *whoosh* of his pulse.

Ping.

The doors judder open. A young woman steps out, nearly stopping Fisher's heart. He turns his face away as he steps into the car. The doors remain open for a moment, and he fumbles for the close button, stabs at it with his thumb. The doors slide closed and the car ascends.

When the doors open on the twelfth floor, he peeks out at the corridor and, seeing no one else, quickly walks out. His hands are sweating. When he gets to No. 1205, he slips on the work gloves, glances left and right, and tries the door handle. It's unlocked, like Shota said it would be. He's trembling all over.

He remembers the feel of the cold, hard steel under his ear last night. If he doesn't do this, they'll kill him.

He takes a deep breath, as though he's about to dive into the depths of an ocean. Then he quickly lets himself in and pulls the door shut behind him.

It's dark inside the room and like an oven, a good ten degrees hotter than it is outside. The air is stale and smells faintly of shit. Fisher can hear nothing but the pounding of his heart.

He pulls the neck of the hoodie up over his nose. The place isn't much bigger than his own. There's a tiny unit bath to Fisher's left, and through the open plastic door he can see a toilet, sink, and bathtub with the shower curtain drawn. To his right is a kitchenette. Dirty dishes piled in the sink, the gas burner in the little alcove next to it covered in layers of accumulated grease and grime.

In front of him is a closed *shoji*—a paper sliding door. He steps to it, the floor creaking under him. He freezes and keens his ears. Shota had said there wouldn't be anyone inside the apartment, but Fisher's not taking any chances. He raises his left fist, ready to blast whoever might be in there. Licks his lips and swallows, then with his right hand slowly pulls the door open an inch, then another, until the room comes fully into view.

There's no one inside the six-mat room, and the knot of tension in Fisher's gut loosens a degree. He scans the room. It's a landfill site in miniature. Trash piled a foot deep on the *tatami*. Fast-food wrappers, Styrofoam containers, plastic bags, and PET bottles. Old newspapers and magazines. Empty beer cans, an old laptop with a slashed screen, a coffee mug with a layer of green mold crusting the bottom. Ancient VHS tapes, DVDs, and plastic video game cases.

The place looks like any of the succession of shit holes Fisher had lived in with his brother, Danny, after their parents died. The two of them had moved around a lot as Danny went from job to job. They lived in dump after dump, Danny and his friends strewing their trash everywhere, just not caring.

It takes Fisher a moment to snap out of the memory, and when he does his eyes land on what he's looking for: a black Nike gym bag sitting atop a *kotatsu*—a low table equipped with a heater—in the middle of the room, an island in a sea of garbage. His pulse thuds in his neck as he kicks some cans and bottles out of the way, reaches down, and picks it up. It's heavy, about thirty pounds. It can only be one thing: drugs.

He shoves the thought away, then takes the bag and hurries to the door. He's about to put his shoes back on when the smell hits him again, stronger here in the *genkan*. Shit or...something rotting. Decomposing.

It's coming from the bathroom. *Just get the hell out of here*, he tells himself. But he can't. He steps over to the open bathroom door, and the stench is so strong, he has to cover his mouth and nose with the hoodie again. The toilet and sink are empty. He reaches over and pulls back the shower curtain and lets out an involuntary "Ah!"

Crammed in the tub in a sitting position is the shirtless body of a man in sky-blue sweatpants. His hands are bound behind him, and his distended belly presses against his thighs. His whole head has been wrapped in so many layers of plastic wrap that his features look smeared.

Fisher scrambles away, fighting the urge to vomit. He bursts out the door, then stops short. He's forgotten the gym bag. He swings the door back open and steps inside again, forcing himself not to look over at the bathroom as he reaches down for the bag. Once outside again, he throws the strap over his shoulder, and then he's running down the corridor, past the elevator and to the door to the stairwell.

Did Shota set him up?

Huffing and puffing, he reaches the first-floor landing. There's a door marked "Exit" at the end of a short hallway. To the left of it is another door with a little white sign beside it that says "Trash Collection." He runs to the exit, grabs the doorknob, and as he turns it, the door to the trash collection room swings open, and out steps an old woman in an apron. Fisher manages to look away just as she glances at him.

A shard of ice spears his chest. Did she see his face? All the people who saw him on his way into the building and now this old woman, whose eyes he can feel like lasers on his back. He pictures her telling the cops later about the big foreigner she saw with a gym bag on his back.

He exits the building, head full of bees, and it's all he can do not to break into a sprint. He hurries down the sidewalk, more people everywhere as he scans the street for the black Mercedes, the weight of the sweat-soaked hoodie and the bag on his shoulder feeling like a hundred pounds.

The Mercedes isn't there. All he sees is a glut of taxis.

Taxis. A delivery truck. A cop car.

Oh shit, a cop car.

CHAPTER EIGHTEEN

FISHER STOPS IN his tracks. The patrol car is parked at the curb fifty feet ahead, and he can see two policemen inside, one young-looking, the other older. The older one smiling and nodding as the younger one, also smiling, talks. The younger cop glances over at Fisher, and he realizes he's staring at them.

Fisher averts his gaze and continues walking, hoping they don't decide to get out and question him.

It wouldn't be the first time. Getting stopped from time to time for no particular reason is simply a fact of *gaijin* life in Tokyo. One evening three or four years ago, Fisher decided to get some air after he and Lisa had a big argument—over what, Fisher can't remember, but it was probably his fault, probably something selfish and impulsive and stupid. It was a warm night, and he walked to a little park around the corner from their apartment and sat down on a bench. It wasn't that late, maybe 9 p.m., but there was no one else in the park at that hour. A young policeman strolled by, caught sight of Fisher alone on the bench, and doubled back, pulling out his *tonfa*—essentially a billy club with a perpendicular handle attached at one end. He asked what Fisher was doing there, and Fisher explained in

Japanese that he'd just gotten into an argument with his wife and came out to cool down a bit. The cop proceeded to grill him. Where did he live? What was the fight about? Why did he come to this park? Fisher was pissed but he bit his tongue and answered the questions. "Well, you should go home now," the cop finally told him.

Heart racing, he walks past the black-and-white, eyes fixed on a Lawson's convenience store up ahead. If they stop him, it's over. They'll look in the bag, find the drugs or whatever is in there, arrest him on the spot.

At the entrance to Lawson's he shoots a glance over his left shoulder as the automatic doors slide open, just in time to see the car pull away from the curb and drive off.

He closes his eyes for a moment, takes a deep breath, then turns on his heel and continues walking. He takes the phone from his pocket and dials Shota. It rings and rings. What if he doesn't pick up? A knot of fear twists in Fisher's gut.

Shota finally answers after the ninth or tenth ring. "You got the bag?"

A taxi honks its horn at a guy on a motorcycle. Fisher jumps, startled.

"What the fuck is going on?!" he shouts into the phone, looking this way and that as he moves.

"What are you talking about? Did you get the bag or not?"

He lowers his voice. "Yeah, you piece of shit! I got your bag! It was next to the dead guy in the bathtub!"

"What?"

"There was a fucking dead guy in the bathtub!"

"I don't have time for this bullshit. Bring the bag to the rear entrance of Club Deluxe in forty minutes."

"Fuck you."

"What?"

"You heard me."

Shota sighs. "I have no idea what you're talking about, but I want that goddamned bag."

Fisher pictures all the people who saw him going into the building. The old lady who saw him coming out.

He looks left, then right, then left again. People everywhere. *Eyes* everywhere.

Shota says, "I can hear you hyperventilating. Settle the fuck down. Don't lose your shit, and everything will be fine."

No. Nothing is fine. Fisher pinches the bridge of his nose as he walks. "I give you the bag and I'm done."

Shota says, "This is not a negotiation, asshole." He switches to Japanese. "You do understand that, right?"

A man in a suit coming toward Fisher is staring at him with a funny look on his face. Fisher steps over to the metal guardrail bordering the sidewalk, a hollow feeling settling into the pit of his stomach as he realizes Shota is right. He's in no position to dictate terms. He just committed burglary. He's got the bag he was forced to steal on his shoulder, and there's a fucking dead guy in the apartment he stole it from. Countless people saw him go into the building, and at least one person might very well have gotten a good look at his face when he'd gone out. Shota knows where he lives, so he can't go home. And he can't hide, because where would he go, and what's he supposed to do with the bag? The thought of what might be in it sends a shiver down his neck. He obviously can't go to the cops, either. He's trapped.

"No more fucking around," Shota says. "Be at the club in forty minutes."

❦

Fisher buys a ticket outside the entrance to the Ginza Line and gets on the next train bound for Asakusa. He stands near a set of double doors, sets the gym bag down between his feet, and lets the cool air from the AC wash over him. He looks down at the gym bag, and a slow wave of cold dread rolls through him. What's inside it? He pushes the thought away. He doesn't want to know.

At the first stop, in Omotesando, he transfers to the Chiyoda Line. From there, he goes one more stop to Nogizaka and gets off. It's nine thirty when he exits Nogizaka Station and walks east on Gaien Higashi Dori. He passes the Ritz Carlton, part of the big glitzy Tokyo Midtown complex that sits where the old Ministry of Defense used to be. The crowd here is more grown-up, more professional than the one in Shibuya, with its hipsters and nerds and wannabes and *furiitaa*—part-time workers. Midtown at night is crawling with men and women on their way to the hundreds of restaurants and clubs cramming the back streets and alleyways radiating in every direction. All of them oblivious to all the dark happenings underneath the bright, shiny surface.

Like Fisher had been two days ago.

He hasn't walked a minute before he's drenched with sweat again. Hoodie soaked, shorts looking like he's pissed himself. The strap of the gym bag is rubbing the top of his shoulder raw. Fisher switches it to the other shoulder, feeling the contents of the bag shift. Morbid curiosity oozes cold into his mind. He slips the strap off his shoulder, grabs the scruff of the bag at the top with both hands, and shakes it once, hard.

Don't, he tells himself. You don't want to know.

The problem is, he *does* want to know. A friend of his from Ghana once told him about pulling a guinea worm from his arm and the mix of horror and fascination he'd felt at seeing this horrible parasite emerge from under his skin. The desire to see what's inside the bag feels like that to Fisher. But it's also because whatever is in there controls what happens to him next.

He checks the time. He's got about fifteen minutes before his scheduled rendezvous with Shota and company.

There's a big Starbucks across the street, a two-story affair with a wine bar on the second floor. Fisher went there once with Lisa and the twins several years ago. He was home between fights and remembers it was Chinese New Year, because they walked from there to Roppongi Hills, where a lion dance was being performed. Justin loved it, but James freaked when the lion came up and pretended to bite the top of his head. He and Lisa, exchanging suppressed smiles as they consoled James, barely containing their laughter.

Fisher's eyes are suddenly hot. He wipes at them with his hand. At the next crosswalk he waits for the signal to change, crosses the street, and walks into the Starbucks. He moves quickly past the long queue of customers at the counter, ignores the greeting of a barista who takes notice of him, and goes through a door in the rear of the store to the restroom. It's empty. He goes inside and locks the door and sets the gym bag on top of the toilet lid. Fisher steps back and looks at himself in the mirror above the sink.

Jesus.

He looks like hell. Dark circles under his eyes. His color chalky, except for his right cheek and nose, which are red and swollen. Not a trace of the man who was here with Lisa and the kids years ago. Lisa had been right about him. He'd stepped off a cliff somewhere, and she'd seen him turning into someone else as he fell. She tried to tell him, and he didn't listen. And now he is hitting bottom.

Kaeru no ko wa kaeru. The apple doesn't fall far from the tree.

He takes the hoodie off and stuffs it into the trash receptacle, wondering why the hell he hadn't tossed it earlier. He turns on the faucet and washes his hands and face, then dries off with a handful of paper towels. Then he steps over to the bag and unzips it.

Inside is a black plastic trash bag covering a big rectangular block of something. It's ringed at both ends with duct tape. He runs his hand over the length of the bag. He can feel the edges of thin, brick-like objects underneath the plastic. A knot of dread uncoils in his gut. He should just go. Just zip up the bag and leave. Give it to Shota like he's supposed to and be done with this mess.

Fisher grabs one end of the trash bag. The stubby cylinder is sealed tight at both ends with the duct tape. He doesn't see a way to remove the tape without ripping the bag, so hell with it, he tears a little hole in one end with his teeth and then widens it into a bigger hole with his fingers. He reaches inside and pulls out a vacuum-wrapped bundle of ten-thousand-yen notes. He sticks his hand back in the bag and pulls out another.

There are hundreds of them.

CHAPTER NINETEEN

WHEN HE GETS to the mouth of the long alley that runs behind Club Deluxe, Fisher peeks around the corner, and there's the Mercedes parked fifty yards away, streetlights reflecting in swirls off the car's shiny black surfaces. Catches of muffled laughter waft from a handful of low-end bars and pubs lining the alley. Where the alley dead-ends, maybe fifty yards down from the Mercedes, is parked a black van.

A drunk couple in their thirties passes Fisher, laughing as they zigzag down the street. He waits until they round the next corner and turns in to the alley. As he approaches the Mercedes, the front passenger side door of the car swings open, and Shota climbs out and chucks his chin at Fisher. Matchan gets out on the driver's side and waddles over to join Shota. He stares at Fisher, shifting from foot to foot, as if he's uncomfortable standing in one place.

"Bring it here," Shota says, indicating the bag on Fisher's shoulder. Nerves popping, Fisher starts to shrug the gym bag off his shoulder, glad to get rid of the thing, and then stops himself. Part of him is screaming, *Run, dumbass!* But another part of him needs to know what's happening here. Who was the dead guy in that apartment? Is this all a set-up? The gangsters forcing him to do a robbery and take the fall for the robbery *and* a murder? But in that case, wouldn't they just leave him in the wind for the cops to find? He can't make sense of any of it.

He glances at the van at the end of the alley. Looks at Shota and Matchan again, Matchan still doing his little side-to-side dance.

Shota says, "If you're thinking of running off with that bag, you better fucking think again."

"Who was the dead guy?"

Shota motions with his head at Matchan. "*Told* you. No idea." The two of them start toward Fisher.

An engine roars to life. The van's headlights snap on.

Fisher shields his eyes against the brightness of the lights, panic blasting through him. Are there more gangsters in the van? "What is this?" he says loud, adrenaline making his voice strange.

Shota holds out his hand as he walks toward Fisher, the van now rolling forward. "You run, you're dead. You hear me?"

The van is fifty feet away now, Fisher backing away quickly, heart pounding as he visors his eyes with his hand.

The van's passenger window rolls down. A hand emerges.

With a sudden roar, Shota lunges at him.

Fisher turns to run, his pulse sledgehammering in his head. There's a burst of light, a loud crack ripping through the air. Somewhere a window shatters. They're shooting! He stops and drops into a squat and covers his head with his hands, the image of his parents' bodies flashing across his consciousness, and all at once he's paralyzed. He tries to draw a breath, but his lungs have stopped functioning; everything is frozen. The door to one of the bars opens. A young couple emerges, uncertain looks on their faces.

The *crack* of another shot elicits a yelp from the woman, and the two of them rush back into the bar and close the door.

Run, Henry!

And then Fisher is up and sprinting. *Crack crack.*

Behind him, Shota yelling, "*Yamero*!" Stop shooting! "Get your asses out here and go get him!"

CHAPTER TWENTY

IMAGINE YOU'RE YOUNG. Not a baby anymore, but still on the babe side of childhood, and you live in the woods—literally—with your mom and dad and your big brother, Danny. The four of you sleep in a cavernous, converted barn next to the greenhouse where your folks grow dope, because that's what they do, that's what everyone does up here in the redwoods of southern Humboldt County, in Northern California. You don't know what that means yet, so you're a happy kid living in a green forest straight out of a fairy tale.

Every morning the family rooster, Big Red, wakes you up at dawn with his crowing from the chicken coop. You eat a bowl of your mom's homemade granola mixed with her homemade yogurt, and then you go out and feed the chickens, go back inside, and if it's a school day, you get dressed and walk down the dirt road to the bus stop. It's a thirty-minute ride down a winding, beat-up road to the town of Redway, where your school is. Your teachers are all young and bright-eyed and have long hair and wear homemade clothes, and you have lots of friends, most of whose parents do the same thing as yours do for a living.

Mom and Dad are much older than your friends' parents.

Dad is a short, dark, bald Jewish guy with a potbelly who can build anything. Mom is Japanese-American and on the tall side with shoulder-length silver hair she ties in a ponytail and can hit a quarter from a hundred yards with the .22 Magnum Dad gave her as a birthday present years ago. Danny is twelve years older than you, too old for you to think of him as a brother; he's more like an uncle who's gone a lot and argues with your folks when he's home, mostly behind closed doors because your folks don't want you to hear, and you've learned to tune out the muffled, angry voices, usually at night after you've gone to bed. But once, when you're nine or ten, the arguing wakes you up in the middle of the night and you hear your dad say *Goddamn thief,* real loud, and then Danny says *Hypocrite* even louder, but all you want to do is go back to sleep, so after a few minutes you do, and you don't think of those two words or what they mean until many years later.

On the weekends, you help your folks around the farm during the day, and at night you stay up late with your dad and watch *Kung Fu* reruns on the old black-and-white TV he keeps in the garage. Kwai Chang Caine fighting bad guys in a snow globe, your dad telling you every couple of minutes to reconfigure the rabbit-ear antennas to see if you can get a clearer picture. Your dad digs kung fu too. He practiced an American style of karate called *kajukenbo* in the late sixties and early seventies. Sometimes he teaches you things: how to throw a proper punch, how to execute a proper roundhouse kick.

Time crawls in SoHum, which is fine with you, because you like your school, you like your friends, and you like living in an old barn and swimming in the river in the summer and helping out your folks on the farm, particularly during the harvest in the fall, when everyone has a specific job to do and is so busy but it's like a party that goes on for a whole two weeks.

The grow is small: a hundred or so plants every season, no more, no less, concealed in a greenhouse covered with opaque plastic sheeting. It's not enough to make the family rich, but your folks say it's all you need "to live the good life."

One season, the plants get too tall and are butting up against the plastic sheeting in the greenhouse, so your dad buys lumber and other supplies in Garberville and removes the sheeting so he can increase the height of the greenhouse walls. Until then, they'd been careful and for years had never had a problem, but wouldn't you know it, on the one day the little grow house is open to the sky, a chopper appears out of nowhere, hovers over the property for a few moments, then buzzes off like a sated hummingbird.

Your dad stands there with his mouth open, looking like he's trying to remember something. Then he says *Well, shit*, but your mom, man, your mom starts freaking out, crying and screaming, and you don't know what the heck is going on. You wonder where Danny is, because he's not there, he's never there, and after a few minutes your dad starts saying *It's over it's over it's over*. Just like that, like a chant.

And it *is* over. Just after dawn the next day, you are woken by a deafening roar; it scares the crap out of you, so you clamber down the ladder from the loft your dad built for you, wipe the sleep from your eyes, and join your parents at the door of the barn and you see it: a black chopper, the kind you've seen in the movies, scary and insectile, hanging there in the air above your family's little clearing in the woods like some horror movie dragonfly.

You're pretty sure you know what this is, what's happening, because it's already been a few years since the "Campaign Against Marijuana Planting," began, and CAMP raids are a hazard of the trade, and everybody talks about them all the time; your dad has said it's a game of chance, and even your friend Dillon's dad went to jail last year after he got raided. So you know the helicopter is scoping things out, and you're scared shitless that any moment now you're going to look up and see swarms of camouflaged cops with search warrants and scary-looking guns.

So Dad tells you to get out there and help him, and before you know it, you've helped him tear down the greenhouse, and the funk of the plants is almost overpowering, and you feel like the world is caving in around you. You watch Dad pull up the last remaining boards around the perimeter of the greenhouse, your heart thumping in your chest as you wonder what you'll do, where you'll go. But you also know that whatever happens it's going to be okay, because whatever happens Mom and Dad are here with you and they're going to protect you.

And that's about all you have time to think, because Mom shouts, *They're coming* from the side of the house, and you see her running toward you and Dad with her .22 cradled in her arms.

Run, Henry! she screams. Dad shouts, *Jean! No!* And then you hear a series of loud booms, and she drops to the ground like someone has kicked her feet out from under her.

Dad looks at you, his eyes wild, and you squat right there in the mud and watch him run to Mom, who's not moving, screaming her name *Jean! Jean! Jean!* And he bends down and snatches up the rifle just as men dressed in camouflage just like soldiers emerge from the tree line and *Boom Boom Boom Boom Boom* and then Dad is on the ground next to Mom, and he's not moving either.

That's the end of your fairy tale.

CHAPTER TWENTY-ONE

FISHER'S FEET BEAT the pavement, the picture of his parents lying dead on the ground lingering in his mind like an image stuck in a slide projector. He gets fifty yards and steals a glance over his shoulder.

Two goateed skinheads in white T-shirts and faded jeans are chasing him. Both of them are carrying baseball bats.

People are pouring out of the clubs and bars that line either side of the street, drawn by the unfamiliar sound of the gunshots.

A siren wails in the distance.

The two skinheads are right on his heels, running and shouting at Fisher to stop, their footfalls echoing off the buildings.

The van's engine roars over the voices of the goons behind him as Fisher tries to speed up, fearful that the driver plans to run him down, but he's already running as fast as he can with the bag flopping this way and that, thumping his back with every stride. The alley dead-ends into a narrow one-way street up ahead. He reaches the corner, cuts right, and continues running. He looks back over his shoulder, sees the van a hundred feet behind him. It speeds up, tires squealing, and then an SUV comes from the opposite direction, its horn blaring.

"This is a one-way street!" shouts the driver of the SUV.

Fisher pumps his legs, holding the bag close to his side with his left arm. He can hear the skinheads' footfalls close behind him. A young couple steps out of a bar into the street right in front of him. He darts sideways and barely manages to avoid colliding with them.

One of the skinheads says to the other, "His legs! Aim for his legs!"

The bat hits Fisher's left calf and pops out in front of him. He trips over it and falls, sprawling to the pavement in a skidding forward *ukemi*—a judo break-fall. The gym bag flies up over his shoulder, lands with a soft thud. Fisher's hands and forearms take the brunt of the impact rather than his face, and he barely has time to register the pain in his palms and forearms and elbows and knees before the two skinheads are on him, dancing around and kicking away at his sides and head. Fisher rolls over into a seated position, his right arm behind him, his left out in front, trying to ward off the blows. The skinheads are virtual mirror images of each other but for their goatees, one of which is dyed green, the other red. Identical twins. The one who threw his bat kicks at Fisher's outstretched arm. He's the one with the red goatee. His green-bearded brother is on Fisher's right with his bat cocked like he means to hit one over the fence. On his face is the sneer of a man who was a bully as a kid and stayed that way. He tries to sidestep around Fisher, but Fisher circles on his butt, keeping the guy in front of him where he can see him.

While Fisher's attention is on Greenbeard, Redbeard hops in and kicks Fisher in the side of the face. It jars him, but it's a weak kick, thrown with the leg and not the hip, and the angle is wrong. Fisher pops up to his feet, and Redbeard hops back, saying to Greenbeard, who's behind Fisher, "Now! Crack his skull!"

A woman screams. Someone shouts, "Call the police!"

Fisher whirls around and feels a breeze as the bat whizzes by in front of his face. Greenbeard swings again in the other direction, low and to Fisher's left. He jumps back, curling his torso into a C to dodge the blow, but the end of the bat catches him in the right hip. *Ow*. When he swings again, Fisher takes a big step forward and arcs his left arm up and brings it down hard over the asshole's hands, clamping them along with the bat under his left armpit. Red-faced with rage, the man struggles to pull his hands free. "Let me go, motherfucker!" Greenbeard twists and again tries to extricate his hands from Fisher's armpit. Fisher clocks him with a short right hook to the jaw and then another, and Greenbeard crumples to the ground.

Movement behind him. He spins around. Redbeard stops short and looks at Fisher, then looks down at the ground. Fisher follows his gaze, and there's the bag. Shota tried to set him up, and now he's trying to kill him. No, Fisher thinks. No way is he going to give Shota the money now. He'd rather fucking burn it.

Redbeard is shaking. His head and face are covered in a sheen of sweat. Over his shoulder, Fisher can see the black van is gone. Which could mean they're coming around the other way.

Which means Fisher has to get out of here.

Fisher bends down and reaches for the bag, and as if on cue Redbeard launches himself at him. He comes in low, arms out. Maybe he wrestled in middle school or maybe a friend taught him how to do a double-leg takedown once. Whatever the case, the move is clumsy and slow, and Fisher does what comes naturally: he puts his hands up, braces himself, and when Redbeard is close enough, Fisher grasps the back of his head with both of his hands and rockets his knee into the man's face.

Lights out for Redbeard.

And then Fisher is running again with the bag under his arm. He doesn't get twenty feet before the van's headlights flash at the mouth of the one-way street.

He freezes.

There's a cross-street up ahead. Fisher breaks into a sprint, his heart slamming in his chest as the van gets closer and closer. He makes it to the corner just before the van does, cuts right, and nearly plows into a crowd of people milling around the entrance to a live house. Hipsters smoking, laughing, taking selfies.

The sirens are much louder now.

He looks back in time to see the van round the corner, accelerate with a roar, and then screech to a stop. The driver's side door flies open, and a man gets out just as Shota's Mercedes pulls up behind Fisher. He's sandwiched.

A hush has fallen over the crowd of hipsters, who are looking with an expression of collective alarm at Fisher and the van and the two men getting out of the Mercedes.

Fisher bumps his way through the startled crowd, and once past them turns another corner and nearly collides with an oncoming taxi. The taxi slams on its brakes, horn blasting. Fisher holds his hands up, bows. *Sorry, so sorry.* The red-lit sign in the right bottom corner of the windshield says "Vacant." He waves a hand at the driver.

"Okay if I get in?" he mouths in Japanese. Heart racing. Please please please.

The driver stares for a moment, assessing him with an irritated, uncertain look. Fisher gives him another slight bow. The driver opens the door. Fisher tosses the bag inside and scrambles in, gasping for breath, still in fight-or-flight mode, his veins flooded with adrenaline. The walls closing in.

Shota and Sumo are standing on the corner Fisher just rounded. Both of them looking right at him as the cab goes by. Shota glares at Fisher and points at him like he'd zap him with a death ray if he could. Then Shota pulls his phone out.

Location services! The thought hits Fisher like a mule kick. He pulls the phone out of his pocket, fumbling it as he opens its settings. He turns the GPS off, and immediately the tension thrumming through him loosens a degree.

Eyeing Fisher in the rearview mirror, the cab driver asks him, "Where to?"

There's only one place Fisher can think of to go. Mari's place in Azabu Juban. He remembers dropping her off there after their dinner date a few months ago.

He tells the driver to take him there.

Ten minutes later, Fisher gazes up at Mari's apartment building from the passenger window of the cab, having second thoughts about coming here, thinking of Terry fighting for his life in the hospital, and that it's his fault. All his fault, and now here he is at Mari's, about to put her in danger too.

The heel of his left palm, his right elbow, and his right knee are raw and bleeding and sting like a mother, and there's a dull throb blooming in his right hip. He thinks his left wrist might be broken. Mari will probably know, because she'd told him the night of their date a few months ago that she used to be an ER nurse. She'd gone to nursing school because she wanted to help people. But the trauma of seeing other human beings in extreme physical and emotional pain day after day had been too much for her, and she fell into a depression. She ended up quitting after only a year.

The driver turns in his seat and says, frowning, "One thousand five hundred yen." He's been shooting Fisher suspicious glances in the mirror since they left Roppongi. Fisher had told him he tripped and took a bad fall, but judging from the look on the man's face, Fisher is pretty sure he didn't buy it.

Fisher looks up at Mari's building again. Damn it. He doesn't have any money to pay the driver with, because Shota took his wallet along with his phone. *The gym bag.* He glances down at it. The thought of taking money from it causes a finger of dread to run down his spine. It may as well be a bomb. No, he's not touching it. He reaches for his back pocket, wincing at the dagger of pain in his ribs, and pretends to be surprised to find his wallet missing. "I'm so sorry," he says in Japanese. "I seem to have lost my wallet. I think I probably dropped it when I fell."

The driver's frown deepens. "Huh?"

He's going to have to ask Mari if she can front him the cab fare. "It's okay," he says to the driver. "I'll have my friend bring out the money. I'll go get her. Please wait here." The driver frowns. Fisher gets out, limps to the lobby, and buzzes Mari's apartment. If she isn't there, he's going to have to do a bum rush on the cab driver. He barks an internal laugh. What's a little bum rush when you're on the run from a bunch of *yakuza* with a bag full of their cash?

"*Hai?*"

Thank you, thank you. "Mari, it's Hank."

"Hank? What are you doing here?"

"I'm really sorry but can I ask you a big favor?"

Mari switches to English. "Of course."

"This is really embarrassing, but I lost my wallet and need some money for cab fare. Could I borrow a couple thousand yen from you?"

"Oh. Okay, sure. Give me a minute."

Mari's going to help him, no questions asked, and it's just like her, and her kindness, his putting her in danger like this just by being here, it makes him feel like the worst piece of shit.

She hurries out a minute later, hair up in a towel and wearing an oversized T-shirt, purple sweatpants, and flip-flops. She sees the blood on his arm and his knee and gasps. "What happened?! Are you okay?!"

"I'm fine, I'm fine. Took a little fall, that's all."

She raises her eyebrows. "You fell?"

"Yeah, it's nothing. Just scraped myself up a little."

Mari frowns. "It doesn't look like nothing." As they walk to the cab, she says, "Did you hear about Terry-*san*?"

Guilt churns in Fisher's chest. "Yeah, I heard. It's terrible." His whole left arm is throbbing now.

"I can't believe it."

"Me neither."

The cab driver stares out the windshield, tapping his finger on the steering wheel. Mari leans down and hands him a five-thousand-yen note. He gives her the change and speeds away.

"You're a life-saver, Mari," says Fisher. "Thank you."

Mari looks again at the blood on his arm and winces. "Come on. I have bandages inside."

Fisher hesitates, catching the scent of her shampoo, something floral. He opens his mouth to say something. *Tell her you have to go.*

She rolls her eyes, then takes him by the crook of the arm, careful to avoid the scrape on his elbow, and leads him inside.

CHAPTER TWENTY-TWO

HE'S SITTING ON the sofa in Mari's living room, finishing up the bowl of fried rice she cooked for him as he watches her pour two glasses of iced *mugicha*—barley tea—in the kitchen. The apartment is on the sixth floor, a typical 1DK: one bedroom, a small dining room and kitchen. Little clusters of framed post-cards hang on the walls. There's a glass coffee table on a green shag throw rug in front of the sofa. A bookshelf next to the TV is crammed with what look like vintage Snoopy dolls still in their packages.

After he showered, she'd brought out a clean pair of shorts and a T-shirt for him to wear. Her brother's, she'd said. He was taking night classes at Temple University Japan, a short distance from her apartment, and sometimes he crashed with her. Then she sprayed the scrapes on his palm, elbow, and knee with hydrogen peroxide and covered them with bandages, com-menting that it looked like he'd taken a big fall, not a little one. Fisher made a dismissive gesture, said he was just clumsy, to which Mari responded by raising her eyebrows and nodding several times in agreement. She said it looked like his wrist was probably just sprained because he could still move it, but she wasn't a doctor and he'd need to get it looked at.

"Why did you come here?" she says, wiping the small island counter with a towel.

"The cab turned on to Sendaizaka, and I remembered you lived close by." As soon as the words leave his mouth, his face feels hot because while it's not a lie, it's not exactly the truth, either. The truth is that he's in trouble, and Mari was the first person he thought of.

"I see." She returns the pitcher to the refrigerator and picks up the glasses of iced tea and pads over in her slippers and hands Fisher one. She sits down next to him, and there's the smell of her shampoo again. He realizes this is the first time he's ever seen her without makeup. She has a roundish face that tapers to a pointed chin, light brown eyes, and dimples when she smiles. A graceful sweep to her neck. She's stunning.

"*Itadakimasu,*" he says, and takes a sip of his tea, which tastes wonderful. After the chaos and confusion and terror of the past two days, sitting here with Mari in her quiet, cozy living room—even under the circumstances, even though he knows he shouldn't be here—is blissful in a way he hasn't experienced in what seems like forever.

"*Dozo,*" says Mari, smiling. Please, go ahead.

Fisher takes another sip of tea.

Mari says, "I didn't get a chance to thank you the other night."

Fisher says, "For what?" and then remembers: the grabby guy at Lounge O. "Oh," he says. He makes a dismissive gesture. "You did pretty good all by yourself there. Probably broke that guy's nose."

Mari winces. "You think so?"

Fisher nods.

"Not good for business," says Mari, shaking her head.

"It wasn't your fault. He had it coming. Where'd you learn to throw a punch like that anyway?"

"My brother. He used to box."

"He taught you well."

Mari grins. She tucks her chin and raises her fists.

They both laugh and then there's a moment of silence between them, and Fisher knows they're both thinking of Terry. Mari speaks first. "I hope Terry is okay."

Fisher feels a lump in his throat. "Me too." His eyes find the Snoopy collection. He motions at it, not wanting to fall apart in front of Mari. "You're a Snoopy fan, huh?"

Mari's face lights up. "Yes! They're all vintage." She points to a big doll on the top shelf. "See that one? I bought it last month for two hundred thousand yen."

"Jesus!"

"I know!" She takes her keys from the coffee table, holds them up to show Fisher the Snoopy key chain to which they're attached, and lifts her eyebrows in a Yes-I-know-it's-a-little-crazy expression. Before Fisher can ask her why on earth she would pay so much for a doll, her expression turns serious and she says, "How did you lose your wallet?"

Fisher shifts in his seat. "I don't know. Probably fell out of my pocket when I fell down."

"Where did you fall?"

Every family has one good liar. In Hank's, it was his brother. Danny Fisher could look you dead in the eye and tell you a whopper with such conviction, such sincerity and panache, that even if the details didn't completely add up as he strung you along with whatever bullshit story he was laying on you, you *believed* him.

Fisher? Not only does he hate dishonesty, but he can't lie

his way out of a wet paper bag. Once, when he was in the third grade, his dad caught him playing with matches on the side of the house. Fisher wasn't a pyro or anything, just curious, and he'd collected a bunch of dry twigs and used a box of matches he'd swiped from Danny's room to get a small fire going. It might have burned the house down and started a forest fire if his dad hadn't caught him when he did. *Henry!* his dad had screamed, and Fisher, standing startled over the fire with the box of matches in his hand, said, *I didn't do it!*

He doesn't want to lie to Mari about what happened. But he can't tell her the truth either. He clears his throat. "Aoyama." He's backing himself into a corner, and he's feeling shittier and shittier about even being here after what happened to Terry. He'll hunker down here for a while longer, swallow his shame and ask Mari if he can borrow some more money and find a cheap hotel where he can hide out for a day or two until he can figure out what to do.

Drilling down, Mari says, "Where in Aoyama? We should call the police box. Someone might have picked up your wallet and taken it there."

And she's right. If he'd actually dropped his wallet, someone would in all likelihood have picked it up and taken it to the local police box. That's Japan for you. Safe Japan. But Fisher's not dealing with Safe Japan right now.

He touches Mari's forearm with his fingertips, noting how soft her skin is. "Nah, it's fine. Don't worry about it. I can go to the police box in the morning."

She gets up and goes to the counter and comes back with her phone. "We'd better call now. The sooner the better." She swipes at the phone's screen, searching, he assumes, for a police box in Aoyama.

His pulse tics. "Seriously, it's late, I've caused you enough trouble."

She says, "It's no trouble!" and puts the phone to her ear.

Fisher gently takes the phone from her hand and ends the call and hands the phone back to her. Mari stares at him with her mouth open. Then she frowns. "What's going on? Does this have something to do with what happened to Terry-*san*?"

Terry. Fisher rubs his chin. He takes a deep breath. "Okay," he says after a moment. "I didn't drop my wallet."

Mari rears back as if Fisher has just slapped her. Her frown deepens. "Huh? What do you mean?"

"I'm in trouble."

"What? What kind of trouble?"

Fisher doesn't say anything. He touches the bruised spot on his knuckles where his hand connected with the gangster's jaw.

She leans forward and touches Fisher's arm. "You can tell me."

Fisher looks up at her. The kindness and earnestness in her expression make him feel guilty about putting her in danger, but they also make him want to kiss her. And he doesn't want to lie to her, but he also dreads the thought of Mari thinking less of him if he tells her what's really going on.

"The really bad kind," he says, and he can almost see the color drain from her face.

"What does that mean? 'Really bad.' Did you kill someone?"

"No!" Fisher says. "Not bad like that." A little voice in his head saying, *Oh, but it is bad like that, isn't it? Hey, looks like maybe Danny wasn't the only good liar in the family after all.* "But it's better if you don't know the details."

The two of them sit there for a moment, eyes locked, and then Mari nods once, as if to herself, and says, "What can I do?"

He just told her he's in serious trouble, yet she still wants to help him. The mix of guilt and desire in his chest intensifies. He shakes his head and says, "You've already helped me."

"You can stay here tonight."

"No," he says. "Thank you." But that's exactly why he came here, isn't it? He knew coming here would put her in danger, and he did anyway because he knew she would invite him to stay.

"Do you have someplace else to stay?"

He's an asshole. But he's got nowhere else to go and no money, and the last thing he wants to be doing is walking around in the middle of the night and risking being stopped by the police or, worse, being found by Shota. "No, it's just... there are people looking for me. They're not nice people."

"Are they the same people who hurt Terry-*san*?"

Suddenly there's a lump in his throat. He rubs his chin again. Runs his hand through his hair. "I think so."

Mari considers this for a moment and says, "Did you tell anyone you were coming here?"

"No, but—"

"Then it should be okay, right?"

He sits there, blown away by how unafraid and ready she is to help him. He knows he's going to stay. He tells himself to at least have the balls not to dissemble. "Okay," he says. "I'll leave first thing in the morning."

Mari smiles. "Okay." She gets up from the sofa. "I'll get the bed ready." She starts for a closed door Fisher assumes leads to her bedroom.

Wait, what? "Um, no, Mari, listen. I-I can't, um, that's not..."

Mari juts her chin out and raises her eyebrows. Then she bursts out laughing. "You thought I meant my bed? Ha ha ha ha ha ha! No, of course not! You have to sleep on the sofa!" She disappears into the bedroom and a moment later brings out a pillow, sheets, and a light comforter and sets them next to Fisher on the sofa, her hand brushing against his thigh as she does this.

While he sits there wondering whether she just touched him on purpose, Mari goes to the kitchen and grabs her purse from the counter, comes back, and sits down on Fisher's left. She snaps open her purse, takes five ten-thousand-yen bills—about five hundred dollars—from her wallet, and holds them out to him. "Here."

"No, Mari, I can't—"

She cuts him off. "You can pay me back."

Fisher looks down at the money in her hand. He nods and accepts the cash, his face burning with shame. He's the lowest of the low. Taking Mari's kindness and giving her what in return? Terry tried to help him too, and look where it got him.

Mari smiles like he's just made her genuinely happy and reaches into her bag again and produces two keys on a ring and places them in Fisher's hand on top of the bills. "I like to sleep late, so I'll probably still be asleep when you leave. You can take these when you leave in the morning. They're spares. Just lock the door and drop them in my mailbox in the lobby or give them back to me next time I see you."

Fisher feels the urge to pull her into his arms. Put his lips to her neck, breathe in her scent. But he sees Lisa and the kids, and just sitting here suddenly feels like a betrayal. "Thank you," he says, accepting the keys.

"*Dou itashimashite*," Mari says, bowing with mock formality. Don't mention it.

Fisher's hand is still resting there on top of hers when she's completed the bow. What the hell is he doing? She meets his gaze, notices he's staring at her, but she doesn't look away.

Instead, her eyes seem to search his for a moment and then flick away. He opens his mouth to say something, but nothing comes out and then the moment is gone and Mari is pushing herself up from the sofa.

"I'll go to bed now. Make yourself comfortable."

"*Oyasumi.*" Good night.

At her bedroom door she turns around and gives him a sly grin. "You can tell me the whole story after things settle down."

Fisher forces a laugh and nods, shame and sadness and hopelessness churning in him. "Okay."

If he's still around.

Because right now it's impossible to see how he's not going to end up dead or in jail. He pushes himself off the sofa, fists clenched, the urge to knock some sense into his own head overwhelming. What's wrong with him? He's going to just throw up his hands, give up without even putting up a fight?

No. Fuck that.

CHAPTER TWENTY-THREE

Roppongi District, Tokyo
Friday, 8:00 p.m.

IN THE BACK seat of the big black Mercedes, Suzuki Jun smokes a cigarette, absently staring out the window as the driver navigates the glut of taxis cramming both sides of Roppongi Dori like plaque in an aging artery.

Throngs of people moving up, down, and around the boulevard in the heat, office workers letting off steam, by now already plastered and talking shit about their bosses, gossiping about their colleagues as they look for the next bar to hit. Out-of-towners and foreign tourists, oohing and aahing at the hustle and bustle, the strobing, colored lights and billboards, blaring bells and buzzers and electronic music. Friends and lovers strolling, the working boys and girls—the bartenders, hosts and hostesses, the dancers and strippers and whores, easily distinguishable by the way they hurry through the crowds toward their destinations.

At a stoplight, Suzuki spots a group of girls in front of a bar where he stabbed a man from a rival gang in 1992. He's always surprised to see the bar's still there. Not many places stay around for that long in Tokyo. The landscape is constantly changing, along with everything else. It makes Suzuki feel ancient.

At fifty-eight, Suzuki is Tanabe-*kai's oyabun*, the big boss. He's got all the perks and accoutrements that come with the job: the big house, the expensive German car, the maid, the personal assistant, the bodyguard. What the rank and file don't understand, though, is that an *oyabun* is really just the guy whose ass is on the line when things aren't going well.

And these days, things aren't going well.

The double-whammy of the anti-organized crime legislation that was passed several years ago and the graying of Japanese society (the result of Japan having one of the lowest birth rates in the world) have put the country's traditional organized crime groups under severe financial strain, and the Tanabe-*kai* is no exception. Suzuki is one of a dying breed, and he knows it, and the memory of the good times is so fresh, sometimes it's painful.

During the "Bubble Years," when the Japanese economy was the second biggest in the world, the Tanabe group was flying high. It had parlayed much of the money it had made over the preceding decade on drugs and human trafficking into California real estate. At the bubble's peak, they owned a golf course near Sacramento, office buildings in downtown Los Angeles, luxury condos in Silicon Valley. Hell, when Suzuki was just thirty-five, still a kid in the minds of the bosses, he already had a Porsche 911.

It was a glorious time. Everyone was rich.

Then the bubble popped, Japan's economy took an epically huge shit, and everyone lost everything. CEOs committed suicide in record numbers as Japanese companies went bankrupt left and right, and the ones that didn't were forced to sell off their overseas operations and return to Japan with their tails between their legs.

Thus was born Japan's decades-long recession, which continues to this day.

The Tanabe-*kai* was forced to liquidate its U.S.-based businesses and sell off all of its properties, and now, thirty years after the bubble popped, the group struggles to stay alive. Extreme pressure from rival groups, the police, and a new breed of gangster called *hangure*—juvenile delinquents able to skirt the law in ways the yakuza can't because they are minors—threaten its very existence.

The girls on the corner are laughing and falling over one another, pointing this way and that, debating where to go next. One of them, a petite thing in a tight black skirt and impossibly high heels, suddenly turns mid-sentence and vomits onto the sidewalk, pauses, spits, and turns back to her dumbstruck compatriots and continues talking as if nothing's happened.

Suzuki's driver, Kei, says, "*Sugoi desu nee.*" Jesus.

Suzuki makes a guttural sound. He takes a long drag off his cigarette and lets the smoke drift out through his nose. Five years ago, he was *wakagashira*, second in command, and had been in the number two post for so long—eight years—that he had all but given up on the idea that he would ever accede to the throne. The *oyabun* at the time, a sly old codger named Iida, had long stoked Suzuki's ambition with his constant bitching and moaning about being tired and ready to hand the reins over to Suzuki so he could retire to his house in the mountains of Nagano Prefecture and spend the rest of his days reading and going to hot springs resorts.

But despite the geezer's complaints about his age and his health, he showed no signs of slowing down, and one day while watching Iida enthusiastically mediate a territorial dispute between two affiliated gangs in Kobe, it dawned on Suzuki that the bastard liked his position too much to simply retire to the countryside and fade away. The reins of power would have to be pried from his cold, dead hands, and his talk of Suzuki stepping up to replace him was just that. It was bullshit. A carrot dangled in front of him that the boss had no intention of ever letting him eat. That being the case, Suzuki had two options. He could either be satisfied with what he had and forget about his dream; or he could find a way to get rid of the boss. But before he could decide which course of action to take, Suzuki's wife, Midori, was diagnosed with brain cancer. It had been just two years since their only child, Kaori, had lost her own battle with breast cancer. Daily life became a dismal gray blur, the inevitable outcome of Midori's illness bearing down on Suzuki like an invisible weight. He couldn't eat, couldn't sleep, couldn't think. For the next six months he sat by Midori's bedside and watched his wife of thirty years wither away, and when she died, so did any remaining ambition in Suzuki's heart.

Or so he'd thought.

Because two weeks after Midori passed, so did Iida. The old man had a massive stroke while getting out of the bath one evening, and suddenly Suzuki was the big boss. His ultimate dream finally come true, and now he no longer wanted it.

His first impulse was to step down. Midori's death had left Suzuki feeling adrift. He could barely manage to get up in the morning and brush his teeth, let alone take the reins of a major organized crime group undergoing massive change. But ten days after Iida died, a Tanabe-*kai* member was stabbed by a member of a group affiliated with the powerful Bay Demons, and Suzuki suddenly found himself trying to prevent an all-out war from breaking out. He spent countless hours on the phone and in meetings, and what he found was that immersing himself in the details of the conflict and its ultimately ridiculously complicated resolution was a welcome distraction from his grief, his pain, and from that point forward, the job became everything to him.

Now, several years and two heart attacks later, not so much.

His phone buzzes. It's Morie.

"Give me some good news," Suzuki says. Someone robbed one of the group's stash houses last night and made off with a hundred million yen. Morie has been tasked with finding the culprit.

"I have news," says Morie, "but you're not going to like it."

There's a pause.

Suzuki rolls down his window, flicks the stub of his cigarette out, and sighs. "Speak."

"We found out who did it." Again, there's a pause. "Out with it. I'm in a bad mood already. Don't make it worse."

"It was your nephew, boss."

"What?"

"I said it was your nephew."

Suzuki massages his left temple with his thumb and sighs. "There's more."

"I'm listening."

"The guy who runs the stash house has disappeared."

It's not hard for Suzuki to put the pieces of this little puzzle together. He'd found out several weeks ago that the operator of this particular stash house was likely ripping him off. He sent Shota to find out if it was true. Obviously, what happened instead was Shota strong-armed the operator into helping him take the money, and now the guy is probably at the bottom of the bay.

"What do you want me to do, boss?"

What to do indeed. Shota has been a pain in Suzuki's ass ever since he was a kid. A never-ending source of trouble. Suzuki had gotten him into international school after he was kicked out of Japanese school. Then he was kicked out of the international school too, so Suzuki started giving him jobs here and there. Deliveries and other simple stuff. Around the same time, Shota began hanging out with a group of ne'er-do-wells, some from his international school days. They went to clubs in Roppongi and preyed on young girls and did drugs and picked fights. The only reason Suzuki put up with the kid's nonsense was that he was his little sister's son. But Junko has been dead for years now, and Suzuki's tolerance for his nephew's antics, which have only gotten worse, has finally reached its limit. "Do you know where he is?"

"We haven't been able to track him down yet, but we will."

"Call me as soon as you do."

"Yes, boss."

Suzuki pulls up Shota's number and hits dial. It rings nine or ten times and goes to voicemail. Suzuki hangs up. He could call Morie back and simply tell him he doesn't ever want to see his nephew again. Morie would get the message. He and his men would make Shota disappear, and that would be that. But Suzuki wants to talk to the boy first. Look into his eyes, which are his little sister's eyes. He wants to look into those eyes and say goodbye to Junko-chan. Goodbye, and that he's sorry.

"Kei," Suzuki says, "take me home."

CHAPTER TWENTY-FOUR

WIDE AWAKE, FISHER stares at the ceiling, listening to the hum of the refrigerator in Mari's kitchen. The Snoopy clock on the shelf says it's 1:00 a.m. It's warm in the living room, but Fisher is shivering. The bag of money is on the floor next to him, and the phone Shota gave him is on the coffee table.

He rolls over on his left side and feels the bruised right side of his rib cage issue a little protest as he pounds the pillow into shape a few times, bunches it up, and sticks it under his head. He thinks about what happened in the alley in Roppongi, goes over it in his mind. He'd been able to push it away earlier when he was talking with Mari, but now it's just him here in the dark and he keeps hearing the gunshots.

Crack crack crack.

Run, Henry!

He fights down a spike of adrenaline and cuts his eyes over to Mari's bedroom door. Ever since they said good night, he's been wondering if she really did want him to climb into bed with her. What is he thinking? He's still married. Not technically, but there hasn't been a day since Lisa split that Fisher has thought of them as being actually divorced. "On hiatus" is how he thinks of it, a bit of conscious self-deception to sustain his belief that they're going to be together again, it's just a matter of time.

Toss.

Turn.

He grabs the remote control from the coffee table, turns on the TV, and mutes the sound. He sits up. The ache in his ribs and hip is joining the sting of the abrasions on his hand, elbow, and knee in a chorus of pain. He swing his legs off the sofa, stands up, and stretches, gently massaging around the humongous bruise that's formed at the top of his right butt cheek. It feels better standing.

What is he going to do? He can't focus.

He paces the length of the living room as quietly as he can. He stops at the window, which affords a decent view of Tokyo Tower. Just down the street from the Tower but blocked from Fisher's view by other buildings is Prince Park Tower Hotel, where he and Lisa stayed their first night in Tokyo eight years ago.

About a year prior to that, a guy from the gym had told Fisher about a friend of his who'd gone to Japan and fought in the Pride Fighting Championship and was now back in the U.S. and getting ready for his first UFC match. Guys were still getting paid pretty well in Japan, the guy said. Why didn't Fisher go there, make a name for himself, and then come back like his buddy?

Yeah, Fisher thought. Why not?

He was recovering from a torn hamstring at the time, one in a seemingly never-ending series of injuries, feeling sorry for himself, and latched on to the idea, and by the time his leg had healed up, he'd convinced himself it was the right thing to do for his career. Japan had the massively popular Pride Fighting

Championship and was a martial arts mecca. He could fight there, maybe actually make a living doing it too, and once he made a name for himself, he'd be a hot property. The best part was that Lisa was born in Tokyo, lived there until she was seven, when her dad's company, one of the big Japanese general trading companies, relocated the family to San Jose.

When Fisher laid his brilliant plan out for her one evening during dinner, Lisa looked at him the same way she did when he'd told her he wanted to fight professionally: eyebrows raised, head tilted, like she was trying to figure out if he'd finally gone nuts. "Do you know anyone there?" she said. "Japan is about connections, Hank. If you don't have connections, you can't do anything. I don't have any family there anymore, either."

Lisa's parents and younger sister had died in a car accident when she was eighteen and in her first year of college. Fisher shrugged. "I'll find a gym," he said. "Once they see what I can do, the connections will come." Lisa just shook her head.

"And I have my secret weapon," Fisher said, pulling her into his arms and kissing her face all over.

Two months later, they were in Tokyo with nothing but the clothes on their backs, Lisa seven months pregnant with Justin and James in the middle of a hot Tokyo summer. She'd always supported him because she thought they were a team, but Fisher had of course only been thinking of himself.

He paces some more. Back and forth, back and forth for several minutes until an image on the TV screen catches his eye and stops him short. It's the outside of the apartment building he was in last night, the same thin brown apartment tower. Police are going in and out of the lobby while a headline at the bottom of the screen reads "Police investigating possible murder." He unmutes the volume and turns it down low.

"...victim was found dead in his apartment earlier today. Police are treating the death as a homicide. A fellow resident has provided investigators with a description of a foreign man seen on the premises close to the victim's estimated time of death. The foreign man is believed to be tall, between thirty and forty years old, and wearing a hooded sweatshirt."

Terror spears the back of Fisher's neck. In addition to Shota & Company, now the cops are looking for him, and Fisher has nowhere to go. He paces again, faster, his heart slamming the inside of his chest like an angrily hurled handball.

Calm. Down.

The news goes to commercial.

Fisher turns the TV off and closes his eyes and forces himself to breathe. The cops are looking for a tall foreigner in a sweatshirt between thirty and forty. Which means they're not looking for him, they're looking for, like, half the *gaijin* men in Tokyo.

Okay.

He goes to the sink in the kitchen, rinses his face with cold water, and returns to the living room and sits down on the sofa. He takes another deep breath. In for a four-count and out. Fisher swings his legs up and stretches out again. He lets his gaze wander the room until it lands on Mari's Snoopy collection. The dolls make him think of Mickey Mouse, which in turn makes him think of Justin and James because, man, they used to love Mickey Mouse.

Fisher remembers the time he and Lisa took the two of them to Tokyo Disneyland with Pete and Keiko Marini and their two kids, Timmy and Soraya. The thought of Marini turns something over in his stomach and makes him want to spit. He hasn't thought of the son of a bitch in a long time. It had been the end of the day, and the kids had found these huge Mickey dolls in

155

the gift shop and commenced a chorus of pleading so loud and persistent that it was as though they'd conspired ahead of time to shake their parents down. Fisher and Lisa and Pete and Keiko ended up buying the dolls for them (Minnie for Soraya) just to shut them up. It feels, looking back now, like it had been a bad day, but Fisher knows that's just his bitterness toward Marini talking, distorting everything. Because it had been a *good* day. A crazy happy day. The kids had a blast, and so did he and Lisa.

Fisher sits up.

If anyone can help him, it's Pete Marini. And if there's anyone he'd rather not ever see again, it's Pete Marini.

Marini does something for the U.S. Department of Defense. Fisher has never been clear on what exactly that is, but he knows Marini's job involves working with Japanese law enforcement, helping them catch international bad guys on occasion, and providing security to visiting dignitaries from the U.S.

The two of them used to train BJJ together at a gym near Meiji University. Every week they would ride the train out from Roppongi, get their rolls in, and then grab dinner afterward. Marini did BJJ for fun, but he also taught it to a group of Japanese cops, and he was damn good at it. Apart from their shared love of BJJ, though, Marini was pretty much the exact opposite of Fisher. He was into flash—flashy clothes, flashy cars, flashy women. Fisher, he's never cared about that kind of stuff. A car to him is something to get you from Point A to Point B; as far as clothes go, he's happy to wear the same thing every day, and he's always been a one-woman man. Still, he enjoyed hanging out with Marini both inside and outside the gym. It was fun listening to his crazy stories, and they shot the shit, traded gym gossip, talked about life in general. He had a serious, important job, which Fisher admired, and despite his penchant for flash, he was down-to-earth. A guy's guy. Plus their wives and kids got along too.

At six two with a superhero build, Pete Marini was more likely to be pegged for a Jersey wise guy than a federal agent fluent in Japanese. With his slicked-back black hair and light blue eyes, perpetual tan and gold chains, he had that cultivated he-man look and easy charisma that, if you believed the stories he told, women found irresistible. But he was always cagey about the details of his conquests—who and where and when, and Marini was, after all, a family man, so Fisher had always thought he was full of shit.

Then he fucked Fisher's wife.

A wave of something as foul as sewage rolls over Fisher. He detests the very idea of speaking with Marini. But he's desperate.

He remembers Marini's landline. If he calls him now, he'll wake him up, but the hell with it. The asshole owes him. He punches the number into the phone. It rings nine or ten times, then goes to voicemail.

"*Please leave a message,*" says the voice of their son Timmy.

Sweet kid, Timmy. A little guy with a mop of jet-black hair, big brown eyes, and an easy smile. Always full of questions. He and the twins used to fish for crawdads in the pond at the local park on the weekends.

"Pete," Fisher says into the receiver, "it's Hank Fisher. I need to—"

There's a click and then Pete comes on, his voice thick with sleep. "Hank?"

"Yeah."

"You know what time it is?"

It doesn't matter that they haven't spoken in more than two

years. The sound of the motherfucker's voice is abrading, like a giant scab being torn off. "Yeah."

He groans and mutters, "Hold on." Rustling noises, then a groggy female voice murmurs something. Fisher can't tell if it's Keiko's voice or someone else's. The sound of a door closing. Then, "This is a surprise. Why're you waking me up in the middle of the night?"

Fisher suppresses the urge to hang up. "I need your help," he forces himself to say. "Can we meet somewhere?"

Marini laughs through his nose. "You need *my* help?"

Again the urge to hang up. "Can you meet me or not?"

Marini sniffs and clears his throat. "You're a piece of work, you know that, Fisher?"

Fisher doesn't say anything. *He's* a piece of work?

After a couple of seconds, Marini chuckles and says, "Yeah, fuck it. Where are you?"

CHAPTER TWENTY-FIVE

THE CAR SLOWS and eases to a stop.

"We're here, sir," says Kei.

Suzuki waits for Kei to come around and open his door for him. Climbing out of the back seat, he says, "Pick me up tomorrow morning at 6:30."

"Certainly, sir," says Kei, bowing.

The house is not the biggest in the neighborhood, but it's certainly the most unique: a modernist-style structure that's always looked to Suzuki like a bunch of haphazardly stacked boxes. *Boxes and boxes*, he used to say to Midori, poking fun at the design she'd dreamed up after poring through hundreds of magazines and talking with four different architects. "You're such a meanie," she would reply in a mock hurt tone, slapping his shoulder.

Suzuki taps the security entry code into the keypad next to the gate. Buzz. Click. The gate opens and Suzuki goes inside and pulls the gate shut and walks up the curving hedged path to the front door. "*Tadaima*," he says in the *genkan*, kicking off his shoes. I'm home.

Footsteps, quick yet soft, and then the housekeeper, Yayoi, appears in the foyer and bows. "*Okaeri nasaimase.*" Welcome home.

Suzuki nods and looks at the swell of Yayoi's tits under her apron.

"Would you like something to drink?" she says.

"Barley tea."

Suzuki follows her into the kitchen, where she gets a glass down from the cupboard and the plastic pitcher of *mugi-cha* from the fridge. She sets both down on the counter, and as she's pouring the tea into the glass, Suzuki presses himself into her from behind. He reaches around and cups her tits.

Thirty-five and single, Yayoi is homely and on the plump side, a quiet woman of limited intelligence with small eyes set in a round face. She's been his housekeeper for a year now, and Suzuki has been fucking her from time to time for the past six months. The first time, he'd come home late as usual, drunk off his ass. Yayoi greeted him at the door, and before he knew it, he'd torn off her clothes and had her right there in the foyer. She didn't seem to mind while he pumped away at her on the floor, and even if she did, she could've quit after that but she didn't. She was there the next day, and the day after that. Suzuki figured either she needed the money or she liked being his secret sex friend.

Yayoi stops pouring as Suzuki nuzzles her neck and takes in her smell, always fresh and clean, and presses his erection against her.

"Here?" she says in a surprised tone.

Suzuki is silent as he undoes his belt and unzips his fly and pushes his pants down just past his ass. He unties Yayoi's apron and hikes up her skirt and pulls down her underwear. He pushes her forward against the counter. Without looking back at him, she pushes the glass of tea and the pitcher out of the way and grips the edge of the counter.

He finishes with a grunt in twenty seconds, wipes himself off with a paper towel, which he drops on the floor, and pulls his pants up and leaves Yayoi standing there like he always does. It's a satisfying feeling, being able to bend his maid over and fuck her whenever and wherever he wants to. It's different with his mistresses, all of whom he can see at his pleasure but are much younger and prouder, high-maintenance pets who want to be wined and dined and given expensive clothing and handbags and shoes and such.

Suzuki grabs the glass of barley tea, downs it in a few gulps, and returns the glass to the counter with a clink. He wipes his mouth with the back of his hand and with the same hand slaps Yayoi hard on the ass. She gasps.

"You know you like it," he says, turns, and walks away.

As Suzuki leaves the kitchen to go upstairs, he is unaware of Yayoi's gaze, a dead-eyed look that follows him until he's left the room, whereupon she yanks her underwear up, walks quickly to the bathroom, and cleans herself. Then, heart racing, she returns to the kitchen and plucks the glassine envelope from the drawer into which she surreptitiously dropped it after emptying its contents into the old man's tea, carries it to the bathroom, and flushes it down the toilet.

If the old man had come up behind her three seconds earlier, he would have seen her gently shaking the poison into the glass, and she has no doubt he would have killed her on the spot.

She goes to the hallway, where earlier she'd put all of her things in her backpack so she'd be ready to go. She takes off the apron and stuffs it into the top of the backpack. When she's halfway to the station, she pulls a phone from her pocket and taps out a text with her thumb:

It's done.

She hits the send button.

CHAPTER TWENTY-SIX

IT'S DONE.

Shota has been staring at the words on the screen for the last five minutes.

The old bastard is finally gone. The drug Yayoi slipped Uncle Jun is a highly concentrated form of pentobarbital, the drug used in executions and doctor-assisted suicides in the U.S. Developed in China, it was smuggled into the country on a fishing boat. It is not undetectable. But that doesn't worry Shota. It's well known that Uncle Jun had heart problems. There was even an article in one of the tabloids last year that mentioned his last heart attack, and in any event, the police are not going to waste taxpayer money investigating what looks like death by natural causes of a well-known *yakuza*.

So Shota should feel happy right now. Elated. But he doesn't feel that way at all, because with the old man out of the way, things are going to get crazy fast, and Hank Fisher has his fucking money. No money means no guns, and no guns means Shota can't execute his plan.

His phone buzzes, jerking him from his reverie. He glances

at the screen and feels a pang of worry when he sees it's Bobby, the guy with the guns.

"Everything is all set," Bobby says. "Sunday."

"Good," says Shota, trying to sound enthusiastic. Bobby and his friend from the base are to bring the guns in a moving truck to a self-storage place in Hachioji. Shota is to bring the money. "We'll be there."

"Awesome. Everything okay on your end?"

"Of course. Why?" The words come out sounding sharper than Shota intended.

"No need to get pissy. Just checking, that's all. I gotta ask, right?"

Shota says nothing and grinds his teeth.

Bobby says in an amused sort of tone, "Hey, you hear about that stash house that got jacked the other day?"

"Yeah, I heard about that."

"Weird, huh?"

Bobby is prodding, and Shota knows it. He expected it. "Not really. You thought that kind of thing only happened in the U.S.?"

"Yeah, nah, I know. I'm just saying. Whoever did it got away with a lot of cash. And the timing is kind of, you know, odd."

"What are you trying to say, Bobby?"

Bobby's tone shifts from amused to serious. "What I'm trying to say, dude, is if for some reason you can't hold up your end of the deal, it's going to create a very big problem for me, and a very big problem for me would be a very big problem for you."

"One, I put a hundred grand down on this deal. Two, are you fucking threatening me, Bobby?"

"Shota, dude, chill. Just saying."

"I think you're forgetting where you are. This isn't America."

The sound of Bobby taking a deep breath through his nose. Then: "And you're forgetting who you're dealing with, dude."

"What makes you think I won't hold up my end? And what does that have to do with some stash house getting jacked?"

"Look, forget I said anything, okay? Everything's cool. I'm just trying to make sure we've all got our duckies in a row and everything goes smoothly. I'll see you Sunday, all right, brother?"

After he hangs up, Shota thinks about eating one of the dope gummies Tsukahara brought back from L.A. last month so he can unwind, but he's feeling paranoid as it is, so he instead opens a bottle of red, pours himself a glass, and carries the glass and the bottle into the living room. He sets the bottle on the coffee table and stretches his legs out on the sofa and takes a sip of the wine.

He needs his money. He dials one of his guys, a lock-picking genius named Maruto, and gives him Hank Fisher's address. He tells Maruto to find something—anything—that Shota can use as leverage against Fisher. Then Shota hangs up, drinks the rest of the wine in his glass, and refills it. He leans back and closes his eyes.

One thing is for sure: once he gets his money back, Hank Fisher is a fucking dead man.

"Papa?"

Shota opens his eyes and turns his head and sees Ryo standing in the doorway with Sunny tucked under his arm. At five, the boy has stopped carrying the bear around with him 24/7, but he still insists on sleeping with it. Ryo is making that face he makes when he's about to cry, his eyes wide and shining in the light with accumulated tears, the corners of his mouth turned down.

"Did you pee the bed again?"

Ryo frowns and nods once, wordlessly, the motion sending the tears pooled in his eyes streaming down his face.

Shota rises with a sigh and goes to his son and pats his shoulder once. "Come on, let's go change your sheets."

CHAPTER TWENTY-SEVEN

Fisher can hear Mari snoring in her room. It's loud, more of a roar than a purr, but he finds it soothing. He feels drawn to her in a way he hasn't felt about anyone other than Lisa. He reaches for the doorknob and stops himself, feeling pulled in opposite directions.

He pictures Lisa and the kids, and his stomach flip-flops. No. Getting them back is what's most important—after he manages to get himself out of this situation, that is.

He's meeting Marini in forty minutes, so he clicks on the TV and quickly flips through the channels, looking for an update on the murder investigation. Unable to find anything other than the weather—they're saying it's going to be even hotter today—he turns off the TV and gets up and goes to the bathroom. He takes a leak and then rinses his face with cold water, checking himself in the mirror. The swelling on his forehead has gone down quite a bit. The bruises on his hip and ribs have bloomed a nasty shade of purple.

After changing the bandages on his hand, elbow, and knee, he returns to the kitchen and helps himself to a glass of barley tea, rinses the glass out, and places it on the dish rack next to the sink. Then he takes Mari's key and the money she's loaned him from the coffee table, grabs the gym bag, and jots a message on the whiteboard on the fridge: *Thanks Mari. I owe you one.* He draws a little heart below the message, wondering if he'll ever see her again, and suddenly he's filled with sadness. He breathes a long breath, then goes to her door and places his hand on it. He stands there for a moment listening. Mari's snore has settled into a deep, steady hum. A riptide of regret pulling at him, he walks back into the kitchen and stops at the fridge. He considers his message for a moment and then erases the heart.

Maybe in another life.

He slips on his shoes and lets himself out as quietly as possible, closes and locks the door, and takes the elevator down to the lobby, where he drops Mari's keys into her mailbox. The street outside is dark and empty. He leaves the lobby and walks quickly up a steep hill called Sendaizaka, past the Korean embassy and high-end apartment complexes.

He waits next to a vending machine near the entrance to Arisugawa Park. A little tug-of-war breaks out in him, part of him saying he should leave right now so as not to endanger Marini too, another part saying fuck him.

The asshole rolls up five minutes later and stops at the curb. The car is a black U.S. government-issue Chevy Suburban with a fat black push bumper and left-hand drive. Fisher goes around the right side of the car and opens the front passenger door. Hip-hop music plays low on the stereo. The heavy smell of cologne hits his nose.

Marini is dressed in a black T-shirt and cargo shorts. He's wearing a chunky gold watch on his wrist. It's been more than two years since Fisher last saw him, and he looks the same, except the once-perfect hair is graying at the sides, and even in the dim light from the dash, Fisher can see it's thinning out on top. He's still a big fucker, with the same wide shoulders, thick neck and arms, and barrel chest. There are guys with muscles and then there are guys like Marini, whose muscles have muscles.

Fisher hesitates. The old, buried anger now dug up and lying exposed on the dirt like dry kindling. This was a mistake. More than two years gone by, and just the sight of the man makes Fisher want to smash something.

Marini sees it. Lifts his eyebrows as if to say, *What you wanna do here?*

Fisher has no other choice. He sets the gym bag on the floor and climbs in and pulls the door shut.

Marini turns the volume down, then looks up at him and extends his hand. "Long time."

Fisher stares at his hand for a moment, then averts his gaze, as if distracted by something outside the window.

Marini chuckles. "That's how it's gonna be, huh?" He puts the SUV in drive, and they pull away from the curb.

Yeah, asshole. That's how it's going to be.

It happened one Saturday while Fisher was away at a training camp. Marini's son Timmy had come over to play with Justin and James. Keiko was busy running errands and had sent her husband over at the end of the day to pick Timmy up. When Marini arrived, the three boys were still playing at a little park down the street. He and Lisa got to talking in the kitchen about the kids and school, Japan, America, marriage, life. The way Lisa described it later, she'd asked Marini if he wanted a refill on his coffee, he said sure, and when she got up and came around to his side of the table to take his mug, he grabbed her by the hips and pulled her onto his lap.

Fisher had always thought Marini had a thing for Lisa. He'd seen the way he looked at her sometimes when the two couples went out for dinner. Little hungry, sidelong glances when he thought no one was looking. Laughing too hard at Lisa's jokes. Fisher had playfully mentioned this to Lisa a few times, but she dismissed it, said he was imagining things.

Yeah, no.

Fisher got home relatively early that evening. The gym was only forty minutes from home by train, but preparing for a fight was exhausting work, and home was a distraction he didn't think he could afford. His last fight had been yet another loss, and his desperation to chalk up a win, to put his career back on track and show Lisa he could do what he'd promised her he would do, had become all-consuming. So for the previous month, he'd done nothing but eat, sleep, and train. The kids were already in bed, but Lisa was up. She was quiet, and it looked like she'd been crying. He ignored it at first, figuring she was upset at something the kids had done and probably upset at him for not having been there when whatever had happened happened. Whatever it was that was bothering her, he was too worn out to deal with it right now. She washed dishes silently in the kitchen for several minutes and then stopped and stood there for a long moment, totally still, and when she turned around she burst into tears and everything spilled out of her. She told Fisher what had happened with Marini, that he'd kissed her and…she went silent for several seconds and then began saying over and over how sorry she was. Everything went black for a moment, as if Fisher's brain had simply shut down, and when the lights came back on, he said, "You fucked him."

Lisa's face fell. "What?"

She'd stabbed him in the heart. They'd been together for

twelve years, married for ten. "You fucked him!" Louder this time. She stared at him for a moment, her expression seeming to cave in on itself, her silence her confession.

He stalked back and forth across the kitchen. "You fucked him!" Shouting now at the top of his lungs.

As Fisher glared at her, Lisa looked down and covered her mouth. She choked out a sob. "I—"

"Fucking whore!"

She jerked like she'd been stabbed.

One of the kids woke up and started to cry, Fisher hearing it and not caring, all wrapped up in his own little world of hurt. He'd never said anything as vile to her before. For a moment, watching his words sink in gave him an intense feeling of satisfaction. The joke was on her now. Then her face crumpled and she began to tremble, and the feeling was gone and all he felt was anger. He snatched a glass from the table and hurled it at the wall. It shattered, a big shard ricocheting and barely missing Lisa's face. She screamed, and now Justin and James were both awake and crying hysterically.

He stormed out and walked. He walked for hours, ending up in Shibuya, where he bought beer at a convenience store and then checked into a private room at a twenty-four-hour Internet café and got plastered for the first time in years. Then he went out and caught a cab and gave the driver directions to Marini's house. Once there, he stood across the street and waited. Fisher didn't know how he was going to do it, but he'd decided he was going to kill Marini. He'd wait for him to leave for work, flag him down as he backed out of the driveway, and then… what? What was he going to do? The more he sobered up as he waited, the more it became clear it was stupid. *He* was stupid. Fuck Marini. Fuck Lisa. Fuck everyone. Fisher caught another cab and went back to the Internet café and crashed.

He went home a few days later, still drunk. The kids were at school. Lisa looked awful, eyes swollen and red from crying and lack of sleep. He sat on the sofa in the living room, smoldering in his own self-righteousness while she did something in the other room. They were both orphans, and they'd somehow found each other, and he'd always thought there was something about that that made their bond unbreakable. But she'd broken it. Shattered it like a piece of cheap pottery. He wanted her to suffer, to feel crushed, like he was feeling.

A few minutes later, she came in and sat across from him and asked if she could talk with him.

"Fuck off," he said.

She sat there quiet for a moment and began to weep. "You scared me, Hank. You scared the kids."

He stood and left the room, part of him filled with self-loathing, but fuck her.

He took the sofa that night, got no sleep. The next morning, before the kids woke up, Lisa came and stood next to him, sniffling, her eyes puffy and teabagged. "I need to talk to you," she said.

He sat up, a stew of anger and hurt and despair churning in his gut. "There's nothing to talk about," he said.

"I didn't—"

"I told you to Fuck. Off." He'd decided to leave her. She fucked everything up, he thought. Let her reap what she'd sown.

She stood there for a long moment, blinking, tears rolling down her cheeks, lips pressed together. Then she said, "*Wakatta.*" Okay.

He started sleeping at Internet cafés, leaving after the kids went to bed and coming home early in the morning before they woke up. He couldn't even look at her. She'd abandoned him, made him feel like he was twelve years old again and all alone. So he punished her, waging a war of silence on her that became mutual after a few weeks. Around the kids they put on their best happy faces, but they didn't speak at all when it was just the two of them.

This went on until about two months later, when Lisa dropped the kids off at school and then came back and told him she was leaving. They were in the bedroom, Fisher rummaging in the dresser for a change of clothes. She was taking the kids, she said. They were little but they weren't dumb, and they knew things weren't right between her and Hank and it was affecting them. Fisher knew that Justin had bitten a boy at school the other day. Did he not see the connection? And James had been wetting the bed for weeks. Did he even know that? She was sorry but they were leaving.

Fisher went berserk. *She* was leaving *him*? How fucking dare her. This was all *her* doing. *She* fucked someone else. He screamed at her, his rage feeding on itself, multiplying and twisting into something huge and ugly that got away from him, and the next thing he knew, he was smashing a small wooden chair the boys used to pieces on the floor. He punched a hole in the wall, upturned the sofa, then picked up their big plasma TV and threw it on the floor, Lisa pleading for him to stop, stop, stop.

He left that morning, thinking she didn't have the balls to leave. A week later he came back to find the apartment cleaned out and Lisa and the kids gone, a note on the table reading:

The rent is paid through next month but you'd better start looking for another place right away. There's enough food in the fridge to last you a week or so. Please don't look for us.

CHAPTER TWENTY-EIGHT

FOR SEVERAL AWKWARD minutes, they drive in silence, the only sound in the car the muted thump of a hip-hop song. They pass the Australian Embassy and turn right on Sakurada Dori, then left in front of the police box at Mita Dori.

With one hand on the steering wheel, Marini adjusts the AC and then takes a box of mints from his front shirt pocket, flips open the lid with his thumb, and pops one into his mouth.

A black and silver pendant embossed with the words "Route 69" dangles from the rearview mirror, swinging lazily with every motion of the car. Fisher remembers the pendant, remembers laughing the first time he saw it. He remembers Marini's reaction to his laughter too: *My favorite number, dude! All day every day v-jayjay!*

Fisher's throat clenches, the old anger rising up hot inside him. Once amusing, now the pendant feels like a taunt. He suppresses the urge to grab the thing and chuck it out the window.

Marini holds the box of mints out to him, and he rejects the offer by looking away. He shifts in his seat, his foot bumping against the bag of cash at his feet. An image floats up, Marini fucking Lisa on the kitchen table. The picture in his head no less painful than it was two years ago. He pushes it away. Yeah, it hurts, but he realized what he'd lost when Lisa and the kids left, and he knows that she wouldn't have done what she did if he'd just been there for her. None of which makes it any easier to sit here with this repellent scumbag, but he has to or he might never see his family again.

Marini shrugs, puts the mints back in his pocket. He looks out his window, sniffs, and says, "One of my students at the Keishicho, he's got this CI who works with some gangsters. This CI, he tells my student yesterday about an American dude put a Tanabe-*kai* lieutenant in the hospital last week."

The Keishicho is the Tokyo Metropolitan Police Department. By one of his "students," Fisher assumes Marini means one of the TMPD cops he teaches tactical martial arts a couple of nights a week. Part of Marini's job is liaising with the TMPD on matters that bear on American citizens. He once told Fisher about the cooperative relationship the TMPD has with the U.S. government. The arrangement has something to do with the U.S.-Japan Status of Forces Agreement, or SOFA for short, part of the mutual security treaty between the two countries. SOFA is also why Marini is one of the few foreigners who can carry a gun in Japan outside of the country's U.S. military bases. Fisher never saw him wear a holster, and he's not wearing one now, but he remembers that Marini keeps a pistol in the glove compartment.

They pass the Rainbow Bridge on-ramp and turn in to an empty pay parking lot next to the structure's massive base. From the bridge's underside a hundred feet up, floodlights cast a ghostly pallor over the lot. Marini puts the Suburban in park and turns the music off. He peers out the windshield, taps the steering wheel with his hand. "So," he says, "my guy said the American was an MMA fighter. It was you, right?"

Fisher nods.

"I didn't make the connection until you called." Marini looks at Fisher. "How the fuck did you get mixed up with these guys?"

Fisher grips the edge of the seat with his hand. Tells himself to put aside his revulsion and distrust and give Marini the whole story. He's got no choice. Marini is his only hope. He draws in a long breath and begins to talk.

When he gets to the part about the guys in the van opening fire on him in the alley, Marini turns to look at him, eyebrows raised, and says, "I heard about that. You were there?"

"What part of 'They shot at me' did you not understand?"

Marini pops another breath mint, returns the box to his pocket, and rolls the mint around in his mouth.

When Fisher is finished talking, it goes quiet in the car. Marini nods to himself like he's keeping time with the beat of some tune only he can hear.

After a minute of this, Fisher says, "So what do I do?"

Marini looks at him, raises his eyebrows, and cocks his head. He looks down at his lap, his shoulders shaking with silent laughter. When he looks at Fisher again a couple of seconds later, his face is red and he brings his fist up to his mouth.

Fisher glares at him.

Marini lets out a couple of coughs meant to disguise his laughter, clears his throat several times, then finally lets go. "Ho ho ho ho! *Cough cough.* Ho ho ho ho ho!"

Fisher wants to punch him in the side of the head. Like. Really. Bad.

A half minute passes before Marini notices Fisher glaring at him, and he stops laughing. "I don't like the way you're looking at me, Hank." His eyes flick down to Fisher's hands, and Fisher becomes aware that he's balling them tight into fists. "Settle down, dude," Marini says.

"Fuck you," says Fisher, his voice quavering with anger.

"Hey, you called me and I came, didn't I?"

Fisher looks away, stabbing the fingertips of his right hand into his thigh. He did come. Fisher has to give him that. "Either you can help me or you can't. Just do me the courtesy of not fucking with me. You owe me that much."

Marini turns his head to look out the window, but not before Fisher catches the grimace that appears on his face. Like he's eaten a rancid bug. He turns back to Fisher and says, "All right. Okay." He fiddles with the AC, adjusts the vent next to the window. "Did anyone see you go in or out of the apartment in Yotsuya?"

Fisher pinches the bridge of his nose and makes a scoffing noise. "There were people everywhere. So, yeah, I'm pretty sure."

"Any of them get a *good* look at you?"

Fisher remembers the old lady and sighs. "One, maybe. I took the stairs down to the first floor. There was an old lady coming out of the trash room when I got there, but I was wearing a hoodie and had my head down, so I don't know."

"Okay. Have you told anyone else about this?"

"Is that a serious question?"

Marini nods, staring unfocused out the windshield. He chews the side of his cheek. After a moment, he says, "You know anything about what's been going on with the Tanabe-*kai* recently?"

"Why would I?"

"Yeah, no reason, I guess. There's some drama between Suzuki and his nephew."

"Shota."

"Yep. Crazy fucker, as you now know firsthand. It's pretty well known that he and his uncle don't get along, and more important, he's not in the line of succession. Shit's *super* hierarchical in these *yakuza* groups. You know, *nenkou joretsu* and all that."

Marini is referring to Japan's seniority system. Fisher recalls the moment in Suzuki's office when Suzuki told Shota to shut up, and he has to agree: the corporate world isn't the only place where the seniority system is alive and well.

Marini says, "Anyway, he's been working with a band of knuckleheads from his school days. They call themselves 'Spiral.' Kind of a *hangure* outfit but a little older than usual. They're all either bad boys who got themselves kicked out of the international schools or *kikokushijo* who got involved in gangs and drugs overseas and then brought that shit back with them to Japan when they repatriated. A lot of these guys speak native English, and it comes in very handy for them. They do big business smuggling all sorts of shit into the country—drugs, guns, you name it."

Fisher has read about *hangure*. They're groups of juvenile delinquents, usually middle and high school dropouts, who do certain types of jobs for traditional Japanese organized crime groups. *Kikokushijo* are Japanese returnees, people who went with their families to live overseas for a period of years, usually because their dad was sent there on a job assignment.

"So what does all this have to do with *my* situation?"

Marini arches an eyebrow. "I don't know that either, but you sure picked an interesting time to mess with them."

Fisher cuts his eyes over to Marini. "I didn't *mess* with them. It was an accident, goddamn it."

Marini shakes his head. "Doesn't matter. You fucked up one of their guys. And now things are all fucked up."

"This is so helpful. Thank you. I feel so much better."

"What, you want me to lie to you?"

Fisher can't think of anything to say. He can't think, period.

Marini sniffs and wipes his nose with a knuckle. Looks out his window, leans forward, and looks out Fisher's window. He checks his rearview mirror and motions with his chin at the gym bag on the floor in front of Fisher.

"Let's see what you got there."

Fisher hesitates. Marini knows now that Fisher is in serious trouble. But all they've been doing until now is talking. Once he sees what's in the bag, he's going to realize just how deep the shit Fisher is in goes. Fisher takes a deep breath. He's got no other options. He sets the gym bag on the center divider.

Marini unzips the bag, pulls up the end of the black plastic trash bag, and finds the hole Fisher tore in it yesterday. He reaches inside the bag and plucks out one of the plastic-wrapped stacks of cash. He turns on the ceiling light and whistles low as he turns the money over in his hands a few times.

"You know what this is?"

"Um, money?"

Marini drops the stack into his lap and pulls out another. "Drug money's my guess." He slaps the palm of his free hand with it a few times. "Look at that." He stares at the cash in his hand, and there's something different in his eyes, a sharpness that wasn't there a moment ago.

Fisher's stomach flip-flops.

Marini returns the two bundles, zips the gym bag up, sets his hand on it, and looks out his window. He pats the bag like it's his pet golden retriever. He points toward the bay. "Over there."

Fisher looks where Marini is pointing, but all he can see is the dark expanse of Tokyo Bay, and beyond it, the twinkling lights of Odaiba Aqua City. "What?"

"The Bay. That's where the *yakuza* dump bodies. Chop 'em up, weigh 'em down, drop 'em in the drink."

A jolt of adrenaline races through Fisher, from his gut up into his chest and throat, all the way up to his head, making his scalp tingle. All at once, he can hear himself breathing, and he's aware of how he's situated in the passenger seat: where his left hand is in relation to the gym bag, how close his right hand is to the door latch.

Fisher remembers the gun in the glove box, and feels another surge of adrenaline. Marini is going to kill him and take the money. But despite the fact that every cell in Fisher's body is screaming at him to get out and run like hell, Fisher still wants to believe that Marini is one of the good guys, a professional who wants to help him, and that maybe he's only a complete and utter dickhead on a personal level.

His mouth dry, Fisher swallows and his throat clicks. "Kind of risky, isn't it?" he says, hoping Marini can't hear the tremor in his voice. "They must have CCTV cameras all over the place out here."

Marini's lips form an upside-down Tony Soprano smile. "Nah. The cameras are mostly near the overpasses." He points at a concrete path that runs alongside the water and traces it with his finger. "Not even down there." He draws a long, slow breath in through his nose and lets it out.

For a moment it's quiet in the cab. Fisher stares out the windshield at the dark waterfront, listening to the whoosh of his pulse, unsure what to do. Then Marini shifts in his seat, and out of the corner of his eye, Fisher sees a flash of something metallic in his hand. He doesn't wait around to see what it is. He snatches the bag by its strap with his left hand as he opens the door with his right. He shoulders the door open and jumps out and runs.

"Hank!" Marini calls out behind him. "Where you going, man?"

CHAPTER TWENTY-NINE

HE RUNS UNTIL his knee, hip, and ribs are screaming, which is about a hundred yards, after which he hop-skip-jogs as fast as he can, grunting each time his right foot hits the pavement. He turns to look over his shoulder every few yards to see if Marini is following.

There's no one behind him.

But he keeps up his herky-jerky pace for as long as he can and turns in to a side street, and then another, and another, until it's clear that Marini isn't coming after him. Then he slows to a limp, heart thumping, out of breath, and heads back toward Mita, where he catches a cab on Sakurada Dori. He tells the driver to take him to the first place that pops into his head:

Shibuya.

His heart pounds as the cab rolls smoothly through the dark streets, his thoughts scurrying like rabbits fleeing a pack of predators. Fear and paranoia, confusion and hopelessness clouding his mind. What now?

He wipes the sweat from his face with the hem of his shirt, shoots a glance at the driver. A tiny old man with huge glasses, he can barely see over the steering wheel and seems too focused on his driving to pay Fisher any attention in the rearview.

Fisher forces himself to take deep, slow breaths, the animal fear loosening its grip on him a little in the coolness of the AC.

The driver turns right off of Roppongi-Dori onto Meiji-Dori, then left at Miyamasu-Sakashita. Normally clogged with throngs of bar- and club-hoppers, lovey-dovey young couples, and wide-eyed foreign tourists, the streets of Shibuya are weirdly empty at this hour.

From his window Fisher sees the sign for Takarajima 24, an Internet café. It's the same Internet café where two years ago he'd holed up after Lisa hit him with the news that she'd slept with Pete Marini. He decides he'll crash there. But first he needs to stash the gym bag somewhere.

In the U.S., Fisher occasionally heard people—usually white people—say that Asians all look alike. Funny thing is, to a lot of Japanese people, all foreigners look alike. If he hadn't spent a significant amount of time talking with drunk Japanese people, this probably would've come as a surprise to him, but it's true. Today there will probably be hundreds, if not thousands, of big, curly-headed foreigners traipsing around Tokyo with gym bags slung over their shoulders, and if you lined all of them up in a row, a lot of Japanese people would think they looked pretty indistinguishable.

But even in deserted Shibuya, in the middle of the night, this doesn't make Fisher feel safer. Not when he's got a deranged *yakuza* group and a very probably crooked pseudo-cop after the contents of the gym bag on the seat next to him.

He has the cab driver drop him off at the curb in front of the Hachiko entrance to Shibuya Station. One of the most crowded spots in Tokyo most of the day, there's hardly a soul this early in the morning. Fisher goes straight past the unoccupied police box to the left of the entrance to a bank of twenty-four-hour coin lockers just outside the turnstiles. He pays eighteen hundred yen from the money Mari lent him—about nineteen dollars—for a large locker in the bottom left corner and taps the month and day of Lisa's birthday in as his passcode. Then he stuffs the bag of money inside and closes the door.

From Shibuya Station, he walks up Dogenzaka to a big twenty-four-hour Don Quixote store, a national chain that carries a chaotic mash-up of groceries, sporting goods, clothing, cosmetics, electronics, and just about anything else you can think of, all of it crammed tight into every bit of available floor and wall space. He walks into the store, grabs a basket. He finds a corner nook stuffed with hair care products and grabs a pair of scissors and a cheap electric hair clipper and tosses them into the basket, along with a razor and shaving cream. Then he picks up a box of bandages and some disinfectant spray for the scrapes on his hand, elbow, and knee. He finds the men's clothing on another floor and picks out two T-shirts, one light blue with the word "Omelette" on the front, the other plain gray. A green baseball cap and a pair of cheap wraparound sunglasses. Then he goes to the grocery section and gets two *bento*—lunch boxes—with *karaage*—Japanese fried chicken—a couple of bottles of water, a few bananas, a protein bar. He pays for his items, the woman at the register barely looking at him as she takes his money.

From the store he walks directly to the Internet café, pays the middle-aged guy behind the counter 3,955 yen for twenty-four hours, and carries the gym bag along with his two bags of groceries to the end of a narrow hallway to his room. Once inside, he wolfs down one of the lunch boxes and downs one of the bottled waters, then stretches out in the recliner and closes his eyes.

He tries to puzzle out what to do next, but after hours on the run, he's got nothing left in the tank.

Sleep first, then think.

Exhaustion pulls him down, monster claws in black cottony gloves.

Justin and James are perched at the top of a towering tangle of monkey bars, eyes wide with fear, holding hands and looking this way and that for a way down.

Justin says, *Papa!*

James says, *Help!*

Fisher runs around the monkey bars, desperate to find a way up to help them, but the lowest rung is at least twenty feet up. The boys are crying like he's never heard them cry before, a primal wail that sends a jolt like lightning through him. Above him is a bar low enough to grasp. He reaches for it and his hand passes through it like it's a hologram. Oh God.

Hey, a voice says.

It's Lisa's voice. *Lisa?* Fisher looks around for her, and all he sees is cracked concrete and a mangy yellow swing set. He turns back to the monkey bars and they've vanished, and so have his children.

He wakes up gasping for breath.

It takes him a second to remember where he is—in a tiny windowless room at Takarajima 24. He's stretched out on a reclining leather chair in front of a computer console with two monitors, one for TV viewing, the other for web-surfing. Shelves stuffed with *manga* comic books and DVDs line the walls on either side of the console, and on the desk is a basket containing a room key, a ballpoint pen, a notepad, and a condom. There's a sink with a mirror next to the door, and just down the skinny hall are a communal bathroom and a shower.

It's 7:23 a.m.

He's been asleep for a couple of hours, and the image of Justin and James screaming at the top of the monkey bars hovers in his brain. His nose is stuffed up, and his mouth and tongue feel like sandpaper. He sits up and wipes the sleep from his eyes. He plucks a few tissues from the box on the desk and blows his nose. He reaches for what's left of the now lukewarm tea, uncaps it, and takes a swallow. Then he eats the protein bar and polishes off the tea.

Everything hurts. The scrape on his right palm feels hot and inflamed, as do the abrasions on his right elbow and knee. The pain in his hip has subsided to a dull ache, but his ribs remind him of the bruise there with a sharp jab of pain every time he breathes in too deeply. His neck and back are stiff and sore, and his feet hurt from all the running on pavement he's been doing. He really should run more regularly.

He turns on the TV and absently flips through the channels. Goddamn it. He shouldn't have called Marini. Asshole blew up his life and Fisher calls him for help? What had he been thinking?

No, dipshit, you *blew up your life.*

And not just his own life. He's blown up Terry's too. Is Terry okay? In the message Fisher left Laura the other night—how many nights ago was that?—he asked her to call him back, but Shota took his fucking phone. He needs to call her again. He picks the phone Shota gave him up off the desk. It's an old model, white and nicked up and stripped down with no password protection. He pushes the home button, and a column of call received notifications gooses his adrenaline. It's Shota's number. *Fuck you, asshole.*

He blocks the number and considers dumping the phone and getting a new one and then remembers there's no such thing as a disposable "burner" phone in Japan. Getting a new cell phone in this country is a complicated, time-consuming process that requires a valid ID and a credit card, neither of which he has, because Shota has his wallet too.

His eyes drift up to the basket on the desk and land on the condom inside. Lonely people come to these places to fuck and chill out, not to hide from bad guys.

He remembers what Marini said last night about Shota and his uncle not getting along. Again he recalls that moment in Suzuki's office when Suzuki told his nephew to shut up. *You are mine now.*

Fisher had interpreted Suzuki's words to mean that he would have to do something for the gang, so when Shota told him to go into the apartment and retrieve the bag of money, he'd assumed it was on his uncle's orders. Is it possible that Shota had done it without Suzuki's knowledge?

It occurs to Fisher that he could go to Suzuki and tell him what happened. But he doesn't know where Suzuki is. Besides, what if he's wrong and the burglary had been on Suzuki's orders after all? He'd be fucked, that's what.

Akio's words come back to him: *You should get out of the country.*

No, that's not going to happen. He is going to see his family again, and this means he's staying, period.

But maybe, just maybe, Akio can help him out here. Maybe Akio can get in touch with Suzuki for him, find out whether it's safe to approach him. A tiny spark of hope flickers in Fisher's mind.

And then an image pops up on the TV screen, and all the air goes out of him.

It's a police sketch of a man in a hoodie.

CHAPTER THIRTY

IT'S ROUGH EVEN for a police sketch. Bushy hair poofing out from under the hoodie. The head angled slightly downward, not a lot of facial detail filled in. The man in the drawing could be a foreigner, maybe not. It is, after all, a rough drawing.

But seriously, like, shit. That thing about all foreigners looking alike to Japanese people? Yeah, well, pretty sure it doesn't apply to Japanese cops who are working off of an eyewitness description.

The old lady in the apron at the bottom of the stairs in the apartment complex had obviously gotten a look at him after all, and based on the drawing on the TV screen, it was a pretty good look. *Chill.* He massages the back of his neck.

Relax.

It's unlikely anyone will be able to ID him from a sketch.

Clicking off the TV, he pushes himself out of the chair and steps in front of the mirror above the small sink by the door. His hair is a tangled bush, his beard a matted mess. His eyes are puffy and bloodshot with bruised-looking bags underneath. The goose egg on his forehead has begun to subside, but his right cheekbone is red and swollen where the red-bearded skinhead kicked him last night. He looks like crap.

More important, he looks like himself.

There's an outlet at the base of the wall next to the sink. He takes the hair clipper out of one of the plastic grocery bags and removes it from its package, plugs the thing into the socket, and goes to work. He buzzes his hair down to about a half inch and then uses the scissors he bought to hack away as much of his beard as he can before scooping up the trimmings and dumping them in the trash can. Then he shaves and goes down the hall, where there's a small shower. He washes the scrapes on his hand, elbow, and knee, taking care not to let the water hit them directly. He towels off and returns to his room, where he applies the antibacterial ointment and fresh bandages to the abrasions and checks himself in the mirror again.

Fisher hasn't seen his face in a long time, and it's jarring. After Lisa and the kids left, he stopped getting regular haircuts and trimmed his beard only occasionally. He just didn't care anymore. In any case, his new clean-shaven look will make it harder for someone to connect him to the police sketch. And hopefully harder for Shota and his knuckleheads to spot him.

It's just after 9:00 a.m. He'll go to Akio's place in Omotesando. If Akio isn't up by now, tough shit.

He puts on Mari's brother's shorts and is pulling his new blue T-shirt over his head when the phone buzzes. He jumps, confused because he's blocked Shota's number. He steps over to the console, picks the phone up. No Caller ID. He lets it ring a couple of times before he hits receive.

"Hank?"

The sound of Marini's voice throws him, and then he remembers he used this phone to call Marini from Mari's apartment last night.

"Yeah."

"Dude, what the fuck? Why'd you run off like that?"

"Let me see… Oh, I remember now. It was the fucking gun you were about to stick in my face."

Marini laughs. "What gun?"

"I saw it in your hand, asshole."

"Dude, that's nuts. If I wanted to kill you, you really think I'd splatter your brains all over the interior of my government-issue vehicle? That's just stupid."

"You know what's stupid? You expecting me to just sit there after telling me that stuff about gangsters dumping bodies in the bay because there's no surveillance cameras out there."

Marini says, "I wanted you to understand how bad these people are."

"Yeah, I'd kind of figured that out already."

"Fair enough. Look, I'm just trying to give you a hand here. You called *me*, remember?"

"I've been making a lot of bad decisions lately."

"You know what? Whatever."

"Goodbye, Pete." Fisher moves his thumb to end the call.

"Hey, Hank?"

His thumb hovers over the button. He returns the phone to his ear.

"Been watching the news?"

Fisher says nothing. So Marini has seen the news reports too. One after another, his options are blinking out of existence.

Marini says, "That's what I thought. Listen, now that Suzuki is dead—"

"Wait, what? What do you mean Suzuki's dead?"

"Died last night. Heart attack, apparently."

Fisher doesn't know whether to feel more freaked out or relieved. "What's that mean for me?"

"Hard to say. But shit's going to get crazier now that Shota's free to do whatever the fuck he wants. Listen brother, if the bad guys don't get you, the cops will, and don't think they won't track you down. You're a big *gaijin*, and they're good at what they do. Plus—and this isn't public yet—but I heard they got a fire lit under their asses because it turns out the dead guy in that apartment was the son of somebody important."

This just kept getting better and better. Fisher closes his eyes and massages his temples with his free hand. "Who?"

"Ever heard of George Fukuda?"

A chill runs down Fisher's back. George Fukuda is a beloved former comedian and television personality who chucked his career to run for a seat in the lower house of the Diet, Japan's parliament. He won handily and now represents his home prefecture in the south of the country. "Oh fuck."

"'Oh fuck' is right. This shit you're in is fathoms deep, brother."

Fisher feels like his head is going to explode. He doesn't trust Marini, but right now he's open to suggestions. "So what do you suggest I do?"

"First thing you should do is give me the bag. Last thing you want is to be caught with all that money."

"And if Shota's guys catch me and I don't have all that money, I'm dead." And Marini is suddenly a million dollars richer.

"Let me take care of that end. Trust me. I can help you. I'll work my *yak* connections, call in some favors, and get Shota off your back. And I'll talk to my guys at the National Police Agency, make sure the trail from Fukuda's body doesn't lead them to you."

Is it possible that it wasn't really a gun Fisher saw in Marini's hand last night? "What's in it for you, Pete?"

Marini says, "I'm not going to lie. I got another four years until retirement. It'd be nice to go out with a bang, you know what I'm saying? I get credit for getting a load of illicit drugs and cash off the street *and* helping to solve a murder and a shooting? I make the NPA look good, make the U.S. look good. The muckety-mucks can hold it all up as a shining example of cooperation between America and Japan, talk about how the relationship is as strong as ever, *blah, blah, blah.* Everybody loves Pete Marini. I get to ride off into the sunset with a plum executive job at one of the big security firms or a corporate asset protection gig."

Bullshit. Like Fisher's supposed to believe that Pete Marini's ultimate dream is to stop chasing international criminals and rubbing shoulders with muckety-mucks so he can settle into a boring desk job at some company in Butthole, U.S.A.?

Marini used to joke that when he retired he would divorce his wife, move to Phuket, and spend every night with a different woman. "Or," says Fisher, "you could keep the cash and move to Phuket like you always talked about."

Marini is silent for a minute, then says, "Yeah. Yeah, I could. Guess you'd have to trust me."

There it is again: *Trust me.* The idea rolls around in Fisher's head. He wants to believe Marini. He really does. He's drowning in the middle of the ocean, and Marini has just thrown him something that looks like a life preserver. The problem is, Fisher can still see the look in Marini's eyes when he was looking at all that cash in the gym bag last night, and the more he focuses on that image, the more the life preserver looks like a suicide vest. "I'll think about it," Fisher says and ends the call. Suzuki is dead. So much for his plan to reach out to him through Akio. But maybe Akio can still help him somehow. He puts on the green baseball cap and pulls the bill down low. He puts the money Mari lent him in one pocket and the phone in the other. He takes the room key from the basket on the desk, lets himself out, and locks the door behind him.

The kid at the reception counter is playing a game on his phone. He barely looks up as Fisher goes by. The doors swish open and Fisher steps out into the morning heat, headed for Akio's place. He's going to get his life back, and Akio is going to help him, goddamn it.

CHAPTER THIRTY-ONE

HE TAKES THE Yamanote Line one stop to Harajuku and walks from there up to Omotesando Street, where he turns right into the narrow street adjacent to Jubilee Plaza. Fisher moves past the classy cafés and hip eateries, clothing stores and sports shops that line both sides of the narrow street.

It's doubtful Shota's goons will be looking for him here, especially on a Saturday morning. Even if they are, Fisher is fairly confident that with his hair and beard gone, the green cap pulled down low on his forehead and the sunglasses hiding his swollen face, they won't spot him, at least not right away. But that doesn't stop him from checking over his shoulder every minute or so as he walks, or prevent the sudden tightness he feels in his chest every time he catches someone looking at him.

He walks again, reading the brand names on the store-front signs as a distraction, rattling them off in his head: Saint Laurent. Armani. Gucci. Chanel. Dior. Omotesando is where Tokyo's fashionistas, artists, wannabes, and looky-loos come to shop, eat, stroll, and be seen. The buildings range from funky faux-clapboard to shiny glass and concrete. The place is too cool for school, which explains why Fisher has always felt out of place here. And why Akio doesn't.

Akio. Jesus. The poor guy is already in trouble with the Tanabe-*kai* because of Fisher's fuck-up. The other night on the phone, Akio had said the gang would probably beat the shit out of him. Said they'd probably run his business into the ground too. What if they've already beaten the shit out of him? Or, now that Fisher is on the run with the stolen money, something worse?

A knot of dread forms in Fisher's stomach.

Akio's condo is in an old but ritzy *gaijin manshon*—a ridiculously roomy apartment complex built with foreign corporate expats in mind—called Park Place Residence, in a quiet enclave in the Jingumae neighborhood. Fisher was here once for one of Akio's infamous blowouts. He had heard the rumors. Booze and drugs, models, loud music, dancing and debauchery. Akio had invited him several times before, but Fisher had always begged off. He's not a party guy, because he discovered in college that he's not a nice guy when he drinks, so he doesn't drink. He also discovered in college that parties are terrifying without booze, so he doesn't normally go to parties. And what business does a family man have going to parties anyway?

Akio didn't invite him again until last year. Lisa and the kids had been gone a year, and Akio's then-current girlfriend, a (surprise) model named Tina, had by that point made it her mission to pair Fisher up with one of her friends. Initially, Fisher told Akio thanks but no thanks, but Akio kept at him about it until Fisher finally said why not. He went out and bought a shirt and some slacks for the occasion so he'd look halfway normal, if not hip, only to go and end up walking out the door after an hour or so. The music was too loud, the people were obnoxious, or maybe Fisher was just too old, and the girl Tina introduced him to talked nonstop about herself for a half hour before Fisher finally excused himself and made his escape.

Before he left the party, Akio flashed Fisher that smile of his and gave him a big hug, and Fisher felt a little better, osmosis or something, he doesn't know. What he does know is that Akio is one of the nicest, most radiantly alive people he knows, and he feels horrible that he's going to ask him for help when the guy is in as much trouble as Fisher is. But goddamn it, he has to.

The complex is quiet when he arrives. He walks up the short stone path and takes off the cap and sunglasses as he goes through the glass doors and into the lobby. He crosses a wide marble floor bordered on three sides by sky-lit bamboo trees and meticulously pruned shrubbery behind glass walls and makes his way to the set of tall double doors that lead to the interior of the complex. He punches Akio's room number into a console next to the doors. It rings nine or ten times before the intercom automatically ends the call.

Akio keeps late hours. Maybe he's still asleep. Fisher enters the number again. Again the call is disconnected after nine or ten rings.

A middle-aged woman in pink sweats and running shoes trots in from outside, huffing and puffing. Fisher turns away from the console and walks away, careful to look in the other direction as he passes the woman, but she's already intently tapping away at her phone and doesn't give him so much as a curious glance. He stops, turns, and waits as she enters her security code. There's a buzz and the double doors open, and the woman quickly walks inside, still looking at her phone. On his tiptoes, Fisher bolts for the doors, barely making it inside before they slide shut, the woman oblivious to his tailgating.

He waits for her to turn the corner, and then takes the stairs up to Akio's floor.

There are only four apartments on this level, two on each side of a long hallway. When Fisher arrives at Akio's place, the door is ajar. It's dead quiet inside. Something isn't right. Fear scratches at the back of his skull, sending little bursts of electricity down his spine. He pulls the door open, steps inside.

"Akio?"

Silence.

His nerves fire crazily at the exact moment a cloying, coppery smell hits his nose. A wave of roller-coaster fright smacks his stomach. Swallowing hard, he slips off his shoes and steps into the living room and immediately sees Akio lying faceup on the floor. He's pale, with one glassy eye open. Blood from a huge, yawning gash across his neck has soaked the plush carpet around his head.

Fisher gags, stumbles back a step. He claps a hand over his mouth, then makes a dash for the bathroom and vomits into the toilet. Dizzy with panic, he returns to the living room, averting his eyes from his friend's body. The curtains are closed, and the only light comes from lamps on tables at either end of a leather sectional. But it's more than enough light for Fisher to see the place is a disaster. Pizza boxes and crumpled food wrappers and empty beer cans litter the floor. Something odd about the sofa catches his eye. It's got a zebra-hide look he doesn't remember seeing the night of the party last year, and it takes a second for him to realize it's because the thing has been slashed to ribbons. Fisher looks around. That's not all that's been destroyed. The gigantic TV built into the opposite wall has been smashed. The art hanging on the others has been slashed like the sofa.

An erratic rushing sound fills his ears, crazy gusts of wind, and then he realizes it's his own gasping.

Oh God. Who did this?

Another question slams into him, freezes him at one end of the mauled sectional:

Are they still here?

He keens his ears, heart slamming his ribs like a caged beast. Scans the room, slow. Past the dining room, he spies a butcher block knife holder on the bar counter fronting the kitchen. He starts toward it and then stops. If the killer was still here, he would've heard Fisher throwing up in the bathroom. He grabs the knife anyway and looks in every room, pulse thumping, then returns to the living room and poor Akio.

Fucking Shota and his crew did this. They came here looking for Fisher and their money, and when they didn't find him, they wrecked Akio's apartment and killed him. He pictures Shota pulling a knife across Akio's neck. Arterial blood spraying from the wound.

Breathing fast, Fisher squeezes his eyes shut. It's his fault. He might as well have slashed Akio's throat himself.

He's spinning. The room is spinning.

He drops to a knee, his vision tunneling, the circle of light at the end of the tube becoming smaller and smaller.

Run, Henry!

The tube widens. The dizziness abates. Fisher pushes himself to his feet, unsteady, and goes to the door. He turns the door handle and lets himself out and freezes.

Does this place have CCTV? Frantic, he glances up and down the hall, looking for cameras. None. Then he remembers the middle-aged woman. Shit. But there's no time to worry about it now.

There's an exit at the end of the hall opposite the one he entered a few minutes ago. Fisher starts for it, then remembers something and doubles back and with the hem of his T-shirt quickly wipes down the door handle and pulls the door closed.

By the time Fisher arrives back at the Internet café, he's made up his mind.

He's going to accept Marini's offer to help him.

CHAPTER THIRTY-TWO

"Boss, that's him."

Masa is pointing at a big guy in a blue T-shirt and green baseball cap walking up the alleyway toward the Internet café.

They're parked curbside at the bottom of Dogenzaka Hill within view of the entrance to the Internet café where Hank Fisher has apparently been holed up, Shota in the front passenger seat, Matchan behind the wheel, Tsukahara, Masa, and Yuki in back. Bouncing his knee and chewing his lower lip, Shota looks in the direction Masa is indicating and sees a skinny kid in jeans and a T-shirt walking up the sidewalk, a guy of about thirty in an apron spraying water over the pavement in front of a pub, and a big lumbering man with a shaved head under a baseball cap. He sniffs and wipe his nose with the heel of his palm. "Where?"

Fisher was spotted here in Shibuya by a Spiral associate who works as a tout for a local hand-job parlor. The associate followed Fisher to the Internet café, but according to the guy at the reception counter, the asshole stepped out earlier this morning. Fisher hasn't checked out yet, which means he's coming back, but Shota is getting antsy because they've been parked here for two fucking hours, waiting for the asshole to return from wherever the fuck it is he ran off to.

"There," Masa says.

Uncle Jun's only been gone a day, and already there are rumors flying that one of Sato's guys is going to make a play for control of the Tanabe-*kai*'s human trafficking and protection businesses. The pieces of the pie are going to get snapped up fast, and if Shota doesn't get his money quick, he's going to end up with none of it.

Shota sees the guy Masa is pointing at and feels a flash of anger. The fucking guy looks nothing like Fisher. He's about to tell Masa he's a fucking idiot because Fisher has a big head of curly hair and a bushy beard and looks like Sasquatch, whereas this guy has no beard and looks clean-shaven under his cap. Then the guy takes the cap off, wipes his face on the sleeve of his shirt, and Shota sees that indeed it is Hank Fisher. He balls his fist and smacks it into the palm of his other hand.

If you want to grab somebody in Shibuya, you want to do it early in the day, when the streets are virtually empty. Like right now.

Shota raps his knuckles on the dash twice and says to his crew, "Go get that fucker."

CHAPTER THIRTY-THREE

"*Oi*," SAYS A voice from the mouth of the alleyway. Hey!

Fisher glances to his right. A black van is stopped at the curb. The doors of the van fly open and out hop the two guys from the other night. His breath hitches in his chest.

How did they find him?

Fisher turns on his heel, ready to run, and there's Shota, Tsukahara, and Matchan approaching from the other end of the alley.

He stops, heart beating fast. These are the people who killed Akio.

The blue-bearded skinhead repeats, "*Oi!*" Hey! He and his brother are dressed in matching gray summer suits and actually don't look half bad in them, though their faces are a mess from the other night when they tried to clobber Fisher with their bats. Which, thankfully, neither of them is carrying today.

A couple of teenage boys step past the skinheads and start up the alley, then, sensing trouble, exchange a startled glance and turn back around.

The five men are getting closer. It's a squeeze play, and there's nowhere for him to go, but he doesn't care. A torrent of rage lifts him, begins to carry him away. He wants to kill them. All of them. He puts his hands up and says, "Okay, okay," thinking, *Let's go, motherfuckers.*

Glowering at Fisher, Redbeard points at the ground and says, "On your knees."

Fisher doesn't move. His pulse drums loud in his ears. If they take him down, they're going to fuck him up. He *wants* them to. He takes a step forward. *Come on.*

"Don't even think about it," Shota says.

Tsukahara reaches into his pocket and produces a switchblade and clicks it open. Two more metallic clicks draw Fisher's attention to the skinheads. They, too, have blades in their hands.

Fear twists in his gut.

The five men hurry forward and stop eight feet away, forming a semicircle around him. He imagines what getting stabbed is going to feel like, then thinks of Terry, then of Akio with his head nearly cut off on his living room floor. Fisher deserves worse.

Shota says in a low tone, "Down on your stomach."

"Fuck you," says Fisher. He feels his hands trembling, not from fear but from anger.

Shota's frown deepens. He bites his lower lip and chucks his chin at Tsukahara. Tsukahara nods and then holds his knife up for Fisher to see.

Sunlight glints white off the blade. Fisher lowers a knee to the ground. He's sure Shota's assholes are going to tune him up now, but he doesn't care. He doesn't think they'll kill him. Not until they get their money. He lowers the other knee, heart thudding with fear and anger, then slowly stretches out on the pavement, feeling the heat through his clothes.

Matchan lumbers up and puts his foot on his upper back.

The twins pull Fisher's arms behind him and zip-tie them. He gets ready for his beating, but instead Matchan helps him to his feet, and the five men escort him through the crowd on the sidewalk to the van.

≈

Traffic is bumper to bumper on Dogenzaka.

The inside of the van smells like leather, cigarettes, and cologne. Reggae music plays low on the stereo as they move slowly up the hill, Matchan behind the wheel, Shota next to him in the passenger seat talking low on the phone to whom Fisher assumes is his son.

"I know I said we'd go, buddy. We'll go next week instead, I promise."

Fisher is in the middle row of seats, next to Tsukahara. Behind Tsukahara, in the rearmost seat, are Redbeard and Greenbeard. "Yes, they do the light show every day. I know. Yes. Yes. No."

Fisher shifts in the seat. His shoulders ache because his hands are bound behind his back with a zip tie, which forces him to sit in an awkward hunched position to avoid having to lean back on his hands, which makes the pain in his ribs even worse. Worst of all, though, is the feeling of doom that's settled over him. He can't see a way out of this. If he doesn't give them the money, they're going to cut off his ears and probably keep cutting things off until he does. And once he does, they'll just kill him then.

"Okay, Daddy loves you." Shota ends the call, sets his phone down on the center console. He produces a pack of cigarettes and a lighter from his jacket pocket, shakes out a cigarette, lights it, and takes a drag. He turns in his seat to face Fisher and lets the smoke drift out of his mouth. "Where's my money?"

And there it is. Suddenly Fisher remembers Marini's words last night, about the *yakuza* chopping bodies up and dumping them in Tokyo Bay. The money is all that stands between him and a watery grave. He looks down at the floor and shakes his head. He really didn't think it would end this way.

"Fuck," Shota says, spitting the word. He jerks his head at Tsukahara.

Tsukahara moves his right arm across his body like he's reaching for the door and slams his elbow into Fisher's face. His frame of vision jitters like a TV on the blink. The inside of the van whirls once and then rights itself.

Shota says, "How'd that feel?" Although the coppery taste of blood fills Fisher's mouth, the blow didn't catch him flush. He runs his tongue along the inside of his upper lip and finds a jagged tear there, and a dull throb is emanating from the left side of his nose, but otherwise he's fine. He sees Terry. He sees Akio. Fuck these assholes. He locks eyes with Shota then leans over and spits a stream of blood onto the carpet.

Tsukahara clucks his tongue. "*Chikusho!*" he says between clenched teeth. Fucker! He seizes Fisher's left ear and twists it. It hurts. But it's all relative because everything else hurts too.

Shota takes another drag off his cigarette, squinting, and motions for Tsukahara to stop. Tsukahara gives Fisher's head a shove as he releases his ear.

Shota says, "Money. Where is it?"

"Why'd you kill Akio? He had nothing to do with this."

Shota flicks ash from his cigarette into the ashtray in the dash console. He looks at Fisher for a moment, his gaze utterly dead. He brings the end of his cigarette up to his lips, blows on it until it glows red, then without hesitation places the burning end on Fisher's right knee.

"Ah!"

Shota takes another drag from the cigarette. Looks at the end of it again and says to Tsukahara, "Pull his shorts down."

The anger and bravado he'd felt a second ago are suddenly gone like smoke, blown away by a typhoon blast of fright. He's not going to sit here and have his dick cut off. Tsukahara turns toward him, but before he can comply with his boss's command, Fisher says, "It's in a coin locker."

Shota motions for Tsukahara to stop. "Where?"

"The station."

"What station?"

"This one," Fisher says. "Shibuya." The feeling of doom settles over him again, seeping into his bones now.

CHAPTER THIRTY-FOUR

TEN MINUTES LATER, they're parked at the curb in front of Magnet, a new mall across the street from the Hachiko Square entrance to Shibuya Station.

Through the windshield, Fisher watches the throngs of people massing at the corners of Shibuya Crossing, waiting for the light to change. It's the world's busiest pedestrian crossing, people pooling on each side of the five crosswalks until they reach a kind of critical mass, and then red goes to green and they spill out into the intersection like water bursting from multiple dams. Then it begins again.

Pool. Flood. Repeat.

On a normal day, it might be interesting to sit here and watch these dams bursting over and over, but it's not a normal day, and Fisher feels like he's high above Niagara Falls, about to be pushed over into the roaring abyss.

It's quiet in the van for a few moments, Matchan's breathing as he plays a game on his phone the only sound. Then Shota says to Fisher without turning in his seat, "Which coin lockers?"

Shibuya Station sprawls over a couple of city blocks, and there are too many coin locker places nestled in its nooks and crannies to count. The one where Fisher stowed the bag is literally a minute's walk from where they are right now, just inside the Hachiko Square entrance to the station. Fisher considers lying. If he sends Shota to the other side of the Station, maybe he can make a run for it. He thinks better of it when Redbeard thunks the barrel of the gun into the back of his head. Reluctant, Fisher points toward the station entrance. "The ones in the Hachiko entrance. Right across from the turnstiles. Large locker in the bottom left corner."

Shota turns and looks at Fisher and arches his eyebrow. "Out of all the coin locker places in that station, you choose the one right next to a police box." He clucks his tongue.

Fisher shrugs. He'd forgotten about the police box. He'd paid no attention to it earlier this morning when he stashed the bag. No cops were on duty yet that early, so Fisher, panicked and exhausted as he was, didn't give it a second glance. Through the fog of his gloom he sees a tiny ray of hope.

Shota holds his hand out. "Key."

"It's a passcode. Zero five one seven."

Shota nods. He opens his window and flicks the butt of his cigarette out into the stream of pedestrians flowing up and down the sidewalk. It hits a gangly boy holding hands with a tiny girl in a dress that looks like a gunny sack. They both look over, frowning slightly, and then hurry along, glancing once back over their shoulders before disappearing into the crowd.

Shota says, "It better be there."

"It's there."

A man in a tie-dye muscle shirt appears in front of the van. He's got a buzz cut and a wispy mustache and he does not look happy. He pounds once on the windshield. "*Konna yaro!*" Hey, motherfucker!

"Who's this asshole?!" says Tsukahara. Four more men appear beside the man in the tie-dye shirt, seemingly out of nowhere.

From the back seat, Slugger says, "They're DNZ!"

Confused, Fisher tenses.

The five men spread out along the front and sides of the vehicle. One on the driver's side, a short guy with chubby cheeks, tries to open Matchan's door and finds it locked. He tries the side door too, and then slams his fist into the door.

Boom!

It's a rival gang. Fisher's heart kicks with hope-fueled adrenaline.

Then all five of them begin pounding on the van.

Boom! Boom-boom! Boom! Boom! Boom!

Wait, drawing the word out in his head.

On the sidewalk, heads in the crowd turn to look. Matchan says, "Boss," pointing at the guy with the chubby cheeks, who's holding a can of spray paint. Chubby cheeks smirks, gives the can a few shakes, and then quickly sprays the letters "DNZ" wide across the windshield.

Shota says, "Fuck!"

The next thing Fisher knows, the doors fly open and everyone is piling out of the van.

Everyone except him.

A riot breaks out in front of the van, ten men throwing down in the street. A small crowd separates from the stream of passersby on the sidewalk to watch them. Kids mostly, their eyes wide and mouths agape. A few are holding their phones up, recording the melee. Things like this rarely happen in Japan, and for them to happen in broad daylight in front of a crowd is surreal, like something out of a movie.

The sliding door on Fisher's left is wide open. This is his chance.

Over on the right, Matchan picks up the chubby cheeked guy and slams him up against the front of the van.

Boom!

A woman screams.

Greenbeard and a man with Elvis sideburns grab each other by the shirt, punching each other in the face. A few feet away Redbeard is wagging his bat at another guy. Shota and Tsukahara are kicking the shit out of the tie-dye guy, who's in a fetal position on the ground.

"Motherfucker!"

His hands still zip-tied behind his back, Fisher scoots over and swings his legs around and hops out of the van. Horrified stares greet him as he moves toward the sidewalk. The crowd parts to make way for him as he steps over the chain divider. He moves with the foot traffic toward the crosswalk, thinking, *Now what?*

The bag. It's his only leverage, and he gave Shota the locker number and the combination. He has to get the bag before Shota does. But he can't do that with his hands zip-tied behind his back. Tokyu Department Store is straight ahead, looking old and tired next to the shiny new Shibuya Scramble tower rising up on its left like something out of a sci-fi flick. When Fisher is twenty feet from the crosswalk, the light turns red and the crowd comes to a dead stop. He glances over his shoulder, tries to catch a glimpse of the fighting gangsters, but the crowd is blocking his view. He looks at the red light, thinking, *Come on, come on, come on.*

"Excuse me, sir?"

Fisher turns. A tall blond kid with a scruffy beard is staring at him. The kid is dressed in Birkenstocks, cargo shorts, and a sky-blue T-shirt. He has an accent. Scandinavian? Next to him is a blonde girl, almost as tall and dressed exactly the same as the boy. Both of them are carrying big backpacks.

The boy's eyes are full of concern, but his girlfriend is frowning.

Fisher says, "Yeah," wondering what they could possibly want from a handcuffed man who looks like he's just had the shit beaten out of him.

"Do you need help?"

CHAPTER THIRTY-FIVE

THE KID'S GIRLFRIEND tugs on his arm and hisses something in his ear. Fisher doesn't understand the words, but he knows from her expression it's something along the lines of *What are you doing?!*

Fisher turns to show the kid his bound hands. "Do you have something to cut these off?"

The kid exchanges a look with his girlfriend, then shrugs his backpack off and unzips a pocket on the side. He rummages around in it and pulls out a small pair of scissors and steps behind Fisher.

Snick.

His hands free, relief pours into Fisher like cool water into a bone-dry well. He just might make it out of this and see his family again.

The light changes to green, and all at once the crowd is flowing around them and into the street.

"Thank you," Fisher says, looking at each of the kids in turn. He hurries across the street, dodging this way and that to avoid the pedestrians swarming toward him.

The first thing he sees when he reaches the other side is a

cop standing outside the open doorway of the police box next to the station entrance. A wave of panic washes over him. He keeps moving, walks straight past the statue of Hachiko with the old green Tokyu railcar housing the Shibuya City Tourism Association office on his left. He makes a big U-turn and approaches the station entrance. There are two agitated cops outside the police box now. One is talking animatedly to the other as he points across the street in the direction of Magnet, where Shota and his goons are still battling it out with the rival gang.

Fisher keeps his head down and ducks into the station. He walks directly to his unit in the bottom left corner of the bank of coin lockers. He kneels down and punches in Lisa's birthday, opens the door, and yanks the bag out. He reaches into his pocket, pulls out the gangster phone, turns off Location Services, and sticks it back in his pocket. Now what?

He looks over at the ticket vending machines, at the people dropping change into them. The turnstiles are less than fifty feet away. Getting on a train is the quickest way out of here. But Fisher has no money because one of the skinheads emptied his pockets after they'd cuffed him back in the alley. He slings the gym bag over his shoulder. It thuds against his hip and he remembers: he's got plenty of cash right here. The dread he'd felt the other night at the thought of touching the money is gone.

Setting the bag on the floor, he checks left, then right, then quickly kneels next to it. He opens it and pulls out a bundle of ten-thousand-yen bills. He tears one end of the blue plastic wrapping with his teeth, slides a single bill out, then returns the rest and zips the bag closed. He's inserting the bill into one of the ticket vending machines and is about to push the button when he checks over his shoulder and spots the twins in the crowd crossing the street, sunlight glinting off their bald heads.

He tries to insert the bill again, but the machine won't take it. Goddamn it. He turns the bill around, almost drops it. Tries to ease it in, but the machine still won't accept it. He glances over his shoulder again. The twins are approaching the gate, mouthing curses and pushing people out of the way. Greenbeard's eyes suddenly lock on Fisher's and then he's pointing and yelling at his brother and the two of them are running toward him.

The two cops who were in front of the police box a couple of minutes ago are gone. Fisher stabs the Cancel button, throws the gym bag over his shoulder, and quickly moves past the turnstiles and heads in the direction of Shibuya Stream. He doesn't get ten feet before he spots Tsukahara jogging toward him, the patch that had been covering his scalded eye gone.

Fisher doubles back and sees the two cops are back, and the twins are shooting wary glances at them as they approach. He goes left out and heads for the JR gate less than fifty yards away. But when he gets there, Matchan is standing in front of the entrance, scanning the crowd, the foot traffic streaming around him like water around a boulder. Ducking behind a noisy group of foreigners, Fisher walks right past Matchan and into the entrance to Tokyu Department Store and takes the stairs two at a time down into Tokyu Food Show.

Tokyu Food Show is one of Tokyo's many department store basement food centers. Filled with immaculate food stalls and shops, *depachika* are a food lover's paradise. Grilled meats, fish, rice balls, pasta, sushi. But Fisher isn't here for the food. He's here because Tokyu Food Show has several exits, one of which is on the other side of the street.

It's crowded in the air-conditioned basement, Fisher moving quickly past the endless deli-style food stalls lining the narrow aisles. He scans the crowd as he walks, covered in sweat, heart thumping, feeling like every eye in the place is on him.

Try to look more casual, damn it.

He turns to look over his shoulder, slow, catches the eye of a wide-hipped lady with round glasses who arches an eyebrow at him. The majority of the shoppers are female, young working women and homemakers and elderly ladies, out to buy dinner for themselves, their families, their retired husbands. There are lots of foreigners too, tourists mostly, ooh-ing and ah-ing at the exotic offerings on display, which makes Fisher feels a bit less conspicuous.

Fisher continues to move. It's noisy and the aisles are clotted with people. He knows there are some restrooms down here and, not far from them, an exit that leads up to the street, but it's been several years since he was last down here, and he's forgotten what a maze this place is. Pulse thumping in his neck, the gym bag heavy on his shoulder, he turns the corner and pauses to get his bearings in front of a stall selling *yakitori*—grilled chicken skewers. Next to him, a Chinese man is saying something to his wife in Mandarin as he finishes eating the last couple of pieces of chicken from a skewer.

"*Irrasshaimase,*" the man behind the counter says to Fisher. Welcome.

The Chinese guy pulls the last hunk of chicken from the skewer with his teeth, waves thanks to the man behind the counter, and then drops the used bamboo stick into a plastic trash bag hanging from a hook at the end of the counter.

Heart pounding, Fisher looks over the heads of the crowd for a restroom or an exit sign.

A pudgy guy bumps Fisher aside and clicks his tongue.

Fisher shifts his gaze and sees Matchan standing in front of a fruit display, his big face shiny with sweat. His scalp tightens. Matchan signals to the twins, who are in the next aisle over, then points at Fisher.

"Can I help you?" says the man behind the *yakitori* counter.

Fisher gives the man an apologetic no-thank-you bow, then quickly slips his hand inside the trash bag at the end of the counter and grabs the bamboo skewer the Chinese guy threw away. He sticks the skewer in his waistband, drawing a brief startled look from a young girl in a school uniform, and continues down the aisle. He moves as quickly as he can, trying to put some distance between himself and the gangsters. He rounds a corner and sees the restrooms up ahead on the left, a yellow "Cleaning in Progress" sign set up outside the entrance. Fifty yards beyond the restrooms is the exit to the street.

Frantic, he plows through the crowd toward the exit.

Forty yards to go.

"Hey!" a tall western kid with a full beard says as Fisher bumps past him.

Thirty yards.

The crowd thins and the path to the exit is clear. A ripple of relief runs through Fisher. When he's twenty yards away from the stairs, Tsukahara, the guy with the ponytail, emerges from the doorway to the exit. He spots Fisher immediately. Grimacing, Tsukahara reaches into his pocket and pulls out the switchblade he'd threatened Fisher with earlier, clicks it open, and holds it against his thigh. Fisher wheels around and walks back the way he came, only to see Matchan and the skinheads a hundred feet away. The sound of pulsing blood fills his ears.

Fuck. He's cornered.

He runs for the restrooms, apologizing to the cleaning lady as he enters the L-shaped corridor leading to the men's room and enters one of the stalls. He closes the door and secures the latch. Ten seconds later, a voice he recognizes as one of the twins asks the cleaning lady if she saw a foreigner go into a stall. "Yes," she says. "He's in that one."

A moment later: *Knock. Knock.* Then: "Come out of there, dickhead."

Fight-or-flight chemicals pour into his veins. "Hold on a second," Fisher says. He reaches over for the toilet paper and pulls out a long strip, wads it up, then does it again and makes the wad bigger.

Outside the stall, one of the twins laughs. "You gotta be kidding!" The other one laughs too.

Fisher wraps the wad of toilet paper around the blunt end of the bamboo skewer, hoping the makeshift handle will give him enough of a purchase on it. He squeezes the TP around the skewer several times, testing the grip.

"Come out of there now!"

Fisher reaches for the latch. He takes a deep breath and blocks the bottom of the door with his foot, and the moment he unlocks the door, one of the skinheads tries to shoulder himself into the stall. The goon grunts as he puts his weight into the door, and then his brother joins in the effort, and the hinges make a groaning sound and the wood crackles, and then Fisher turns to the side and removes his foot and Greenbeard comes crashing in, barely avoiding slamming into the back wall. Fisher stabs him in the side of the thigh with the skewer.

"Ah!"

Seeing his brother get stabbed with something, Redbeard steps away from the door.

Fisher exits the stall.

Greenbeard says to his brother from inside the stall, "He fucking stabbed me, Yuki! Get him!"

Redbeard's face is scrunched up in anger and fear. He scrabbles at his pocket, and Fisher remembers the switchblade he had earlier. Before the skinhead can get the knife out of his pocket, Fisher jabs the skewer at his face. Redbeard rears back, throwing his forearm up to protect his eyes, and as he does this, Fisher launches a lunging front kick into his midsection that blasts him into the wall.

He has to get out of here. With the bag over his shoulder, he backs quickly away, turns, and runs right into Matchan, bouncing off the huge man like he's run into a thick mattress. With unusual speed for such a big man, Matchan seizes Fisher's shirt with one hand. Fisher reacts without thinking. He grabs Matchan's wrist with his left hand and plunges the bamboo skewer deep into his forearm.

The big man screams, a sound like a mortally wounded cow. He releases Fisher's shirt, and by the time Redbeard and Greenbeard have picked themselves up off the floor, shouting curses, Fisher is already past Matchan. He runs up the corridor, cuts left then right to exit the restrooms, and plows right into Tsukahara, who's been standing guard.

"Ah!" says Tsukahara, his ponytail whipping up as he stumbles backward. He crashes into a group of schoolgirls and lands hard on his ass. The schoolgirls issue a collective scream.

Fisher doesn't look back.

CHAPTER THIRTY-SIX

IN A PAY parking lot smushed between two narrow buildings, Shota watches for Masa, Yuki, and Matchan from the front passenger window of the van, trying not to look at the big red letters spray-painted across the windshield, massaging his jaw where one of the motherfuckers sucker-punched him during the brawl fifteen minutes ago.

A small but increasingly active *hangure* group, DNZ has been making moves on Spiral's territory for the past year, but the attack in front of Magnet was their most brazen move ever, and it had nothing to do with territory. The word is out that Uncle Jun is dead, the Tanabe-*kai* is in flux, and everyone associated with it is vulnerable. This was DNZ taking advantage of the situation, fucking with Spiral simply because they thought they could get away with it. And then those piece-of-shit pussies ran off as soon as those two cops showed up, leaving Shota to explain that no, he didn't want to file a report on the attack or the vandalism, and the cops, whose bemused looks told Shota they knew who he was, seemed only too happy to wash their hands of the matter.

Shota had recognized two of the DNZs. One was a guy

named Nagaoka, a former motorcycle gang member with a reputation for beating women, the other a short, fat-cheeked car thief named Tamura, who's known to have a thing for young boys.

Shota stares for a moment at the tag on the windshield, the dribbles at the bottom of each letter where the paint ran and quickly dried, and feels his blood rise. His jaw is throbbing and he wants to smash something. But it's not DNZ he wants to kill. He can take care of those cocksuckers later. It's Hank Fisher he wants to cut into pieces. Hank Fisher has his fucking money, and the clock is ticking.

Shota hawks phlegm, turns his head, and spits out the window. Rubs his throbbing jaw again and sees Tsukahara, Masa, and Yuki coming up the sidewalk, Matchan lumbering behind them. Hangdog looks on all three of their faces. Masa limping and holding the right side of his ass with his hand, Matchan pressing a bloody handkerchief to his right forearm, looking like he's going to cry.

Goddamn it. Fucking idiots let Fisher get away. His knee bounces and he slams his fist down on the dash, the sudden movement sending a fresh rocket of pain through his jaw. He winces. "Fuck," he says, barely moving his mouth, the word coming out more like *Huck*.

The side door to the van slides open, and Tsukahara and the twins get in. Matchan climbs behind the wheel. The big man is breathing heavily, his face shiny with sweat.

Shota turns in his seat to look at the four of them. "What the fuck happened?" he says, loud enough to draw the attention of a girl walking past the parking lot. Another bolt of pain shoots through his jaw.

"I'm sorry, boss," Masa says. "We lost him."

Shota fixes Masa with a stare. Masa's Adam's apple bobs once. He exchanges a nervous look with his brother.

Yuki motions toward his brother. "Fucker stabbed him with a chicken skewer, boss. Stabbed Matchan too."

Shota shakes his head with disgust. He looks at Matchan, who's looking down, still breathing in labored gusts.

Tsukahara says, "I checked the Internet café again. He wasn't there."

Shota pinches his earring with his thumb and forefinger, spins it one way and then the other. No more games. He points to the spray-painted letters on the windshield. "One of you go and get some paint thinner and wipe this shit off. And get me some Tylenol or something too."

His phone buzzes. He sees it's Maruto, who was supposed to search Fisher's apartment for something to use as leverage against him. "You find something?"

Maruto says, "Fisher's got an ex and two kids. He's been looking for them."

"Meaning what?"

"He doesn't know where they are." Maruto chuckles. "But I do."

"I'm listening."

Maruto chuckles again. "There was a message on his land-line from the PI he hired to find them. Guy named Watanabe. Said he'd finally located the ex-wife and kids but he wanted more money before he'd hand over the address." Another chuckle. "So me and Arturo paid the PI a little visit. Had to smack him around a little, but he gave us the info."

"Good work."

"Thanks, boss. One more thing. We found Gen."

Shota has been so preoccupied with Hank Fisher and his

220

money and everything else, he wonders for a moment who "Gen" is. Then he remembers: Gen, the mousey stash house operator. Shota had told him to go out to the abandoned house near Lake Sagami after they jacked the stash house and lie low there for a day or two. In retrospect, not the best plan since that was where they'd bound the little fucker naked to a chair and gotten him to confess to ripping Uncle Jun off. Instead, Gen disappeared, no doubt terrified they'd kill him. And loose ends being loose ends, that's exactly what Shota had planned to do. "Where was he?"

"His sister's place in Monzen-Nakacho. We got him coming back from 7-Eleven. What do you want to do with him?"

"Let Matchan take care of him."

Shota hangs up, his thoughts already returning to Hank Fisher, a plan forming in his head.

CHAPTER THIRTY-SEVEN

LISA IS GETTING ready for work when the nanny calls and says she's sorry but she can't make it today because she's come down with a bad cold.

Which is a bit surprising because in the year and a half that Lisa has been using Rumi, she's never once no-showed. She knows Justin and James are going to be disappointed. She can hear them moaning already. They adore "Rumi-*chan*."

Rumi apologizes and asks Lisa to tell the boys she'll see them next time. Lisa says, "There's no need to apologize! Take care of yourself and get well. It must be that summer cold that's going around."

"Thank you for understanding," says Rumi. "The girl filling in for me, her name is Fujita."

"Fujita?"

"Yes."

"Okay. Thank you for letting me know."

Lisa ends the call and pours cereal into the boys' bowls and goes to the fridge for the milk as James comes into the kitchen wearing his shirt inside out. Lisa points at it.

"Your shirt is inside out."

James looks down, looks back up, and smiles, and Lisa smiles back at him, and then Justin appears behind him and says, "Ha ha. Idiot."

"Shut up!"

Lisa says, "Stop it, both of you. We don't have time for this. Sit down and eat." As soon as the nanny gets here, Lisa will have her walk the kids to school like Rumi usually does. Then she'll have her walk Brownie and do some cleaning. Then she'll pick the kids up from school and take them and Brownie to the park.

As Lisa makes a pot of coffee, she tunes out the boys' bickering and runs down a mental list of the things she needs to do today. Email outside counsel about an issue that has come up with a supplier. Review a customer's proposed changes to a sales contract. Reschedule tomorrow's lunch with Kaori. Something about the call with Rumi nags at her, though. Two things, actually. The first is that there was something strange about Rumi's voice. Lisa is certain she heard a slight quaver in it, as if Rumi had been on the verge of tears, and the way the girl paused several times during their short conversation reinforced this impression. Second, why did Rumi call and not the agency? Lisa's pretty sure that Happy Helpers Agency prohibits their contractors from directly contacting the families they help. She decides to look at the pamphlet and the agreement she signed with the agency later, maybe after the kids go to bed tonight. It's not a big deal anyway, and now that she thinks about it, maybe Rumi is having some sort of personal issue. Maybe her boyfriend broke up with her, or maybe a friend of hers died, or maybe one of her parents is sick. Who knows?

Justin and James finish their breakfast, and as they're getting their backpacks ready for school, the doorbell rings.

Lisa goes to the intercom and sees a round-faced young woman on the screen. "Fujita-*san*?" she says.

"Yes, I'm Fujita," the young woman says, smiling. She's got big rosy cheeks and a button of a nose.

Lisa buzzes her in. A minute later there's a knock at the door. Lisa opens it, and Fujita-san smiles and bows and says again, "I'm Fujita. Nice to meet you."

Lisa says, "Please come in." Over her shoulder she says, "Justin! James! Come here!"

The boys appear in the hallway, confused looks on their faces.

"Rumi-*chan* has a cold, so Fujita-*san* here is going to help us today."

Fujita-*san* smiles at the boys and says in English, "You can call me Yayoi, okay?"

CHAPTER THIRTY-EIGHT

ANOTHER INTERNET CAFÉ.

On the ninth floor of a rundown building across the street from Meguro Station, this one is more spartan than the last and in place of rooms has narrow cubicles enclosed by six-foot-high walls.

He's been holed up here for the past twelve hours, waiting to hear back from Pete Marini. After escaping from Shota's goons in Shibuya yesterday, he'd stashed the gym bag in another coin locker, this one at Ebisu Station, and then ridden one stop to Meguro and checked into a room, showered, and used Shota's phone to call Marini. He'd gotten Marini's voicemail, left him a message to call him back.

After that, he'd fallen into a restless slumber in the cubicle's obligatory faux-leather recliner, tossing and turning, guilt and fear and anger and hopelessness churning his guts as he thought of Lisa and Justin and James. What would they think if they knew he was hiding like a criminal in a shitty Internet café from a bunch of gangsters who forced him to steal a bag of money?

He thought of Terry and Akio, Terry in an ICU somewhere with tubes going in and out of him, Akio's nearly headless corpse lying on the blood-soaked carpet. All because of him. That thought, in turn, made him think of Mari and the danger she could be in, and suddenly the horror of this possibility woke him like a double shot of espresso. He remembered her number because the last four digits happened to be the same as the last four digits of his old home landline. But he didn't want to wake her up in the middle of the night. His worry for her ratcheted up and up, and now, thirty minutes later, he can't wait any longer. He dials the number.

Mari picks up on the sixth ring. "Hello?" she says, her voice thick with sleep.

"Mari," he says, relieved to hear her voice, "it's Hank. I'm sorry to wake you."

"Hank? Are you okay?"

"I'm fine." His face goes warm with shame. He's the one putting *her* in danger, and here she is asking him if he's okay. "Mari, I don't want to frighten you, but have you seen anyone suspicious-looking around your building?"

Mari pauses to think about it, then says, "No," a slight tone of alarm in her voice. "Why? Is it the bad guys you told me about? Should I call the police?"

Fisher doesn't want to scare her any more than he already has. "I don't think you need to now, but definitely call them if you see anyone creepy hanging around."

"Okay," she says. "But don't worry. I have to go see my parents tomorrow. Maybe I'll stay the night with them."

"That's a good idea."

Mari laughs. "You don't know my parents."

Fisher laughs too, feeling reassured. "I just wanted to be sure you were all right. And to say sorry and thanks again for helping me out the other night."

Mari makes a dismissive noise. "You can take me out to dinner again, okay?"

"Okay," says Fisher, meaning it but knowing it can't happen.

He sits there after they hang up, picturing her brown eyes. Her dimples and the graceful line of her neck. In another life.

He drifts off to sleep again, wakes up a few hours later, groggy and sore all over. He paces the little space, wondering what's taking Marini so long to call him back. Fisher dials him again, leaves another voicemail. He hates the thought of being at the asshole's mercy, still isn't sure he can trust him, but at this point Marini's offer of help is looking like Fisher's only hope. All he can do now is wait for him to call.

He reaches for the mouse on the desk, clicks open the browser. The Yahoo Japan homepage pops up with a list of the latest news items. All nerves, Fisher scrolls halfway down the page and sees the headline he was hoping not to find.

George Fukuda murder investigation: Police say they have several leads.

Heart thumping, he clicks on the article and reads:

The Tokyo Metropolitan Police are following up on several leads in their investigation into the death of Fukuda Akira, son of comedian-turned-politician George Fukuda, a police spokesperson said at a press conference yesterday. Mr. Fukuda, 37, was last seen two weeks ago at a bar he frequented in Kabukicho and was reported missing a week later by his sister.

The article goes on to say that several witnesses saw a big foreigner in the building where Fukuda's body was discovered by the police after they received an anonymous tip that led them to the apartment in Yotsuya. Embedded in the article is a reproduction of the sketch Fisher saw on TV the other night.

Suddenly an elephant is sitting on Fisher's chest. He closes the browser, shuts his eyes, and tries to will his heart to stop racing. Goddamn it. He needs help, and he needs it now. *Marini, where the fuck are you?*

He drinks half a bottle of water, takes several deep breaths, and once he's managed to get his nerves under control, he sits back down in front of the monitor and, for the first time in he doesn't know how long, logs in to his email account. His inbox is crammed with spam. He scrolls through it all, deleting as he goes.

Need Car Insurance?

Click.

Meet Hot Girls In Your Area

Click.

Drive Your Partner Crazy In Bed Tonight

Click.

Then: *Hey, where the hell are you?*

It's from Ken, his trainer—*former* trainer—at Blast MMA. A ripple of trepidation passes over him. Why would Ken be trying to get hold of him? Could the gangsters have paid him a visit too? He moves the cursor to open the message, but the one below it stops him dead. It's from Watanabe, the PI, and it's dated yesterday.

Your ex-wife's mobile number and address are below, it says. *I am very sorry. I recommend that you go to the police immediately.*

Go to the police? What the hell does that mean? He scrolls down the page to the address. Unbelievably, it's in Aoyama, not far from where he works in Roppongi on Monday and Wednesday nights. All this time, and Lisa and the kids were minutes away. He picks the phone up off the desk, looks at the monitor again, and that's when the subject line of another email catches his attention.

Consequences, it reads.

There are two attachments.

Fisher doesn't recognize the address of the sender, but he knows who it is. He opens the email and reads the following:

No more games. I want my money back. Contact me within 24 hours or the next time it'll be one of your kids.

He breaks out in gooseflesh, dread hitting him like a shot of liquid nitrogen. The inside of his mouth dry as dead leaves, he clicks on the first of the two files attached to Shota's email.

The image in the first clip is shaky for the first few seconds. Then it steadies and zooms out, and there are Justin and James in a park. Fisher's heart seems to freeze in his chest. The camera zooms out a bit more, and a plump young woman comes into view. She's sitting on a bench, holding Brownie's leash as she watches the boys run to the slide.

Fisher swallows.

Justin clambers up the steps of the slide, James right behind him. James turns and waves to get the woman's attention. "Yayoi-*chan! Mite!*" Watch me, Yayoi!

The woman waves back, unsmiling. "*Miteruyo.*" I'm watching. She reaches down and scratches Brownie's head.

The video ends.

Fisher is trembling and his pulse pounds in his ears. He doesn't want to know what's in the second video. Please don't let it be what he thinks it is. Please please please.

He clicks on the file. The gray concrete interior of an empty parking structure appears on the screen. Daylight pours in from the open sides. Walking toward the camera with Brownie on his leash is the young woman. Whoever is recording the video is standing between a black Hi-Ace van on one side and a silver BMW on the other. The two cars are backed into adjacent spaces. The side door of the van is open, and inside is a guy with a shaved head.

The woman's head swivels left and right as Brownie trots in front of her, tail wagging.

Fisher gets a sick feeling in the pit of his stomach.

Off camera there's a rustling of paper followed by what he recognizes as Matchan's pinched baritone. "Here, Brownie! I have a snack for you!"

Brownie responds with a little whine of excitement. Fisher knows that whine. He used to sit nearby at dinnertime and patiently wait for the four of them to slip him food under the table. The dog could go five, maybe ten minutes before his patience went out the window and he started whining.

Off camera, another voice says, "Hurry up." It's Shota. He's doing the recording.

No.

The woman and Brownie enter the narrow space between the van and the BMW. The camera does a quarter turn as it pans downward, and there's Matchan, squatting sumo-style, holding a doggy treat out for the dog.

Toy poodles aren't known for being particularly congenial to strangers. Someone must have forgotten to tell Brownie that, though, because from the time he was a puppy, he's been the kind of dog who's so friendly, you worry he'll go off with anyone willing to pay him the tiniest bit of attention. Offer to feed him something and you've got yourself a buddy for life. So it's no surprise to Fisher when he goes right up to Matchan, tail still going like a metronome at warp speed, eats the cookie in one bite, and licks Matchan's hand all over.

Matchan says, "You're a cute little guy!"

Do not hurt that fucking dog.

Matchan gently scoops Brownie up and cradles him with his left arm. He offers him another treat with his right hand. The woman stands there blank-faced next to him, still holding Brownie's leash.

Shota says, "That's enough. Hurry up and do it."

The woman holds the leash out to Matchan, who takes it in his right hand and gives Brownie a scratch on the head. She steps back. Matchan puts his face close to Brownie's head and says, like he's speaking to a child, "*Gomen ne, Buraunii-chan.*" Sorry, Brownie. Then he wraps the leash twice around his fist.

Nauseous and dizzy, Fisher jumps out of his seat, turns away from the screen, and claps his hand over his mouth.

A hissing, gurgling sound from the monitor's speaker. Fisher bites his fist. He screams against his fist and bites down hard and barely feels it as his teeth pierce the skin of his knuckles. Shota's voice: "Hold it away from me, you idiot!"

Fisher turns to the screen again. The frame jounces around a few times, and when it steadies, it's pointed at the skinhead in the van, who's putting the lid on a blue plastic bucket in front of him, Fisher catching a glimpse of brown fur before the door of the van slides shut. The video ends.

Fisher slams his fist down on the desktop. BOOM!

He does it again. BOOM!

The guy next door bangs on the wall again. "Knock it off!"

His breath coming in labored gusts, Fisher re-opens Watanabe's email, scrolls down to Lisa's mobile number, and dials it.

CHAPTER THIRTY-NINE

THE PHONE RINGS five times and goes to voicemail. Fisher hangs up and hits redial.

Same result.

The third time, Lisa picks up and says in a hushed voice, "*Hai.*" Yes? The sudden sound of her voice after so long hits Fisher in the gut, and he stands there stupid and mute, his mouth opening and closing like a fish.

"*Moshi moshi?*" Hello?

Fisher finally collects himself. "Lisa, it's me, Hank."

There's a long pause. Then: "How did you get this number?"

"I'm sorry for calling you out of the blue, and I know this is going to sound crazy, but I need to know where the kids are."

"What? Why? How the hell did you get my number?"

She's confused. She's confused and she's pissed, and Fisher can't blame her. "I-I can explain. I promise I'll explain. Just... please, tell me where the kids are right now."

"They're with the babysitter. Now tell me what the hell this is about. I'm at work right now."

The floor under Fisher's feet slowly rolls. He grabs the top of the recliner to steady himself. He moves the receiver away from his mouth and takes deep breaths.

"Hank?"

Fisher swallows hard. "You have to get the kids away from the babysitter."

Lisa makes a scoffing noise. "What's that supposed to mean?!"

"Just trust me, okay? You have to get them away from her. Take them and the three of you get as far away as possible."

"What the hell are you talking about?"

"I know she takes the kids to the park with Brownie. Is that where they are now?"

"How do you know that?! Are you spying on us?! Jesus!"

"I'm not spying on you! Please, just listen to me! I hired a private investigator to find you. But that's not...look, Lisa, I got into some trouble with some bad people, and this woman... she's with them."

"What does that mean, *with them?*"

"I mean she works for them. She's dangerous. You have to get the kids and go now. You have to—"

"What are you *talking* about?! This is insane! Why are you doing this?!"

His heart sinks. She's right. He sounds like a raving lunatic. "I know it sounds crazy," he says. "But I can prove it. Hold on." He sits in the chair and grabs the mouse with his free hand. He scrolls down and finds the email from Shota and clicks it open and clicks the Forward button. "What's your email address? I need to send you something."

"Enough, Hank. Please. Enough."

"It's two videos. Lisa, please, just watch them and you'll see."

"I don't know what's happened to you, but you need help, Hank. Please get some help."

"Lisa. I'm begging you."

She starts to cry. "Why are you doing this?"

Something inside Fisher bursts. "I don't want to lose you guys!"

Lisa doesn't say anything, and Fisher sits there listening to the sound of her sniffling over the steady thump of his pulse.

When she speaks again a few minutes later, her tone is firm. "You lost us a long time ago."

"No. Don't say that. I know it's all my fault. I messed everything up, and the past two years, without the three of you, the past two years have been...I might as well have been dead, and you were right about the fighting. I couldn't let it go, and it was selfish and stupid and I know that now. But that's not me anymore. I'm done fighting." It's true, he realizes. He's done. And he feels nothing but hope. "I'm a husband and I'm a father, that's what I am, and I want to show you that, you and Justin and James, and I can't do it now because I've got to fix this situation I'm in first, but when everything settles down, Lisa, I'll show you. I love you."

Lisa sighs. "Hank, I'm seeing someone."

He can't speak, and it's a good thing he's sitting down, because he feels dizzy, like he might pass out. He waits until the feeling passes and then says, "Is it serious?"

In a quiet voice Lisa starts talking about how sad she was for so long after they split and how their marriage just wasn't meant to be, and how it had taken her a long time to realize that and come to terms with it, and it made her so sad, and of course she still cares about him, but she couldn't live like that anymore, afraid, and what they both need to do is hang on to the good times, keep them in their hearts, and despite their failed marriage, they produced two beautiful, wonderful boys together, and for that she is so, *so* thankful, and they should both be happy about that, and maybe someday he can be part of the kids' lives again, but not now, not when he so obviously needs help.

He feels like he's been run over. Run over by a truck, and then the driver jacked the thing into reverse and ran over him again. He wipes his cheeks with the back of his hand. He takes the phone away from his face and holds it against his chest while he snatches a couple of tissues from the box on the desk and blows his nose. He balls the tissues up, swivels around, and throws them at the wastebasket. They hit the wall and fall to the floor. He clears his throat again and returns the phone to his ear.

"I'm happy for you," he says, trying to sound like he means it, but it comes out sounding clipped and icy.

"Oh, Hank."

The pity in her tone ignites something in him, and all at once he wants to smash something. Then he remembers why he's calling.

"Just give me your email address, Lisa."

She sighs again. "I have to go."

"Wait—"

Click.

Eyes closed, he sits there with the phone to his ear for he doesn't know how long until he finally places it on the desk and pushes himself out of the chair. He stares at the phone. He looks up at Shota's email on the monitor. This doesn't change anything. He still has to do what he has to do. The question is *how*. Lisa didn't give him her email address, but he has her mobile number, and he can text the clips to her. Fisher opens the phone's browser and logs in to his email account and saves the videos to the phone. He opens the messaging app and types in Lisa's number, attaches the videos, and hits send. A few moments later he gets a message saying she's blocked this number.

Which leaves him with only one other option.

He opens Watanabe's email again and jots down Lisa's physical address on a Post-it. He pockets the phone and his room key and leaves.

CHAPTER FORTY

"SIR, WE'VE ARRIVED."

It's just before 5 p.m. when the cab stops in front of Lisa's building. It looks brand-new, all sleek glass and steel with meticulously landscaped grounds facing a narrow, one-way street. There's a small pond and inviting-looking shade trees and a winding flagstone footpath leading to the entrance.

Across the street, facing the building, is a row of shops next to a small park where cicadas are making a racket that Fisher can hear through the cab's windows.

A Rolls-Royce pulls into the apartment tower's driveway, stops at the entrance to the underground parking garage, and waits for the gate to open.

Fisher is all nerves as he scans the street for signs of Shota and his goons. Seeing none, he looks up at the tower. A condo in a new building like this in Aoyama—you're probably talking anywhere from two to six million U.S. Which means that either Lisa got a *really* good job after she left him, or her boyfriend makes a ton of money. Fisher pictures some rich asshole banker or venture capitalist. He pictures that asshole with Justin and James, playing dad.

"*Koko de yoroshii desuka?*" the driver says. Is this where you wanted to get out?

Fisher apologizes and pulls a couple of thousand-yen bills out of his pocket and sets them on the little tray between the front seats. The driver hands him his change, Fisher tells him to keep the receipt and gets out. The cicadas' high-pitched buzz jumps several decibels, the sun beating down on him as he stares at the shiny apartment building.

Could the gangsters be watching from somewhere nearby, waiting for him? He thinks of Brownie, and then he thinks of Justin and James with the woman in the park and he's filled with rage. He has to get them away from her, away from Shota.

What if Lisa's not home yet and the woman from the video is in the apartment with the kids? She might hurt them and she will definitely alert Shota that he's there. And if Lisa *is* home, she might call the cops on him.

His chest tightens.

He can see a security guard just outside the entrance to the building, which rules out loitering in the lobby until Lisa appears who knows when.

All at once he feels exposed out here on the street.

In the row of shops is a Starbucks. Fisher hurries there and buys a tall coffee and takes a seat next to the window facing the street and waits. Sooner or later, Lisa is going to appear. He'll wait here all night if he has to.

He tries to think about how he's going to approach Lisa and get her to watch the videos, but his addled brain can't seem to process everything that's happened in the last twenty-four hours. So he gives up after a minute or two, thinking he'll cross that bridge when he comes to it. His eyelids feel heavy despite the coffee, and he has to pinch himself several times to stay awake.

A heavily made-up woman in pink sweats and purple tennis shoes emerges from the entrance of the tower cradling a French bulldog in her arms like a baby.

A picture of Brownie floats up, his little body in the blue bucket. Fisher's jaw clenches.

Ten minutes pass. Fifteen. He sips his coffee and watches taxis and bicycle delivery guys roll past on the street, every now and then shooting a glance at the entrance to the apartment tower's garage to see it swallow up or spit out another luxury car. Benzes and Beemers and Range Rovers. No sign of Lisa or the twins, though.

Setting down the last of his coffee, he goes to the counter and buys another. He's about to sit back down when he glances out the window and spots them. The three of them are coming up on the left on their bikes. Justin is in the lead, a big grin on his face. James is pedaling furiously behind him, howling at Justin to slow down. Lisa is bringing up the rear in a loose-fitting blue floral print dress and sandals, trying to keep up with both of them, and if she wasn't there with them, he might not have recognized them right away. They're five or six inches taller, not the little guys he remembers. They've got that willowy, gawky look of boys on the cusp of adolescence. His beautiful boys. He's missed out on two years of their lives. Do they remember him? Something catches in his throat, and suddenly his cheeks are wet. For a moment he's right there with them, it's the four of them on their bikes, back from a trip to the park. The kids laughing at one of Fisher's jokes, Lisa snorting and rolling her eyes.

Hank, I'm seeing someone.

He rubs at his eyes, swallows the lump in his throat. He sits there watching them for another moment, then remembers why he's there, feels his heart race. Lisa and the boys are a hundred feet or so from the mouth of a wide footpath that runs from the sidewalk to the entrance of the building.

Fisher leaves the coffee where it is on the table and exits the store. He stands inside the recessed doorway so the three of them can't see him. He scans the street for the hundredth time, sees no one who looks like a gangster. He needs to make this quick, before they turn up the footpath and go back inside. How should he play this? Lisa already thinks he's gone nuts. If he runs over there, it's going to freak her out, and if he walks over all casual, that's going to freak her out too.

Just go, he tells himself.

Justin and James are now yelling at each other, their voices deeper than he remembers, and even as Lisa is yelling at both of them to stop fighting, Fisher's chest swells with pent-up longing for his sons. He's going to scoop them up into his arms and tell them he loves them and he's sorry he hasn't been able to see them. As he steps out into the street, oblivious, floating, a voice blares in Japanese over a loudspeaker.

"*Please use the crosswalk.*"

He jumps.

A patrol car is on his left, not fifty feet away, the two cops inside looking right at him. Out of the corner of his eye, he sees Lisa and the boys looking his way, trying to figure out what the fuss is about. He smiles lamely at the cops, gives them a little apologetic bow, and returns to the sidewalk. The cop in the passenger seat eyes Fisher as the car rolls by. Fisher smiles and bows his head again—*So sorry, officers*—his heart hammering in his chest. The cop just stares at him as the car continues slowly on its way.

The patrol car rolls to a stop at the end of the street, turns left, and is gone. Fisher looks over at Lisa and the kids, and the three of them are standing there stock still, mouths agape. He raises his hand, tentative, and presses his lips together into what he hopes looks like a smile. Fear for their safety vying with guilt over putting them in danger like this. Thinking, *Please, please, please, just give me a minute.*

Lisa frowns and reaches into the big cloth bag she's got slung over her shoulder. She pulls out her phone, taps at the screen a couple of times, and presses it to her ear, keeping her eyes on Fisher the whole time.

"It's Daddy!" says Justin, and then he and James are both jumping up and down like excited puppies. "Daddy! Daddy! Daddy!"

Joy washes over Fisher. Two years is an eternity to a kid. But his sons *do* remember him.

Lisa frowns, says something to them.

Fisher trots across the street, jogs a few steps toward them on the sidewalk, and stops and holds up his hands. "Lisa—"

Justin and James let go of their bikes and tear off toward him. The bikes crash to the sidewalk. The phone still pressed to her ear, Lisa calls after them, "*Jitensha!*" Your bicycles!

The boys cannon into Fisher. "Daddy's here!" They're all over him, grabbing and pulling at him, jumping up and down. "Come here, you guys!" he says, and he's weeping as he scoops them both up, Justin with his left arm, James with his right. "Look at you! You guys are huge! How are my monkeys?!" They laugh and make monkey noises as he gently rag dolls them for a few moments, noting how much heavier they are. Then he sets them down one by one, takes a knee, and pulls them into a big hug. Kisses the tops of their heads, pure joy washing away, if only for a second, everything that's happened over the past few days.

Lisa glares at him as she speaks into the phone. He can't hear what she's saying, but this isn't good. Is she calling the cops? Her boyfriend? She ends the call and storms up to Fisher.

"What are you doing here? You have to leave."

James says, "Why, Mama?!" followed by Justin. "Yeah, Mama, why? We want Daddy to stay!"

Fisher had thought he might never see them again, and now he's here with them and he doesn't want to let them go.

Lisa says to the boys in Japanese, "You two pick up your bikes and go put them away. Wait for me inside the lobby."

The twins issue a chorus of protest. "But, Mama!"

Fisher thinks of the videos, and the fear smoldering in him just under the surface reignites into panic. Lisa has to take the kids and leave town *now*. He puts a hand on each of their heads. "It's okay, guys. Mom and I just need to talk for a minute."

Lisa says, "No! No, we don't!"

The twins don't move. They look back and forth between Fisher and their mom, frowning, until he squeezes both their shoulders. "Go, guys. Do what your mom says." Reluctant, they trudge off. Fisher pulls his phone out of his pocket, quickly pulls up the videos, and holds the device out to Lisa. "There are two videos on there. Just watch them."

She doesn't move.

"Damn it, Lisa, you and the boys are in danger. You don't believe me, I get it. But you will when you watch these videos. It'll take you thirty seconds. Please. Watch them and I'll leave."

"I don't want to watch your videos, Hank. I want you to leave, and I don't want to see you again. I don't want you around the kids. What I said before about you being part of their lives... you've just shown me that's not possible."

"Goddamn it! Just…okay, just one question. Answer one question, Lisa: where's Brownie?"

"Where's…what?! Here we go again with the crazy questions! No, Hank! Just go! You're sick! You need help!"

"They killed Brownie, and recorded it! That's what's on the videos!" It's as though she and the kids are walking toward the edge of a cliff and he's screaming at her but they can't hear him.

Lisa closes her eyes. Takes a deep breath and lets it out and opens her eyes and says, in the same tone she would use to calm one of the kids during a meltdown, "Hank, get out of here before I call the police."

Fisher reaches out and grabs Lisa's right wrist and tries to put the phone in her hand.

"Let go of me!" she says, yanking her hand away. The phone pops up into the air and drops to the concrete with a loud crack. "Asshole!"

Fisher bends down to pick up the phone.

"You in the green cap! Stay where you are!"

Fisher straightens, turns. The patrol car's red lights are flashing. Pedestrians staring at him, and Lisa, wide-eyed.

All the cops did was circle the park and come back.

A current of fear races through Fisher's body.

Lisa barrels past him and hisses, "Unbelievable!"

The officers get out of the patrol car, both of them frowning, batons at the ready. They take up positions on either side of the car, one in the street, the other on the sidewalk directly in front of Fisher.

Fisher does the only thing that comes to mind:

He turns and runs like hell.

243

CHAPTER FORTY-ONE

ONE AFTERNOON A year or so after the twins were born, Fisher and Lisa packed lunch, put the babies in the double stroller, and went to the outer grounds of the Imperial Palace for a picnic.

Situated on acres of manicured lawn dotted with black pines, the Palace grounds were a kind of oasis in the middle of the central Tokyo when the weather was nice, a getaway from the hustle and bustle of the big city favored by picnickers, sunbathers, strollers, and runners.

Fisher was between fights at the time, enjoying lazy days with Lisa and the kids and eating a lot and getting happily fat. It was a gorgeous day, the afternoon sun shining down on them, just a hint of humidity in the spring air. They laid beach towels out on the grass underneath the parasol they'd brought. Lisa fed the boys, who were fast asleep in the stroller, and then they ate the tuna salad sandwiches they'd made and stretched out on their towels, Lisa nodding off.

Fisher had also brought a pair of Rollerblades he'd found buried in the back of the bedroom closet. He'd bought them in Santa Cruz in the late eighties, and they'd somehow found their way to Tokyo along with the rest of their stuff. He kissed

Lisa on the forehead, asked if she minded if he took a spin around the grounds. It had been years since he'd Rollerbladed, and he wanted to see if he still remembered how. She chuckled, drowsy-eyed, told him to go on and be careful, she was going to take a little nap.

A few minutes later he was flying around the concrete path that circled the outer Palace grounds, cruising, grooving to the music from his iPod blasting in his ears as he moved against the flow of the foot traffic on the path, weaving around joggers and strollers, aware of the ridiculous image he was cutting. Rollerblades were so 1990s. But he was enjoying the weather and being outside.

That's why he didn't notice the pair of cops who tried to flag him down. Fisher raced by them, oblivious, as the two cops took chase and quickly multiplied, four becoming eight and so on, until he had a small army pursuing him. He didn't stop until a couple of minutes later when a wall of blue popped up out of nowhere in front of him, cops screaming and frantically waving their arms at him to halt.

The problem was, Fisher was never a great Rollerblader. Once he got going he was fine, but stopping was tricky. He required a lot of runway. The cops had materialized so suddenly, however, that Fisher ended up plowing into them and doing a spectacular crash-and-burn. And then, faster than you can say *rule-breaking-foreigner*, ten angry policemen descended on him like hornets whose nest has been disturbed, kicking him and clubbing him with their batons, shouting *Baka yaro!*—Stupid asshole!—and demanding to know what he was doing and why he hadn't stopped and didn't he know that he was going the wrong way and didn't he know he should've known that?

An hour later, after seemingly every other cop in Tokyo had

arrived on the scene, after Fisher had produced his foreigner registration card and explained that he hadn't been able to hear them and apologized a hundred times and rinsed the road rash on his knees and elbows with a bottle of water one of the cops gave him, they finally let him go.

The lesson Fisher took from the incident was simple: Don't make Japanese cops chase you.

They *really* hate that.

Fisher is running as fast as his legs will carry him, which isn't saying much because knives of pain are jabbing his knee, hip, and ribs with every stride.

The foot traffic on both sides of the street has come to a dead stop, pedestrians gawking in horror at the big, bad, fleeing *gaijin*.

A hundred yards ahead, two more cops, round the corner on bicycles, pedaling furiously toward Hank Fisher, Outlaw.

The bicycle cops are seventy-five yards away now and closing. Fisher glances to his right. Lisa is walking quickly back inside the apartment building.

Behind Fisher, one of the cops from the patrol car says, "Stop!" in English.

Somewhere a woman screams.

Across the street, a young guy is holding up his phone, recording all this, no doubt so he can put it up on YouTube.

When the bicycle cops are fifty yards away, they skid to a stop and kick out their kickstands. They hop off their bikes and unsheath their batons and move toward Fisher in a tentative semi-crouch.

Sirens wail in the distance.

Sweat rolls down Fisher's sides. He toggles his gaze back

and forth as he runs between the bicycle cops in front of him and the other two behind him. He can see from the way the bicycle cops' eyes are bugging out that they're scared, and this scares *him* because it's pretty clear they think he's the big *gaijin* everyone's been talking about on TV, the man who murdered the man in the apartment in Yotsuya.

It's a game of pickle. Only it's no game. And Fisher's the pickle.

The bicycle cops are fifty feet away now, the cops from the patrol car maybe thirty.

The thought of surrendering flashes across Fisher's mind, and just as quickly he dismisses it. Surrendering won't help Lisa and the boys. Besides, he's a murder suspect now, and it seems insane to think the police would ever believe his story. It's much more likely that he'd sit rotting in a jail cell while the cops tried to get a confession out of him and Shota did something horrible to his family. No, he is not going to let that happen. A burst of panic-fueled energy drives him forward.

The sirens are getting closer.

Fisher has to get out of here. He can either run toward the bicycle cops (Option 1) or try to get past the cops in the car (Option 2). If he goes with Option 1, all four of the cops will give chase and they'll all be going in the same direction, only Fisher will be on foot and they'll be in a car and on bicycles. He likes Option 2 better, because the street is barely two car-widths across, making a quick U-turn impossible, so the cop car will instead have to use the apartment building's driveway to turn around in order to follow him, and in the meantime the other two cops will have to run back and retrieve their bikes before joining the chase.

Go, Fisher tells himself. He runs toward the cop on the

sidewalk next to the patrol car. To Fisher's left is the edge of a rectangular patch of lawn that runs along the sidewalk for fifty yards or so before ending at a tall fence. The cop braces himself. He's a young guy, big across the chest and shoulders, and he's holding his baton horizontal in both hands. Fisher runs as fast as he can, ignoring the pain in his knee, and at the last moment, just before barreling into the cop, he cuts left, his feet sliding as they hit the grass. It's wet, must be freshly watered, and he scrambles and barely manages not to go down.

"*Oi!*" the young cop yells as Fisher blasts by. Hey! The cop's baton sails by in front of him and lands on the grass ten feet ahead. Fisher passes the fence, turns left at the corner, and nearly collides with an old lady coming in the opposite direction. He turns right, past a row of shops, then left. Approaching a FamilyMart, he slows to a trot, pulls the green cap off his head and stuffs it into the trash receptacle next to the entrance. He turns right at the next street and slows to a walk, trying not to attract attention. More sirens fill the muggy air, so many of them now, coming from every direction.

He turns left. He turns right. Left. Right. And there, not fifty feet away, at the end of the street is a subway entrance.

CHAPTER FORTY-TWO

"Dad, I need help," says Ryo.

Shota holds up a finger. "Hold on." For the past thirty minutes, he's been watching his boy try to put together a Lego Dodge Charger, the pieces of which are scattered all over the coffee table. Now, though, Shota's attention is on the TV, where a news program is showing a video clip of four cops running after Hank Fisher.

He chews on his bottom lip, twirling an earring. Fisher has his goddamn money, and Shota has two days to get it from him. Failing that, he's going to lose everything—his hundred grand down payment on the guns, the guns themselves, and any chance he has of putting Spiral on the map before the splinter groups already peeling away from the Tanabe-*kai* carve up the organization's territory.

"Dad, please!"

"Shut the fuck up!" Shota barks out the side of his mouth as he grabs the remote and turns up the volume.

The caption at the top of the screen says the footage was taken by a pedestrian this afternoon. Visible in the background is Fisher's ex-wife's apartment tower in Aoyama.

Shota watches with a mixture of anger, dread, and fascination as Fisher hauls ass toward a scared-looking young cop. It looks like Fisher is going to tackle the guy, but at the last moment Fisher cuts sideways like a football player, slides on a patch of grass, and almost eats it before somehow righting himself and continuing his escape.

So Fisher went to his ex-wife's place to try to warn her after seeing the videos Shota sent him of Yayoi with his kids and Matchan killing their dog. And now the asshole's got every cop in the city after him. Which means that Shota has to find him and get the money before the cops do.

It's time to stop fucking around.

Shota grabs his phone and dials Yayoi and tells her to be ready tomorrow morning. Then he dials Masa and tells him the same thing. He turns off the TV, and that's when he registers the soft sound of his son's sniffles.

Ryo is frowning at the half-completed Lego car, tears rolling down his cheeks as he turns one of the red plastic pieces over and over in his small hands.

Shota clucks his tongue. The fucking guy at the toy store said a smart five-year-old should be able to put the thing together. Shota pushes himself off the sofa and sits down cross-legged next to his boy and musses his hair.

"Okay," he says. "Stop being a little pussy and let's figure this thing out."

CHAPTER FORTY-THREE

Blast MMA
12:30 a.m.
Friday

෴

FISHER SITS AT Ken's desk, his right hand resting on the receiver of the gym's landline. In his left is a hand towel he's been using to wipe the sweat from his face, because the AC in here—an ancient wall-mounted Panasonic unit that Ono, the owner, should've replaced years ago but won't because he's a cheap bastard—sucks.

He'd arrived at the gym a little before midnight. The train had rolled into Tachikawa Station just past eight o'clock, but the gym doesn't close until ten, and Fisher wanted to avoid running into anyone there, so he hung out for a couple of hours at a twenty-four-hour Mickey D's about a minute from the station, pretending to read a magazine he'd picked up at a kiosk while nibbling at a burger and sipping a large Sprite.

The spare keys to the gym were under the doormat at the

bottom of the stairs, right where he'd remembered them. Ken keeps them there for members who want to train after hours. Fisher let himself in, locked the door behind him, slipped his shoes off, and put on one of several pairs of slippers in front of the *geta-bako*—the shoe box. He walked down the hallway to the gym, pulled open the sliding door, and reached in and turned on the AC. Then he grabbed a clean towel from a stack on a shelf in the locker room and shut himself inside Ken's office.

Fisher examines the cracked screen of the phone Shota gave him and feels a pang of guilt for trying to force it into Lisa's hand. He confirms it still works and calls Marini's number. Marini picks up on the second ring, sounding wide awake.

"*Moshi moshi.*"

"Did you get my message?"

"Hey, Hank," Marini says. "Yeah, I got it." His tone casual.

What is this? Is Marini fucking with him? "So why haven't you called me back?"

"Hey, I got a real job, remember?"

A "real job." The implication clearly that Fisher doesn't have one. Asshole. He tamps down his anger. He needs this asshole's help. "Sorry," he says, trying to sound contrite. "I've had a rough couple days."

"No worries. You near a TV?"

There's a small flat-screen TV in the corner. Fisher finds the remote on top of a box of old magazines. "Yeah," he says, turning the TV on.

"Channel four."

Fisher presses the number on the remote and hits enter, and his heart falls to the floor. They're playing CCTV footage of him in the lobby of Akio's building. The video is followed by what looks like a clip someone took with their phone, and it's of Fisher running away from the cops after arguing with Lisa. "Oh Jesus," he hears himself mutter.

"What I thought too," says Marini.

His voice trembling, Fisher tells him about the videos and Shota's deadline and how the PI sent him Lisa's address. When he finishes relaying all this to Marini, he pauses, then says, "I need help. Can you still help me?"

Marini blows a gust of air into the receiver.

There's a pause, and the hesitation Fisher senses fills him with terror and desperation, his only chance of saving his family and getting out of this alive suddenly water threatening to pour through the spaces between the fingers of his cupped hands. "He's going to hurt Lisa and the kids, Pete," he says, his voice cracking. "He'll do it. He killed Akio. He tried to kill Terry."

Marini says, "No, listen. I'm gonna help you, and we're not gonna let that happen. Okay, dude?"

Fisher suddenly thinks of Mari. She's in danger too. "The other night, when you picked me up, I was staying with a friend in Juban. I think she could be in danger too."

"She?" says Marini.

"Her name is Mari. Sekiyama Mari."

"What makes you think she could be in trouble too?"

"Because I fucking stayed the night with her, Pete!"

"Okay, okay, settle down, dude! I'm trying to help you here, Jesus. Give me her address. I'll get one of my cop buddies to keep an eye on her, all right?"

Fisher gives him the address.

"Tell you what," Marini says. "Meet me in front of Hiroo Station at six thirty. I'm gonna help you and everything is gonna be fine. But, Hank? You gotta give me the money. Do you have it with you?"

"No."

"Why don't you tell me where it is. I'll go get it and then we can focus on getting Lisa and the boys out of trouble."

An alarm goes off in Fisher's head. He sees the flash of metal in Marini's hand the other night, a bead of cold suspicion running down the back of his neck. If he tells Marini where the money is and Marini fucks him over, he'll be empty-handed and Shota will hurt Lisa and the kids. "No, I'm not doing that. You'll get it when you pick me up."

"Okay, hey, that's fine, you're playing it safe, bro, I get that. I'll see you in a few hours then, all right?"

Fisher hangs up and switches off the TV and looks at a framed picture next to the phone of Ken, his wife, and their three kids. The five of them are crammed together on a sofa, big, open-mouthed smiles on their faces like someone's just told them something hilarious.

Justin and James are bigger now, but their smiles are the same as he'd remembered. Their laughs too, James's maniacal cackle, Justin's booming HAH HAH HAH! Seeing them today after so long…Fisher's heart swells. And then the fear of losing them comes roaring back, helplessness, frustration, self-disgust in its wake. He can't make Lisa see the danger they're in because she thinks he's gone crazy.

He pushes the chair back and rises, rubbing his face.

Is Marini really going to help him? If he's not, Fisher is dead, but more important, Justin and James and Lisa probably are too.

He turns off the AC and the lights in the office, shuffles down the hallway to the gym proper, and pulls the sliding door open and kicks off his shoes. He steps inside and pulls the door closed. It's nice and cool in here now, and he breathes in that nasty, funky gym smell he knows so well, and all at once a heavy blanket of exhaustion settles over him.

He grabs a red kicking pad from the metal shelf by the door, walks across the mat to the grappling area in the far right corner, and eases himself down onto the mat. He tucks the pad under his head, stretches his legs out, and closes his eyes.

$\approx$

He opens his eyes.

The old classroom clock on the wall says 3:20 a.m.

He's been lying here for hours, unable to sleep, his mind smearing the events of the past few days into a foul mash, the aches and pains all over his body making it impossible to find a comfortable position on the mat.

He finally gives up on sleep and sits up. Stretches a little. Slow, to get the blood circulating. Then he gets up and takes the kicking pad he's been using as a pillow back over to the metal shelves and exchanges it for a pair of gloves. He slips the gloves on and goes over to one of the heavy bags that line the left side of the gym and hits it. Nothing hard, just tapping the bag, basically. Nice and slow.

One. Two.

Like that. Loose. Get the blood flowing.

One. Two. One. Two.

It smarts, but not that bad. He keeps at it, picks up the pace a little.

One-two. One-two.

Pivots on his left foot, throws a low kick for three. His right shin hits the bag with a *whap*. Tiny spark of pain in his knee. A little too hard.

One-two. Three.

Nice and light. No power. Focusing more on the movement, ignoring the dull throb behind his eyes, the shooting pains in his shoulders and elbows and hands.

The fog clears after a while, and Fisher feels a little better. Then the memories come, and it's okay at first. Gauzy remembrances.

His mom's smile.

His dad's big laugh.

The smell of fresh-baked bread filling their converted barn-house.

One-two.

Then the roar of the black helicopters over the farm.

One-*two*.

The crack of gunfire.

One-two.

Fisher's mom falling to the ground, the faraway stare in her eyes as she dies in the mud.

BOOM-BOOM-BOOM!

The flash of metal in Pete Marini's hand.

BOOM-BOOM-BOOM!

Brownie hanging from his leash.

BOOM-BOOM-BOOM!

Akio, dead on his living room floor.

BOOM-BOOM-BOOM! BOOM-BOOM-BOOM! BOOM-BOOM-BOOM!

Fisher collapses to the floor, gasping for breath. Sweat pouring off him and puddling on the mat.

He'd had it all—the best life partner a guy could hope for, two wonderful kids, a warm home. What more did he need? But he couldn't see it, because he was in his own little world, chasing an impossible dream at the expense of everything else, and for the life of him, he couldn't see it.

And now here he is and there's no going back.

But Hank Fisher knows one thing: He's had it with being everyone's punchy clown.

CHAPTER FORTY-FOUR

HE GOES TO the locker room, strips down, and steps into one of the two freestanding fiberglass shower stalls against the back wall. He stands there swaying as the warm water washes over him. It feels so good he kind of trances out, not quite awake but not exactly asleep either.

Ten, fifteen minutes later, Fisher turns the water off. He plucks a towel from a pile of unfolded laundry on the shabby vanity next to the bathroom. He dries off, then finds a pair of shorts and a T-shirt that sort of fit him, plus a gray Blast MMA cap.

Back inside the gym, Fisher checks the time: 4:00 a.m. If he remembers correctly, the trains start running at Tachikawa Station around 4:30.

Time to get moving.

He realizes he needs money and kicks himself for not taking more from the gym bag before he stashed it in Ebisu. He returns to Ken's office, pulls open the file drawer in his desk, and takes the metal cash box out and flips open the lid. Inside is eighty-three thousand yen and change—about eight hundred bucks. He takes all of the bills, leaving the change, and slips them into his pocket. Then from the top drawer he takes out a pen and a pad of green Post-its and writes an IOU and sticks it on the underside of the lid before closing the box and putting it back in the file drawer.

He turns off the lights, closes the sliding door to the gym, and walks down the hallway to the main entrance. He puts the slippers back in the *geta-bako* and his shoes back on. He's about to let himself out when he hears someone coming down the stairs outside.

Fisher freezes.

Muffled footsteps. Whoever's out there is at the bottom of the stairs now.

Fisher's heart thumps. Has Shota somehow tracked him down?

The doorknob jiggles, followed by the slap of the doormat on the floor. The visitor just looked under the doormat for the spare keys, which means it's not Shota, because only members who train after hours know about the spare keys. Neither is it Ken or the owner, Ono-san, because both of them have their own keys.

Silence.

Maybe the person had been hoping to have the gym to themselves and now, having seen that another early bird beat them to it, has decided to bail.

Knock knock knock.

Fisher jumps at the sound, then stands there, motionless, his blood pounding in his ears. Goddamn it. No one can know he's here. A spark of worry for Ken and the other guys ignites in his chest.

KNOCK KNOCK KNOCK.

The sound is like mortar rounds going off in the entryway,

the echo barreling down the hallway. Fisher cringes and curses under his breath. The gym is in the basement of a three-story apartment complex, but it's four in the morning, and if this asshole keeps it up, the residents on the upper floors are going to start waking up.

Just go away, damn it.

KNOCK KNOCK KNOCK.

Shit.

A man's voice booms, "*Sumimasen!*" Hello?! American accent.

Oh for Christ's sake.

"*Hey!*" he says, in English. "*Hello!*"

And Fisher recognizes the voice now: it's Douchebag Dave.

"*Yo! Open up!*"

Unbelievable. Dave is exactly the kind of pushy asshole who will keep this up until either he's let in or someone calls the cops to come and shut him up. Which is the last thing Fisher needs. So he's going to have to open the door. The problem is, it's been less than a week since their little incident, so Dave isn't going to be thrilled to see him. Plus, and more important, if he's been paying attention to the news, he'll likely know Fisher's a wanted man.

Fisher opens the door.

Dave's mouth drops open when he sees him. He squints, and Fisher can almost see the gears turning in his head as he contemplates how to play this. The right side of Dave's face is still swollen, his right eye a palette of painful-looking black, blue, and yellow. He's wearing a red sleeveless rash guard, black shorts, and Nike high-tops. Dave closes his mouth and grimaces like he's just bitten into a stink bug. Then he tilts his head and looks past Fisher into the hallway.

"Anyone here?"

The dig implicit in the question—that Fisher's presence doesn't count—doesn't bother Fisher, because it indicates Dave hasn't been watching the news, which in turn means that Fisher doesn't have to worry about him calling the cops—at least not right away. Fisher glances over his shoulder. "Just little old me."

Dave touches his lip with a thumb, turns his head, and pretends to spit something out. He sniffs. "You're not supposed to be here."

"Oh?"

"Yeah. Ono kicked you out. Maybe you didn't get the memo."

Fisher shrugs. "Huh. Nah, no one told me about it."

Dave says, "Yeah, well," then motions with his head for Fisher to leave. "Time for you to go."

Time for you to fuck off. The words are right there on the tip of Fisher's tongue. Instead, he says, "Yeah, no problem. I was just leaving anyway." He feels Dave's eyes on him as he picks up the duffel bag and throws the strap over his shoulder. He holds the spare key out to Dave as he steps out from the doorway into the stairwell. Dave plucks it from his hand and steps in.

Fisher is halfway up the stairs when Dave calls after him.

"I'll let the cops know you were here."

Fisher stops. He considers running back down and grabbing Dave and...what? What's he going to do? Kill him?

"Do what you got to do, Dave," Fisher says, and continues up the stairs.

CHAPTER FORTY-FIVE

LISA IS ABOUT to leave for work when the doorbell rings.

Pee-pong.

Every doorbell she's ever heard in Japan makes the same sound, but it startles her all the same. No one Lisa knows would ever drop by unannounced, let alone this early in the morning, and adding to her alarm is the fact that she's still not quite right after Hank's sudden appearance and bizarre, frightening behavior yesterday.

The whole episode had left her deeply shaken. It had scared her and frightened and confused Justin and James, and Lisa had spent a good part of last night doing her best to calm the boys down, to deal with the barrage of questions they had. When could they see Daddy again? Why can't Mommy and Daddy live together? Is Daddy in trouble? Is he in jail? Is Mommy mad at Daddy? They'd been so happy to see Hank after so long, and that somehow made all of this so much worse.

When finally the kids were in bed and asleep, she called Jay, the guy she's been seeing for the past three months. She told him she'd had a crummy day but didn't go into detail. An English lit professor at a local university, he's a sweet, caring guy, but they're still getting to know each other and she doesn't want to scare him off by telling him about what had happened today with her ex.

They talked about having dinner this coming weekend, then said good night, and after they hung up, Lisa lay awake for several hours, the scene with Hank in front of the apartment building playing over and over in her head. What could possibly have happened to him to push him over the edge like this? He'd looked awful: bruises on his face, a crazed, desperate look in his bloodshot eyes. All the crazy talk about how they were in danger, that Lisa needed to get the kids away from the babysitter because she was dangerous. How he'd been spying on them—spying on them!—for who knows how long. And that awful stuff about how they—whoever *they* were—had killed Brownie, when Lisa knew that Brownie had run away. Yayoi had been so despondent over it—even more upset than the twins—that Lisa actually felt bad for the poor girl. Brownie was a good dog, but you had to watch him constantly because he'd always had a wayward streak.

Scariest of all was the way Hank had grabbed her wrist and then run off when the police showed up, like an insane person. She could still feel a ghostly twinge in her arm where he'd grabbed her. It had terrified her, instantly taken her back to that night two years ago when she'd told him she was leaving him, and he'd flown into a rage, punched holes in the walls, and smashed their furniture to pieces.

What had happened to the gentle, funny man she'd met and fallen in love with all those years ago? They'd been pretty much inseparable after their first date. They just clicked. Such a cliche, but it was true. They used to talk about how lucky they were to have found each other. Hank's parents had died horribly when he was twelve, and then his older brother was murdered shortly after he and Lisa were married. Lisa's own parents and little sister were killed in a car accident in Nagano Prefecture when she was eighteen. Neither had any other family to speak of. Two orphans brought together by chance and bound to one another like atoms sharing electrons.

The first eight years of their marriage were bliss. They back-packed in Mexico, cleaned a beach on an island in Malaysia after a tsunami, spent a summer hiking and camping in northern California. She got pregnant on their fifth anniversary, gave birth to two beautiful twin boys, Justin Thomas and James Henry, two months after they arrived in Tokyo. It was tough with two babies at first, but because Hank wasn't yet training every single day, he was a mostly stay-at-home dad, which allowed Lisa to start working after a few months. They were a team, and life as a foursome was good.

But when Hank began losing fights, everything changed. He became moody, impatient with her and short with the kids. He spent less and less time at home and more and more time in the gym. When he did come home, he'd toss Lisa a careless "Hey," drag himself across the room, and plop himself on the couch. The kids would try to play with him, and he'd tell them he was too tired. Then he'd spend the rest of the evening sighing as though somebody had died in between looking at his smart-phone and trying to find something to watch on TV. He was hurt all the time too, which was part of the problem. Broken bones. Dislocated joints. Cuts and bruises. A retinal tear that, but for a stroke of luck, would've left him blind in one eye. It seemed like he didn't care about his own health. She'd started to notice articles about fighters and football players diagnosed with CTE—chronic traumatic encephalopathy—after suffering repeated concussions, read how they became moody, depressed, suicidal even. Could CTE be the explanation for the changes she'd seen in Hank?

She pleaded with him to stop fighting. He could start a new career, do something different. Or go back to school maybe. Think about the kids, she'd say. Think about her. He would sit there and quietly listen. When she was finished, he'd say, "I'm okay, Lisa. A few more fights and if I'm still losing, I'll hang it up."

But he didn't.

She grew despondent. Lonely, desperate. And one day she did something stupid that marked the beginning of the end of their marriage: she kissed Pete Marini, a peck that he had turned into something she hadn't at all intended, and everything fell apart. Racked with guilt, she tried to explain to Hank later that night what had happened, and before she'd gotten the whole story out, he screamed at her, calling her a liar and a whore, convinced she'd fucked Pete. She tried to deny it, but he was beyond reach by that point, past all reason. He threw a glass at the wall, shattering it and scaring her into silence, which he took as proof of her guilt.

They stopped talking after that. For the next few months, Hank left at night and came back in the morning, and she had no idea where he went. When the two of them were around the kids, they pretended everything was normal, an unspoken agreement between them. But little kids are more perceptive than adults give them credit for. Justin and James could feel it, knew things weren't right between Mommy and Daddy. When they began acting out—James wetting the bed and Justin getting into trouble at school—and Hank acted like he didn't care, Lisa knew they couldn't stay. When she told him she was leaving with the kids and he went berserk, it only confirmed that she was doing the right thing. Until then he'd been violent only in the cage, but now he'd brought the violence home and was smashing things. What if he smashed her next? What if he hurt the kids? No. There was no way she was going to let that happen.

Pee-pong.

Still in her underwear, she hurriedly pulls on a T-shirt and a pair of old sweatpants. The kids left for school thirty minutes ago with the new babysitter. After dropping the kids off, Yayoi had said she was going to go home. Lisa wonders if maybe she forgot something and has come back? She was surprised when Yayoi showed up again this morning instead of Rumi, but apparently Rumi has the flu, not just a cold. Rumi has been watching the kids for a year now, and Lisa had been worried that the boys would make a fuss about the sudden change, but Yayoi is so bubbly and enthusiastic, the kids just love her.

Lisa goes to the monitor set in the living room wall and sees not Yayoi but two men in dark suits looking up into the CCTV camera. One of them has a shaved head and a neatly trimmed goatee, and the other is a giant of a man, tall and as big around as a sumo wrestler. Lisa has never seen either of them before.

The word that comes to mind as she looks at them on the screen is *chinpira*, the Japanese term for thugs. A chill ripples through her.

She pushes the button on the intercom. "*Hai?*" Yes?

The bald guy with the goatee says, "*Sumimasen! Okusama?*" Ma'am? Excuse me! His voice is way too loud and way too curt for this or any other time of day.

Lisa hears Hank's words: *You and the boys are in danger.* And suddenly her heart is pounding. But no, she thinks, it's just too crazy, so she tells herself to calm down. There must be a rational explanation for why these men are ringing her doorbell.

The bald guy sticks his face right up into the camera. "*Okusama!*" he says, much louder than the first time, so loud that it makes Lisa step back from the intercom. She presses the talk button.

"*Nan desuka?*" she says, loud and harsh to hide the quaver in her voice. What do you want?

The bald man says, "Can you come out? We want to talk to you about something." His tone is downright rude, hostile even, and his use of informal speech, as opposed to *keigo*, the polite form one normally uses with strangers, heightens Lisa's alarm.

Pee-pong.

Lisa steels herself, pushes the talk button again, and says in English, "What the hell do you want?" Thinking, hoping, that this will make them go away.

The bald man steps back, turns, and says something inaudible to his partner, who shrugs his huge shoulders.

Lisa kneads the hem of her T-shirt as she watches the men, panic rising in her chest. Then, to her relief, they turn and walk off. Lisa purses her lips and blows a gust of air from her cheeks. She calls down to the doorman, who confirms that, yes, the men have left the premises. Lisa really doesn't want to be a bitch, but she lets the doorman know she's not happy that the two men were able to get past him. This is supposed to be a secure building, after all. The doorman apologies profusely and explains that the men said they had an appointment with her. Lisa tells him that no, she didn't have an appointment with them, and if they show up again to please call the police.

As she walks down the hallway to the bedroom, a worm of doubt wriggles its way into her head, and she wonders if maybe what Hank said yesterday is true. But she pushes the doubt away when she sees the clock on the nightstand. She's going to be late for work.

❦

Twenty minutes later, Lisa is on her way to Aoyama Station, mulling the best way to achieve a compromise on a somewhat one-sided indemnity clause proposed by a customer.

She walks, dabbing at her forehead with a handkerchief. She considers calling Yayoi and telling her about the men who came to her door but decides against it. She doesn't want to alarm her. Better to wait until tonight when she gets home. It's hot and sticky, and she isn't looking forward to getting on the crowded train, even though it's air-conditioned and even though it's only three stops to work. Traffic on the street is heavy.

Which is why she doesn't notice the black Toyota van parked at the curb until the van's side door is sliding open with an electric whirr.

But by then it's too late.

Before Lisa has time to scream for help, three men fly out of the van and are pulling her into the vehicle.

It all happens so fast.

Which is not to say that Lisa goes easily or quietly. She's no fighter, but the moves and ideas Hank taught her years ago come back surprisingly quickly. She screams once at the top of her lungs to get someone's attention, sees a few startled faces in the stream of morning commuters, but no one stops. The bald men are holding onto her arms, while the fat guy is bent over, trying to grab her legs while Lisa kicks at him as hard as she can over and over until the point of her shoe hits the fat man right in the face. She feels a satisfying crunch and then a bolt of terror when the fat guy barely flinches and, roaring like a wounded hippo, scoops up one of her feet and plants it under one of his massive arms. Lisa launches herself backward into the bald men, snapping her head back in the hopes of head-butting one of them and misses. She screams and kicks the fat man again with her free foot, and then a gag is stuffed in her mouth and Lisa changes tack, going limp in an effort to slip out of their grasp, but it doesn't work and then one of the bald men punches her in the face twice and the world tilts and Lisa sees stars and feels herself go airborne, and the next thing she knows she's inside the van with the door closed.

A few seconds later, the van is moving and Lisa's hands are bound behind her back with what feels like a plastic cord and she registers the fat man behind the wheel and the bald men on either side of her. Every nerve in her body fizzing with fear and panic and rage, and she opens her mouth to say something, and that's when she hears a familiar sniffling and turns in her seat to see, in the middle of the rearmost seat, the babysitter, Yayoi, with her arms around the shoulders of two small figures on either side of her, both with black cloth hoods over their heads.

"*Mama?*" one of them says. It's Justin.

James says, "*Mom?*" and starts to cry.

Lisa's mind goes black save for a single thought: she'll do anything to protect her children from these people. Anything.

CHAPTER FORTY-SIX

FORTY MINUTES LATER, Fisher arrives in Ebisu on the JR Line.

At six in the morning, the sun hasn't even been up for an hour and it's already steaming hot, scattered commuters wiping sweat from their brows with handkerchiefs and fanning themselves with *uchiwa* as they hurry through the turnstiles and off to work.

He's got thirty minutes before he's scheduled to meet Marini in Hiroo. He goes to the bank of coin lockers where he stashed the gym bag. He takes a thousand-yen note from his pocket and is about to pay the locker fee when he feels the phone vibrate in his pocket. He fishes it out. There's a number on the screen ending with 4745.

Mari's number.

A feeling of foreboding worms its way under his skin. He hits Receive. "Mari?"

"Hank! There's someone here!" Her voice a frantic whisper.

"Mari, where are you?"

"I'm in the closet!"

Fisher wheels and runs to the escalator. "Mari, I'm coming."

Over the sound of her soft crying comes a metallic rattling. "*Kowai yo! Kowai!*" she says. I'm so scared!

Then a sound like an explosion, the bedroom door being kicked in, followed by the hiss of a man's voice telling Mari in Japanese to calm down, be quiet, everything is okay. Mari says in English "No!" then, "Help!"

Fisher says, "Mari!"

Three thumps and then a crash. Mari shrieks and her voice is cut short, and then another crash and the sound of shuffling feet, rustling, a series of grunts. Mari whimpering, breathing fast and irregular.

The line goes dead.

Fisher takes the remaining steps of the escalator two at a time. He bumps past a guy in a suit, sprints to the curb, and hails a cab. He tells the driver to go to Azabu Juban, worried he won't be able to make it to Hiroo in time to meet Marini, fearing he'll miss his chance to protect Justin and James from Shota and get out of this mess alive. He banishes the thought from his mind. He's going to protect them, and he's going to live.

But first he has to help Mari.

Fifteen minutes later, Fisher runs into the lobby of Mari's building and takes the elevator up to the sixth floor.

What if she's dead? Panic twists in his chest. Everyone, everything he touches gets hurt.

The elevator doors slide open. He dashes out onto the empty balcony walkway, past the level's four apartments to Mari's place, number 601. He grabs the door handle, expecting to find it locked. It's open. He jerks the door open and steps inside, blood thumping in his temples.

The AC is going, and it's cool and dim and still inside the apartment, the early morning sunlight muted by the still-closed curtains in the living room.

"Mari?"

His whole body buzzes with adrenaline. With a shaking hand he hits the light switch by the door. Standing there in the entrance, he can see straight down the hall into the living room, which is empty. He steps up into the hallway without removing his shoes, and a chill runs through him.

"Mari?"

He moves quickly toward the living room and hears a soft, gurgling rattle that makes his hair stand on end. Oh no. He hurries to the end of the hall and turns left into the kitchen and stops.

Mari is lying faceup on the floor in a big puddle of blood between the island counter and the cupboard. Her oversized T-shirt and sweatpants are soaked red, her eyes half open.

"Mari!"

Frantic, he drops to his knees beside her. His eyes find a steak knife lying parallel to the baseboard under the counter. *Oh Jesus.*

"Mari! Stay with me!" He looks up and down her body and counts one, two, three, four, five places she's been stabbed. Two on the right side of her stomach, under her rib cage, one on her right forearm, and two on her right shoulder. Blood is pumping steadily from the one under her rib cage. He has to stop the bleeding somehow. He pops up, slips in the blood on the floor, and almost falls. Heart in his throat, he yanks open drawers, searching for something to use to stop the bleeding.

Nothing.

He pulls open a cupboard door and spots a stack of dish towels. He snatches them, kneels beside Mari again. He pulls up Mari's shirt and applies two of the towels to the freely bleeding wound under her rib cage.

Ambulance.

Mari's landline is on the counter. Fisher rises on his knees, trying to keep pressure on Mari's abdomen as he reaches up and scrabbles around with his hand until it lands on the phone. He grabs it and pulls it off the counter and sets it on the floor. Pinches the receiver between his ear and shoulder and dials 119, Japan's emergency services number.

His pulse thuds thick in his ears. "My friend," he says to the operator, his voice high and tight with panic, "stabbed!" It's the only Japanese word that comes to him. He looks down at Mari. Her face is pale. He can't let her die. Another Japanese word comes to him: the word for ambulance.

"*Kyukyusha!*" he says, gasping for breath.

"Sir, please calm down and give me the address."

He doesn't know the address, so he says, "Azabu Juban," and gives her the name of the apartment building and unit number. The operator asks him questions about Mari's injuries, then instructs him to get some clean towels and press them onto the wound. Fisher tells her he's doing that already. She tells him to wait for the ambulance.

The towels in his hands are soaked now. He tosses them away and replaces them with two fresh ones. Mari lets out a little groan, winces, and turns her head away ever so slightly. "I'm sorry, baby, I know it hurts. The ambulance is coming."

If she hears him she doesn't show it. With his free hand he brushes away a strand of hair plastered to her pale face. Her skin is clammy. He remembers the way her face lit up the other night when she was talking about her vintage Snoopy collection. Her easy laughter. How he'd touched her hand and how she didn't look away when she noticed he was staring at her. The thought of never seeing her again feels like a fist around his heart.

Sirens sound outside, surprisingly close, two of them blaring a discordant duet.

Keeping the pressure on her abdomen, he takes Mari's left hand in his and gives it a gentle squeeze. "They're coming, baby. You're going to be okay." Her hand moves, a barely perceptible squeeze back. "I'm here," he says.

The hum of the elevator and then the echo of hurried footfalls in the corridor outside the apartment. A loud knock on the door.

"It's unlocked!" Fisher shouts in Japanese, his voice breaking. Three paramedics rush in carrying a stretcher, radios squawking. One takes over for Fisher, holding the towel on Mari's stomach, and the other prepares the stretcher. Fisher moves away, keeping his eyes on Mari while he answers the third man's questions: What's her name? When did this happen? Does he know who did this? How long has he been here? Fisher can hear himself respond, but it's as if someone else is talking while he watches them attend to Mari, mentally pleading for her to hang in there, as if she might be able to hear his thoughts. It's only when the paramedic asks Fisher for his name that he looks up and sees he isn't a paramedic.

He's a cop.

Fisher's heart stutters. He turns his face away and looks down as the cop continues his questions. The room tilts and slowly spins.

"Sir?" the cop says, concern in his voice. "Are you okay? Did you hear me?"

Fisher focuses his gaze on Mari, not wanting to give the cop a full view of his face. "No, I'm sorry, what did you say?" Another voice in the hallway draws his attention. He looks over. There's another cop, talking on the phone.

"I said I'm going to need you to come with us to the station to answer some more questions." The other cop walks into the room and talks in a low tone with his fellow officer.

Fisher is trapped. If he goes to the police station, the cops are going to figure out who he is. He'll be fucked, which means Lisa and the kids will be fucked.

The paramedics are loading Mari onto the stretcher now. Fisher addresses one of them. "Is she going to be okay?"

"It's hard to say," the paramedic says, "but her pulse is strong, and that's a good sign."

Fisher goes to her and takes her hand. "You're going to be okay, Mari." He addresses the paramedic again. "What hospital are you taking her to?"

"Nisseki, if they'll take her." The Red Cross Hospital.

Fisher glances at the two cops, who are talking quietly by the sliding glass door now. He sees the faces of his kids. He's got to protect them. It doesn't matter what happens to him.

He has to go, and it's now or never.

He steps into the entryway and walks right out the door.

CHAPTER FORTY-SEVEN

CAP PULLED DOWN low on his forehead, he walks quickly up Sendaizaka Hill, humming with panic. He checks over his shoulder. No sign yet of the two cops he just ditched. But Hiroo Station, where he's supposed to meet Marini, is a twelve-minute walk, and any second now they're going to be chasing him on their bikes.

A young guy in a beige suit hurries along on the other side of the street, headed in the opposite direction. He slows when he sees Fisher, his eyes going wide with horror.

Fisher looks down at himself, sees Mari's blood all over him. It's on his hands and arms and the front of his shirt and on his knees. He looks like he's just murdered someone.

A car zooms by.

Breath catching in his chest, he ducks into the vestibule of a liquor store that hasn't opened yet. Yanks his shirt off, uses it to hurriedly wipe off as much of the dried blood on his hands and arms as he can, then balls it up and tosses it onto the ground. Then he darts out and breaks into a sprint up the hill toward the South Korean Embassy.

Immediately he sees a security guard in front of the embassy entrance. Directly across the street from the guard is a cop standing at attention with his *jo*—a four-and-a-half-foot-long wooden staff carried by the riot police. Both of them are looking right at Fisher.

Heart pounding, he slows his pace to a fast jog, looks straight ahead, and forces himself to breathe rhythmically, hoping they don't notice the blood on his hands and arms and knees. *Hey fellas, just out for my morning run.*

No such luck. They gawk at him as he runs past, but neither of them moves.

Fisher recalls reading somewhere that the duties of a Japanese riot cop are strictly circumscribed, meaning if he's guarding an embassy and a crazy, blood-covered foreigner runs past him, he can't give chase. That's cold comfort, though, because a cacophony of sirens goes up, a shrill wailing that seems to come at him from all directions. He kicks faster, adrenaline surging in his veins.

When he reaches the five-way intersection at the top of the hill, he spots a tiny public restroom on the second side street to the left. He goes there, slips into the men's room, turns on the faucet, and frantically splashes water onto his arms and legs, washing the blood away.

The too-close squeal of bicycle brakes. The squawk of a radio. A man's voice shouting, "I'm at the intersection. I don't see him."

Maybe he should just go outside and give himself up. Bring all of this to an end. But if he does that, will the cops believe him? Will they protect Lisa and the kids from Shota? Why would they? He's the guy they've been looking for, the one they suspect of murdering that man in the Yotsuya stash house, and now they're going to think he's also the one who attacked Mari.

No. Giving himself up is out of the question. He wheels around. There are two stalls. Next to the stall on the left is a storage closet. He opens the door. The closet is two and half feet wide and three and a half feet deep. There's a bucket on the floor, a mop resting in the corner. Fisher gently pushes the bucket aside with his foot and squeezes himself into the tiny space and quietly pulls the door closed.

The radio squawks again, louder, and then the cop's heels click on the tiled floor. The sound of the stall doors being opened, one at a time. There's a pause. Fisher practically holding his breath, waiting to be discovered like a trapped animal, internally chanting, *don't look in here don't look in here don't look in here.*

The scuff of the cop's shoes and then the sound of him pedaling away on his bicycle and Fisher can breathe again. But not for long, he knows. He pulls out his phone. It's already a quarter after seven. He was supposed to meet Marini in front of Hiroo Station fifteen minutes ago. He pulls up the number, hits redial.

"Dude," says Marini, "I've been waiting. Where are you?"

"Public restroom at the top of Sendaizaka. You have to come get me. There are cops everywhere."

"Hang tight, I'll be right there."

The Suburban arrives six minutes later, Marini's music thumping low. Fisher bursts out of the stall, dashes out of the restroom, dives into the back seat of the SUV.

"What happened?" Marini says, giving him a startled glance before pulling away from the curb. He eases the car down a narrow street toward Shirokane. He pulls his shades down on his nose with a finger, eyes Fisher in the rearview, brow knit with consternation, the Route 69 pendant dangling there beneath his gaze. "What happened? Why are you all wet? Where's your shirt?"

Fisher rubs his face with his hands. "Just go."

Marini turns, glances down at Fisher's feet, obviously looking for the bag. Not seeing it, his frown deepens for a fraction of a second.

The AC inside the SUV is blasting. Fisher takes his cap off.

Marini shoots him another glance. He takes a rag from the glovebox and holds it out to Fisher. "Don't think I've ever seen you without hair."

Fisher mops his brow with the rag, ignoring the comment.

They come to the stoplight at the top of Sendaizaka Hill.

"Hank."

"Yeah."

"I gotta ask."

Fisher opens his eyes. "Yeah?"

"Where's the money?"

"Meguro Station."

"Meguro Station," repeats Marini.

"I put it in a coin locker."

Marini nods. "Okay, good. That's good. What do you say we run over there and get it and then we'll go somewhere you can rest and we can talk. That sound all right?"

Fisher isn't even listening at this point. He keeps seeing Mari on the floor of her kitchen, blood pumping out of the wound in her stomach. Suddenly he remembers his call with Marini last night. He'd given him Mari's address, and Marini had promised to send someone to protect her.

I'll get one of my cop buddies to keep an eye on her.

He stares at Marini. Had it been a lie? Anger surges up into his throat. "Where was your buddy, Pete?"

Marini frowns at him in the rearview. "Huh?"

"You said you'd send a cop to keep an eye on my friend

last night," says Fisher, clenching and unclenching his jaw. "Remember?"

Marini's frown deepens. One hand on the steering wheel, he makes a placating gesture with the other. "Hold on."

"She was stabbed! Where the fuck was your guy?!"

"What are you talking about?"

Fisher's head fills with a red fog. "Someone broke into her apartment and tried to kill her," he shouts. "You told me last night you'd make sure she was safe!"

"How do you know this?"

"I was just there!" Fisher leans forward and grabs the top of the front passenger seat. "I found her on the floor. She was bleeding out. I called 119 and..." Tears well in Fisher's eyes.

Marini's mouth drops open. "Jesus. Hank, I —"

"Where was your friend, Pete?" says Fisher, his voice hoarse with emotion.

Marini turns right onto Meiji-dori Boulevard, pulls over, and puts the car in Park. He turns in his seat and faces Fisher. "I called my buddy like I said I would, okay? I gave him the address, and he was supposed to keep watch outside her apartment. But there was a bank robbery this morning, okay? First one in a long time in Japan. He must have gotten pulled away. I'm sorry, Hank, I really am, brother."

Anger and confusion churn in Fisher's chest.

Marini shakes his head like he's pissed. "It was Shota, Hank. It had to be."

He's right, Fisher thinks. It had to be Shota. His crew stabbed Terry and left him for dead and then they cut Akio's throat. It can't be a coincidence that Mari was attacked with a knife. The gang must have gone to Lounge O looking for information on Fisher's whereabouts. Threatened the girls and gotten Mari's address from one of them. Guilt pangs in Fisher's chest.

They arrive in Meguro ten minutes later and park curbside in front of Atre 2. Marini turns in his seat. "We're going to make sure no one else gets hurt, but you have to trust me."

Fisher nods.

"What's the locker number?"

Fisher tells him and gives him the combination.

Marini gets out of the car and runs off. He returns with the bag in less than five minutes, puts it in the back of the SUV, and climbs back behind the wheel.

Ten minutes later, they pull up in front of a ten-story apartment tower not far from the Tengenjibashi freeway entrance. Marini parks in one of the four parking spaces out front. He cuts the engine, grabs a blue hoodie from the passenger seat, and hands it to Fisher. "Put this on."

Fisher does as he's told. Marini retrieves the gym bag from the cargo area of the vehicle, and Fisher follows him into the building. The lobby has that new building smell. They take the elevator up to the tenth floor, then Marini leads Fisher down a carpeted hallway to the room farthest from the elevator. There's a security keypad next to the door. Marini punches in the code, then opens the door and steps aside to let Fisher in.

The lights are on. At about four hundred square feet, the place isn't much bigger than Fisher's own apartment in Shinjuku. The difference being that this place isn't a rat hole. It's got a small, albeit real kitchen, recessed lighting everywhere. Beige plush carpeting in the living room, with a comfy-looking sofa and chair, big flat-screen TV on one wood-paneled wall, and a print of that famous Ansel Adams shot of El Capitan on the other. A hint of spice in the air, some kind of macho potpourri or something. It's a nice place. The rent can't be cheap. How can a government employee afford a place like this?

As if he's read Fisher's thoughts, Marini says, "Friend of mine owns the place. He lives down in Okinawa most of the year, only comes up to Tokyo every once in a while. I get to use it the rest of the time." He takes a bottle of water from the fridge, tosses it to Fisher, and gestures toward the living room. "Make yourself comfortable. Try to relax, all right?"

Fisher's head feels like it's full of buzzing insects. He couldn't relax if he wanted to. He keeps thinking of Lisa, Justin, and James, keeps telling himself that he has to get them to safety before they end up like Mari. Oh God, Mari. But beneath his twitching nerves is an undercurrent of fatigue so deep, it makes his bones ache. He needs to sit for a moment. Just for a moment so he can catch his breath and clear his head. He goes to the sofa and takes a seat, opens the bottle of water, and drains it in a few thirsty gulps. The sofa like quicksand under him. Pulling him down.

Marini's voice from the kitchen: "I'm going to put this in the bedroom, okay?" He pats the bag under his arm.

Fisher nods, suddenly drowsy. Whatever you say, Pete. He closes his eyes. Immediately he sees Mari lying in a pool of blood, followed by the image of Lisa and the kids on the sidewalk outside their apartment tower. He opens his eyes.

No. He can't sleep. He tries to rise, but it's as if his legs are giving his brain the middle finger. *Fuck off, we're not going anywhere.*

Sounds from the kitchen. Marini rummaging around in the fridge. Did he already take the bag into the bedroom? "You want a sandwich?" Marini says over his shoulder. "Got some roast beef."

Fisher's stomach growls at the mention of food. He doesn't remember the last time he ate. He hears himself say, "Sure," and feels the velvet fist of exhaustion close tight around him. He decides he has to trust Marini. He can't protect Lisa and the kids without the man's help.

But first he'll rest here for a little longer.

Marini works on the sandwich, talking the whole time. Fisher's brain is too addled to make sense of the words. He leans back into the sofa, floating. Eyelids heavy, but everything else light as a feather. He can't help his family if he's running on fumes, can he? A few minutes' rest, that's all he needs. When he wakes up he'll be recharged and ready to go.

By the time Marini brings the sandwich over to him, he's fast asleep.

CHAPTER FORTY-EIGHT

FROM THE WINDOW of his second-floor office in Kabukicho, Aikawa Yasuhiro watches three sparkly girls down on the street, dressed to the nines with perfect hair and perfect faces, walking and talking, pointing this way and that. Girls out for a night on the town.

They pass a fat foreigner in a tent of a T-shirt standing outside a 7-Eleven store, Yankees cap on his head, snow-white mustache that makes him look like an old walrus. He stares at the three girls with sad, hungry walrus eyes. His mustache moves, and the girls turn in unison, flash him a collective look of disgust, and run off.

Aikawa chuckles. He can't blame Mr. Walrus for trying. Kabukicho is a red light district after all. He imagines it's probably hard for foreigners to tell the whores from the good girls.

Good girls and bad girls. Touts and tourists. Hosts and whores.

Kabukicho's got them all.

Originally a swamp called Tsunohazu, Kabukicho became a duck sanctuary in the Meiji Period (1868 to 1912), which gave way to a water purification facility in 1893, then a school for girls in 1920. Then came the war and Uncle Sam's firebombing of Tokyo, and the area was burnt to the ground like most of the rest of the city and most of its people too. After the war, a failed plan to build a kabuki theater inspired the name that would eventually become associated with the area and a different kind of swamp. Nowadays, the place is full of bars, nightclubs, host and hostess bars. Massage parlors, strip clubs, brothels, and peep shows.

It's also home to the offices of 120 different organized crime groups, including Aikawa's.

His phone buzzes. It's Hashimoto, no doubt calling to give him the latest on Hank Fisher's movements.

"I just sent you a video," Hashimoto says.

Aikawa puts the phone on speaker, sets it down on his desk, then settles into his ergonomic chair and opens the messaging app on his laptop. The icon for the video pops up. Aikawa clicks on it and watches with surprise and amusement as Hank Fisher runs shirtless up Sendaizaka Hill with what looks like blood all over his hands and shirt.

"What's he doing? Is that blood?"

"I think so."

Aikawa shakes his head, watching Fisher on the screen pumping his legs and arms as Hashimoto and Ryu trail a hundred yards behind him in their car. Incredible.

"We followed him from Meguro to an apartment building in Azabu Juban," says Hashimoto.

Fisher reaches the top of the hill, turns left into a side street, and ducks into a tiny public restroom. The video ends. Aikawa hits replay and strokes his big chin. He feels a migraine coming on. He started getting them when he was in his teens, and it wasn't until he was well into his thirties that he finally saw an orthodontist who told him the headaches were likely caused by his pronounced underbite. A malformation of his jaw, it could be fixed but would take several surgeries, the orthodontist had said, and even then there was no guarantee that the migraines would stop. So Aikawa decided to live with them.

He takes a bottle of Tramadol from the top drawer of his desk, shakes out a pill, and dry-swallows it. Rolls his shoulders a few times and massages the back of his neck.

Hashimoto is still talking. "He goes inside, and me and Ryu wait for him to come back out. Ten minutes go by, fifteen, twenty. We're thinking, anytime now he's gonna come out. Then we hear the sirens. First we don't think nothing of it, probably another geezer kicked the bucket. But the sirens keep getting closer and closer and then we see the fire truck coming up the street, lights flashing. Thing pulls up right outside the building Fisher went in. Couple cops on bikes race up, park, and run inside with the paramedics. Me and Ryu, we're waiting there in the car for, like, ten minutes, and then all of a sudden Fisher comes charging out all covered in blood. He takes off like a shot, then he stops, rips off his shirt, and runs again. Ryu and me, we're tripping."

This Hank Fisher character is something else. First, he injures Sato, one of the people he's working for, at the meeting the other night at Club Deluxe. Aikawa was there, saw the whole thing happen. One moment Sato was standing there looking lost amid the chaos of the brawl that had broken out, and the next Fisher had thrown him on his head. According to Aikawa's sources, the very next day Fisher was strong-armed by Aoyama Shota into stealing a gym bag full of money from one of his uncle's stash houses. Whereupon Fisher made off with the stolen money, leaving a dead body behind.

It's crazy. Like something out of a TV show.

What happened next, though, was even crazier. Suzuki found out his nephew was behind the robbery and put a hit out on him. *A hit on his own nephew.* Then, a day later, the old man dropped dead from an apparent heart attack. Emphasis on *apparent,* because the word on the street is that Aoyama had the old man killed in a pre-emptive strike.

Nice family.

Anyway, rumor has it that Fisher is running around with a hundred million yen, and Aikawa would very much like to relieve him of it. So when a one-armed bookie named Emoto called him two days ago, saying he'd spotted Fisher going into an Internet café in Meguro, Aikawa sent Hashimoto and Ryu out to tail him. So far, though, they've followed him around for the past forty-eight hours and gotten not one glimpse of the infamous bag of cash.

"What happened after he went into the bathroom?"

"Another foreigner comes rolling up in a black SUV and picks him up. We follow them back to Meguro, and they park outside the station, and the big guy gets out and runs down into the subway. And here's the good part: Guess what he was carrying when he came back out?"

CHAPTER FORTY-NINE

FISHER WAKES WITH a start from a dreamless sleep, no idea where he is. He sits up. It's nearly dark outside, fading dusky light visible through the open curtains on his left. He looks around the room: big flat-screen TV. El Capitan on a wood-paneled wall. He's at Marini's place. A jumble of images cycles through his brain: Mari, covered in blood; Akio's bloody corpse; Terry with tubes going in and out of him; Brownie's body in the blue bucket; Justin and James in the video with the chubby woman in the park.

Where's Marini? How long has he been asleep? He springs off the sofa. "Pete?"

The bedroom door opens and Marini walks out. He smiles. "Hey, you're up. Dude, you were out like a light."

"What time is it?"

Marini checks his watch. "Seven thirty."

Panic seizes Fisher. He's lost the whole day.

"I stepped out for a few hours after lunch, and you were sawing logs," says Marini. "Came back about four, and you were still out." He goes to the kitchen and opens the fridge.

Heart pounding, Fisher says, "We need to go. Now."

Marini comes into the dining room carrying the sandwich he'd made earlier for Fisher on a plate. "Go where, Hank?"

"To Lisa's. We should go and just get them."

Marini sets the sandwich down on the table. "You already tried to do that, remember? You think we can just waltz over there now and ring the bell and they'll just come with us? You want to kidnap them? Is that it?"

Fisher remembers the look of anger on Lisa's face when he grabbed her wrist and tried to get her to watch the videos Shota sent him: *Asshole!* Marini is right. Short of kidnapping them, there's no way to get Lisa and the twins to safety. "I don't know," he says, his voice clipped with frustration, "but we have to do something."

Marini says, "Don't worry, dude. I have an idea." He gestures at the sandwich. "Why don't you get some food in you first; then we can talk."

Fisher looks at the sandwich. Suddenly he's ravenous. He grabs it and devours it, eating so fast, he barely tastes it.

Marini watches him with a bemused expression.

Swallowing the last bite of the sandwich, Fisher looks at Marini, expectant, fully awake now, resuscitated by the rest and the infusion of calories.

The sound of a toilet flushing. A faucet running.

Fear slams into Fisher like a battering ram. He shoots a glance at Marini as he pops up out of his chair. He fucking knew it, he knew Marini was going to double-cross him. Fisher jerks his head toward the source of the noise in time to see a door open and a man emerge from the bathroom. He's tall and wiry. Grizzled with a salt-and-pepper buzz cut, hooded eyes, and a mustache over a thin line of a mouth. He's wearing a white T-shirt under a thin blue blazer and faded jeans. Fisher glances toward the door, gets ready to run for it.

"Hank!" says Marini. "Chill!"

Synapses firing all at once, Fisher's eyes flick back and forth between the grizzled man and Marini. "What the fuck is this?"

The grizzled man stares at him, expressionless, perfectly still.

Marini says, "This is Nitta-san. He's a friend."

A friend? Fisher shakes his head. If this guy is a friend, why didn't Marini tell him about him earlier? "Nuh uh. No way."

Marini widens his eyes in a pacifying expression and motions toward the dining table. "Hank, sit." His tone calm, soothing.

"Who is he?" says Fisher.

Nitta reaches inside his blazer and produces a leather wallet, flips it open, and shows Fisher a badge.

Oh fuck.

Fisher is suddenly dizzy with fight-or-flight. He looks back and forth between Marini and the cop. There's nowhere to go. It's as though he's unwittingly stepped into one of those movie booby traps where you're walking along in the forest and suddenly you're yanked off your feet and hanging upside down from a tree. His mouth fills with a bitter taste. Marini's betrayed him after all. How could he be so stupid? He grimaces and looks at the cop. "I didn't kill anyone." Marini and Nitta look at each other, then back at Fisher.

Nitta says, "I am not going to arrest you." He has a gentle rasp of a voice, like polished gravel.

Marini says, "Dude, we know you didn't kill anyone. Besides, if I wanted to turn you in, I'd have done it soon as I got the bag. Half the TMPD's after you."

It's true. Marini could've had him arrested as soon as he got hold of the money, but he didn't. So then what is this?

Marini says, "I can understand you being paranoid, brother. But you got to trust me here. I want to help you."

Fisher's throat is parched. He stares at Marini. He still doesn't trust this man. Not even close. But it's worth hearing him out because Fisher is out of options. "All right."

"Good."

"How are you going to help me?"

Marini gestures at the dining table. "Sit down and we'll explain everything."

Keeping his eyes on the two men, Fisher takes a seat.

Marini and Nitta sit on either side of him. Marini looks at Nitta, then back at Fisher. "We're going to work those *yak* connections I told you about, get the gang off your back." He chucks a thumb at Nitta. "Nitta-san here is with the Organized Crime Unit. He knows all those clowns *personally*."

Nitta nods.

"And he's already running interference at TMPD. He's going to get you out from their crosshairs."

"How's he going to do that?"

Marini waves his hand like *don't worry about it*. "He'll take care of it."

"What about Lisa and the kids?"

"We'll get them to a safe location, make sure they stay there until all this blows over."

"When?"

"Soon as we work out the details, brother."

"Fuck the details. Why can't you just send someone for them right now?"

"First things first. We're going to take Shota down, and we need your help to do that."

"Fuck that! He's going to kill them!"

Marini shakes his head. "He won't."

"You don't know that!"

291

"Yes, I do." Marini points to the bedroom. "Because I know he's fucked without that money. Do you know what it's for?"

"Of course not. How would I know that?"

"It's for guns, dude."

With a shiver, Fisher remembers the crack of the gunshots in the alley where Shota's men tried to kill him a few days ago.

Marini continues. "Shota's got a guy on one of the U.S. bases who's agreed to sell him five hundred guns."

This surprises Fisher. A *yakuza* buying one or two guns from a shady American soldier he can imagine. But five hundred? He's never heard of anything like that. "Here in Japan?" he says. "How is that even possible?"

Marini turns to Nitta. "Nitta-san, tell him."

Nitta fixes Fisher with a hooded stare. "You are correct. Obtaining firearms is extremely difficult in Japan. However, it is not impossible. Organized crime groups have many ways to do it. They can smuggle the guns into the country by disassembling them and shipping the parts together with other products. But that is very difficult. An easier way is to find someone on one of the U.S. military bases here in Japan who can provide the weapons. This is also difficult, but it is easier than smuggling."

Marini nods. "That's what Shota did. He's already made a down payment of a hundred grand. A *nonrefundable* down payment."

Fisher tries to imagine five hundred guns suddenly on the streets of Tokyo. He pictures people getting shot in dark alleys, American-style mass shootings on the trains.

As if he's read Fisher's mind, Nitta nods gravely and says, "It is a very dangerous situation."

"What's he plan on doing with them?"

"We don't know," says Marini. "But with Uncle Jun gone,

the Tanabe-*kai* is breaking apart. It's a good bet Shota's going to make a play for control of whatever territory he can get his hands on."

"It will be a war," says Nitta.

Marini says, "If Shota doesn't come through with the rest of the money, not only does he lose a hundred grand, but the American is going to be pissed because now he has to find another buyer, and it's not like he signed an NDA or anything with Shota, so no way is the guy going to keep his mouth shut about it. And once all the little Tanabe-*kai* splinter groups catch word that Shota is trying to buy guns, how much you want to bet that they pause their little turf wars so they can take him out?"

Fisher softly thumps the fingers of his right hand on the glass top of the table. There's no reason for him not to believe any of this. But if it's true, there's also no reason to believe Shota wouldn't hurt Lisa and the kids to lure Fisher out and get the money back. What if he killed one of them? He takes a deep breath, holds it a moment, and lets it out. He rises from his seat and walks over to the sliding glass door. Outside is a small balcony, over which he can see the Tengenjibashi on-ramp to the Shuto Expressway. Beyond the freeway stretches the residential neighborhood of Shirokane. He turns and looks at Marini and Nitta. "I'm supposed to call him. What's your plan?"

Marini looks at Nitta then back at Fisher and nods. "He's going to tell you to meet him somewhere. You take the money with you and you go. You won't see us, but we'll be right behind you the whole way. You hand over the money. Nitta and his boys sweep in and arrest these assholes. End of story."

Fisher almost laughs out loud. "Just like that, huh?"

Marini holds a hand up as if to say *Hear me out.* "We're

293

going to put a transmitter in the bag. We'll know exactly where you are at all times."

How many movies has Fisher seen where a bug is placed in a bag or some poor schmo is wired and the gizmo stops working? Or the bad guys discover it? "I'm not going anywhere until I know my family is safe."

Before Marini can respond, Fisher's phone buzzes against his leg. Paranoia arrows into him. He fishes the phone out of his pocket. Two banner notifications from an unknown caller stare up at him from the screen.

OPEN NOW.

His throat goes dry. He clicks the first one open. There's an image file attached. He taps it with his thumb, and a photo appears on the screen: Justin and James sitting on a bench with their backs against a concrete wall, a small metal table in front of them. Justin is looking into the camera with a bewildered expression. James is frowning, his mouth turned down at the corners, the face he makes when he's mad and is about to cry. Both of them are holding boxes of chocolate-covered pretzels. Lisa sits next to them, rigid on the edge of the bench, hands behind her, probably cuffed. Her eyes are red-rimmed, her lips pressed into a grim line.

Fisher can't breathe. He staggers a step, puts his forehead on the cool surface of the sliding glass door. He opens the other file, and the floor falls away under his feet. In the second picture, Lisa, Justin, and James are sitting on the same bench, but they have black hoods over their heads. Looming behind them is a huge man in a suit. His head is not visible, but Fisher doesn't have to see the face to know it's Matchan.

His knees buckle, his terror for his family snapping and popping in him like a live creature being fried in oil.

There's something on the table in front of Lisa, Justin, and James. He expands the photo and his heart freezes.

It's Brownie's leash.

Anyone who was ever in a schoolyard scrap knows how bad it sucks when you get the wind knocked out of you. The sudden force of the blow causes your diaphragm to spasm, which for several moments makes it impossible to refill your emptied lungs, and you feel like you're going to die.

"Hank."

This doesn't feel like that. This feels like Fisher doesn't have any lungs at all, like they've been ripped out of his chest and stuffed into his mouth.

The room spins crazily.

"*Hank.*"

Fisher turns around and holds the phone up to show Marini. Marini and Nitta both rise from the table and rush over to Fisher. Marini takes the phone from Fisher's hand, studies the picture for a moment, and then shows it to Nitta. They exchange a look Fisher doesn't like at all. The phone buzzes again. Marini looks at it, then locks eyes with Fisher and says, passing the phone back to him, "Stay calm."

Fisher glares at Marini and flips him the bird, then turns back to the window and presses Receive.

"You get the pictures?" Shota says, in his DJ baritone.

Fisher opens his mouth to speak. His lips form the word *yes* but no sound comes out.

"*Hey.* You there?"

"Yes," says Fisher, his voice a hoarse whisper.

"So we understand each other now?"

"Yes."

"They're cute kids. Be too bad if something happened to them."

No no no. He struggles to breathe, sucking air like a fish. "I'll give you your money," he finally gasps.

"Yes, you will," says Shota. "Be at the entrance to the Oedo Line at Roppongi Station, with the money, at eleven sharp. Come alone. We'll be watching you. If we see anyone even near you, Matchan is going to do to your kids what he did to their doggie."

Click.

CHAPTER FIFTY

FISHER STANDS THERE with the phone in his hand, his face as white as a sheet.

Marini thinks the poor asshole might pass out. "You okay, brother?"

Fisher says, "I need to use the bathroom."

Marini says, "Of course."

When the bathroom door closes, Nitta says, "*Aitsu, daijobu ka?*" Is he going to be okay?

The sound of Fisher running the faucet.

Marini makes a dismissive gesture. "Don't worry, he'll be fine." He walks into the kitchen and texts Shota: *All set on our end. You?*

Shota's reply comes a couple of seconds later: *Good to go.*

Marini chuckles. Fucking liar. Aoyama Shota is smooth, but he's not nearly as smooth as he thinks he is.

This isn't the first time Marini and Nitta have done business with Shota. Their relationship goes back several years, in fact. It's been grunt work, mostly, a hodgepodge of shakedowns, muscle work, the occasional drug deal. None of it good for much more than a couple extra grand in pocket money now and then.

But money is money.

Once, a couple of years ago, Marini and Nitta got their hands on several hundred tabs of yaba—low-quality meth mixed with caffeine—and sold it all to Shota at a ridiculous markup. Another time, they trashed the house of a club owner who owed Shota's crew protection money. Most recently, they beat up a guy Shota was convinced was putting the moves on his then-girlfriend. Actually, it was Marini who tuned the guy up. Nitta stood by and watched because he won't engage in violence unless it's payback for someone putting the hurt on a woman or a kid. Marini has always gotten a kick out of the contradiction— Nitta, the sorta-peace-loving but otherwise crooked-as-fuck cop.

Anyway, Shota's jobs were all small-time stuff until he contacted Marini a month ago and said he wanted to buy guns.

Marini asked him what kind and how many, expecting the answer to be a couple of handguns. And indeed, Shota said he wanted pistols, but then he asked how many a million dollars would buy him.

A. Million. Dollars.

Marini's balls tingled as he imagined himself on the beach in Phuket, tropical drink in hand, a harem of whores tending to his every need.

He didn't believe it at first. Neither did Nitta. They both thought Shota was full of shit. There was no way he had that kind of money. Marini told Shota he wanted a down payment, nonrefundable, of a hundred grand or no deal, expecting the asshole to balk, which he did at first.

But then he actually came up with the money.

Things aren't nearly as expensive in Japan as they used to be. Marini knows places where you can get laid in a small but clean hotel room for a hundred fifty bucks. He also knows restaurants where thirty bucks will buy you a feast. Depending on what it is you're buying though, a million bucks is still worth a lot less than it is just about anywhere else.

Especially when what you're buying is guns.

Not that Marini ever had any intention of spending that much on Shota's guns. No fucking way. He was going to soak Mr. Earrings.

Marini knows a guy on one of the bases, goes by the name Dee, who can get him anything, and in bulk. You want four cases of Cap'n Crunch? Dee's your guy. A year's supply of American-size Tampax? Same. You need ten pairs of tactical night vision goggles? Talk to Dee.

Marini knew Dee could get him guns too, because Dee had told him so. Marini arranged to meet him at a Denny's out in Chofu, and over pancakes he popped the question: If Marini had—hypothetically speaking, of course—say, three hundred grand to spend on handguns, could Dee fill the order?

Dee speared a syrup-drenched piece of pancake into his mouth and smiled as he chewed, because wouldn't you know it, he knew just where to get five hundred old Beretta M9s. Perfect, thought Marini. The Beretta M9 had been the U.S. Army's handgun of choice until recently, when it plunked down a little more than half a billion dollars to upgrade to the Sig Sauer P320.

Now, the M9s were being phased out.

Which meant they were out there on the white, gray, and black markets. And apparently five hundred of them had fallen off the back of a truck, so to speak, and were sitting in a warehouse on one of the U.S. military bases in Japan, waiting to be shipped to some third-world country.

Dee said Marini would have to take the weapons as-is. He

couldn't guarantee their condition. And his price was four hundred grand for all five hundred.

Three fifty, Marini countered.

Done, said Dee.

Marini called Shota, said he could provide the guns but Shota had better come up with the rest of the money. Shota said not to worry about it, and they set up the meet.

That was three days ago.

And then, what do you know, Marini gets a call in the middle of the night from Hank Fisher, who, it turns out, is in deep, deep shit. Which in and of itself tickled Marini pink, because the bullshit that happened after he had tried to fuck Lisa ended up costing him his marriage. But, so, he listens to Fisher's sob story, and everything goes from good to fantastic for Pete Marini. Fisher tells him about the "one-time job" he did for the Tanabe-*kai* and how he completely fucked it up, accidentally putting one of the very guys he was working for in a coma, and *then* it got even better. Fisher ended up being used by Shota to jack a stash house and steal the very million bucks that Shota intended as payment for the guns he's agreed to buy from Marini. Which was *perfect*, because it meant that now Marini could call Dee and tell him the deal was off, because Shota couldn't come up with the money after all. Dee was pissed, but not too pissed; Marini gave him half of Shota's hundred-grand down payment for his trouble.

And now there's a million bucks in untraceable *yakuza* cash sitting in Marini's bedroom.

Until today, he'd been trying to reel Fisher in so he could snag the money. No easy feat given that he's a person of interest in two murder investigations: the dead guy in the stash house, and poor Akio.

Oh yeah, and now the girl in Azabu Juban. Unless she's still alive, in which case it could be a problem if she got a good look at Marini's face. But Fisher said she was bleeding out when he found her, so Marini's not too worried, and he isn't planning on sticking around for much longer anyway.

It's all coming together.

There is one small wrinkle, though. Nitta is expecting to get half of the cash. But Marini has no intention of giving the cop any more. Because who has done all the work on this deal? Marini. Shota came to *him*. Dee was *his* connection, and so was Fisher for that matter, and he's worked his ass off running around, setting everything up, reeling Fisher in. The only thing Nitta has done is keep his ear to the ground, and Marini is not about to fork over half a fucking million bucks to the man for eavesdropping on his Organized Crime Unit buddies while they gossiped around the watercooler.

He's going to have to do something about old Nitta. And it's kind of a shame. They've been a good team over the years. But a man's gotta do what he's gotta do.

He reminds himself there's also the matter of Fisher's kids and Lisa. Marini remembers when he'd pulled Lisa into his lap that day—how long ago was it? Two years? The way she let him kiss her at first, and then pushed him away when he slipped her a little tongue, even scratched his face when he tried to put his hand down her pants. The little cock tease. And all the drama that ensued afterward. It was hilarious. Fisher had acted like such a pussy. He'd been so convinced that Marini had fucked her. Whatever, dude. Marini honestly doesn't know whether Shota will make good on his promise to kill Lisa and the twins when he discovers that Fisher doesn't have his money. What he knows for certain, though, is that Shota will kill Fisher when he sees what's in the bag.

And Marini will be right here in this room, with the money, when it happens.

After that? Watch out, Phuket, 'cause here comes Pete Marini.

He has to stop himself from giggling. Sometimes the way the universe works is so fucking cool.

The bathroom door opens. Fisher emerges looking only slightly less shell-shocked.

Marini gestures toward the dining table and says in a sympathetic tone, "Sit down, brother, let's figure this out."

PART THREE

CHAPTER FIFTY-ONE

AT ELEVEN SHARP, Fisher stands outside the entrance to the Oedo Line at Roppongi Station as per Shota's instructions, dread and resolve playing catch along the length of his spine.

Shota calls at 11:01. "Take the Oedo Line to Shinjuku. I'll call you again in ten minutes."

The phone buzzes again as he steps off the train at Shinjuku. Shota tells him to take the Oedo Line back the way he came and ride it to Shiodome Station. Then Shota tells him to take Yurikamome, an automated light rail, to Shibaura-futo Station. From there, he is to walk about four hundred yards to Kaigan Park, a small park overlooking Tokyo Bay.

He's one of only two passengers to get off at Shibaura-futo. His mouth dry and sweat pouring down his back, he takes the stairs down to the street, hikes the heavy gym bag up on his shoulder, and moves briskly in the dim light under the elevated expressway, passing several warehouses and waterfront apartment towers.

Utterly alone he walks, nerves frying like they've been hooked up to a giant battery. Marini and the cop had argued with him when he told them that Shota had warned him to come alone. Marini said that was crazy. Said there was no reason Shota wouldn't just kill him once he had the money. And why did Fisher come to Marini in the first place if he wasn't going to accept his help? Don't be ridiculous, he said. Backup from the TMPD would be out there with them. They'd hide a transmitter in the bag and stay far enough away not to be detected by Shota's crew but close enough to swoop in as soon as the gang appeared in the park. They would strike so hard and fast, the gang wouldn't know what hit them. Once Shota was in custody, he would tell them where Lisa, Justin, and James were, and they would be safe.

Fisher refused. How could Marini be so sure? He kept seeing the photo of Lisa, Justin, and James, Brownie's leash on the table in front of them. It was too risky. Too many things could go wrong.

Now it's just him.

Traffic whooshes on the expressway overhead, but down here on the street, the only cars are a few taxis parked at the curb, their orange out-of-service signs lit up in their windshields.

His plan is simple: the money for Lisa and the kids. He'll hide the bag somewhere in the park and he'll tell Shota where it is only after he's let them go.

He's almost to the park when a horrifying thought occurs to him. What if Marini switched bags on him? He'd taken the bag into his bedroom this morning, and Fisher didn't see it again until he brought it out just before Fisher left.

Up ahead is a mostly empty Times pay parking lot with a tiny security guard station that looks closed for the night. He steps behind a low wall abutting the edge of the lot and sets the bag down. He bends over and unzips it, looks inside, and feels the ground beneath him fall away. Blank paper cut into hundreds of cash-sized bricks stare up at him, bluish white in the dim light.

All at once he's dizzy. Like a hologram suddenly switched off, his simple plan to save his family has blinked out of existence. His hand shoots out and grabs the top of the wall to steady himself as the world tilts, black spots spinning crazily before his eyes.

That whole conversation with Marini and the cop had been bullshit, their arguing with him an act. And he'd fallen for it, hadn't he? Hook, line, and fucking sinker. He sees the flash of metal in Marini's hand the other night. It was a gun, you dumb shit. He fucked you over, and goddamn it, you *knew* he would. And when Shota finds out you don't have his money, he's going to kill your family.

No.

Fisher slowly straightens. He's not going to let that happen. He takes a deep breath and, letting it out, gets down on a knee and places a palm on the duffel bag. He runs his hand over it, feeling the contours of the bogus cash bundles inside. Marini did a pretty good job of recreating the rectangular block into which the actual bills had been stacked and packed. Fisher unzips the bag, removes one of the bundles, and examines it closely. Printer paper is all it is, cut into the shape of currency and held together by a paper band.

An idea.

He reaches into his pocket, pulls out the eighty-three thousand yen he borrowed from the cash box at Blast MMA last night. He takes one of the ten-thousand-yen notes and places it on top of the little stack of paper in his other hand. It fits perfectly. Heart thumping, he slips the bill under the paper band, then uses the remaining ten thousand yen notes to do the same thing to seven more of the bundles. When he's done, he puts the rigged bundles money-side-up in the duffel so that when Shota unzips it, he'll see what looks like his cash. So long as he doesn't pull the zipper down too far.

Fisher closes the duffel, slings the strap over his shoulder, and walks, half his brain singing with hope, the other half twitching in fear. He crosses an access road with a guardrail, tall, unruly weeds growing along its base. Another parking lot scattered with yellow service vehicles and finally, farther along, just south of the massive support structure under the east end of the bridge, the entrance to the park.

As parks go there's not much to the place. A copse of scruffy trees and overgrown shrubbery fronting the water and a fenced-in dirt playing field behind it. A truck yard on one side and a dock on the other. A few outbuildings border the dock, some old office buildings standing dark behind them. The overall effect is of a little green thumb sticking out into the bay from a massive fist of concrete and steel.

His whole body hums with tension. He walks past a long, narrow shed with weathered wood siding, then down the well-lit asphalt path around the rear of the playing field. It's dark back here, the only illumination coming from the lights dotting the bridge high above. Past a small parking lot on the left is a big clump of shrubs against the chain-link bordering the field. He takes a furtive look around and, seeing no one else, stashes the bag behind the shrubs.

He walks up an asphalt path to a chest-high steel fence that skirts the waterfront. It's a moonless night, the lights of Odaiba twinkling on the other side of the bay. A damp salt wind blows in his face as water laps at the base of the embankment five feet down. Several hundred feet above him, traffic whooshes on the Rainbow Bridge.

A truck's horn blasts somewhere up on the bridge.

Fisher jumps.

He checks the time: 11:57. He turns his back to the water and scans the park, his eyes moving left to right and back. Three minutes to go and no sign of Shota.

A cruise ship is making its way up the bay, all lit up like a giant floating birthday cake.

He walks slowly toward the dock, the water on his left, the thicket of trees on his right. Marini was right about one thing. There are no CCTV cameras out here, not that he can see.

Don't worry, brother.

He imagines his hands around Marini's throat, the man's face purple, his tongue lolling out. Lisa, Justin, and James crying in a concrete box. Mari covered in blue surgical sheets, belly sliced open. Terry lying half dead in an alley. Akio's head haloed in blood. Brownie strangled and discarded like a piece of garbage.

Fisher smacks his face hard with both hands. Pull yourself together.

Directly ahead, across the water, is a cement factory with a tall smokestack jutting up into the sky. Fisher reaches over with his left hand and drags his fingers a foot or so along the top of the steel fence. It's sticky from the salt air. He takes his hand away, wipes his fingers on his shirt.

The lights around the park go out.

He looks about, frantic. There's still enough light from the underside of the bridge to see, but the sudden relative darkness is disorienting and it takes a moment for his eyes to adjust. A flicker of movement in the trees draws his attention. He takes several steps forward, craning his neck and squinting into the murk.

A shoe scuffs the pavement behind him.

Fisher spins around and there's Shota standing at the fence, looking out over the water.

"Where's my money?"

Fisher's heart thuds in his chest.

Shota makes a show of looking at Fisher's hands, scanning the ground for the gym bag.

A crunch of leaves draws Fisher's attention to trees. Masa and Yuki, the twins he fought in the restroom of Tokyu Food Show, are standing there, heads shining dully in the dim light. A tall man emerges next to them, a machete hanging loose from one of his hands. Another man appears a few yards away, then another, and another. They keep coming, seemingly out of every nook and cranny of the park.

Fisher's whole body is trembling now. There's nowhere to go. "Let my wife and kids go, I'll tell you where the money is."

Shota glares at him, works his jaw for a moment. The little army is about ten feet away and has formed a semicircle around the two of them. Fisher counts nine of them. He sees a few knives in addition to the machetes, a couple of baseball bats. He can make out their faces now. The tall one is closest to the dock on the left. He has a faux-hawk, no eyebrows, and a beard. The guy next to him is almost as tall but fat with a buzz cut. Masa and Yuki hold baseball bats. The rest of them look young. Really young. Fisher would be surprised if most of them aren't still in their teens. They're visibly nervous, fidgeting, ready to chop him to pieces. *Run, Henry!*

Shota turns to the tall guy. "Bring him," he says, then walks off in the direction of the park entrance.

The line of thugs parts like a curtain to let him by, and once he's past them, they reconfigure themselves into a kind of gauntlet. Eighteen eyeballs lock on Fisher. The younger ones can't seem to stay still, shifting from foot to foot, swinging their weapons, rolling their heads on their shoulders like they're getting ready to step into the cage.

The tall guy frowns and points with his blade. "*Konna yaro! Tsuite ike!*" Go, asshole!

Fisher walks.

CHAPTER FIFTY-TWO

LISA, JUSTIN, AND James sit huddled on a dirty futon, sweating in the heat, glancing up occasionally at the fat man who stands guard in front of the metal door.

The room is bare concrete, and a little fan in the corner chops away ineffectually at the soupy air.

Sitting between the twins, Lisa fans each of them in turn with a hand, wiping her own brow now and then with a dirty rag she found on the floor next to the futon.

Her head hasn't stopped pounding since one of the bald men punched her in the face. But the pain is no competition for the raging ocean of anguish and helplessness threatening to drown her. Hank tried to warn her and she didn't believe him, and now her babies are in danger. Where is he? Is he okay? She should've listened to him, but how could she have known? Goddamn him! He's the reason they're here!

They'd ridden blindfolded in the van for about thirty minutes and then were led on foot here, and it was only then that the cloth sacks were taken from their heads. She smelled the ocean and motor oil and sweat and urine. As Lisa directed her attention to Justin and James, she saw out of the corner of her eye that the two shaven-headed men, the fat man, and the smirking tall man with the diamond earrings were in the room with them. The babysitter must have stayed either in the van or outside the room. Oh God, the babysitter, she thought. What Hank had told her had all been true, and these people had somehow gotten to Rumi and threatened her, forced her to call in sick. Justin's and James's faces were red and wet from crying, and when Lisa saw that both of them had wet their pants, she went blind for a moment, her field of vision a wall of red, and she saw herself jumping on the one with the earrings and sinking her teeth into his neck and tearing his throat out. She heard him tell the fat man to stay in the room with her and the boys. He left and returned an hour or so later with the bald men and made Lisa, Justin, and James sit on a bench and took pictures of them.

The fat man licks his lips and swallows nervously, shifting from foot to foot, Lisa's head ringing with Hank's words: *Get the kids away from the babysitter. Get as far away as possible.*

She wants to scream.

She looks up at the fat man. There's a reddish purple knot under his left eye, where she kicked him earlier. She wishes the kick had taken his eye out. He mops sweat from his big, round face with a soggy handkerchief. He looks miserable, and not because of the heat. He won't make eye contact with Lisa, and he's got this anguished look on his face, like he's ashamed to be in here with them.

Justin and James have been oddly quiet for the past few minutes, but now James starts crying again, big, choking sobs. "Mama," he says, "I want to go home." Then Justin cries too, a loud chorus of terrified sobbing. "Me too."

Lisa turns and faces them, sitting on her knees. She reaches out and pulls them into her, buries her face in their hair. Then she releases them and lifts their chins and says, feeling their breath on her face, "We're going home soon, okay? I promise."

The words ring hollow in her ears, and she suddenly feels sick. Goddamn it. What is she going to do? The inside of her mouth feels like sandpaper. She picks up one of the three bottles of water the fat man brought for them earlier. She unscrews the cap and hands the bottle to Justin, does the same for James, and tells them to drink. Then she takes a drink from her own bottle.

James takes a sip of his water, wrinkles his nose, and says, "Mom, it's warm."

Justin says, "I'm not thirsty."

"Come on, you guys, it's hot. You have to drink."

Justin fumbles with his bottle, drops it. The water spills out onto the concrete floor. He looks up at the fat man, eyes wide with terror. "I'm sorry."

For the first time since they were brought here, the fat man looks at them. His eyes are slits encased deep in fat in an almost perfectly round face. He has no neck, his head a huge misshapen thing that seems to sit directly on top of his massive, sloping shoulders. The overall impression he conveys is terrifying. But the expression on his face is strangely childlike.

"*Chotto matte ne*," the fat man says in a high, almost feminine voice. Just a second. He turns and walks out the door and quickly shuts it behind him.

Lisa jumps up, heart slamming in her chest. If they're going to get out of here, they have to get past the fat man first. This room is in a garage of some sort. She knows this because before their hoods were removed, she heard the distinct rattle of a roll-up door. Her eyes dart around the room, looking for something she can use as a weapon.

"Mom," Justin says, sniffling. "What are you doing?"

There has to be something.

"Mom!"

She holds a finger to her lips. "*Shhh!*" Think think think. When she's at work, she makes to-do lists. Every project gets its own list of action items, which she crosses out as she goes. She paces the room, mentally cataloguing everything she sees. There's the futon they're sitting on, the sheet, the card table, and the wooden bench on which she and the boys were made to sit when the man with the earrings took pictures of them an hour ago. Otherwise, the room is empty. The card table is a flimsy metal thing. She could pick it up and throw it at the fat man, but even if it hit him, it wouldn't hurt him. The bench is too heavy for her to pick up, and she doubts it would hurt him either, even if she could.

From outside the room comes the muffled rattle of the roll-up door, quickly followed by the sound of men's voices and the scuff of shoes on concrete.

Lisa freezes.

She hears two voices. One is deep like a DJ's. That one belongs to the man with the earrings. The other voice is slightly higher, and she recognizes it instantly.

Hank.

CHAPTER FIFTY-THREE

THE TALL GUY with no eyebrows pulls a key from his pocket and unlocks the outbuilding's roll-up door, bends down, grabs the handle, and heaves it, the door clattering and squeaking on its way up.

Fisher passed this place on his way into the park earlier. Fifty feet long and twenty feet wide, it's a low-slung, flat-roofed barn with five evenly spaced, blacked-out windows that run its length. A small white sign next to a roll-up door says "Oil Fence Storage" in black *kanji*.

He can hear himself panting over the sound of his pulse hammering in his ears. Maybe they've already killed Lisa and the boys and their bodies are inside and now they're going to kill him.

No Eyebrows reaches inside and flips a switch. Overhead fluorescents flicker on, light spills out, and a tangle of shadows springs out across the pavement.

"Inside," Shota says.

Someone shoves Fisher from behind. He stumble-steps into the shed and sees several big stacks of folded plastic tarp on a low shelf that hugs the near wall. There's something on the floor in front of him, but his eyes don't seem to want to look at it, and it takes an act of will to lower them from the splintering slats in the walls to the thing on the floor.

A small man with a bowl haircut is lying barefoot on his back in a torn T-shirt and shorts. Around his neck is a rope. The whites of his eyes are blood red, and his mouth is an open oval shape.

Fisher can't breathe.

Shota walks over, nudges the corpse with his foot. "Say hi to Little Gen. He ran the stash house you robbed for me." He looks up at Fisher. "You remember Matchan, don't you?" He motions at the body. "He has a thing for strangling people. Me, I like to use a knife, but Matchan, he likes to squeeze the life out of people with those big hands of his. Right now he's with your ex-wife and kids."

They're alive. Relief and terror rip through Fisher's body. All at once it's as though he's standing on the ledge of a skyscraper, looking down.

"Where. Is. My. Money?"

Where are they? Eyes wild, Fisher looks around the space. There's another roll-up door directly opposite the one he was pushed through, leading, he assumes, to the dock. A forklift is parked all the way down on the left. Next to the forklift is a door. Adjacent to the wall on Fisher's right is a long workbench, on top of which are a number of large tools: several pipe wrenches, a rubber mallet, screwdrivers, c-clamps of varying sizes. Next to the workbench, partially hidden by a tall, empty shelving unit, is another roll-up door just like the one they entered through.

No sign of Lisa, Justin, and James.

The taste of fear is in his mouth, metallic and cloying. Fisher feels like he's choking on it.

Wherever they are, he has to get them out of here. How, goddamn it?

He looks at Shota, who's staring at him. It's the same death-ray stare he gave Fisher in Roppongi after Fisher escaped by hopping in a cab and speeding off.

A cab, he thinks, remembering the taxis parked out on the street, their drivers catching naps. That's it.

He meets Shota's gaze and shakes his head. "I want to see them. Then I want you to put them in a cab and let them go." He pulls the phone out of his pocket and holds it up for Shota to see. "Tell Lisa to call me when they're safe. She calls, I'll tell you where the money is, but not a moment before that."

Shota squints at him for a second; then he barks a laugh.

Someone kicks Fisher hard in the lower back and sends him stumbling to the cement floor, where he lands hard on his hands and knees next to the corpse. Fisher starts to push himself up, and the tall guy steps forward, machete raised.

"Down," the tall guy says. Under the fluorescent light, his faux-hawk looks like it could use a good combing, and there's something stuck in his beard. Fisher can see a spot of stubble where he missed shaving his right eyebrow, and for a moment he has the crazy urge to point this out to him.

Instead he says, "Fuck you."

There's a *swoosh* of air behind him and then pain explodes in his left arm. "AH!" He drops to a knee, barely feeling his kneecap thud against the concrete. He glances at the kid who swung the bat. He has it cocked and ready to swing again. Someone on the other side of Fisher kicks him in the gut. Fisher isn't ready for it at all, and the force of the blow knocks the wind out of him and then seemingly everyone is joining in, kicking and stomping him until he curls up into a ball.

They keep at him like that, soccer-kicking him, bolts of pain bursting like gunshots all over his body until one catches him in the jaw, and everything goes black.

CHAPTER FIFTY-FOUR

A BURST OF static comes over the radio, followed by Hashimoto's voice:

"They took him to a shed near the park entrance." Pause. "They all just went inside and closed the door. What do you want us to do?"

Aikawa leans forward and stubs out the remains of his cigarette in the ashtray. Hashimoto and Masuzawa had followed the black SUV from Meguro to an apartment building in Hiroo this morning and then watched from across the street as Fisher and the other big *gaijin* went inside the building, Fisher wearing a hoodie, his friend carrying the black gym bag. They sat there in their car and waited the whole damn day for Fisher to come out.

Hashimoto finally called Aikawa a little before 7 p.m. and told Aikawa that a cop named Nitta, known around town as a member of the TMPD's Organized Crime Unit, had just walked into the building.

Aikawa's heart sank, the opportunity to make an easy hundred million yen seemingly gone like a puff of smoke. He felt a migraine coming on, sighed, and told Hashimoto to keep an eye on the place to see what happened. And lo and behold, a few hours later, Hashimoto called again and told him Fisher had left the building with the bag on his back, practically running toward Hiroo, Nitta, the cop, and the other *gaijin* nowhere in sight.

They followed Fisher to Hiroo Station, where Masuzawa shadowed him on the train all the way to Shibaura-futo and from there to Kaigan Park, where the fighter had hidden the gym bag in some bushes and then walked off to the edge of the waterfront. According to Masuzawa, at one point on his way to the park, Fisher stopped, looked in the bag, and tossed his cookies, the sight of a hundred million yen in cash apparently too much for the poor bastard. Meanwhile, Hashimoto had picked up Tanaka and raced out to Shibaura-futo and joined Masuzawa, and Aikawa ordered the three of them to grab the bag from where Fisher had hidden it and get the hell out of there.

But before they could, Aoyama Shota showed up with nine of his young knuckleheads. According to Hashimoto, Shota's gang has just escorted Hank Fisher to a shed on the other side of the park, and the money now sits in bushes right where Fisher stashed it, ripe for the taking.

Aikawa grabs the handset and presses the push-to-talk button. "Get the bag."

"Yes, boss."

"Then I want you to block the doors to the shed and light it up."

"Sorry?"

"I said I want you to set it on fire."

There's a long pause.

Aikawa feels a prickle of irritation at the man's hesitation. "Is there a problem?"

Hashimoto says, "No, boss. No problem."

"Go then."

CHAPTER FIFTY-FIVE

FROM HIS PERCH on top of a big rig in the truck yard next to Kaigan Park, Hashimoto watches Masuzawa and Tanaka through his binoculars as they make their way toward the shed with the can of gasoline.

Once several years ago, Hashimoto had run out of gas. He'd been in a stolen car in the parking lot of a shopping center in Gunma Prefecture in the middle of winter, and it had just started to snow, and he had no money on him. Three hours he spent in that parking lot, freezing his ass off, until one of the crew came with a can of gasoline. Since then he's always kept a full gas can in his trunk.

And it's a good thing, Hashimoto thinks, because when the boss says he wants something done, he wants it done *now*.

Hashimoto adjusts the focus on the binocs. Masuzawa and Tanaka are now on either side of the shed's closed roll-up door. Tanaka squats down next to the lock. Hashimoto can see it's one of those right-angle jobs with a padlock. Tanaka removes the padlock, which is hanging open from the latch hole; then he closes the latch, re-hooks the padlock through the latch hole, and locks it.

Hashimoto puts the binocs in his backpack and hurriedly climbs down from the top of the big rig. He jogs to the fence, hops over, and lands in a patch of weeds at the northern edge of the park. Then he walks a hundred feet to the row of chest-high bushes where not thirty minutes ago Hank Fisher hid the gym bag.

The lights that dot the underside of the bridge cast a sickly glow over the park, and the strip of walkway abutting the hedge is cloaked in shadow.

Even in the dim light, though, it takes Hashimoto less than a minute to find the bag. He hefts it up, slings the strap over his shoulder, and radios the boss. "I got it," he says.

"Bring it to me," says the boss.

CHAPTER FIFTY-SIX

LISA STARES AT the door, hands on her head, heart tapping furiously in her chest. Hank is out there. She heard him scream, she knows it was him. She heard other voices too. They're going to kill him, and then they're going to kill her and the kids too.

Should she pound on the door? Yell Hank's name? She puts a hand to her forehead. No, she tells herself. There's nothing she can do for him. And she knows better than to think he's capable of helping her and the kids. Yes, he'd tried to warn her about the danger they were in and never mind the fact that he was the reason they were in danger in the first place. But look at the way he did it—freaking her out with that call out of the blue, frightening her even more by showing up at her building and then actually becoming violent, grabbing her wrist, and then running away from the police like an insane person. It was all proof that he hadn't changed one bit. And the realization pained her, because she knew that in his own way he was trying to save them. But Hank's own way was to act without thinking, to be a walking bomb, ready to detonate without warning, and that was exactly the problem.

So she has to get Justin and James out of here by herself. She considers having them stand to the side of the doorframe and dash out as soon as the fat man opens it, but then what? Then they have to get past the man with the earrings and all the other people she hears on the other side of the door.

Think, she tells herself, fighting tears of fear and frustration. *Think, damn it.* One thing at a time. They first have to get out of this room.

"Mom," James says behind her. "Look what I found."

She turns and sees James holding up a silver nail. His eyes are still red from crying, but his tone is pleased. Ever since he was eighteen months old, James has been a little scavenger. He can't go anywhere without picking up all manner of things along the way. Dead bugs, dry leaves, a pretty rock, dropped change. Lisa and Hank used to joke that he would discover hidden treasure and strike it rich someday.

Lisa takes the nail out of James's hand. "Where did you get this?"

"It was under the futon," he says, defensive.

The nail is thin and about four inches long. Not much of a weapon, but it's their only chance. Suddenly Lisa is thrumming with adrenaline. She knows what she has to do. But oh God, she doesn't want the kids to see her do it. She kneels down in front of them and takes each of their hands. "Boys," she says, trying to keep the quaver out of her voice. "I want you to turn around and look at the wall and don't turn back around until I tell you to, okay?"

"Why?" the boys say almost in unison.

"Just do what Mama says. Promise me. No matter what you hear, you won't turn around."

"Okay," Justin says.

James hesitates, frowning.

Lisa knows from his expression that he's trying to make sense of all this. He's cautious and logical, and he needs an explanation. She puts her hand to his cheek. "I might have to hurt the big man and I don't want you to see me do it. So promise me."

James's frown dissolves. "I promise."

The doorknob rattles.

Lisa jumps. "Do it now!" she whispers, frantic. "Turn around!"

The door opens, and the fat man walks in with three new bottles of water. He closes the door with his foot.

Lisa rises, the nail hidden in her right hand. Hank told her once that in a fight for your life, fighting fair will get you killed. You must fight dirty. This is a fight for her children's lives. She will do anything and everything to get them out of here. She turns to the fat man, smiling. "Thank you," she says, pretending to reach for one of the waters as she steps forward.

The fat man dips his head. *You're welcome.*

Lisa leaps at him, screaming at the top of her lungs. His head jerks back in surprise as he throws a big hand up to ward off whatever's coming, and he stumbles backward, slamming against the door.

BOOM!

Her limbs coursing with sudden animal strength, Lisa stabs the fat man's hand. He yelps in pain, yanks the hand back. With his other hand he seizes Lisa by the hair and jerks her toward him. Pulse rocketing, she feels nothing as she plunges the nail into the fat man's left eye with the ferocity of a wildcat protecting its cubs. He makes a high-pitched, keening sound and then falls to his knees, covering his ruined eye with both hands.

This is her only chance.

Justin and James are huddled against the wall, hands over

their ears. Lisa grabs them by the scruff and pulls them to their feet. "Up! Up! Come on, boys!" They look at her, wide-eyed with shock and terror, and she wants to squeeze them, tell them she loves them and she's sorry and it's going to be okay. But there's no time. She makes them stand behind her while she sidesteps past the fat man, who's on his knees now, still reeling in pain. She reaches for the doorknob, turns it, and pushes the door open. There's a forklift outside on the right. She makes the boys go out first, tells them to stand by the forklift; then she steps out herself and closes the door.

She doesn't see the tall man with no. eyebrows behind the forklift until it's too late.

CHAPTER FIFTY-SEVEN

THE SCREAM IS unlike anything he's ever heard. A banshee cry, shot through with animal rage, it jerks him back up into consciousness.

For the first time ever, he was knocked out.

He's on his side now, curled into a semi-fetal position with his hands duct-taped behind his back, pain from the beating he just took singing out all over his body.

Shota's voice: "What the fuck was that?" His crew, who have formed a circle around Fisher, jerk their heads toward the sound.

That was Lisa's scream, Fisher realizes with a surge of panic. It came from the metal door next to the forklift on the other side of the shed. Oh Christ, she's in trouble. Are the kids in there with her? He uncurls himself on the floor, daggers of pain stabbing him in multiple places up and down his back, and pushes himself up onto his knees. Then: BOOM!

Something—*someone*—slamming up against the door

"Fucking Matchan," says Shota. "What the fuck is he doing in there?"

Fisher's blood freezes. The fat man is hurting Lisa, hurting Justin and James. Maybe already killed them. He strains against the duct tape around his wrists, breathing in gasps, twisting his arms so forcefully, he feels his skin tear.

There's a loud yelp from behind the metal door, followed by a high-pitched bleating, the sound of a lamb or a goat being tortured.

"Goddamn it," Shota says. He points to the tall guy. "Go see what the fuck is going on."

Tall guy runs off toward the forklift.

Fisher's wrists have gone slick with blood and sweat. He keeps working them, biting down on the pain. A kid with a shaved head and a wispy mustache steps forward from the circle and kicks him back onto the floor.

Suddenly the sound of Justin and James screaming fills the shed. "Let her go!"

Fisher roars, pushing himself onto his knees again, the pain he felt a second ago a tiny, distant thing. He sees the tall man approaching, pulling Lisa behind him by the hair, Lisa screaming, Justin and James running after them, sobbing. They know they can't help their mom, and the anguish Fisher hears in their voices slashes at his soul. He knows the horror of this pain, of being helpless in the face of your parents' final moments, and now his own children know it too, and if only he'd been the father they needed and deserved, he could've spared them this torment and none of this would be happening.

Every eye in the shed now directed at the source of all the commotion, Fisher frantically twists his wrists, every heartbeat a detonation in his ears. But the duct tape is too tight. "Boys!" he says. "Lisa!"

"Daddy!" the boys say in succession.

Lisa says, "Hank!"

Matchan's bleating continues like background music to a horror movie.

"It's going to be okay," Fisher says. A fist clips him in the side of the head. It's not a powerful punch, but after the kick in the jaw, it makes his vision go sideways for a split second.

"Leave my daddy alone!" James says.

"Somebody grab them," Shota says, making a dismissive motion at Justin and James. Masa and Yuki storm over to the boys and grab them by the arms. The boys immediately squirm, trying to extricate themselves from the gangsters' respective grips.

"You hurt them, I'll kill you," says Fisher, his pulse pounding.

Masa makes a *Tsk* sound.

Matchan stops bleating for a moment and starts up again. Shota makes a face. "What's wrong with him?"

The tall guy tilts his head at Lisa, smirks, and holds up a small silver nail. "She stabbed him in the eye with this."

Shota squints at the nail and scoffs. "Bring her here and go and get that fat ass."

The tall guy drags Lisa over to where Shota is standing and forces her to her knees.

Fisher looks at Lisa. Her hair is plastered to her forehead with sweat, her eyes are red and puffy, and the left side of her face is swollen. He did this to her. *I'm so, so sorry.* She looks up at him as if she's just heard his thoughts, rage and panic and hurt in her eyes, and under the intensity of her gaze, something dies inside him, and in the next instant, something new rises in its place, something calm, cool, and clear-eyed. He twists his wrists, feeling the adhesive on the inside of the tape begin to give way to the blood soaking his wrists.

The thug closest to Lisa on the right, a teenager with plucked Spock eyebrows, puckers his lips at her and makes a kissing sound.

Lisa whirls and spits in his face.

Her utter fearlessness fills Fisher with pride, but just as quickly the pride is replaced with raw fear for her life. He works his wrists with renewed vigor, twisting them, turning them as he pants through his nose. He has to get them out of here. He casts a quick glance over his shoulder at the workbench and spots the big pipe wrench lying on top of it. Next to the workbench is the second roll-up door behind the shelving unit.

"Bitch," the thug says. He wipes his face on his T-shirt, then raises his fist and steps toward her.

Fisher's breath catches in his throat.

Shota says, "Stop."

The kid freezes. He bites his lower lip and steps back.

Heart slamming in his chest, Fisher works his wrists. Duct tape is water resistant but not waterproof, and that's why it's now bunched up at the top of his hands, having lost its purchase on his bloody wrists. As soon as he breaks free, he's going to tell Shota where the bag is, and when Shota sends one of his men to go get it, Fisher is going to run and grab the wrench off the workbench. The gangsters will come after him, and when they do, he's going to signal to Lisa to take the kids to the roll-up door behind the shelves.

Just then, the tall guy returns with Matchan, escorting the big man by the elbow. Matchan's bloody left hand covers his left eye. His whole face is covered in blood, and from his open mouth drifts an unearthly warbling sound. The tall guy steps away from Matchan, leaving him standing there looking forlorn and alone.

Shota glowers at the fat man.

Someone laughs.

Shota glances at Justin and James, then looks up at Masa

and Yuki. "Cover their eyes." Masa and Yuki do as they're told, Justin and James silent except for their sniffles. Then in one quick motion, Shota pulls a pistol from the small of his back and shoots Matchan in the face.

Fisher jumps, the explosion echoing through the shed.

Lisa screams and the boys cry out as Matchan's huge body crumples to the concrete with a thud. Shota swings his arm down and points the gun at Lisa's head, looks at Fisher, and raises his eyebrows.

A giant fist closes around Fisher's heart and squeezes. "Bushes!" he says, loud but barely hearing his voice through the ringing in his ears. "It's in the bushes next to the truck yard."

Shota stares at Fisher for a moment, then removes the gun from Lisa's head and says to the tall guy, "Go get it."

Fisher's head buzzes. He has to make his move before the tall guy comes back with the bag full of blank paper. The thugs around him are angling their faces up, alternately looking at the ceiling and each other with confused expressions. Something's wrong. Whatever it is, Fisher takes advantage of the distraction and works his wrists furiously behind his back. Blood hammering in his head, he wrenches them up and down, twists them left and right. Left, right, left, right, left, and finally one of his hands slips free.

One of the thugs beside Fisher says quietly to the guy next to him, "You smell something burning?" The gangsters look at each other, wrinkling their noses.

Fisher can smell it too. It's faint, but something is definitely burning.

The sound of muffled banging on metal.

Fisher looks over and sees it's the tall guy kicking the bottom of the roll-up door. "Boss, the door is stuck!" the tall guy says.

Fire. Panic buzzes in Fisher's head.

Shota turns, walks a few paces to the left, away from Lisa and toward the roll-up door, his back to Fisher. He lifts his nose and sniffs the air.

"Open the door!" someone says.

"It's locked!" another voice says.

Shota standing there with his back to Fisher, gun dangling by his thigh.

And all at once, the smell is almost overpowering. Shouts go up, the gangsters scattering like confused soldier ants.

NOW. Fisher leaps to his feet. It takes him less than a second to close the distance. He kicks the gun out of Shota's hand. The gun clatters to the floor somewhere, Shota yelping with pain. He turns around and Fisher blitzes him with a flurry of blows. Shota drops. Fisher wheels around. Everyone in the shed is coughing now, and suddenly Fisher is coughing too. The air in the shed is hazy with smoke, and for a panicky moment he can't see Lisa or the kids, and then he sees them over by the workbench, the three of them coughing, Lisa looking frantically around. Fisher starts toward them, stops, looks over his shoulder. Shota's getting to his knees.

The smoke is getting thicker, the other gangsters running around, frantic, looking for a way to escape. They pound at the windows, hammer the roll-up door with their fists.

Fisher looks up at the window nearest him and through the opaque glass sees the yellow glow of flames.

Black smoke rolling in now, heavy and acrid. The sound of glass breaking.

Fisher hacks and coughs, his eyes burning. He looks for Shota again, can't see him through the smoke. There's no time. The buzz of panic in his brain is suddenly a roar. He wipes his eyes with his hand, peers through the smoke, searching for his family. "Lisa! Justin! James!"

"Hank!" says Lisa. Cough! Cough! Cough!

The guy with the wispy mustache stumbles by, wheezing and coughing, then disappears into the smoke. Above the noise and chaos, a clatter goes up from the back of the shed, followed by the slam of metal on concrete.

Fisher remembers the roll-up door behind the shelving unit. He can barely see anything. He crouches low, sees a small shadow and another next to it. "Justin!" He coughs violently. "James!" He moves toward the figures, his lungs filling with burning smoke, and he can't breathe and he can't see anything and everything goes dark, just like, he thinks crazily, in a movie theater just before the show is about to begin.

CHAPTER FIFTY-EIGHT

BENT OVER A patch of weeds a hundred feet from the burning shed, Shota hacks and coughs and vomits until there's nothing left in his stomach to purge. His eyes sting, and the taste of smoke fills his mouth, his nose, his goddamn brain.

The fire is consuming the wooden structure like a starving beast, popping and cracking and producing a heat so intense that Shota has to turn his face away.

He'd managed to pick himself up after Fisher hit him, grab a gun someone had dropped, and escape through a second roll-up door in back, leaving the others behind. He'd known about the door, but none of the others had. Too bad. Maybe they'll find their way out, maybe they won't. Right now, all he cares about is the money.

Shota walks a few steps, rubs at his eyes. Another fit of coughing hits him so hard, it doubles him over. He clears his throat and spits repeatedly, and when the fit finally subsides, he hears sirens in the distance.

He has to move fast.

Fisher said the bag was in some bushes near the truck yard. Shota knows exactly where that is. He sets out in that direction, and before he makes it even halfway, he spots a man walking toward the entrance to the park. On his back is a knapsack. In his hand is a gym bag.

There are restrooms up ahead. Shota quickly walks to them and peers around the corner, hoping the man didn't see him too. Fortunately, the guy is focused on the fire, which is now a full-fledged conflagration. The man stops for a moment and with his back to Shota stares at the flames shooting into the air.

The sirens are getting louder.

Good night, Shota thinks. He pulls the pistol from his waistband and moves quickly if not silently, but it doesn't matter because the sound of his footsteps is drowned out by the crackling of the raging fire and the noise of the traffic on the bridge overhead. Shota gets within ten feet of the man before the man notices him, and by then it's too late. Shota shoots him twice in the face as he turns around.

The man drops to the ground.

Shota fires two more rounds into the man's chest, and it feels so good, cathartic, really, that he fires some more and then some more and, finally satiated, he grabs the bag and walks away, feeling, for the first time in days, happy.

CHAPTER FIFTY-NINE

BLACKNESS AND CHAOS and noise all around.

He's far away on a dead planet, lying at the bottom of a sea of oily, acrid smoke, drowning in it, because he can't breathe, and his lungs are on fire, and this is the end.

Get up.

A small voice. Not that of a grown-up, but neither is it that of a little kid.

Come on, get up.

It's more insistent this time, the cracking voice of a boy on the cusp of adolescence, a kid who watched helpless as his parents were shot down like dogs in another life a long time ago.

There was nothing you could do, the kid says. *But there is now, so get your ass up.*

He coughs, and then he's briefly losing consciousness again, and everything is moving farther away.

Get up!

He opens his eyes. Remembers something he read or saw in a movie and rolls over onto his stomach and presses his face to the floor and inhales and it's a little better, and he crawls forward, flat on his stomach, reaching out one at a time with his hands. He coughs again, violent, racking coughs. Crawl. Cough. Crawl. Cough. He touches cloth, grabs hold of it, and tugs. There's a shriek and then fingernails claw at him, rip the skin on top of his hand.

"Lisa!" Fisher's heart bangs against his ribs. He can barely see her through the smoke, a dark form sitting huddled with two smaller forms at her side. Justin and James.

"Lisa!"

"Hank!"

Briefly he's able to see that they're huddled under the workbench, ten feet away from the shelving unit, behind which is the other roll-up door.

"There's a door!" he says, scooping James up with one arm. He helps Lisa up. She takes Justin's hand. Eyes burning, tears streaming down his face, Fisher leads them, James coughing into his neck. He moves in a crouch, holding his free hand out in front of him until he reaches the wall. He gropes along the wall until he feels the metal edge of the roll-up door. A fit of coughing hits him. He sets James down and holds his wrist, doubling over.

Panicked shouting and coughing echo in the shed.

Fisher spits, wipes his eyes, straightens. Through the haze, he sees Lisa and Justin move past him to the door. Pulling James along he follows her, the two of them coughing and retching. When they get to the door, Fisher sees the shelving unit has been pushed aside and the latch on the door is unlocked. He realizes with a prickle of fear that Shota must have gotten out and gone to look for the money. Justin is standing beside Lisa, crying, coughing. Fisher leans down and says loud to both of the boys, "Stay right here!"

Lisa is already trying to heave the door up to no effect.

Fisher leans down next to her, grabs the bottom of the door, and together they heave. Nothing. It's stuck. Lisa turns away, coughing and choking. Fisher leans over and tries again. Goddamn it. It won't budge. Panic swamps his senses. He straightens, looks around for something to use to pry the door up, sees nothing.

There's no time.

He squats down, gets his fingers under the lip of the door, and with all his might heaves again. With a groan of metal the door rises an inch. He screams as he heaves again, and with a scrape of metal the door rises another six inches and then rattles up. Lisa and the kids tumble out onto the gravel outside the shed, retching. Fisher tumbles out after them, salt air hitting his face.

Sirens blare in the distance.

The shed is burning, yellow tongues of flame snapping and flicking out from the oily black smoke billowing up into the air.

Fisher gulps several breaths of fresh air, picks himself up off the ground. He helps Lisa and the kids up, and the four of them run.

⊷

Five minutes later, they're in a tall bank of weeds abutting a chain-link fence.

The shed burns a hundred yards away, enveloped entirely in flame now, spewing roiling clouds of smoke that billow and drift out over the water. The heat coming off the fire is so intense, Fisher can feel it on his arms and face as he coughs and gags and wipes the film of tears and gunk from his eyes.

Lisa is coughing in violent spasms, Justin and James sobbing as they hack and cough and spit into the weeds.

Fisher reaches over and gives each of the boys several firm

pats on the back, nerves rapid-firing, making him alert to Shota's presence somewhere out here. He may already have found the bag and discovered he's been tricked.

The fire cracks and pops.

Blinking furiously, Fisher rises and scans the park, eyes stinging. To his left is the shed, engulfed in flames. To his right, some restrooms, the dirt playing field behind the chain-link fence. He turns, surveys the trees and shrubbery, the paved path fronting the water. There's no sign of Shota, no sign of any of his men, either. Fisher pictures them running around in the burning shed, panicked, desperate for a way out. Burned alive, Fisher thinks with a shudder. All of them except their boss, who saved his own ass and left them behind to die. And now he's out here somewhere.

The sirens are close now.

He feels a small arm wrap around his leg, looks down and sees James, crying softly and rubbing his eyes. Lisa is helping Justin blow his nose on her shirt. Fisher kneels and rubs James's back, then reaches over with his other hand and rubs Justin's too. Relief flooding into him, Fisher looks at his sons and realizes with a brief sick feeling that he almost lost them. "Are you guys okay?"

"Yeah," says James.

"My throat hurts," says Justin.

"Hang on, kiddo, we'll get you some water."

All at once, the noise of the sirens crescendos and then stops. There's a hiss of brakes, followed by the urgent shouts of the firemen, the echo of their running footfalls.

"Here come the firemen, guys," he says, forcing himself to make his tone sound relaxed as he watches Lisa wipe soot from their faces.

James says, "Where did the bad guys go, Daddy?"

They're dead, son, Fisher thinks. *All but one.* His eyes find Lisa's. Her expression is tight.

"The one with the earrings," she says, "I saw him run out of the building."

Fisher nods. A renewed sense of resolve settles over him. Cool. Hard. Controlled. He's going to find Shota and end this.

He stands up and waves his arms at the firemen.

"Over here!"

CHAPTER SIXTY

SHOTA IS SITTING in his car, staring at the stack of paper in his hand. He flips through it with his thumb one more time, because he still can't believe his eyes.

Unfortunately, he's not seeing things. Each and every sheet in the rubber band-bound bundle is perfectly blank. It's printer paper, cut to roughly the same size as ten-thousand-yen notes.

Blood pounding inside his head, Shota fishes another stack out of the gym bag. Same. He grabs another. And another. Same and same.

All blank.

His face twitching with rage, Shota jerks the bag open and shakes out the rest of its contents. The stacks of useless paper tumble out, cascade onto the seat, his lap, the floor of the car. He turns the bag inside out, pulls at it this way and that, and then he's trying to rip the fucking thing apart, spitting and making animal noises through his teeth until finally he hurls it against the passenger side window and sits there huffing in his seat.

He'd been so sure he finally had the money, and to have come this far and gone from feeling on top of the world minutes ago to *this*. Shota takes out his gun and holds it with both hands in his lap. A wedge of pale moonlight shines dully on the matte-black barrel. All his plans have been for naught, because without the money, he's done. He might as well end it right here.

But no.

Not yet.

There's one thing he needs to do.

CHAPTER SIXTY-ONE

THE FIREMEN LEAD the four of them out of the park to an ambulance parked next to one of two rumbling fire trucks. The scene behind them at the shed is pandemonium as the firefighters struggle to put the fire out, the air filled with their shouts, the rumble of the fire engines, the whoosh of water being sprayed from the fire hoses.

A light southerly wind is carrying the smoke from the fire out over the park, the smell of it thick in the air as it billows up, clouding a section of the Rainbow Bridge above the park.

One of the firemen, a kindly slope-shouldered guy in his fifties with bushy eyebrows that jump when he talks, helps Lisa and the boys up into the ambulance. He gets them seated, and while he helps them put on oxygen masks, Fisher turns and leaves.

He walks the perimeter of the park, quiet, blood humming in his ears, his senses on full alert as he scans the bushes, the trees, the playing field for signs of Shota.

Nothing.

He circles the park, giving a wide berth to the ongoing battle with the now-dying fire.

Steam hisses over the hum of the fire engines, the slightly less tense voices of the firefighters.

He walks toward the elevated freeway behind the park and comes to a gravel parking lot behind an old office building where a small truck is parked. He moves around the truck to the fence that runs along the back of the lot and peers down at a set of concrete steps on the other side. The steps lead down to the dock, where a coast guard vessel and two small boats with outboard motors are moored.

Traffic whooshes on the expressway above him. Water laps at the base of the dock below.

Where are you, Shota?

CHAPTER SIXTY-TWO

SHOTA GETS OUT of the car to head back to the park, and that's when he sees Hank Fisher moving quickly up the sidewalk toward where Shota is parked.

A smile spreads across Shota's lips, his teeth shining in the dim moonlight. He scoots down in his seat and watches Fisher over the top of the steering wheel. A few seconds later he turns off the path and disappears behind an old office building, but it's okay, because Shota knows the only thing behind that building is a fenced parking lot, and beyond it, the water of Tokyo Bay.

There's nowhere for Fisher to go.

Moving furtively up the sidewalk to the office building, Shota feels a tingle of anticipation. He reaches the building and takes a peek around the corner, and there's Fisher at the fence, a truck parked about ten feet behind him, staring out at the water like he's got not a care in the world.

A mixture of rage and panic floods his veins, and yet part of him can't deny a grudging admiration for the motherfucker. The guy has been pulling rabbits out of his hat ever since he took off with the money.

But you're out of bunnies now, aren't you, motherfucker?

Shota hasn't had much practice shooting. You have to go to Hawaii or California to do that. But he figures at this distance— no more than fifty feet—it shouldn't be hard to hit Fisher, even in the dark. Shota steps around the corner and raises the pistol.

Fisher turns and they lock eyes.

Shota smiles.

CHAPTER SIXTY-THREE

THE CRUNCH OF shoes on gravel freezes Fisher. He turns and sees Shota standing fifty feet away, gun in his hand and aimed at Fisher's head.

Fisher's pulse thuds once in his neck. Out of the corner of his eye, he registers the truck parked ten feet away. He snaps his right foot backward, pivots, and executes a leaping forward roll over his right shoulder and comes out of the roll in a crouch behind the cab of the parked truck.

Shota fires a shot at him. *Crack!*

Fisher barely hears the sound. Heart thumping a measured beat, he places his hands on the passenger-side door of the truck, and quickly pops his head up and peers through the window.

Shota is still standing in the same spot with the gun in his raised hand, a bright, empty look in his eyes. "After I do you, I'm going to find them again and kill them," he says, his voice higher than usual and ragged-sounding. "Make no mistake about that. And all you had to do was give me back my money." The threat to Lisa and the kids sends a bolt of rage through Fisher's body. He fights it down, the flame of his anger dying quickly as his thoughts collapse into an icy point, and then a steely calm settles over him, as if a kind of cold fusion reaction has been triggered inside him. He shifts his weight from his left foot to his right, gravel crunching under his feet, and is suddenly keenly aware of the size and shape of the rocks under his sneakers. There are fifty feet between him and Shota, and it's dark, and he's willing to bet that Shota hasn't had a lot of shooting practice.

Shota fires again. The shot goes wide and hits the front fender of the truck.

Crack-clang!

Yeah, Shota is a shitty shot.

Fisher squats down and grabs a handful of the sharp rocks.

Another shot: *Crack-crunch!*

Small shards of glass from the passenger window rain down on Fisher's head. Heart banging in his chest, Fisher says, loud: "I have your money! Stop shooting!"

Crack-clang! Crack-clang!

"Stop!" says Fisher. Still crouched, he sidesteps along the bed of the truck until he reaches its corner, sticks his hand up, waves, then points down into the bed. "It's in here."

Shota issues a bitter-sounding chuckle and fires again.

Crack-clang!

This time the bullet passes through the fender, nearly missing Fisher's head. Pulse thundering in his ears, he says, "Goddamn it, stop! No bullshit. I bought another bag and filled it with paper. Stashed the real one in here before I met you in the park."

Shota chuckles again. "Is that right?"

"Yes. Why do you think I came here?"

Shota sighs noisily, a tired sound. "I don't have time for this. It's in there, you bring it to me."

"No way. You'll just shoot me. You come and get it yourself."

Shota grumbles something, and then Fisher hears the gangster's footsteps in the gravel.

The footsteps stop.

"I don't see nothing in there," Shota says. "Enough. Stand up where I can see you."

Fisher squeezes the rocks in his hand, feeling their sharp edges cut into his palm. Shota takes another step forward in the gravel, and that's when Fisher sucks in a big breath, rises, and hurls the rocks at the gangster as hard as he can, his arm whipping around too fast for Shota to perceive what's happening until the rocks are hitting him. One raps him in the forehead, blood running instantly from the gash it leaves behind. Another hits him in the middle of his chest, and yet another tags him right in the balls. Shota throws his hands up to protect his face even though it's too late. The pistol flies out of his hand and clatters to the ground six feet away.

Fisher is already running at him at full speed, adrenaline juicing the muscles in his thighs.

Seeing Fisher approach, Shota's eyes go wide. He reaches around and pulls a *tanto* from behind his back. Holding the short sword up in front of him, the gangster scrambles backward, trips, and almost falls. He raises the sword up over his head as he recovers his balance and slashes downward when Fisher comes within striking distance. Fisher stops short, hops back. The tip of the sword nicks the top of his chest. Pain sings out over his left pectoral. With a scream of rage, Shota swings the sword in the other direction, trying to cut Fisher in half. Fisher jumps back again, avoiding the blade entirely this time. Shota slashes at Fisher again and misses again, and this time Fisher darts in and seizes the gangster's wrist with both hands in a classic two-on-one grip.

Fisher glues himself to the outside of Shota's arm, and as Fisher stretches the arm out and down, with all his strength he jams the top of his head into the side of Shota's face and sprawls his entire weight forward against Shota's shoulder and arm, forcing the gangster toward the ground.

Shota scrambles back and manages to stay on his feet and circle away from the pressure of Fisher's head as he uses his left hand to blast Fisher with a series of short, sharp uppercuts. Fisher turns his face away, burying it into Shota's neck, but not before one of the punches grazes his chin. After the kick in the face in the shed, it stuns him, but he somehow manages to keep hold of Shota's wrist and circles to the left and headbutts him in the side of the face.

The two men struggle in an awkward dance until Shota manages to get his free left hand on Fisher's face and push it away as he attempts to jerk his right hand, which is still gripping the handle of the short sword, out of Fisher's grasp. But Fisher doesn't let go. Shota claws at his face, manages to stick his thumb in Fisher's right eye socket. Fisher rears his head back, his left eye zeroing in on the thumb.

A lightning flash of memory: Douchebag Dave biting his thigh in the gym.

Fisher opens his mouth and seizes Shota's thumb in his teeth and bites down as hard as he can.

"AHHHH!"

Shota jerks and flails like he's been set on fire. Fisher spits a mouthful of Shota's blood, feels his energy ebbing as spasms of pain from the beating he took in the shed pop all over his body. He starts to lose his grip on Shota's wrist. He's got to end this now.

As Shota tries to straighten himself, Fisher shoots his left leg out, back-kicks Shota's right leg up, and drives his weight forward against Shota's arm and shoulder. Shota crashes forward at the exact moment his right wrist—and with it, the *tanto*—slips from Fisher's hands. The two men collapse to the ground with a thud, Shota face-first, with Fisher on top of him. Shota lets out a bloodcurdling shriek and goes still. Fisher sees the man's right arm is pinned underneath him. He eases his weight off Shota's back, rises slow, and quickly steps away as Shota rolls to his side. and that's when Fisher sees the *tanto* half buried in Shota's abdomen, just under his sternum. Blood already gushing from the wound and staining his shirt.

Shota looks down at the knife in his guts, hyperventilating. "Fuck," he says. His eyes flick up to Fisher. "Help me."

Fisher looks down at the man, at the dark blood spilling out of his stomach, and feels a twinge of pity, of guilt, of obligation. He glances toward the park entrance, where the paramedics are tending to Lisa, Justin, and James. He thinks of the gun Shota had held to Lisa's head not twenty minutes ago. He thinks of Terry. Of Akio. Of Mari. And the twinge is gone.

"Oh fuck," says Shota. Blood pours freely out of his stomach onto the ground, the sound of water trickling out of a hose. His face has gone pale, and there's a distant look in his downcast eyes. His legs move once, slowly. And then he stops moving.

A long moment passes, Fisher trying to figure out what it is he's feeling as he stares at Shota's body and decides he feels nothing but relief.

On the way out of the park, he passes what looks like Shota's Mercedes. On the ground all around it are the bound stacks of blank paper. He bends down, picks one up, and stuffs it in his pocket. There's someone he needs to pay a visit.

CHAPTER SIXTY-FOUR

THE BLACK SUBURBAN isn't there when he arrives at Marini's apartment building.

A thrumming tension dulls the pain flaring all over his body as he takes the elevator directly up to the tenth floor. He knocks on the door.

No answer.

He pounds on it.

Nothing.

He turns to the security ID panel next to the door and tries punching in different combinations starting with "000000." Each time, a red light flashes, the device bleating three times in quick succession.

His pulse tics. Will the alarm be triggered if he enters the wrong code too many times? He rubs his temple with his thumb. What combination would Marini use? His kids' birthdays? Fisher doesn't know them.

A sudden flash of memory: The Route 69 pendant hanging from Marini's rearview mirror.

My favorite number! All day every day v-jayjay!

Sixty-nine every day. As in, sixty-nine, twenty-four seven? It's stupid and a long shot but Fisher goes ahead and enters 247069 and gets the red light and the beep-beep-beep. He pauses, then enters 069247. The little light on the panel turns green.

Beeep.

He slowly cracks open the door, sees the lights are on inside. "Pete," he says.

Nothing.

He steps inside, wary, and closes the door. He scans the room. The place looks the same as it did when he was here earlier. The tidy kitchen and dining room, the recessed lighting, the puffy sofa and chair and flat-screen TV and the Ansel Adams print.

The bedroom door is ajar.

"Pete?" says Fisher again, every synapse on high alert.

Still nothing.

Fisher goes to the bedroom door and pushes it open. Inside is a queen-size bed, a single nightstand with a small lamp on it to the left of the bed. On the other side is a small yoga mat, several sets of kettlebells, and a collection of heavy-duty rubber resistance bands in a cardboard box. On top of the bed is an open suitcase stuffed with clothes.

Where is the money?

There's a walk-in closet with a sliding door across from the bed. Fisher slides the door of the closet open, and his breath catches in his throat.

On the floor lying faceup on a blue plastic tarp is the cop, Nitta. His T-shirt and blazer are soaked through with blood, and Fisher sees he's been stabbed multiple times. Heart thumping, he steps inside the closet, squats down beside the cop, and touches his fingers to his neck. There's no pulse that he can feel. He puts the back of his hand to Nitta's mouth and feels nothing.

He exits the closet and sees something on the floor at the foot of the bed, under the bedspread. He bends down and lifts the bedspread up. It's another suitcase, this one navy blue canvas. He tugs it out from under the bed. It's heavy. Fisher unzips it. Neatly packed inside are the bound stacks of currency.

He rises and something inside the suitcase on the bed catches his eye: a tuft of short white fur tucked in with Marini's balled-up underwear. Fisher grabs it and, as soon as his hand touches the soft synthetic fur, feels the cold metal ring attached to it, he knows what it is.

It's Mari's Snoopy keychain.

His stomach lurches. He'd given Marini Mari's address when he called him from the gym last night.

From the living room, the sound of the front door being opened.

He stuffs the keychain into his pocket, then steps over to Marini's fitness set and wraps the fingers of his right hand around the handle of one of the smallest kettlebells on the floor. He picks it up, hefts it a few times. It weighs about five pounds.

Fisher walks to the door and opens it quietly and strides into the dining area.

Marini is unpacking a bag of groceries at the dining room table with his back to Fisher. On the table are a big roll of duct tape, a package of heavy-duty trash bags, a bottle of bleach.

At the sound of Fisher's tread on the carpet, Marini turns and sees him, and a startled expression ripples across his features. An ever-so-slight widening of the eyes, followed by the tiniest furrowing of the man's brow. And then the expression is gone, replaced by a look of puzzled amusement.

"Holy fuck, dude, you scared the shit out of me." Marini's eyes flick to the kettlebell in Fisher's right hand. "You working out?"

Fisher says nothing.

"You look like hell. How'd you get in here?"

Fisher says nothing.

Marini raises his eyebrows. "Well, I'm impressed. Guess I'm gonna have to change the code now, huh?" Fisher's heart is tapping a steady, measured rhythm in his chest, a molten fury smoldering in his gut.

Marini glances at the open bedroom door and stiffens. His expression turns serious. "Listen to me, Hank. It was Nitta."

A storm rages in Fisher. He keeps it at bay, eyes locked on Marini.

Marini frowns. "He was crooked, Hank. I had no idea. I'm sorry I brought him into this, brother. We brought the bag straight here from Meguro and I put it in the bedroom. Remember? You saw me. I didn't even look inside it." He holds his hands up for emphasis, palms facing each other. "I stepped out while you were asleep. Nitta stayed behind and that's when he must've made the switch. I found out about it after you left and I confronted him. He pulled his gun on me. I had to kill him. It was him or me. And now I'm in a real fix here, Hank." He shakes his head. "I was just trying to help you, and look where it got me."

It amazes Fisher how convincing Marini sounds. He's an even better liar than his brother Danny was. The molten rage in Fisher's gut catches fire. He reaches into his pocket and pulls out Mari's Snoopy keychain and holds it up for Marini to see.

For a split second, Marini's brow creases in confusion and then his expression turns serious again. His mouth opens like he's about to try to explain this away too, and then it closes and he meets Fisher's gaze with a dead-fish look. Something like electricity passes between them, a charged moment of mutual recognition that this is where things end.

For a second the two men stand there staring at each other.

The only sound Fisher can hear is the rush of blood in his ears. He gauges the distance between them to be about ten feet. Marini glances at the dining table. Fisher follows his gaze and sees Marini's pistol sitting there on the table next to the bottle of bleach. Marini shifts his weight, pivots, and runs for the table. Fisher runs after him and gets there a moment too late. Marini grabs the gun. Fisher swings the kettlebell up and slams it down on Marini's hand.

"Ah!"

The gun falls to the floor with a clunk. Marini staggers back. He bites his lower lip, looks at his hand, shakes it out. The side of his mouth hitches up in a half smile that doesn't reach his eyes. And then with no warning, Marini launches a lunging front kick at Fisher. But he's too far away, and Fisher sees it coming. Fisher sidesteps to the left, away from the kick. Marini's foot grazes Fisher's ribs, and as Marini's momentum continues to carry him forward, Fisher swings the kettlebell at Marini's face with all his might. Marini ducks, the kettlebell barely missing his head.

"You're slow, Hank. Dumb, used up, and slow. That's why Lisa left you."

Fury coils in Fisher's gut. He fights it down. He makes an anguished sound and swings the kettlebell again.

Marini hops back, dodging it. "I fucked her right on your kitchen counter, Hank. It was sooo easy. *Too* easy. I mean, she pulled my pants down and started blowing me right there. *Hungry*, dude. Like she was starving for a *real* man. I actually felt kinda sorry for her."

Fisher issues a cry of rage and charges Marini. Marini takes a step back and lobs a punch at Fisher's head with his good hand, which is exactly what Fisher wants him to do. He ducks, the punch goes wide, and Fisher swings the kettlebell up hard.

This time it hits its mark.

There's a sickening *crunch* as the iron ball connects with Marini's left cheek. He makes a sound that's a cross between a groan and a grunt and falls face first to the floor and lies there silent.

Fisher rolls him over onto his back. He's out cold. Blood pours from a huge gash under his left eye, and there's a round depression under his cheekbone. Fisher's face is hot with suppressed fury. It would be easy for him to finish Marini off. Two or three blows to the skull would do it.

No.

His anger suddenly gone, like a campfire doused with water, he uses one of the resistance bands from the bedroom to bind Marini's hands behind his back, then goes to the kitchen, fills a glass with tap water, and pours it on Marini's face.

Lying on his side, Marini groans. His eyelids flutter a few times and he looks up at Fisher and sticks his left arm up as if to ward him off. "Oh fuck. What'd you...? Oh fuck." He coughs once. Tries to get up, frowns with the realization that his hands are bound, then gives up. Fisher pulls his phone out of his pocket. He'll dial the police. They'll come and arrest Marini and this nightmare will be over and his family will be safe once and for all.

Marini opens his mouth, squints his left eye, and blood gushes from the gash under it onto the floor. Marini inhales sharply. "Oh my God, Hank," he says, voice cracking. "I think you really hurt me. Oh my God."

Fisher's finger freezes midair. Suddenly he can see exactly how this is going to play out: The cops will come, and Marini will point at Fisher and demand the cops arrest him. He'll try to pin the blame on him for everything. Nitta's murder. Akio. Mari. And all of the death and destruction at Kaigan Park. Would the cops believe it? Fisher doesn't know. But he's not taking any chances.

He kneels a couple of feet away from Marini, turns his back to him, and thumbs the screen of the phone before setting it down on the floor. Then he picks the kettlebell back up. The handle feels hard and slick in his grip. He uses the hem of his shirt to wipe the handle dry as he stares down at Marini, wipes his hand on his shorts, and then takes the handle in his hand again and squeezes it hard. He hits the palm of his left hand with the ball of the weight, making a smacking sound.

"You're going to tell me the truth now."

Marini looks at the kettlebell, then up at Fisher. He swallows. Fisher starts to raise the kettlebell.

"Okay!" says Marini. "Just settle down, okay? I needed the money. You ran off the other night, and I didn't think you had anyplace else to go, and I needed that money. So I went to Akio's, and he wouldn't tell me anything, so I roughed him a little bit and he fought back and—"

Fisher is confused. "*You* killed Akio?"

"I had to."

Fisher sees Akio's neck slashed open. The desire to hurt Marini, to make him pay, is overwhelming. "And Mari?" he says, his voice trembling.

"I thought maybe you'd stashed the money at her place. I went there and picked the lock. My bad, okay? I shouldn't have done that. I found her hiding in her bedroom. I tried to tell her I was a friend of yours and I needed to see you, but she completely freaked out. I wasn't thinking! I just wanted the money and she went fucking crazy. She just started screaming and screaming and I thought she was going to wake her neighbors up, so I had to shut her up."

Fisher's hands are shaking. "By stabbing her over and over."

"If she hadn't gone crazy on me, it wouldn't have happened! It was an accident, Hank. You see?"

Blood is trickling freely out of the gash in Marini's cheek and puddling on the floor under his head. The entire left side of his face is bright red now.

Fisher nods, his fury dissipating, replaced by the same steely calm he felt in the park earlier. "I see." He motions with his head toward the bedroom. "What about Nitta?"

Marini closes his eyes. "He wanted half of the money."

"So you killed him."

"Yeah," says Marini. He makes a noise that's half sigh, half chuckle, then sucks in a breath through his teeth. "God that hurts. Cracked me a good one, didn't you? Fuck. Ha ha." He closes his eyes again. "Mm. Yeah." He opens his eyes again. For a moment he stares at Fisher, his gaze bright and cold. Then the corner of his mouth hitches up. "Lisa came so hard when I fucked her that—"

Fisher cuts him off. "Look at this!" he says, glancing down at the phone on the floor. Smiling, he picks it up and turns it around so Marini can see the little timer running on the screen. He'd turned the recorder app on before setting the device on the floor. "Weird. Must have hit record somehow before you started talking." He presses stop.

Marini goes quiet.

Fisher dials 110, explains to the operator that there's been a murder, gives him the address, then hangs up and waits for the cops to come.

Every minute or so, Marini barks a laugh and then goes silent again. Blood trickles from the gash under his eye, and his cheekbone has become grotesquely swollen.

It's only a couple of minutes before sirens begin to wail in the distance. Seems like sirens are all Fisher's been hearing the past four days.

Right now, though, it's the sweetest sound he's ever heard.

⟡

He answers questions at the police station late into the afternoon, breaking occasionally for snacks and coffee, helping the cops piece together everything that's happened over the past week.

He plays Marini's confession for the officers, and they take the phone into evidence. Then Fisher goes over the whole story several times. From the brawl at Club Deluxe to the bag of money he was forced to steal from the stash house and the body he found there (indeed the body of George Fukuda, the son of the famous comedian-turned-politician, who had been the stash house operator's lover and had apparently been killed by him after a quarrel), to his discovery of Akio's body, the videos Shota sent him of the kids with the babysitter (who has yet to be found) and of Brownie being killed, to finding Mari unconscious in her apartment and being taken to the shed in Kaigan Park, where Shota threatened to kill Lisa and the kids. And, finally, to his discovery of Detective Nitta's body in Pete Marini's apartment and his fight with Marini.

Fisher asks about Mari. Is she okay? The man he pegs for the most senior officer in the room, a tall, good-looking guy in his fifties with silver hair and hooded eyes named Kawamura, tells him she's in stable condition, and Fisher suddenly finds himself choking back tears. What about Terry? Kawamura tells him Terry is okay too, then goes on to explain that ten people in all, including Shota, were found dead at the park after the fire. Kawamura asks what, if anything, Fisher knows about Shota's death, Fisher tells the truth: Shota pulled a gun on him, Fisher threw a handful of rocks at him, and charged him. Shota then pulled a knife. They fought, Shota fell and stabbed himself. Kawamura seems satisfied with this answer and asks no further questions about Shota.

Fisher asks what will happen to Marini, and Kawamura tells him his fate is uncertain. Because of the Status of Forces Agreement between Japan and the U.S., it's not clear which country will have jurisdiction over his case. Two witnesses had seen him coming out of Akio's apartment around Akio's estimated time of death, and the knife he used to kill Akio had been found and appeared to be the same weapon he used to attack both Mari and Detective Nitta. The recording Fisher made will certainly strengthen the case against him, and whether Marini ends up being tried here in Tokyo or in the U.S., he faces charges of murder and attempted murder, not to mention a long list of other charges. Assuming the two witnesses and Mari are willing to testify against him, if convicted, Marini will be looking at many years in prison.

Before Fisher is released, Kawamura asks him to please not leave town. "I think we will need to ask you more questions."

"Don't worry," Fisher says, "I'm not going anywhere."

CHAPTER SIXTY-FIVE

IT'S AFTER 5:00 p.m. when he gets home, the sun still hot as it sinks to the west over the city.

Bone-weary, stiff and sore from the lumps and bumps and bruises all over his body, he showers, washing away the soot and blood on his skin, shaves, and applies bandages to the abrasions on his wrists, moving slow as a sloth. He's felt less banged up after five rounds of getting his ass whupped in the cage. But in his chest is a lightness of spirit he's never felt before. Lisa, Justin, and James are okay. Mari is okay. Terry is okay.

He'd been informed before leaving the police station that his family had been discharged from the hospital. He used a pay phone to call Lisa and asked if he could come and see the kids. She didn't say anything for a moment, and Fisher steeled himself. He understood her reluctance, but it was still going to hurt when she said no. But she said yes.

He then called Nisseki Hospital and tried to find out about Mari's condition, but the receptionist refused to give him any information because he wasn't immediate family.

Finally he rang Laura, who told him without a hint of resentment or rancor in her voice that Terry had suffered a perforated colon and lost part of his small intestine, but it looked like he was going to be okay, and he was getting out of the ICU tomorrow. He told Laura how sorry he was, and she told him not to beat himself up too much about it. She said Terry had told her when he woke up after the surgery that he'd confronted the gangsters outside Lounge O; otherwise, they probably wouldn't have stabbed him.

He dresses in a blue button-down shirt, jeans, and sneakers, then goes down the street to a little diner and wolfs down a meal of fried mackerel, rice, and miso soup. He pays for his meal and heads for the station.

⁓

Justin and James are both fast asleep in their beds when he arrives, sawing logs. They used to sound like two cats purring. Now it's a little rougher, a little louder, like the growls of two little tandem motors. They're exhausted from their ordeal, and now Fisher stands between his boys' beds, feeling both crushed with guilt and amazed at how much they've grown. He whispers to Lisa, "They're so big."

Lisa nods. She's wearing a T-shirt and sky-blue sweat pants. Her left cheekbone is swollen and turning a deep shade of purple. Dark circles underline her eyes.

He steps over to James's side of the room. Leans over and resists the urge to reach out and touch his head. He wants to pick both of them up and squeeze them.

"Please don't wake them up," says Lisa.

He turns to step away from James's bed.

"Dad?" James's voice says behind him.

Fisher's heart leaps. He turns back around, and James is up

on an elbow, rubbing his eyes with his other hand. Fisher smiles at him. "Hey, kiddo!"

James pops up to his feet and crashes into Fisher, wrapping his arms around him. "Daddy!"

Fisher glances at Lisa and winces.

Lisa sighs and makes a dismissive gesture with her hand. Says in a hushed tone, "It's okay." Then addresses James in Japanese. "*De mo ookina koe wa yamete! Niichan okiru kara!*" But be quiet! You'll wake up your brother!

"Shhh!" Fisher says, squeezing James back as he kisses the top of his head.

Justin pops up like a jack-in-the-box. "Too late! I'm already awake!" He scramble-dashes across the room and launches himself at Fisher, and then the two of them are climbing all over him. "Hey, guys!" Fisher says as he fights back tears. He pulls them in tight and tickles them and smothers both of them with hugs and kisses.

Horsing around with his boys, he feels like he's levitating. Lisa looks on, haggard, her expression betraying her irritation at the fact that the kids are wide awake now. Fisher can see she's exhausted and her face must hurt like hell, and getting the kids to settle down so they can get back to sleep isn't going to be easy.

Growling, James jumps on Fisher's back, wraps his arms around his neck. Justin clamps himself upside down on Fisher's right leg.

Lisa says, "Okay, you two. Say *oyasumi* to Papa."

Eyes bright, Justin says, "Aw, Mom! Can't we stay up a little longer?"

Followed by James, who says, grinning, "Yeah, five more minutes!"

Fisher ruffles their hair. "No, mind your mom. You guys need to get back to sleep."

James grabs Fisher's right wrist with both of his hands, grips it tight, and looks pleadingly into his dad's eyes. "Are you spending the night?"

Justin says, "You can sleep in my bed, Dad!"

James says, "No, he'll sleep in my bed!"

For a brief moment Fisher feels a flutter of hope as the question hangs there in the air, and then he looks up at Lisa and she shakes her head.

"No, guys," Fisher says. "Not this time."

"Aww!" they say in unison.

"Are you coming back?"

Fisher shifts on the bed, clears his throat. "Uh…"

Without looking at him, Lisa says, "Say good night, boys."

Guess that's a no. On the verge of tears again, Fisher pulls Justin and James in for a last hug and kiss before he goes. "Mind your mom, guys. I'll see you soon, 'kay?"

He follows Lisa down the hall to the huge living-dining area, where she gestures for him to have a seat on the sofa. She takes a seat on the love seat across from him, and Fisher says, "Can I just say one thing first?"

Lisa nods.

"I know you didn't sleep with Pete." The suspicion that he'd been wrong about whatever had happened between her and Marini had nagged at him for a long time, like a tiny sliver buried so deep you can't dig it out, so you forget about it until, having worked its way up to the surface, it becomes impossible to ignore.

She presses her lips together and nods again.

The moment of realization had finally come last night when Marini was taunting him. He'd felt a flash of rage, and then it hit him: Marini was full of shit. He always had been. "You tried to tell me, didn't you?"

"I did."

A mix of shame and regret and sorrow sweeps over Fisher. He'd wronged her in the worst way. "And I wouldn't listen."

"No. You wouldn't."

"I'm truly sorry, Lisa. For everything. I was a selfish prick. You and the boys deserved better."

Tears well in her eyes. "For a long time I was so angry at you." She frowns at him. "I'm still angry, Hank." She points toward the kids' bedroom. "What they've been through, what they saw…" She wipes her eyes with her sleeve. "I don't know if I can ever forgive you for that."

Fisher nods.

"But I know I can't stay angry at you, either. It's not good for me or for them. And they need you. I know that. They've really missed you."

A tiny flare of hope goes up in Fisher's heart.

Lisa gets up from the love seat, takes several tissues from a box on the counter, blows her nose, and sits back down. "But I don't know. After everything that's happened…" Lisa lets out a long sigh. "I just don't know if being around you is what's best for them. I need some time to think about it."

The flare of hope dims. The possibility of not being able to see the boys again brings a thickness to his throat. "I understand."

She walks him to the door.

An awkward moment passes between them, Fisher not sure if he should try to hug her, and then she steps forward and hugs him. The embrace isn't without warmth, but there's a formality to it, a stiffness that tells him that what they once had is gone forever. Hurt pangs inside him, but it's dulled by the realization that he'd already known for a long time it was over between them.

"I'll be in touch," Lisa says.

Fisher nods. "Okay."

He passes through the lobby and exits the sliding doors into the muggy night. Down the flagstone path to the sidewalk, headed for Aoyama Station, he walks.

He's not going to lie. He feels like shit.

But maybe he can be a father to his sons.

He passes a police box. The cop inside looks up from his desk and watches Fisher for a moment. Fisher's heart flutters once in his chest, and the image of Pete Marini's blood-covered face flashes across his consciousness.

Fisher nods at the cop.

The cop nods back and returns to his paperwork.

Fisher keeps going.

CHAPTER SIXTY-SIX

Nisseki Hospital
7:30 p.m.

MARI IS ASLEEP when Fisher steps into the room.

He moves quietly through the doorway, a sick feeling in the pit of his stomach. He's been telling himself that she'd be okay, but the sight of her now in the hospital bed, tubes going in and out of her, tells him that that had been wishful thinking, and he's torn up inside, beside himself with grief and guilt for being the reason she's here.

Mari's roommate, a girl of about ten whose leg is up in a cast, is watching TV. She turns her head as Fisher enters the room, her eyes widening in surprise at the sight of the big *gaijin*. Fisher raises his hand. "*Konnichiwa*." Hello. He says it quietly, almost a whisper, so as not to wake Mari.

"*Konnichiwa*," the girl whispers back.

Mari is snoring as he approaches the bed, the same soft sound he heard coming from her room the other night. A young guy with long hair is sitting beside her bed. He's wearing a dark red T-shirt emblazoned with the Temple University Japan logo, khaki pants, and sneakers. He looks Fisher over and rises from his chair.

Fisher offers his hand. "My name is Hank Fisher," he whispers. "I'm a friend of Mari's. You must be Hiroshi."

The young man nods and shakes Fisher's hand. "Nice to meet you," he says with barely a trace of an accent. "My sister has told me about you. You're the fighter, right?"

Fisher shakes his head. "Used to be." He focuses his attention on Mari and feels a lump in his throat. "How is she?"

Hiroshi explains that Mari underwent emergency exploratory surgery the morning of the attack. The two stab wounds on the right side of her stomach had pierced her liver, but fortunately the lacerations had both missed any major arteries. The wounds on her shoulder and forearm were superficial. The upshot was that they would keep her in the hospital for a while for observation.

"She was lucky," he says.

The lump in Fisher's throat swells, and tears well in his eyes. He presses his lips together and wipes them away with the back of his hand.

Seeing this Hiroshi gives him a sympathetic smile and gestures at the chair next to the bed. "I'm going to go get a cup of coffee. Please have a seat."

"Thank you."

Fisher stands beside the bed and watches Mari sleep for a while. He wants to tell her how sorry he is. He also wants to tell her that she's all he's been thinking about. How would she react to hearing that? She'd probably tell him she never wants to see him again. And you know what? He'd deserve it. He remembers her generosity the other night. So kind, so willing to help him even after he told her he was in trouble. He'd taken advantage of her kindness and put her in danger, and look what happened.

Maybe coming here was a bad idea. He reaches into his pocket, pulls out the Snoopy keychain, and places it under her hand, lingering for a moment, noting how cool and smooth her skin is.

She abruptly stops snoring and stirs. Her hand twitches, and then her fingers close around the Snoopy keychain. She slowly turns her head and opens her eyes, and when she sees Fisher, she smiles.

CHAPTER SIXTY-SEVEN

Eighteen months later
Ebisu, Tokyo

⋘

IT'S A WARM Sunday morning in May, and they're making pancakes.

Fisher's new place is on the tenth floor and overlooks a neighborhood of closely packed houses and apartment buildings. The sun is bright in the living room window, and Mt. Fuji is visible in the distance, so sharply outlined against the cloudless blue it feels like you could reach out and stick your finger in it.

The recipe is his mom's, and it's simple: flour, milk, yogurt, eggs, cooking oil, baking powder, baking soda, vanilla essence, and butter.

Like, a *ton* of butter.

He says to James, "Put some more butter in there, kiddo." Seated on a stool at the island counter, James is mixing the wet ingredients in a big stainless steel bowl. Justin, who sits across from his brother, has already blended the dry ingredients in a separate bowl, and Fisher can tell by the way he's drumming his fingers on the countertop and throwing impatient glances at his phone that he'd rather be watching a YouTube video. But Justin knows better, because it's Sunday morning.

And Sunday mornings are about pancakes. It's a new tradition they've started: Sunday Pancake Club. Make the pancakes. Eat the pancakes. Enjoy the day together.

He polishes off his coffee, goes over to the coffeemaker, grabs the pot, and refills his mug.

James says, "Dad, there's already three tablespoons in there." The kids aren't having nightmares as often now. Neither is Fisher. He winks at James. "Put in a couple more tablespoons." With all the butter *in* them, you don't need to put butter *on* them.

James makes an exasperated *If you say so* face. He measures out two more tablespoons of butter, chunks them into a cup, and puts the cup in the microwave for a few seconds.

Without looking up from his phone, Justin says, "Cholesterol, Dad."

He and his brother will turn eight month after next. Fisher has them almost every weekend now, and he's seeing the people they're becoming, and it makes him happy. Warm, smart, funny as hell.

Fisher gives Justin a dismissive wave, lifts the hem of his T-shirt up, and slaps his spare tire with his other hand. "Cholesterol can't touch this."

"Dad," James says. "That *is* cholesterol." He laughs and then Justin laughs and then they shake their heads in the exact same way, reminding Fisher, as they do every once in a while, that they're identical twins. They're so different in so many ways he sometimes forgets.

"True that," he says, laughing with them. His MMA career is over, and his training schedule is pretty hit and miss these days. He works at a small law firm, and apart from a jiu-jitsu class he teaches a couple of nights a week at Ken's new gym, he spends most of his waking hours with his butt in a chair, proofreading memos and translating documents from Japanese to English. It's not super exciting, but he can't complain. Life's been pretty damn good the past year and a half. Most of the time, the madness and fear of that week he spent running for his and his family's lives seem like a distant memory. Occasionally he'll see a report on TV about the ongoing turf wars between rival Tanabe-*kai* factions. Every now and then an update on Pete Marini, who now sits in a Japanese jail somewhere awaiting trial. Fisher prefers not to think about him, so he doesn't.

He thinks about his friend Akio, though. He misses his smile, his charisma, the kindness under all that flash. He'd gone to the funeral a week after the fire. An unusually large number of women were in attendance. Classic Akio to the very end.

The doorbell rings.

He sets his coffee down, immediately nervous. The kids are meeting Daddy's girlfriend for the first time today. Will they like her? Will *she* like *them*?

He goes to the intercom and buzzes her in. She knocks a minute later. He opens the door and Mari steps inside. Her hair is pulled back into a ponytail, and she's dressed in faded jeans and a light green blouse. A cooler bag is slung over her shoulder. She smiles, showing her dimples, and it's one of those smiles that takes a face from merely lovely to radiant.

"Hey," she says. Fully recovered from her injuries, she's in the process of applying to Temple University, where she wants to study business like her brother.

He takes the cooler bag from her, sets it on the floor, and leans in to kiss her, taking in the scent of her shampoo. They've been seeing each other steadily ever since she got out of the hospital. Fisher is crazy about her. She accepts him for who he is, they make each other laugh, and there's a naturalness to their being together that just feels...*right*. That's why he really hopes Justin and James will like her. That she'll like them.

She smiles. "Have you guys already started?"

"You're just in time." Fisher turns. "Guys! Come here!"

A moment later, the kids appear in the doorway, shuffling their feet, uncharacteristically bashful.

"Mari, this is Justin and James."

"Hi, Justin! Hi, James!"

Justin leaps forward hopscotch-style, lands with a thump, and says, "Hi!"

James gives Mari a tentative wave, eyeing her suspiciously.

Mari meets James's gaze and lifts her eyebrows, then gestures at the cooler bag on the floor. "I brought something you guys might like. It's kind of cool." She bends down and unzips the top of the bag, then lifts out a small plastic terrarium. Inside it is a huge rhinoceros beetle—a *kabutomushi*. It's coffee-brown and almost the size of Fisher's palm. It's got a tremendous horn jutting straight out from its head, like something out of a Godzilla movie.

The boys go nuts.

"Whoa!" James says, his standoffishness completely gone.

"It's huge!" says Justin. "Is it a boy or a girl?"

Mari says, "It's a boy." She kicks off her shoes, steps up into the entryway. "You guys want to hold it?"

James's expression suddenly turns serious. He regards the beetle warily. "Will it bite?"

374

Fisher smiles, proudly noting James's cautiousness. The kid thinks before he acts.

"No, it won't bite," says Mari. "Come on!"

The three of them go into the living room, Fisher trailing behind. He stops in the doorway, watching as Mari removes the lid of the terrarium, reaches inside, and gently picks the big beetle up and places it in James's palm. His brave, cautious boy stares at it, eyes wide with fascination.

"Let me hold it too!" says Justin. Justin is fearless, and sometimes that worries Fisher. But James picks up the bug and gently sets it down on his brother's hand, keeping his own close by, just in case.

"Careful," he tells Justin, and Fisher realizes he doesn't need to worry—his boys will look out for each other.

Mari grins over her shoulder at him, flashes a surreptitious thumbs-up, then turns her attention back to the boys. "Careful not to hurt him."

Fisher smiles and heads into the kitchen to pour her a cup of coffee, thinking there was no need for him to be nervous. Everything's going to be just fine.

ACKNOWLEDGMENTS

HEARTFELT THANKS TO:

Tak Ishikawa, longtime training partner and brother from another mother, for believing in this book from the beginning and for helpful feedback on the initial ideas that started me down the path to writing this story. Any resemblance between the character of Terry Nishikawa and Tak is entirely coincidental ;-).

My friend Keith Vargo, for encouragement, insight into what it's like to train at a Japanese MMA gym, and helpful feedback on an early draft. Keith is an amazingly accomplished martial artist, fighter and author, whose books span an incredible array of martial arts-related subjects and should grace the shelves of anyone even mildly interested in the fighting arts: https://www. keithvargo.org

Paul Sorci, friend and training partner of many years, for insight into what it's like to do security-related work for the US government in Japan and for the idea for the scene under the Rainbow Bridge with Pete Marini. For the record, Paul is a good human, and other than his general badassness, shares nothing in common with the character of Pete Marini ;-).

Tiffany Yates Martin, editor extraordinaire, for helping me make this book so much better than it would otherwise have been. Tiffany's book Intuitive Editing is fantastic and should be read by all aspiring authors. Her website is also an amazing resource: https://foxprinteditorial.com

David W. Rudlin, friend, inveterate foodie, and author of the great Inspector McLean mystery series. David was the first person to read Ways to Die in Tokyo from beginning to end and provided me with invaluable feedback as well as assurances that, with some work, the book would be good enough to show other humans.

My friend Jonathan Siegel, for constant encouragement and for helpful comments on the manuscript. Jonathan's book The San Francisco Fallacy: The Ten Fallacies That Make Founders Fail is a must-read for entrepreneurs and anyone interested in start-ups and business in general.

My friend Barry Eisler, for the inspiration, encouragement and helpful suggestions. I've been a fan of Barry's awesome thrillers since he published his first way back in 2002. https://www.barryeisler.com

My dear friend, Michael Van Zandt, who passed away unexpectedly in July 2021, for the encouragement, conversation and laughter. I miss you Mikey.

Sam Rogan, my friend and expert on Tokyo's hidden nooks and crannies, for showing me several little-known and fascinating spots in and around this great city. Unfortunately, none of them made it into this book, but they may very well appear in the next.

The following people, who have variously helped, encouraged, or inspired me over the years and/or throughout the writing this book: Barry Bergmann, Richard Cerruto, Herman & Jennifer Chu, Ralph Gracie, Ed Higashi, Makio Inui, Eri Fukaya, Osuke Honda, Devin Fields, Hengtee Lim, Alan "Gumby" Marques, Adisa Banjoko, Alicia Ogawa, James Peters, Abasa Phillips, Mike Prudencio, Sandro "Batata" Santiago, Brice Soriano, Matt Twigg, Chica Twigg, Keith Watanabe, Shinji Yamasaki, Dan Zoot, and all my friends and training partners over the years at Ralph Gracie Jiu Jitsu Academy, Santa Clara PAL Judo Club, Axis Jiu Jitsu Academy, and Carpe Diem Brazilian Jiu Jitsu Academy.

My dad, for his unceasing support and encouragement from the very beginning of this project, and his regular reminders that he's "waiting for the book."

My late stepdad, Don Torrence, who I know would have gotten a kick out of reading this thing.

My mom, for the encouragement and support over the years. Hope you like it, Mom.

My late stepmom, Bonnie Schinaman, who in her day was an avid reader and I know would have enjoyed the story.

Finally, this book would never have come to be without the constant support and encouragement of my wife, who makes everything possible, and my sons, Kai and Eigen, who provided smart, funny and brutally honest feedback and ideas during the years I spent writing it. I am privileged and proud beyond words that you are my sons.

ABOUT THE AUTHOR

Thomas Ran Garver is the pseudonym for Thomas H. Schinaman. A long-time resident of Tokyo, Schinaman was born and raised in Northern California. He has a B.A. in Japanese language from the University of California, Santa Cruz, and a J.D. from Santa Clara University School of Law. He has had a lifelong interest in the martial arts and has been training Brazilian Jiu-Jitsu since 1995. He holds black belts in Brazilian Jiu-Jitsu and Judo. Ways to Die in Tokyo is his first novel.